Dosha Dhatu Mala Vignyan

Integrative Human Physiology

Dr Hanmanthrao S Palep

Popular Prakashan
www.popularprakashan.com

Published by
Asmita Mohite for
POPULAR PRAKASHAN PVT. LTD.
301, Mahalaxmi Chambers
22, Bhulabhai Desai Road
Mumbai - 400 026
info@popularprakashan.com

First Published 2022
First Reprint February 2022
Second Reprint October 2025

(4534)
ISBN: 978-81-950882-1-8

Cover design and layout: Anjali Sawant

PRINTED IN INDIA
by Manipal Technologies Limited
Manipal, Karnataka - 576104

This book is dedicated to my beloved wife Mrs Lalita Palep.

She shared all of life's trials and tribulations through more than five decades of togetherness with rock solid determination and joy.

सत्यमेव जयते

भारत के उपराष्ट्रपति

VICE-PRESIDENT OF INDIA

December 13, 2021

Dear Dr. Hanmanthrao Sambaiah Palep ji,

Namasthe!

Thank you for sharing a copy of your book, "Dosha Dhatu Mala Vignyan – Integrative Human Physiology".

I appreciate you for the publication.

Yours sincerely,

Naidu

(M. Venkaiah Naidu)

Dr. Hanmanthrao Sambaiah Palep
Manoj Co-op. Housing Society
Shankar Ghanekar Marg
Near Ravindra Natyamandir
Mumbai – 400 025.

BHAGAT SINGH KOSHYARI
GOVERNOR OF MAHARASHTRA

सत्यमेव जयते

RAJ BHAVAN
Malabar Hill
Mumbai 400 035
Tel. : 022-2363 2660
Fax. : 022-2368 0505

17 December 2021

APPRECIATION

I am pleased to know that Dr Hanmanthrao S Palep has authored the book "Dosha Dhatu Mala Vignyan - Integrative Human Physiology".

Ayurveda is not just an ancient science, it is a living tradition of healthcare of Bharat since time immemorial. A majority of the Indians use Ayurveda in their day to day life for preservation of good health and prevention of diseases.

I understand that Dosha Dhatu and Malas are the foundation of Ayurveda. Explaining Ayurveda fundamentals in terms of human physiology is a very daunting task. It is reassuring that Dr Palep has done this work with remarkable dedication. I have no doubt in mind that the book "Dosha Dhatu Mala Vignyan- Integrative Human Physiology" will prove immensely helpful to both Ayurveda and modern medicine students, teachers as well as researchers.

I congratulate Dr. Hanmanthrao S Palep for his efforts in bringing out the book and wish the publication success.

(Bhagat Singh Koshyari)

Dr Hanmanthrao S Palep
Mumbai

॥ ॐ ॥
राष्ट्रीय स्वयंसेवक संघ
प्रधान कार्यालय : डॉ. हेडगेवार भवन, महाल, नागपुर - 440 032
दूरभाष: (0712) 2723003, 2720150 Email-sachivalay@hedgewarbhavanngp.in

कार्तिक शु. 6 / यु. 5123 10.11.2021

नागपुर

Health is a concern that engulfs entire humanity. Everybody is prepared to do anything and everything to get cured of illness and stay healthy. In a country like Bharat reaching every individual is a very arduous if not impossible task and hence it is a necessary but yet to be accomplished goal. In fact the accomplishment is not even in sight in far future. The vast expanse of our land and mind boggling numbers of our population render the task nearly unachievable.

But that is true only when we think of only one Pathy as a valid system for curing diseases. Allopathy, for eg. has a particular theory of how diseases are caused and therefore a particular way of treating diseases. That may not be the only valid theory. Therefore we find that in certain ailments Ayurveda finds an effective cure and in some other ailments the Homeopathy may offer the wonder cure. Then there are individuals who respond more readily to a particular system of treatment than other.

The cost incurred in treatments can vary for different systems and now the medical world has started realizing that the science of wellness is more important as prevention is better than cure.

So to summarize the conclusion of the human experience as regards to staying healthy and disease free is that we have to employ various systems of curing diseases as well as systems of wellness, even their combinations to provide an affordable health care which is accessible for all.

Dr. Hanumantrao S Palep is a learned and experienced Professor of both Allopathy and Ayurveda. The noble object of providing accessible and affordable health care the various systems of treatment will have to transcend their egos and apprehensions about other systems of treatment. For that a certain understanding of the basic knowledge of such systems should be available to the proponents of other systems in the paradigm they can understand. The book 'Dosha Dhatu Mala Vignyan, Integrative Human Physiology' written by Dr. H. S. Palep is a very successful attempt in that direction. Various authorities in medical field have praised the book. I support Dr. V. V. Prasad (MD Ayurveda) in his wish that Dr Palep hopefully would come out with more such books. I also express the same opinion as Dr. Y. S. Nandanwar (MD OB/GY) that all medical students, health care workers and medical practitioners must read this book to obtain the understanding in Human Physiology in the context of Ayurveda.

Mohan Bhagwat

वैद्य राजेश कोटेचा
Vaidya Rajesh Kotecha

सचिव
भारत सरकार
आयुष मंत्रालय
आयुष भवन, 'बी' ब्लॉक, जी.पी.ओ. कॉम्प्लेक्स,
आई.एन.ए. नई दिल्ली–110023

Secretary
Government of India
Ministry of Ayush
Ayush Bhawan, B-Block, GPO Complex
INA, New Delhi-110023
Tel. : 011-24651950, Fax : 011-24651937
E-mail : secy-ayush@nic.in

MESSAGE

The Indian Traditional Healthcare System is of great antiquity. It is the culmination of Indian thought of medicine which represents a way of healthy living valued with a long and unique cultural history, as also amalgamating the best of influences that came in from contact with other civilizations. Like the multifaceted culture in our country, traditional medicines have evolved over centuries blessed with a plethora of traditional medicines and practices.

Ayurveda is the oldest and well-documented Indian health-care system with a comprehensive approach to health and homeostasis. Essence of any science is a continuous quest for new knowledge through research, development and newer applications. Ayurveda is meant to be open for new ideas, principles and knowledge for continuous and systematic progress of the science. Current medical research emphasizes personalized medicine and systems biology. Ayurveda can provide a universal perspective to the nature of life, health, and even to cell and molecular biology. Ayurvedic paradigms can be explored to elucidate cellular and molecular genetics mechanisms. Ayurveda itself proclaims, 'Paratantra avalokana', 'gaining insight into allied sciences is also of the utmost importance'. Acharya Sushruta in his first compendium chapter 4 mentioned that study of different or allied medical science should be done as one cannot determine the purport of a particular science by studying that science alone.

The integration of the key principles of Ayurveda and bio-medicine without losing the vital fundamentals of both the systems is a key to achieve the goal of Universal Health care. This is a challenging task that needs great insight in the field of Ayurveda and intellect nourished with modern tonic. The Book entitled "**Dosha Dhatu Mala Vignyan-Integrative Human Physiology**" is a good attempt in this direction and this will surely give a better understanding of the fundamental concepts of Ayurveda. This will be a ready source of information for all the stakeholders of Ayush as well as other scientific communities.

I place on record my appreciation and best wishes to Dr Hanmanthrao S Palep for his excellent efforts in bringing out this publication.

राजेश कोटेचा

(Rajesh Kotecha)

New Delhi
7th December, 2021

वैद्य जयन्त देवपुजारी
अध्यक्ष
VAIDYA JAYANT DEOPUJARI
Chairman

भारतीय चिकित्सा पद्धति राष्ट्रीय आयोग
आयुष मंत्रालय, भारत सरकार
National Commission for Indian System of Medicine
Ministry of Ayush, Govt. of India

APPRECIATION

There is no doubt that the book written by Dr H. S. Palep, Dosha Dhatu Mala Vignyan, Integrative Human Physiology is a very successful attempt to explain Ayurvedic principles in western science terminology. This is need of the hour as our students are having science background till 12th standard of education & hence are well acquainted with the western thought process in science. They are unaware of the Indian thought process as they remained unexposed to it during their education.

Another community who likes this type of presentation is scientific community or those who are curious about eastern sciences like Ayurveda as they are well acquainted with western scientific terminology & concepts. It may be difficult for them to accept the existence of parallel scientific thought process. What is important is to understand the Ayurvedic terminology in its proper scientific context with reference to Ayurveda. Terminology is always associated with thought process & hence a word used as terminology has a definition & a word which is not used as a terminology has a meaning. Ayurvedic Biology & Ayurgenomics are the two upcoming branches related to Ayurveda. They are working in silo. In my opinion what is required is combined efforts with synchronization & the persons like Dr Palep may take initiative in this regard.

Another important word used in this book is 'integration'. Unfortunately, in Ayurveda fraternity there is no consensus on what is integration. For this also we need focussed efforts. When the whole world is talking about integrative medicine then there shall not be two meanings of the word integration.

How to sensitize students to read such type of books is another question. The teachers may take initiative for this purpose. I hope, this work will help to make the practice of Ayurveda more popular & fashionable in near future.

Vaidya Jayant Deopujari

कार्यालय: 61-65, संस्थानिक क्षेत्र, जनकपुरी, डी-ब्लाक नई दिल्ली - 110058 / Office: 61-65, Institutional Area, Janakpuri, D-Block, New Delhi - 110085
दूरभाष/Phone:- अध्यक्ष/Chairman, कार्यालय/Office, पंजीयन/Registration, फैक्स/Fax, 28525156, 28525464, 28522519, 28520878, www.ncismindia.org, chairman@ncismindia.org

महाराष्ट्र आरोग्य विज्ञान विद्यापीठ, नाशिक

MAHARASHTRA UNIVERSITY OF HEALTH SCIENCES, NASHIK

दिंडोरी रोड, म्हसरुळ, नाशिक - ४२२००४ Dindori Road, Mhasrul, Nashik - 422004

MUHS

Tel:(0253) 2539193/6659235 ☎ Student Helpline:0253-2539111/6659111/100

Website: www.muhs.ac.in, E-mail: academicayurved@muhs.ac.in

डॉ. सुनिल ह. फुगारे
एम.एससी. पीएच.डी.
उपकुलसचिव

Dr. Sunil H. Fugare
MSc. Ph.D.
Deputy Registrar

जा.क्र.मआविवि/ई.३/ १०२६ /२०२५ दि.२५/०८/२०२५

प्रति,

अस्मिता मोहिते,
पॉप्युलर प्रकाशन प्रा. लि.
३०१ महालक्ष्मी चेंबर्स,
२२ भुलाभाई देसाई रोड
मुंबई - ४०० ०२६
मो. नं. : ९८२०७००२७०
ई-मेल : asmitam@popularprakashan.com

विषय :- "**Dosha Dhatu Mala Vignyan**" या पुस्तकास मान्यता प्रदान करणेबाबत...

संदर्भ :- १) आपले दि. ०४/०१/२०२५ रोजीचे पत्र
२) दि. ११/०४/२०२५ रोजीच्या अभ्यासमंडळाच्या बैठकीचे इतिवृत्त

महोदय,

उपरोक्त विषय व संदर्भीय पत्राच्या अनुषंगाने आपणास कळविण्यात येते की, आपण संदर्भीय पत्रान्वये, विद्यापीठ मान्यतेस्तव सादर केलेल्या वैद्य. हणमंतराव एस. पालेप लिखित "**Dosha Dhatu Mala Vignyan**" या पुस्तकास मान्यता मिळणेकरीता विषय दि. ११/०४/२०२५ रोजीच्या प्रि-क्लिनिकल अभ्यासमंडळाच्या बैठकीमध्ये सादर केला असता "**Dosha Dhatu Mala Vignyan**" या पुस्तकास "पुरकपुस्तक" म्हणून मान्यता प्रदान करण्यात आलेली आहे.

आपणास कळविण्यात येते की, सदर पुस्तकाच्या मान्यतेस प्रसिध्द्‌ी द्यावयाची असल्यास, प्रसिध्द्‌ीमध्ये विद्यापीठाने दिलेल्या मान्यतेचा "पुरकपुस्तक" असा स्पष्ट उल्लेख करावा.
याची कृपया नोंद घ्यावी.

आपला,

[signature] : ९३।८

उपकुलसचिव

प्रत माहितीस्तव: परीक्षा नियंत्रक, म.आ.वि.वि., नाशिक

Contents

Foreword

"People who cling to an ancient past have their pride in the antiquity of their accumulations and in the sublimity of their high-walled surroundings...some lover of the truth breaks open their enclosure and floods it with the sunshine of thought and life. Ideas cause movements, but they consider all forward movements to be a menace against their warehouse.

– ***Sri Rabindranath Tagore***

More than three decades back, we launched a national programme on "Ancient Insights and Modern Discoveries in Life and Health Sciences." This was called 'one of the most important projects undertaken in independent India' by Lok-Nayak Jay Prakash Narayan. This initiative in some sense was much ahead of its time. But it succeeded in initiating the new fires of research from the old but blazing embers.

A critical mass of some outstanding minds got inspired by the programme. Some of these are Prof. R.D. Lele, Dr R. A. Mashelkar, Dr M.S. Valiathan, Dr Rama Vaidya, Dr Bhushan Patwardhan, Prof. Sharadini Dahanukar, Dr H. S. Palep, Dr V. Prakash and several more. A fresh breeze of synergy between Ayurveda and Biomedical Sciences was blowing across the nation and the world. The antipathy between different medical 'pathies' started thawing for the first time. Some remarkable research institutions were taken up by the R & D leaders.

Once again, after the challenge of COVID-19 pandemic, the nation has woken up to the inadequacies of any single health system in handling major challenges. The Niti-Aayog has coined a new slogan, "One Nation – One Healthcare". As a consequence, the old intersystem animosities have surfaced again. A healing touch is needed to take healthcare forward.

To assuage such a health divide in India, we need to encourage all genuine and intelligent efforts to build bridges of communication. The competence to be architects of such bridges requires dual expertise in education, competence and authenticity in diverse systems of medicine. Our medical educational system is not conducive to have experts with such qualities. There are only a small number of specialists educated both in Ayurveda and Modern Medicine. Dr H.S. Palep is one of them.

For decades, he has taken initiatives to provide avenues and platforms for *Tadvidya Samvad* -experts' dialogues for integrative healthcare.

In the present book, Dr Palep has tried his best to provide an understanding of integrative physiology of Ayurvedic basic principles in terms of modern sciences. The book will generate more ferment and critical debate on the views expressed, with an eye to "One nation – One Healthcare system". Scholars of different domains of healthcare can learn much from the simple elucidation of Ayurvedic axioms underlying the logical structure of the system.

– ***Prof. Ashok D. B. Vaidya***
MD. PhD, FAIM

Research Director, Kasturba Health Society-Medical Research Centre, Mumbai

Adj. Professor, Transdisciplinary University of Health Sciences and Technology. Bengaluru

Drexel University College of Medicine, Philadelphia; Gujarat Vidyapeeth, Ahmedabad; and Saurashtra University, Rajkot

Former Regional Medical Director (South Asia)-Ciba-Geigy

Medical-Research Director, Bhavan's SPARC
V. Asst. Professor, Yale Medical School

Acknowledgements

The inspiration to write this book came from a realisation that Ayurveda is no more of an antiquarian interest and that we need the genius of Ayurveda today more than ever before.

Understanding Hindu shastras was essential in learning the real importance of Ayurveda. My teacher, late Vaidya Vasudev Vyas guided me to understand sankhya and vaisheshika foundations of Ayurveda. Late Dr Pranjivandas Mehta (M.D., M.S.) was an inspiring personality. I had met him while I was an undergraduate student. His English translation of Charak Samhita was of great help to me. Late Prof. C. Dwarkanath's book on dosha, dhatu and mala vignyan provided me the correct understanding of Ayurvedic foundations. Ayurveda and Modern Medicine by Prof. Dr R. D. Lele has brought out many new concepts of current sciences. My friend late. Prof. George St. Laurent III of Washington University gave me many new insights in understanding of new developments in genetics, semiotics and information transfer mechanisms in humans. I am deeply indebted to all of them.

I owe my gratitude to my wife, Dr Lalita and my family for all their co-operation. My daughter Dr Manisha contributed all the hand drawn anatomical illustrations.

My association with stalwarts, my teacher, Prof. Dr R. D. Lele and Dr Ashok Vaidya helped shape my views in a big way to understand Ayurveda from the view point of a modern medicine.

I thank my students Vaidya Dattatreya Muzumdar and Mandar Muzumdar for providing needed references.

I thank another student, Snehal Funde for typing tables in this book.

I very profusely thank Shriman M. Venkaiahji Naidu, Honourable Vice-President of India, for perusing the book and sending his blessings. I am very grateful to Shriman Bhagat Singhji Koshyari, Honourable Governor of Maharashtra, for his appreciation of the book.

I am greatly indebted to Param Pujaniya Sarsanghchalak of Rashtriya Swayamsevak Sangh, Shriman Mohanji Bhagwat. He has painstakingly reviewed the book in great detail and has blessed this book with his appreciation.

I am grateful to Vaidya Shriman Rajeshji Kotecha for his valuable opinion and appreciation of the book. I am also grateful to Vaidya Shriman Jayantji Deopujari for having reviewed and appreciated the book.

I thank Dr Y. S. Nandanwar, Dr Ashwin Gumaste, Dr Chandrakant Katiyar, Vaidya V. V. Prasad, Dr Sharad Gogate and Dr Rammohan Rao for painstakingly reviewing this book.

Of course the most important support I received is from Shri. Ramdas Bhatkalji and his personal involvement in publishing this book. Mr Harsha Bhatkal, Dr Anu Sheth, Mr Vijay Thakur, Ms Armaity and the entire team at Popular Prakashan have worked hard to bring out this book. I sincerely thank them from the bottom of my heart.

It will not be possible to acknowledge all the people by name. I thank each and every one of my friends and well-wishers.

Introduction

Ayurveda, the Hindu system of medicine, is the proud heritage of India. It literally means the science of life. The uniqueness of this system is its holistic approach to life that is centred on nature and its rhythms. One can trace its origin to antiquity. Ayurveda was revealed to the great Rishis, who desired the benefit of long life (*Ayush kameeya*) for all people, at least 6000 years ago. *Ayu* is derived from the root "*Eti gachati iti Ayu*," meaning one which is on the move. Life or *ayu* is that which preserves the body, organs of the senses and actions, mind and *atma*. It is also called *dhari* and *jeevitam*.

The word Veda sounds more like a philosophy than a science, whereas *vidya* is science. Ayurveda is a blend of philosophy, art and the science of human life, both in the states of health as well as disease. It is one of the most ancient codified medical systems in the world. It encompasses eight specialities, *viz.*, *kaya* (internal medicine), *baala* (paediatrics), *graha* (planetary or unknown causes; mental and as well infectious diseases), *urdhwanga* (head & neck), *shalya* (surgery), *damshtra* (toxicology), *jara* (geriatrics), *vrishya* (rejuvenating medicine).

The ancient Hindus believed that life is a mixed bag of experiences, which can be wholesome, unwholesome, happy and sorrowful. Therefore it becomes necessary for man to learn and know, what is appropriate as well as safe and beneficial for a healthy, happy and long life. Ayurveda provides all the answers towards this goal in terms of life style, diet, drugs and procedures. It has evolved through a relentless quest, extending over millennia, by the seers of yore. Thus it is timeless experiential wisdom that has crystallised for the prevention of disease and relief from suffering. Any sort of suffering, either physical or mental is disease, and health is happiness. The objectives of this science are to ensure the maintenance of positive health by an individual and also to provide relief from disease.

Ayurveda defines health as a state when the key elements, *viz.*, *doshas*, *agni*, *dhatus* and *malas* are in a state of balance or equilibrium in an individual, his soul and mind are in a state of happiness and bliss and his organs of cognition and conation are functioning perfectly. This state is called *sama*, meaning a state of harmony and equilibrium in all the body constituents. This *sama* state is the homeostasis of milieu interior of modern medicine.

Sama dosha samagnischa sama dhatu mala kriya l
prasannatmendriya manah swasthamityabhideeyate ll

The holistic approach of Ayurveda considers man and his environment as inseparable entities. Man is a combination of the corporal body, mind and soul. *Sthoola shareer* is the corporal body. *Sookshma shareer* is the astral body, the mind and *Kaarana shareer* is the soul or causal body.

The evolution of Ayurveda in terms of its philosophy and development

Ayurveda has its firm foundations in Hindu theology. It has evolved from the *Vedas*. The *Vedas* represent man's quest for understanding himself in relation to the Universe. (Who knows what truth is, or who may here declare it? What is the proper path that leads to the place of divine forces? - *Rigveda 3.54.5*).

In the beginning the elements of nature were worshipped as gods. Gods were created by man in his own form depicting his beliefs, values and ideals. There were gods for power, wealth and health, misery and death. They believed in their divine power. They feared their wrath, which could lead to diseases. They devised *mantras*, divinations, incantations, charms and amulets to propitiate them. Simultaneously, the empirical use of herbs, minerals and animal products were experimented with, as they discovered remedies for various diseases. The scientific enquiry continued and the knowledge grew so as to understand many scientific facts pertaining to life. They understood the cyclic nature of life. The *Rigvedic mahamrutyunjaya mantra* explains the cyclic nature of life, whereby the seed grows into a tree and tree bears the fruit. The seed from this fruit grows again into a tree in the ever recurring cycles of death and new life. Thus the seed is a described as the causal body of a tree. The seer who composed the *mantra* affirms that there is nothing like death, (*Urvarika miva bandhanat mrityur mukshiyamamrutam).*

They also understood that this universe depends on the sun for all energy (light and heat) through solar radiations. A Rigvedic prayer to the Sun god describes the Sun as the soul of the Universe, *(Surya atmah jagatah)*. They also understood the fact, that the Sun is the creator, *(Asau Adityo Brahmah).*

Apart from *mantras*, the *Atharva Veda*, the last of the four *Vedas* describes various empirical methods for treating diseases by the use of plants, herbs, animal products and minerals. The *Upanishads* form the foundation for the highest level of scientific and philosophical enquiry of creation that led to the development of the Hindu model for life in this universe. With the development of six *darshanas*, *viz*., *sankhya*, *vaisheshika* and *nyaya,* yoga, *mimamsa* and *uttaramimamsa*, the rishis rationalized and systematised these various scientific developments. *Sat* or the *Brahamn* is the core central theme of this model. *Sat* is the true existence that prevails in all the three time zones, *i.e*., past, present and future without any change. *Brahamn* is the cosmic consciousness that operates the whole of this universe. Thus *Brahamn* is described as *Pragnyanam*, the supreme infallible knowledge. It is the software program that synchronises and operates the entire cosmos. This consciousness and intelligence combine is called *Brahamn*. It is the eternal truth with no beginning or end. *Brahamn*, being the embodiment of cosmic wisdom, is considered as principal cause for creation. *(Pragnyanam Brahamn* is one of the four significant statements or *maha vakyas* from the *Rigveda)***.** This true knowledge is infinite and all-pervading in the universe as a matrix.

"Satyam gnyanam anantam Brahamn"

Knowledge is the actionable awareness and is created through a number of steps of information processing. The first being the coding, the next is receiving the information in the mind systems and storing and retaining it for further processing. The ability to recall the stored information is called *smruti* or memory. Thinking, pondering and contemplating on this information is the job of the mind, (*vimarshatmakah manah*). Then the intelligence vets this information and gives judgement, (*nishchayatmakah buddhi*). Important aspects of mind systems are *dhee* (emotional control), *dhruti* (volitional control), *smruti* (memory), *buddhi* (power of judgement) and *vivek* (the experiential wisdom of right decision making).

John Ecceles, an eminent scientist also believes that consciousness and intelligence are not the same, but are distinctly different. He believes that the self-conscious mind, a self-subsistent entity integrates the multifarious activities of the neuronal machinery to give the unity of conscious existence from moment to moment, (Ref. *Man and Medicine* by Farokh Udwadia, Pg. 449).

This sentient *Brahamn* is the efficient cause for inducing the unmanifest material cause, *prakruti* into a dynamic mode, which in turn is the cause of the manifest world. It is how the life systems in this creation began. *Brahamn* is also known as *purush*. The union of the non- material sentient *purush* with the unmanifest material *prakriti* symbolises the consummation of the female by the male. The male is the symbol of *Brahamn* or *purush*. The female is the symbol of *prakruti*. The combination of these two results into life systems. Hinduism used this concept to create many iconographic symbolisms. Phallic worship of Shiva is but one example. The *Shivalinga* has two parts, the *linga* (phallus) and *yoni* (female genital apparatus). Universe is the macrocosm and a man is a microcosm. According to *pinda* (embryo/atom/man) and Brahmanda (macrocosm/universe) *nyay* (law), the laws that operate for both micro and macro cosmos are common. In another artistic presentation, the sky blue waters of the ocean, called *ksheer sagar* (ocean of milk) is shown as the abode of Lord Shri Maha Vishnu reclining on a thousand headed serpent representing knowledge. The god Brahma, the creator of the universe is shown seated in a lotus that emanates from Lord Vishnu's navel. Shri Mahavishnu is known to be in three forms, *viz*., Brahma, the cosmic programmer, seed (embryo) and foetus in utero. All living and non-living beings including man form the microcosm. The representation of Brahamn in man is his *atma*, the soul. It represents the combination of consciousness and intelligence. Consciousness is superior to the mind. This individual consciousness or *atma* was considered to dwell inside the heart of every individual as the representative of the divine spirit or *Brahamn* by the ancient Hindu civilization. Aristotle too like our own philosophers considered the heart as the seat of the spirit. *Atma* carries with it the burden of memories of past lives and is responsible for determining one's life span and capabilities. In essence the description of *Brahamn* fits in to a form of a software that programmes the whole of the life span of an individual. This concept of *atma* in man is somewhat similar to the current understanding of the genome. The genes carry information and knowledge transmitted as a chemical memory in DNA through innumerable generations from the time the first egg was fertilized in this universe. The genome is the library of these memories and instructions.

How Ayurveda influenced systems of medicine in other parts of the world

Hindu scriptures have influenced all the ancient civilizations, *e.g.*, Sumerian, Assyrian, Egyptian, Chinese, Greek, Roman and Persian *etc*., in a big way. They all worshipped identical gods. Even the philosophies professed by these civilizations had many things in common. The philosophy of metaphysical speculation and mathematical rationalization of Socrates, Plato, Pythagoras and Descartes has much in common with our own *sankhya* system. *Vaisheshika* principles are utilized by yet another Greek theologist, Lucretius Carus, during the first century before the Christ. He stated that the whole of the universe is made up of invisible atoms in continuous motion. The whole universe in constant motion is referred to as *samsaara* by ancient Indians. Just as Hindus worshipped *Dhanwantari* (the god of health) with divine origin, these other civilizations had *Madruk*, *Imhotep*, *Confuscius* and *Aesculapius*. The twin gods, the *Ashwinikumars* had their parallel in the twin patron healer saints, Cosmos and Damian. Even the five proto-elements, which are considered to be unique to our philosophy and Ayurveda find their echo in all other civilizations. Empedocles in the 5th century B.C. believed in four elements of the universe, *viz*., earth, air, fire and water. The Chinese believed in wood, fire, earth, metal and water as the proto-elements. They believed in Yin and Yang, the two opposing and complimentary forces, comparable to *purush* and *prakriti*, which control all the body mechanisms. Balance of these forces resulted in health. Qi of the Chinese is equivalent to our own concept of *prana*. The Greeks believed in four elements other than *akash* and only in four attributes or *gunas* out of the twenty believed by the Hindus. These four attributes were hot, cold, wet and dry. Even the *tridoshas* of Ayurveda find their echo in the four humours of Hippocratic medicine. Susruta added one more *dosha*, the *rakta* (blood), which appears to be in line with Greek medicine. The ancient Persian civilisation was famous for its medical school of Jundishapur. The great Indian physician of this school was Al-Harith. Could then this Al-Harith be the same person, who authored *Harith Samhita*? History records that in olden times many Hindu physicians were the court physicians in Persian and Arab lands. Ayurvedic texts were translated into many languages.

The unique contribution of Ayurveda is to categorise personality types based on the preponderance of a particular type of *dosha* at the time of conception, called *prakruti* or constitutional type. It is important to identify it from the point of view of both disease prevention and therapeutic strategies. There are seven such personality types. Recently, the journal, *Nature Human Behaviour*, has reported that a study of 1.5 million respondents revealed four cluster groups of personality types, namely, average, reserved, role models and self- centred. These groups are even considered useful for hiring managers for different health care programs.

Many procedures have been recognised as Hindu techniques, *e.g.*, plastic surgery of the nose. Intuition based concepts, backed by experiential wisdom created a huge volume of knowledge of medicine, which was further categorised into eight specialized branches of Ayurveda *(Ashtang Ayurveda)*, which included obstetrics, gynaecology, paediatrics, ENT and general surgery with plastic surgery etc. A number of famous text books were compiled, *e.g.*, *Charak Samhita*, *Sushruta Samhita*, *Kashyap Samhita*, *Ashtang Sangrah*, *Hriday*, *etc*. The *sutra* in poetic verse form is also unique to Ayurveda. The aphorisms of Hippocrates and versification of rhyming poetic rendering of medicine in Italy by the Salerno School are evidence of the influence of the Hindus. Ayurveda remained the fountain head of medical knowledge full of great concepts. It thrived for nearly more than 1700 years after Christ. These classics were translated into many languages of the east and west spreading the knowledge far and wide all over the globe. Through centuries in the first millennium after Christ many more efforts at updating the knowledge continued. Foremost among them were *Bhavaprakash Nighantu*, *Sharangdhara Samhita*, *Ravana Arka Prakash*, *Naadishastra*, *etc*.

Ayurvedic education in India

When we peruse the ancient *Samhitas*, it is clear that the entire works appear as a compilation of questions from students and answers by the master. Medical seminars, debates and conferences were conducted. There were rules for arguments and discussions during these seminars (*Tadvidya sambhasha*). All the great works of Ayurvedic literature are the result of these scientific pursuits. Many interesting questions were asked. A pupil asked Punarvasu Atreya in *Charak Samhita*, as to how the different tissues of the body having different consistencies and colour and are transformed from the colourless liquid like *rasadhatu*. One of the three mechanisms advanced by the teacher for these conversions was the method of conversion of milk to curd. Technology was primitive.

The explanation looks more in tune with common sense and experience than a scientific mechanisms for different biological processes. During the period of the Renaissance in Europe, many new discoveries in basic sciences were made, totally changing the face of medicine in the west. Whereas in India during this period further enquiry and progress stopped, because of continued foreign aggression and the resulting turmoil. The political, economic and social fabric of the country was completely destroyed. The renaissance medicine has cracked so many secrets of the nature, life and their mechanisms, laying solid foundations for the development of the sciences of anatomy, physiology, biochemistry, pathology, immunology, pharmacology, molecular biology etc. Many mechanisms, which were earlier not understood, are now easily understood. Thus mechanism of conversion of milk into curd, a question that was asked in *Charak Samhita*, is explained by enzymatic conversion by modern biochemistry. Revolutionary developments in basic sciences have helped medicine in the west to make the progress in leaps and bounds. Ayurveda had no benefit of these advances. Vaidyas remained totally ignorant of these advances that changed global medicine, and Ayurveda remained stagnant.

Ayurveda or Ayurvidya?

There is a large section of Ayurvedic scholars, who still believe that the Ayurveda is a complete science, with its own paradigms for investigation and management, with a totally different biological approach from that of modern medicine. According to them these two streams of medicine, *viz*., modern and Ayurvedic medicine can only run parallel but can never be absorbed into each other. Hence there is no need of any interaction or supplementation of other knowledge to traditional Ayurveda.

Almost a century ago the great scholar and legendary freedom fighter, Lokmanya Bal Gangadhar Tilak coined the word Ayurvidya. In his opinion, it was necessary that Ayurveda took into account modern scientific developments in medicine, to make it a better and more adequate science for the health care needs of the country. He was probably the earliest proponent of an integrative approach to Ayurvedic medicine as a solution to our country's health care system.

Though growth of scientific knowledge has reached its acme in the 21st century, one cannot say that we have reached a stage of finality in our quest for knowledge. Desmond Morris, (English Zoologist) said that quest is second nature to the human species. We never stop investigating. We are never satisfied that we know enough to get by. Every question we answer leads to yet another question. This has become the greatest survival trick of our species.

Max Planck stated that science cannot solve the ultimate mystery of nature, because in the final analysis we ourselves are part of nature and therefore part of the mystery we are trying to solve. Charak also said in *Viman Sthana* that the science of life shall never attain finality. Therefore humility and relentless industry should characterize one's endeavour and approach to the knowledge. The entire world consists of teachers for the wise and enemies for the fool. Therefore the knowledge conducive to health, longevity, fame and excellence coming even from an unfamiliar source should be received, assimilated and utilized with earnestness, (Translation of *Charak* by Dr R. D. Lele, *Ayurveda and Modern Medicine*).

Of all the ancient civilizations only the Chinese and Hindus protected their heritage with great zeal and resolve. Hence both of them remained as live civilizations, and their medicine also survived. The Chinese have integrated their ancient medicine into their current contemporary medicine very intelligently. This resulted into global growth of this medicine in a big way. Indian medicine on the contrary could not make its impact globally. It has just a 2% contribution to the global markets.

With all the modern developments in medicine is it worth while looking back in to Ayurveda? Dr Pranjivandas Mehta, the great modern physician, who rendered the English translation of *Charak Samhita*, stated that Ayurveda is not just of an antiquarian interest, but it has suggestions for future medicine. This is in tune with what T. S. Eliot said, "Time future is contained in time past". Conceptually Ayurveda is very advanced. One example will prove the above statement of mine. The objective of antenatal care in Ayurveda is to bring a well born (*sujat*) healthy baby into the world, resulting in a superior and healthy population *(Supraja)*. Such a healthy baby should be able to excel in the race endowed with superior physical and mental prowess *(Shreshtam apatyam)*. There can be no better defined objective possible for antenatal care. Prof. Barkar of Southampton University has proved the validity of this ancient objective of Ayurveda by establishing the role of good antenatal care and optimum birth weight in prevention of middle aged diseases, *e.g.*, hypertension, heart diseases and diabetes mellitus. Many ancient concepts can now be proved by modern clinical and investigative tools. In this book many such Ayurvedic concepts, which hitherto appeared ridiculous, are explained on a modern scientific basis paving the way for integrating the two streams of knowledge. What is important is to understand the Ayurvedic terminology in its proper scientific context. *Prithvi Mahabhoota* by definition is characterized by its attribute of aroma. Basic to the chemistry of aroma is the carbon atom. Thus *prithvi* can now be equated to carbon. Therefore in this text it is attempted to explain the chemistry of the *panch mahabhootas* within the frame work of *Sankhya* philosophy. Modern science and the modern medicine are not antagonistic to Ayurveda. In fact knowledge of them enhances the understanding and validity of many of the Ayurvedic precepts. Throughout this book many Ayurvedic precepts are explained on a modern scientific basis. The merits of Ayurveda are being recognized by modern scientists. John Fagan, chief scientific officer, IDNA (licencing authority for GMO testing and certification) believes in the potential of Ayurveda. He says, "Your traditional knowledge base appears to me to be the most valuable resource that India has. If you look at the knowledge contained in Ayurveda and other Vedic traditions, you will find a whole system that has been greatly undervalued at this point of time and this body of knowledge, I feel, has the potential to transform India and the world."

What ails Ayurveda in India today? Ayurvedic education in India yesterday and today

Institutional medical education was first started by the British in the nineteenth century. It is interesting to know that the first three medical colleges were established in Kolkata, Chennai and Mumbai. The medium of instruction was in the vernacular languages. Grant Medical College had begun with Marathi as the medium of instruction with the participation of local vaidyas. Gradually western medicine was taught in English and it has now developed into a modern mainstream allopathic institute of India. In due course of time Ayurveda was totally discarded in this modern education system. Slowly Ayurveda came to be less favoured and less popular in its own country of origin. Vaidyas kept the knowledge secret and restricted its teaching only to their families. During the freedom struggle, the patriotic zeal of the people helped in the revival of interest in Ayurveda. Many Ayurvedic courses were started, which also had a large content of allopathic education. The integrated education of medicine took root in the country and many colleges were started all over India. In the sixties, under some political pressure, the government of India reversed its policy, leading to strict compartmentalization of the different systems of medicine. Independent councils were formed for each branch, resulting in colleges teaching a pure Ayurvedic system with barely any modern medical knowledge. Students who passed out of junior colleges with a background of physics, chemistry and biology were admitted to these colleges. Once admitted to an Ayurvedic college, the philosophical language of Ayurveda appeared totally alien to them. This resulted in apathy in learning and understanding the various subjects in the Ayurvedic course. Thus students had a poor knowledge of both Ayurveda and modern medicine. Ayurveda has now been relegated to the position of a complementary and alternative system. Presently under political patronisation, the number of Ayurvedic colleges have mushroomed, so that they now number more than two hundred all over India. These colleges instead of helping Ayurveda to make progress, caused a decline in its prestige and status by producing large numbers of practitioners, who suffered a severe inferiority complex through no fault of their own. They were also seen as second class doctors in society.

I underwent training in Podar Medical College (Ayurvedic), where the training was integrated. Frustrated as being seen as a second class medical practitioner, I had to opt for readmission into a modern medical college on the merits of my marks in inter science. Fortunately, I obtained a post graduate degree in modern obstetrics and gynaecology and was able to rise to the position of Honorary Professor at the prestigious Grant Medical College, Mumbai. Simultaneously, I got an assignment as a part time teacher in Podar Ayurvedic College in the subject of *streerog*, *prasutitantra* and *kaumarabhritya*. This assignment rekindled my interest in understanding Ayurveda on the basis of modern scientific parameters. A better understanding of biochemistry, physiology and modern pharmacology helped in an improved understanding of Ayurveda. Clinical research on various herbs in different pathologies with successful results resulted in a greater faith in Ayurveda.

This renewed faith propelled the momentum for the creation of a scientific research foundation of Ayurveda. I created twenty new research based Ayurvedic formulations, some of which became very popular with modern consultants all over the country.

A mathematical problem can be successfully solved by using arithmetic, algebra or geometry, depending upon the nature of the problem. A common result can be achieved by any of the methods. Similarly human health problems can be approached through different systems to get the desired results. Every system has its plus points and its draw backs. A prudent approach would be to integrate different knowledge systems for the larger benefit of humanity. All over the world, interest in Ayurveda is growing. Many Ayurvedic herbs and formulations are undergoing research all over the world. In our own country because of the tight compartmentalisation, the modern practitioner is totally ignorant of the great treasure of knowledge of this ancient science. An Ayurvedic practitioner is taught only a bare minimum of modern medical knowledge, so he ends up practising quackery. This has often lead to two warring camps, which are trying to restrain the other from practicing the others system of medicine. Unless a practitioner of modern medicine can understand and evaluate Ayurveda using a modern clinical and investigative model, Ayurveda can never become main stream medicine. To properly understand Ayurveda one needs a good base of biochemistry and physiology. Hence Ayurvedic colleges need to be supplemented with these departments. A true integrative approach is the need of the day to help Ayurveda progress and reach its state of glory again.

Another important problem which needs to be addressed immediately is the fast disappearing wealth of the forests in this country. This has already resulted in the loss of many valuable species of medicinal herbs and plants. Due to this it has become common practice for suppliers of Ayurvedic herbs to substitute many medicinal herbs with spurious ones. Proper sourcing, identification, collection and storage methods are very important for plants growing in the wild. Cultivation, using newer biotechnological methods *e.g.*, tissue culture has become the pressing need of the day in view of increased global demand for Indian medicinal plants. Ayurveda students need scientific training in all these aspects during their undergraduate studies in college.

I have tried my best to bring this integrative approach in this textbook. It is hoped that this will stimulate many more people with the dual background of Ayurveda and modern medicine to work on these lines and make the practice of Ayurveda more popular and fashionable in times to come.

I conclude this introduction with a plea to the authorities to include the principles of Ayurveda in all modern medical colleges and start departments of modern physiology, biochemistry, pathology, pharmacology, pharmacy and herbal biotechnology in all Ayurvedic colleges so that main stream medicine becomes truly integrative.

Jai Hind

– ***Dr H. S. Palep***
Mumbai
06/9/2019

Part - I

The Scientific Foundation of Ayurveda

Chapter : 1

Indian Philosophies

Ayurveda is the science of life. Let us now understand human life (*ayushya lakshanam*) from the perspective of Ayurveda.

Shareer indriya satwam atma samyogo dhari jeevitam l
Nityagascha anubandhascha paryayih ayuh utchyate ll (Cha. S. 1-42)

Life is that which upholds the union of the body, organs of sense and action, mind and *atma* all together. It is also known as *nityaga* and *anubandha*. Life is called *nityaga* (that which exists always) due to the fact that it exists without being absent even for a moment till death sets in. *Anubandha* is its association to its next life based on the theory of *karma*. Life distinguishes humans, animals and plants from inorganic non-living things.

Who is the *chikitsa purush* (the subject for therapy) according to Ayurveda?

Satwam atma shareeram cha trayametat tridandavat l (Cha. S. 1- 46)

Just as a tent requires three poles, the so called *purush* needs three foundation poles, *viz*., *manas* (mind), *atma* and body. The union of all three is called *chikitsa purush*, who is treatable.

What are the signs of life in a living human being?

Pranaapanau nimeshaadya jeevanam manasogatih l
Indriyantara sancharah preranam dharanam cha yat ll

Deshantaragatih swapne panchtwa grahanam tatha l
Drushtasya dakshine akshinaa savyenaapagamastatha ll

Itcha dvesha sukham dukham prayatna schetana dhrutih l
Buddhi smrutih ahankaro lingani param atmana ll (Cha. Sha. 1-69 -71)

Inhaling and exhaling air, opening and closing the eyes, thinking capacity of the mind, complex interactions of *indriyas*, inspiration, initiation and resolve to act, travelling out of the body in dreams, death of the body, synchronized vision from both the eyes, desire, hate, happiness, sorrow, initiative and effort to achieve the objective, consciousness and strong resolve, intelligence, memory and ego are all the signs of life in a human being, which are *atma* derived.

Let us study some fundamentals of Ayurveda from the very foundations of Hindu philosophy.

Origins of life and the universe have occupied the thoughts of intellectuals from time immemorial and still continue to be topics of enquiry. The seers and savants of ancient India deliberated and debated on this subject and established a number of different schools of philosophy. The foundations of Ayurveda rest on all our original *darshanas* or philosophies. Therefore it is essential for a student of Ayurveda to know the basics of these philosophies, therefore we will describe them briefly.

These philosophies can be broadly categorized into two groups, *viz*., *astika* (those that believe in the *Vedas)* and *nastika* (those that do not believe in the *Vedas*). Prominent amongst the *astika* philosophies are *Sankhya*, *Vaisheshika*, *Yoga*, *Nyaya*, *Purva Mimamsa*, and *Uttara Mimamsa*. Buddhism, Jainism and *Charvaka* are the *nastika* philosophies or *darshanas*.

Sankhya: This school was founded by Kapil *Mahamuni*. According to this philosophy the cause of creation is the conjunction of dynamic material *prakriti* with the sentient *purush*. This speculative thought described 24 constituents of life, which will be discussed later in greater detail.

Vaisheshika: This school was founded by the *Maharishi*, Kanad. Kanad described the *anu* (atom) and *parmanu* (sub atomic particle) for the first time in the history of mankind. He hypothesized that the interaction and union of these particles (*parmanus*) resulted in the creation of this universe. The union of the particles occurred either physically or chemically. In a physical union the different particles can be separated back to their original forms. Once a chemical union occurs, the particles cannot be separated back into their original form. This he termed as *pilupak*.

Yoga: This school was founded by *Maharishi* Patanjali. This is a complimentary science to Ayurveda. It is a holistic approach to the body, mind and soul. From the view point of yoga, the cause of the universe is irrelevant. The most important object is relief from the pain and sorrow of mankind. Life is after all a mixed bag of experiences which are wholesome or unwholesome (*hitahitam*) and also those that cause pleasure or pain/sorrow (*sukham* or *dukham*). Yoga believes that the mind is at the root of all problems, for they reside in the thoughts generated in the mind. Hence control of thoughts is of utmost importance for relief from sorrow and to attain pleasure, peace, and happiness. For this purpose the yoga school developed eight fold techniques.

1. ***Yama:*** Setting up rules for self conduct.
2. ***Niyama:*** Disciplined practice of the rules laid down for the proper conduct of life or in other words living a life of strict discipline.
3. ***Asana:*** Practicing different physical exercises in different body postures.
4. ***Pranayama:*** Practicing breath control.
5. ***Pratyahara:*** Withdrawal from the worldly objects of enjoyment.
6. ***Dharana:*** To fix one's mind and focus on a single object.
7. ***Dhyana:*** Meditation or deep concentration on a particular object.
8. ***Samadhi:*** Final stage of total surrender to almighty and receiving eternal bliss.

Vedic scholars paid great attention to the mind or *manas*. The words, *manu*, *manas* and *manushya* (man) have a common origin. The serpent was a symbol of knowledge in all the ancient cultures. *Kundalini* in yoga is located in the spine and is represented by the aroused hooded serpent. Mind power is the ultimate knowledge. They equated *kundalini* to the power of the mind. If one looks at an anatomical specimen of the brain and spinal cord, one can immediately spot its resemblance to a hooded serpent. From the above it is evident that although the precise anatomy and functions of different parts of the brain are not described, it appears that yoga understood the power of the mind and its location in the brain and spinal cord. From below upwards, *i.e.*, from the *mooladhara* to the *sahasrara* chakra, the central nervous system formed the basis for the power of *kundalini*. It is interesting to know that all the nerves emanating from the spinal cord travel in a semi-circular fashion from the back to the front supplying all the tissues. In my opinion the *chakra* concept is based on the semi-circular arc of all neural reflexes. The various *chakras* (circles) that control different parts of the body functions at different levels are described by yoga. Many of them are currently co-related and correspond to the different autonomous nerve plexuses connecting to the central nervous system. Yoga is mainly concerned with mind control. We will now study the mind and its secrets.

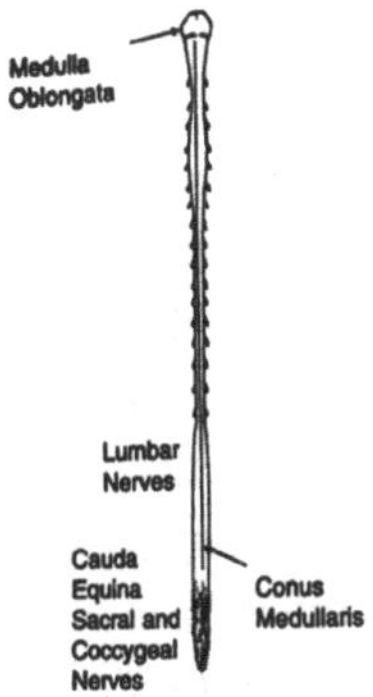

Fig. 1 : Spinal Cord

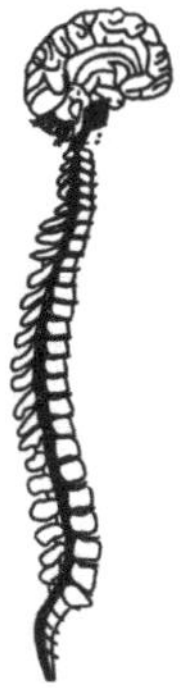

Fig. 2 : Brain & Spinal Cord

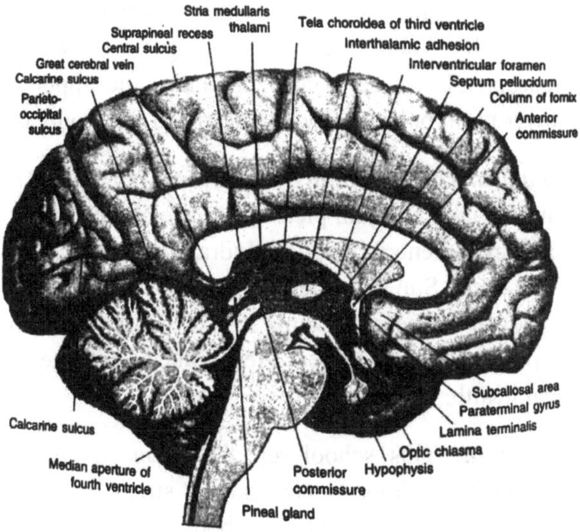

Diagram of brain & spinal cord

Compared to all other mammals, nature has bestowed man with a very highly developed brain. The brain is divided in two parts, *viz.*, a lower brain and higher brain. The lower brain comprises the hypothalamus and hippocampus. It controls the basic behavioural instincts of man. Love, hatred, sorrow, fear and anger are all the emotions, which are controlled by these lower centres of the brain. The cerebral cortex controls all the higher functions, *e.g.*, memory, intellect etc. The higher brain, comprised of the cerebral cortex, is made up of a thousand million neurones and an equal number of glial cells. With axons and dendritic cells they form billions of interconnections. Thus the brain controls all functions of cognition and conation in an absolutely synchronized manner. Different parts of the brain perform different functions. The left side of the brain is responsible for speech. The right brain is responsible for understanding nonverbal images and ideas. The frontal lobe is the seat of intelligence and the posterior part of the brain is the seat of the visual centre. Yet the brain acts as one functional unit. Hence the mind or *manas*, whose functional unit is the brain, is described as unitary by our ancient seers. At one time it can focus on only one object. Yoga practice enables the electrical activity of the brain to be synchronized and appropriate biogenic amines, the neurotransmitters are released. Thus without any doubt, yoga helps an individual to improve his own physical and mental abilities and skills. Yoga practice according Dr B. Rama Moorthy, a reputed neurophysician, helps to synchronise the upper brain control over the lower brain bringing about a balanced emotional control.

Purva Mimamsa: This school advocates rituals (*yagna* and *karmakanda*) to propitiate the gods, to gain pleasure, peace and prosperity. Each part of the body is represented by a god. Indra, the king of gods is believed to control the mind. Sun is located in the eyes. Fire is located in speech. Vishnu resides in the heart. Brahma resides in the head. Propitiation of the gods appears to be more or less a technique of management of mental and physical health.

Uttara Mimamsa: This school rejected *karmakanda* or the rituals. It is also called the school of *Vedanta*. Its stress is on achieving true knowledge. It hypothesises that the body and soul (*atma*) are two different entities. The body is a perishable entity, whereas the *atma* (soul) is eternal. Adi Shankara was a great proponent of this school of thought. *Vedanta* school believed that the universe is a myth (*mithya*) and only *Brahmn* is the reality (*Brahamah satyam jagan mithya)*. Just as gold ornaments of different forms depend on gold for their existence, the universe exists, because all existence is rooted in the efficient cause. This cause is called *sat* or *Brahmn*. Therefore the cause (*sat*) is the reality and not the result (universe). This argument is called *Satkaryavad. Uttara Mimamsa* draws heavily from the *Upanishads*. The *Upanishads* have dwelt on the subject of creation. *Upanishadic* enquiry into creation is described in the next chapter in detail.

Nyaya: This is logic. It believed in the relationship between cause and effect and that God is the cause of the universe. This school devised various proofs for establishing the facts. These are *pratyaksha* (direct evidence), *anuman* (inference), *upamana* (example), *yukti* (intelligent reasoning and deduction) and *aapta praman* (textual evidence/expert opinion).

Pratyaksha praman

Aatmendriya mano arthan sannikarshat pravartate l
Vyakta tadaatve ya buddhih pratyaksham sa niruchyate ll
(Cha. Su.11/20)

Direct observation or perception by the intellect is defined as that arising out of conjunction of the self (soul), mind, organs cognition and their objects together.

Anumana praman

Vahnirnigoodho dhoomena maithunam garbha darshanat l
(Cha. Su.11/21)

One can infer the existence of fire by seeing the smoke. Similarly seeing the signs of pregnancy one can infer a previous sex act. When direct observation is not possible, inference helps us to diagnose many conditions.

Yukti praman

Jala karshana beeja rutu samyogaat sasya sambhavah l
Yuktih shaddhatu samyogat garbhaanam sambhavastatha ll
(Cha. Su.11/23)

With a combination of water, tilling, sowing seeds and seasons, the crops will grow. Similarly the combination of the five proto-elements with the soul gives rise to a new birth. This knowledge is *yukti* or reasoning.

Aapta praman

Rajah tamaabhyam nirmuktat tapo yagna balenacha ye l
Yesham trikaalam amalam gyanam avyahatam sadaa ll

Aaptaah shishta vibuddhaaste teshaam vaakyam asamshayam l
Satyam vakshanti te kasmat asatyam neerajastamaah ll
(Cha. Su.18/19)

Persons who are free from passion and ignorance, always powered by penance and sacrifice, have a knowledge of the three time zones (past, present and future), are pure minded with unclouded knowledge, truthful, authoritative and whose words are unimpeachable are called *aaptas*.

Pratyaksha is very limited and *apratyaksha* is vast, *(pratyaksham hi alpam)*. By indirect knowledge one can appreciate much more. By seeing the smoke one can infer the presence of fire. Though we see this whole universe functioning, we are unable to see its creator (the cause). Without a creator (cause) the creation (the effect) is not possible. In the same vein, the fact that the creator or God exists can be deduced on the basis of inference.

Buddhism and Jainism do not believe in the existence of God. Adi Shankara expanded the concept of the union of *prakriti* with *purush* and its automaticity in causation of the universe to an extent to negate the existence of *Ishwara* (God). In his own times he was called *prachanna* Buddha (incognito Buddhist).

Another interesting philosophy was that of the *Charvakas*. This school believed in absolute materialism. It believed in only one life. Death was the end of life. The object of life was its full enjoyment. According to this school of thought, it was justifiable to 'sell one's own house to enjoy drinking *ghee'*.

Ayurveda adapted the concepts of the *Sankhya* and *Vaisheshika* models of the evolution of life and the universe.

The *Upanishads* form the bedrock of Hindu philosophy and are considered to be the highest level of Hindu theological and spiritual learning. A dispassionate study of these scriptures shows that in reality they are more in the nature of scientific inquiry into the secrets of creation. The various philosophies named above, especially *Sankhya* and *Vaisheshika* are referred to in the *Upanishads* and *Brahmasutras*. On a deeper study, all the spiritual treatises appear as a beautiful blend of science and spiritualism.

Why is it that the study of these philosophies is essential for an Ayurvedic student? An Ayurvedic student needs to understand not just the mind and body, but also a third element, the *atma* (soul). Additionally a good physician needs to understand the purpose of life and its values, his duties towards the self, the society in which he lives and the world or *jagat* at large. Through various examples and real life stories, the *Upanishads* explain the fundamental laws of life. Therefore studying *darshanas* and the *Upanishads* will be of immense benefit to a student.

(Additional Reading : Padarth Vidnyan)

Chapter : 2

The Upanishads: An Enquiry into the Secrets of Creation

Athato Brahmn jignyasa

Jignyasa is the quest for knowledge. It is the preamble of every *Upanishad.* This chapter deals with the enquiry into the mystery of creation and its creator. The *Upanishads* are termed as *para vidya*, superior knowledge. The *Vedas* and *shastras* are considered as *apara vidya*, inferior knowledge. They are also regarded as *Brahmn vidya*. The word *Brahmn* relates to the creator and the creation of this huge universe. *Vidya* is defined as that which liberates a person from ignorance. In other words it is a science. Indeed the *Upanishads* are the life sciences deciphering consciousness, intelligence, the origins of life and the secrets of creation. Therefore understanding the *Upanishads* has relevance to learning Ayurveda. The central theme of study of the *Upanishads* is to answer the question, "Who am I?" And also what is one's own relation to the universe. The *Upanishads* claim that studying them will enable a person to gain knowledge of whatever earlier was unheard as it becomes heard and whatever was unthought till then as it becomes thought.

Yenaashrutam shrutam bhavatyamatam matam l
(Chandogya Upanishad)

Studying the *Upanishads* entailed a strict code of conduct for students. One year's faithful service to the *guru*, observing strict penance with continence or sexual abstinence (*brahmacharya*) were requisite qualifications to enter the *gurukul*, (Rishi Pippalada in the *Prashnopanishad*). Knowledge is required to be established based on various proofs substantiated by evidences or *pramanas*. Learning was evidence based. Since perceivable direct evidence, is limited, one requires indirect evidence to obtain complete knowledge. The four *pramanas* are *pratyaksha* (direct), *anumana* (inference), *yukti* (intellectual deduction) and *aapta* (authoritative textual evidence/expert opinion). Humility was the corner stone of learning in the *gurukuls*. Teachers of the *Upanishads* were humble enough to acknowledge the limitations of their knowledge and always encouraged students to approach more knowledgeable gurus at the end of their training with them.

Let us now dwell on some of the secrets of creation.

Shunya vad: asatkaryavad: There were scholars, who believed that creation began from a void or non-existence or *asat* or *shunya* (zero). The modern big bang theory of creation also states that in the beginning there was non-existence and darkness and creation started with the big bang. Whereas our *darshanas* state that from the state of nonexistence, existence cannot arise. This is the fundamental difference between the two thoughts.

Satkarya vad: The *Upanishads* claim that existence was ever present. *Sat* means existence. Only *sat* in the unmanifested state existed at the beginning of creation. It was in a state of non- expression, but not non-existence. There can be no possibility of creation from the *asat* or non-existence. This *sat* is also called *Brahmn* or the original cause of creation. The entire creation is the result of the will of this singular *sat* to become many. *"Ekoham bahusyat*"

To prove this point let us look at the following examples. Different types of pots are made from mud, different types of ornaments from gold and different types of tools and instruments from iron, all bearing different names and forms. However, despite their different names and forms they have their origin in mud, gold and iron respectively. The cause lies in the original material not in the name and form. Therefore creation exists in a subtle cause that is *sat*, which is not always perceived by us.

Brahmn is defined as the infinite, unchangeable and everlasting true knowledge. (*Satyam gyanam anantam brahma - Tattiriyopanishad).* Thus *Brahmn* or the creator is simply the world of knowledge.

Let us now understand what is meant by knowledge. It is awareness, familiarity or understanding of something, such as facts, information, descriptions of skills, which is acquired through experience, education, by perceiving, discovering or learning. It can mean theoretical and practical understanding of a subject (Wikipedia). In simple terms actionable information is knowledge. No action is possible without knowledge. Even creation is essentially a program based on knowledge.

Another meaning of the word *sat* is also truth**.** Truth is that which does not change with the passage of time, past, present and future.

There is another truth that is relative to time and space, which is called *ritam*. There is only one thing which is changeless in absolute terms, the perfect knowledge, the *sat* or *Brahmn*. Everything else changes with time.

Brahmn is perfect knowledge. The *Aitareya Upanishad* refers to a *maha vakya* (a very significant sentence) from the *Rigveda*, which defines *Brahmn* as *Pragnyanam* (perfect knowledge). It is beyond the mind. The objects of the mind are *dhee* (receiving information and emotional response), *dhriti* (retaining information and well considered, steadfast resolve to act), *smruti* (memory/recall of information), *chintan* (thinking/processing information) and *buddhi* (intellect/judgment). *Vivek* is experiential wisdom behind any decisive action. Thus, knowledge is finally acquired through a number of these intricate mind processes.

Brahmn is all pervading perfect knowledge or cosmic consciousness. It is the cosmic intelligence filling the entire universe as a matrix. It is said to possess sixteen phases or *kalas*. These are sentience (*sangyanam* or *chetna*), ignorance (*ajnanam*), knowledge (*vignyanam*), eclectic response and presence of mind (*prajnyanam*), the ability to understand and memorise (*medha*), vision (*drishti*), fortitude (*dhruti*), intelligence (*mati*), ability of original thinking (*manisha*), sorrow (*juthi*), memory (*smriti*), intent (*sankalp*), resolution (*kratu*), speedy action (*aashu*), desire (*kama*) and passion (*vasana*). These are all the higher functions of the mind powered by *Brahmn*. All these functions of the mind enable a person to perform his duties in a coordinated manner. This principle of intelligence and knowledge operates on two planes, namely at the level of the macrocosm as well as at the level of the microcosm. It is based on a law called *pinda brahmand nyaya* of *Sankhya* philosophy. This law states that what is true for an atom is also true for the whole universe.

The *atma* represents the microcosmic *Brahmn* in the living. It is immortal. The *Katopanishad* states that the intelligent *atma* is unborn, without death, everlasting without any origin and is subtler than the subtlest and greater than the greatest. It is seated in the cavity of *hriday* of all mortal beings without any physical form, but can travel the farthest distances without hands or feet.

The *Kaivalyopanishad* describes *atma* as pure knowledge, which can see without the eyes and can hear without ears and travels to far off places sitting at one place. From what is stated herein with regards to the concept of *atma*, it is a non-material powerful and sentient agency, which empowers the body with consciousness, intelligence and the capacity to process information into knowledge.

The *Kenopanishad* describes *atma* as the eye of the eye and ear of the ear. The sense organs by themselves are incapable of their functions without being powered by the *atma*. *Atma* thus is the source for all perceptions, knowledge and actions. Knowledge helps even in controlling great forces of nature, *e.g.*, wind, water and fire etc.

The *Kathopanishad* states that *atma* is superior to the mind and intellect. Beyond *atma* is *mahat*. The word *mahat* signifies an element of infinite dimensions. Is *mahat* then the all pervading matrix of consciousness filling the entire cosmos? Beyond the *mahat* is unmanifest *prakruti*. Beyond the *prakruti* is the *purush*. This description from the Kathopanishad is the step-ladder model of creation of the universe. This description applies to a single celled micro-organism as well as to the whole cosmos.

The seed has the blue print of a tree. Uddalaka Aruni was a great rishi. Shwetaketu was his son. Shwetaketu returns home from the *gurukul* having completed his studies of the *Vedas* and the *shastras*. His father now wanted to test his son. He asked Shwetaketu to cut open a tiny Banyan seed, and describe what that tiny seed contained. Shwetaketu could not visualise anything tangible inside the seed. His father, Uddalaka, then explained that what was not visible to the naked eye inside that seed was in fact the causal body of the tree. Therefore he concluded that the seed is the causal body of the tree. The seed or embryo is a single cell. The tiny seed contains the blue print of the large Banyan tree, similarly a human embryo contains the total genomic programme of the human body comprising seventy trillion cells!

Then what is *purusha*?

Purey shareere shayati iti purusha l

Puri literally means city. The entity which resides (sleeps) in this city of nine gates is *purusha*. The body is an allegory to the so called *nava dwara puri*. These nine openings are the mouth, two eyes, two ears, two nostrils, anus and genito-urinary orifices. Thus the dweller of this city is *purusha*. Therefore the body is not the *purusha*. The use of the word *shayati* is very interesting. It signifies that the *purusha*, though sentient is non-potential. This *purusha* is *atma*, which is the microcosmic manifestation of the cosmic *purusha* of the macrocosm (*Brahmn*). The cosmic *purusha* is the *sat* or the *Brahmn*, the real cause behind all creation. It is pure consciousness, the super intellect or perfect knowledge that controls the cosmos. It is the cosmic intelligence or the unified field in the modern language of physics. It is the *Brahmn* of *Vedantins*.

The *Charak Samhita* states that the *atma* is the principle of consciousness and knowledge and is the source of all life. It is subtle and self born. It is not dissolved by death and it enters into new wombs in the form of a seed to take new forms of life. It carries with it the burden of past lives. It determines the life span, the intellectual and physical features and capabilities of a person on the basis of accumulated karmic information of previous lives. This description of Charak aptly fits into the modern understanding of the genome and hereditary transmission of genes. Genes are the basic physical and functional units of heredity transmitted from one generation to another. A gene is a sequence of nucleotides in DNA. The DNA spiral carries with it information and instructions in the form of chemical memory. This genetic information has been continuously transmitted over billions of years since the union of a male gamete (sperm) with that of the female (ovum) for the first time at the beginning of creation. A person is the genes he is made up of. It is the genes, which determine one's life span and abilities. A person suffers diseases of genetic origin because of gene mutations. In other words, the genes obviously carry the memories (burden) of previous lives.

The traditional method of introducing oneself starts from the first known lineage of oneself. The author traces his lineage from the ancient rishis of Vedic times, *viz*., Angirasa, Haritambarisha and Yavan. The word Yavan refers to a Greek. Yavana was a rishi of Greek origin. Hence the Hindu religion and thought appears to be universal in nature, rather than being restricted only to the Indian sub-continent.

The *Bhagavat Geeta* has referred to creation as an inverted Peepal tree (*Ashwatha*). The Peepal tree is an evergreen tree with a long life span. The family tree also has a very long life span. In this family tree, the roots are above and it grows in descending order with the shoots facing downwards. The Peepal tree here is more in the nature of a poetic symbolism and a beautiful example of blending the arts with science.

The proposition that the *atma* does not die is explained on the basis of the causal body. The seed is the causal body of a tree. *Mamrutam* of *Maha Mrityunjaya Mantra* means negation of death and continuous and never ending cycles of life (*samsara*). Even in the apocalypse (*pralay*) the genetic code is preserved in the form of a seed and creation springs once again. The seers who composed the *Upanishads* have compared this phenomenon to a web spun by a spider, which is also capable of dissolving it into itself and again recreating it at will.

What is the location of *atma* in the body?

It is located in the deep cavity of *hriday*, which is not necessarily the anatomical heart of human beings. It is connected through one hundred and one main branches (*nadis*) and seventy two thousand sub-branches all over the body. It is the chief central intelligent software mechanism that commands and controls all the functions and actions in the body as one unit, where each body cell is intelligent. Neurones, cardiomyocytes and hepatocytes are all intelligent enough to perform their prescribed functions, which are specific and different. Yet they are all well co-ordinated and synchronized under one single control. *Atma* is that power, which empowers the mind to control more than seventy trillion cells of the human body in a well co-ordinated way. Different texts quote different locations of the *hriday*, from the anatomical heart to the brain enclosed in the cranial cavity. Where this principal control is precisely located in our body and what its form is, is unknown despite all the progress in science. It is for this very reason that the *Upanishadic* perceptors have explained this phenomenon in the words *neti*, *neti*, meaning not this, not this. The statements 'I am *Brahmn*' and 'you are the *Brahmn*' (thou art that; that meaning *Brahmn*/*atman*) only reinforce the fact that everything that exists is *Brahmn*. The reality is *Brahmn* (cause) and the world is merely an elusive expression of Brahmn *(atman)*, *(Brahma satyam jagat mithya)*.

What is the relation of an individual (*jivatma*) to *Brahmn* (*paramatman*)?

Jivatma (individual or personal self) and *paramatman* (representation of the cosmic intelligence) are compared to two birds perched on the same tree. One enjoys the fruits of *karma* (actions) sunk in ignorance equating itself with the body, sensual desires and attachments to worldly things, this is the *jivatma*. The other, the *paramatman* simply remains as a spectator. One can always see this phenomenon as the sane voice, which many times opposes the will. This can also be compared to a catalyst in a chemical reaction, wherein the catalyst does not undergo any chemical change. *Atma* therefore is an adynamic surveyor or biocatalyst. *Brahmn* is described in the *Mundakopanishad* as *sakshi*, (witness), who witnesses an action without actually playing any role in the act.

The *Mandukya Upanishad* describes AUM, the *pranav mantra* and its relation to the three states of consciousness in great detail. The first state is *vaishwanara*, which is the waking state of consciousness, where a person is conscious externally (*bahi pragnya*). It is the process of receiving information from the external world through the sense organs and also responding to all this information through various actions. *Ahankar* of the self is believed to work through the right eye says the Rishi. What is the significance of the right eye to *ahankar* is not clearly understood by us as yet.

Taijasa is the second stage, or dream state. This *taijasa* works from the mind. It is the state of *antar pragnya*, which experiences the subtle objects.

The third state is called *pragnya*, which is a state of deep sleep. It is also called *pragnya ghan*, meaning mass of consciousness. It is full of bliss and joy. It works from the space inside of *hriday*.

The fourth state is of *turiya*. It is representation of the true self/*atma*. It is in the space between the two sounds of AUM. It is a sound without sound. In the words of Tao, it is the sound of one hand clapping. It is the state of supreme bliss, which is without any attachment and miseries. It is incomprehensible.

As an analogy to information technology of today, the concept of *atma* appears as the software file and the mind and body are the hardware. Modern technological progress today has made it possible to transmit thoughts across the globe and perform various acts through robotic arms by a mere thought process. This technology is called cyborg technology. This technology of the virtual world can be compared with *asparsha yog* of the *Mandukyopanishad*, the sensation of touch without actually touching, or clapping with one hand.

The renowned pscycho-analyst, Carl Jung postulated in his philosophy of integrated life and living, the presence of a collective unconsciousness, a repository of centuries of experiences and impressions belonging to a race. It is this collective unconsciousness that determines attitudes, actions and responses of an individual to different situations. Charak's concept of *atma* carrying the burden of previous lives is nothing but the knowledge that has accumulated through experiences and impressions over the centuries, transmitted as hereditary information as chemical memory in DNA through genes from generation to generation. It is similar to the collective unconsciousness of Carl Jung.

Rene Descartes said "I think, therefore I am," (*cogito ergo sum*). According to him consciousness was responsible for life. Whereas Karl Marx was of the opinion that life was superior to consciousness, because of the reason that man's ability to think and the quality of his thoughts depend so much on his living conditions. The living conditions of a person virtually limit his intellectual growth. A person's intellectual development is affected by the environment. We all know that soon after fertilization, gene imprinting occurs in an embryo, which is responsible for the intra uterine growth programme that dictates all the aspects of an individual for his entire life span. This programme defines one's physical and mental abilities as well as the life span. Environmental stress, poor nutrition in the early state of pregnancy, in an expectant mother, adversely affects the foetal growth resulting in babies with poor intellectual development and low birth weight. Thus life depends upon both nature and nurture which play complimentary roles to each other.

Chapter : 3

Creation of Life

How is life created?

Ayurveda has adopted the concept of creation as stated in the *Upanishads*.

The *Chandogya Upanishad* states that the *sat* willed to become many. Union of the non-dynamic *purush* with the unmanifest dynamic *prakruti* resulted in *mahat*. *Mahat* is the all pervading matrix of consciousness. From *mahat*, the *ahankar* is created. *Ahankar* is the ability to recognize the self from the non-self. *Ahankar* thus bestows immune power and the capacity of self-assembly, self-replication, multiplication and finally self perpetuation. Self assembly is the property of all biomolecules. A cell is formed through this process of self assembly of biomolecles. This is followed by cell duplication, multiplication and perpetuation resulting in the multitude of living species on this planet over the billions of years of creation. *Ahankar* drives the mind systems through its three primal qualities, *viz*., *satwa*, *rajas* and *tamas*. These primal qualities are different levels of coding and processing systems of information and knowledge generation. In different proportions they create different forms of characters and the species. *Rajas* and *tamas* are two opposing levels of coding and processing systems that generate knowledge, based on which the different species, characters and forces are formed in the universe. *Satwa* is the most balanced well organized quality of the coding and processing system.

Tamas: It is defined as confusion, delusion and darkness. In mind systems, it represents a very crude order of coding and processing of information by the mind resulting in perverse understanding with a low level of knowledge generation. It can also be compared to Brownian motion of particles (particles in motion without any fixed direction moving hither and thither). It is the most powerful of the three *gunas*. Of the five proto elements (*pancha mahabhoota*), *tamas* is predominant in *prithvi*. It keeps matter in the solid state. It can be compared with the nuclear force, which keeps protons and neutrons together in the nucleus.

Rajas: At level of the mind it is an initiator of vigorous activity. It is also a powerful force. It is comparable to the electro-magnetic force. *Vayu mahabhoota* is rajas predominant.

Satva: It is subtle and luminous. At the level of the mind it is total clarity. It is like a liquid crystal. It is an organizing force. *Akash*, the principle of sound is *satva* predominant. The resonance factor of sound is responsible for all the transformation reactions in the periodic table. This factor converts hydrogen into helium, which is responsible for radiations from the sun that sustain our lives. Carbon, which is basic to all life, is activated by this resonance factor. That is why, the resonant sound of AUM is called *pranav*, meaning the creator of new life. The *ahankar* produces the five *tanmatras*, through different proportions of these *trigunas* (qualities). The five *tanmatras* are *shabda* (primordial sound), *sparsha* (tactile perception), *roopa* (visual perception), *rasa* (taste perception) and *gandha* (olfactory perception). The *Upanishads* and *Sankhya* philosophy have stated that these *tanmatras* produce the respective *gyan indriyas* (organs of cognition), *viz*., ears, skin, eyes, tongue and nose. They are also the cause of the respective *pancha bhootas* or the proto-elements, *viz*., *akash*, *vayu*, *tej*, *aap* and *prithvi*. The *tanmatras* are the different sense perceptions, which are the objects of the mind. All these *tanmatras* in reality are non mechanical entities. How then are they able to create in actuality, the mechanical realities in the universe? This is the real mystery of creation. James Jeans, a renowned physicist in his book, "*The Mysterious Universe*" says that, "matter is the manifestation of mind". The universe is more like a great thought than a great machine.

Padarthas are the objects of perception. *Vaisheshika* philosophy has described seven of them. 1. *Dravya* (substance). 2. *Guna* (attribute). 3. *Karma* (action). 4. *Samanya* (genus - principle of assimilation). 5. *Vishesha* (species - principle of differentiation). 6. *Samavaya* (inherent inseparable combination). 7. *Abhava* (non-existence). *Abhava* is rejected by *Sankhya* on the basis that all the matter that exists in this universe is either in the form of positive or negative mirror images. Temperature exists in positive and negative forms as hot and cold respectively. The twenty attributes, that are described, starting from *guru* (heavy), *laghu* (subtle), *ushna* (hot), *sheeta* (cold) *etc*., are the ten pairs of opposites. Modern science concurs with this approach of *Sankhya*. For example anti matter is the negative mirror image of matter. The mirror image of the proton is the anti-proton, the electron has the positron and the neutron has the anti neutron as their mirror images respectively.

There are nine substances or *dravyas*, *viz*., five *maha bhootas* (proto elements), *atma*, *manas*, *dik* and *kal*. *Kal* is time. Time is defined as an indefinite progress of existence and events that occur in apparently irreversible succession from the past through the present to the future. This linear understanding of time in terms of past, present and future is essentially an occidental concept. Time in the context of all the oriental philosophies is circular (*kala charka*). It has neither a beginning nor an end. It is termed as *akal* (time less). *Dik* is the three dimensional space. *Kal* and *dik* are the time space continuum, which is the fourth dimension, as stated by Einstein. These dimensions are inseparable from matter. With reference to biology, biological time is the period through which an infinite number of species are expressed over billions of years of this creation and space is the biosphere.

Pancha mahabhoota

***Akash*:** It is not space as it sounds. It originates in *shabda tanmatra*, which is the resonance of sound. The quality of *akash* is sound, (*shabda gunam akasham*). The power of sound was understood by all the ancient cultures. *Vedas* declare that the word was the first to exist. Even the Bible concurs with this. The *Mandukyopanishad* states "*Omityed aksharam/ Sarvam omkaram eva*". This primordial sound of AUM or every spoken word is imperishable. All existence is within the sphere of sound. It is present in all the states of consciousness, *viz*., the waking state, dream state and deep sleep. AUM is the resonance of sound that pervades all life. Music has great equalizing, harmonizing and healing powers on the mind and body. It is essentially for this reason that sound is referred to as *Nada Brahmn*. Fred Hoyle described the resonance factor of sound, whose function is nucleo-synthesis or fusion reaction. This factor is essential for the formation of all the elements of the periodic table. It is an essential factor for activation of the carbon atom, which is the basis for all organic life. Sound is a great organizing force without which no matter can be formed. It is important for the organization of molecules and cell structures. Even our body equilibrium rests in the vestibular apparatus of our inner ear. Modern researches have shown that the genome can be translated into audio format and a genetic signature in sound can be made of a person. Ultra sound is a very powerful tool, it is also a disruptive force, with which a huge building can be demolished.

Vayu: It is created from *sparsh* (the sense of touch) *tanmatra*. *Vayu* is the most vigorous of all the *mahabhoota* since it is *rajas pradhan*. Of the *panchpranas* the *vyana* is the *vayu* says Pippalada in the *Prasnopanishad*. It circulates all over the body through thousands of channels connected to *hriday*. *Vayu* is air, which is a mixture of nitrogen (80%), with oxygen and other minor gases forming the remaining 20%. Nitrogen is essential for the formation of protein. Proteins are the building blocks of the body. The body is a very subtle combustive machine. For all the oxidation processes in the body oxygen is required. It is how the body consumes the fuel to generate energy. Modern biochemistry has shown that the combination of nitrogen and oxygen, called nitric-oxide (NO) is one of the important neurotransmitters in the body, which acts on both the afferent and efferent segments of the nervous system. This NO is produced in the vascular channels by the endothelial cells. The discoverers of this work were awarded the Nobel Prize. Discovery of NO has proved one more scientific insight of the *Upanishadic* seers.

Tej: It is created by the *roopa* (sight) *tanmatra*. It is the result of the radiations from the sun. The chemical composition of this universe is chiefly made up of hydrogen (90%), helium, an inert gas (8.9%), carbon (0.03%), nitrogen (0.01%) and oxygen (0.07%). Hydrogen is the corner stone of this creation. With the help of the resonance factor two hydrogen atoms undergo fusion reaction resulting in the release of energy with the formation of helium. This is the same fusion reaction that is used in making a hydrogen bomb. Every minute many hydrogen bombs explode in the sun to make it shine brilliantly and provide the radiation energy for the sustenance of this universe. Apart from visible light the other types of radiations are ultraviolet, infrared, cosmic rays, electric discharges, heat waves and shock waves etc. It is for this reason that the Hindu scriptures considered the sun as the cosmic *prana* (the very life of the cosmos). It is also described to be the soul of the universe (*Surya atmah jagatah*) and considered as *Brahmn* (*Aasau Aadityo Brahmah*).

Aap: This is formed by the *rasa tanmatra*. It is the life giving water. The first speck of protoplasm is therefore believed to be born out of the oceans. A. Oparin, a Russian scientist hypothesized that, life evolved from the hydrocarbon polymers under the effect of solar radiation and ultrasound generated by the tidal waves in the waters of the ocean in the presence of atmospheric air. A major proportion of the bodies of all living organisms is made up of water.

Prithvi: This is created from *gandha* (aroma) *tanmatra*. The entire aromatic chemistry revolves round the carbon atom. No aroma can exist without carbon. It is the dictum of organic chemistry. Hence it is common sense to equate *prithvi* to carbon. The excited state of carbon is basic to life and hence the entire organic world is carbon based. Yet another variety of life, which is silicon based is also known to exist. It exists at the core of the earth at very high temperatures. Interestingly both these elements share the same chemistry. Both can store information and are capable of recall. Examples are gramophone records and silicon chips.

These five *mahabhootas* form the energy and matter of this creation. Interplay of the consciousness, energy and matter resulted in life, which is explained by the *prana rayim* interactions in the *Upanishads*. *Prana* is the sun and *rayim* is the moon or the matter. The moon only shines because of light reflected from the sun. Rishi Kanada, the preceptor of *Vaisheshika* philosophy stated that the *paramanus* (sub-atomic particles) interact with each other and combine physically or chemically in different proportions of the *satwa, rajas* and *tamas gunas*, which results in creation. Kanad defined the subtle *anu*, the atom for the first time in the history of mankind. He also further reduced matter to sub-atomic particles (*parmanus*). The word atom in physics has its origin in the root, *atam* or *atma*. *Atma* was the subtlest of the subtle.

From the above discussions on matter we can conclude that the chemistry of the *panchbahutic* universe is based only on four elements, *viz*., C, H, N, O and two forms of energy, *viz*., light from the sun and sound.

A. Oparin has demonstrated that DNA can be produced in the laboratory by exposing the hydrocarbon polymer in a solution of salt water, simulating sea water, to ultra violet rays simulating the sun and ultrasound simulating tidal waves in the presence of air. His experiment conclusively proves the scientific correctness of the *Upanishadic* hypothesis of creation.

What is *prana*?

Prakrshena ananti iti praanah l
Agni soma vayu satwm rajah tamah pancha
indriyani bhootaatma iti praanah l

That which enables the body to ceaselessly discharge all its functions and actions is *prana*. It is the combination of fire (*pitta*), water (*kapha*) and air (*vata*), *satwa*, *rajas* and *tamas*, all the sense organs and the life creating soul and *pancha mahabhoota* that creates this life force. Essentially the force that enables all the life functions is *praana*. The living systems are created by the union of *atma* or *purush* with *prakruti* and the life systems work through the agency of *prana*. It is an independent force. Just as the combination of software and hardware requires electricity to function, similarly life and living organization also require a force to make life function. We must remember that the living body is a community of seventy two trillion, conscious, intelligent cells. Every living cell has electric potential. Each cell is comparable to a battery cell with 1.4 millivolt electrical energy. Cells conduct electric current. The cell membrane has a positive charge outside and negative charge inside. Thus the cell membrane acts as a barrier to molecular transfer from inside to outside or *vice versa*. Ayurveda has identified two energy sources in the form of *tej* and *akash mahabhoota*. The sun and sound are powerful energy sources. The rays from the sun are a spectrum of electromagnetic waves ranging from infrared (IR), visible light and ultraviolet (UV) rays. Sound energy through its resonance is responsible for fusion of nuclei (property of nucleo sysnthesis). It is responsible for activated carbon atoms. Activated carbon is the basis for all the life on earth. The whole universe is connected through the webs of energy fields. Modern physics recognizes four types of fundamental forces in nature. These are nuclear force, electromagnetic force, electro-weak force and gravitational force. According to Ayurveda there are five forces that uphold life. These are called *pancha pranas*. These five *pranas* are *prana*, *apana*, *udana*, *vyan* and *samaana*. These *pranas* are different from the five types of *vayus*.

Prana is the most powerful and is born out of *atma*. *Atma* represents the sentient and also the primordial source for all kinds of living beings and things. Thus *atma* is different from *prana*. *Prana* is a force that upholds life. It is described as that which burns like fire, shines like the sun, rains as the clouds and rules as Indra. It enters the body by the action of the mind. It can be compared to the most powerful force, the nuclear force, which binds protons and neutrons together in the nucleus of an atom.

The power of nuclear fusion and fission are well known in terms of the hydrogen bomb and the atom bomb respectively.

Apana is the downward attraction towards the earth. It is comparable to the gravitational force. All biological processes are affected by changes in the gravitational fields. Even the cell size will vary with the gravitational force and is inversely proportional to the strength of the gravitational field. Higher altitudes are associated with low gravitational force.

Udana is the levitating force of space, which is characterized by weightlessness. Is it equivalent to the electro weak force? A hypothetical force is postulated to explain both the electromagnetic force and weak nuclear force as two aspects of a single force. The weak force allows fusion of the proton and neutron.This is responsible for the radiations we receive from the sun.

Samaana is the force located in the interspace between the earth and the sun. This force is responsible for digestion of food, providing nutrition to the whole body and the seven *dhatwagnis* (seven flames). This is probably comparable to the electromagnetic force. This acts between charged particles whether or not they are moving and is the combination of electrical and magnetic forces. It has both qualities of attraction and repulsion. This force regulates physiology, biochemistry and molecular biology in living beings. It defines the three dimensional structure of proteins, causes muscles to contract etc.

Vyana, the last *prana* is *vayu*, the air. Oxygen from the atmospheric air is used by the body for internal combustion, which is responsible for the generation of combustive metabolic energy in the body.

Through *prana*, the living systems are sustained. With the addition of *manas*, the thinking process begins. *Manas* is the subtle and single mind, whose objects are *dhee*, *dhriti*, *smriti*, *chintan* and *buddhi*. At the source of all of them is the sentient self or *atma*. The time space continuum is the fourth dimension of space. The fundamental property of time is its irreversibility. Time in reference to creation is that interval in which an infinite number of species of living beings manifested over billions of years of existence.

Nature magazine has reported on the research by Susan Blackmore regarding out of body experience (OBE). New medical developments of brain mappings have shown that by stimulating an area behind the ear known as the angular gyrus, one gets a feeling of lightness and a sensation of floating towards the ceiling, whereby a person can observe oneself and the world from a point outside their own body. This state of OBE can be compared to the astral body, which is different from the gross, corporal body. Such experiences are also described in our scriptures. Whether the practice of AUMkar can result into stimulation of centres located in the angular gyrus or any other such centre in the brain and thereby help in achieving the state of bliss as described in the scriptures could be an interesting subject of research.

(Reference: Blackmore S.J. (1984) - Psychological theory of the OBE, Journal of ParaPsychology, Vol. 48, p 201-218. Blackmore S.J. (2002) - Nature,Vol. 419, page, 269-70.

How is this creation sustained?

The *Upanishads* have recognized that food is an essential ingredient to sustain creation. The *Bhagawat Geeta* quoting the *Taittiriyopnishad*, states that the procreation of living beings, the mind, the *sat* or knowledge, the whole world and all functions and actions depend solely upon food. The sun's heat converts water into rain clouds. Rains nurture the plants on earth, which are the source of food for the whole of the animal kingdom. Semen is formed from the food, which when introduced into uteri results in the birth of all the living beings. Thus the life cycle sustains creation, (*Annaad vai praja prajayante)*.

Purusha is *anna rasa maya*, meaning the human is totally made out of nutrition (*chyle*), (*Purush anna rasa maya* - *Mundakopanishad*).

Taittiriyopanishad has bestowed *annam*/food, the status of the *Brahmn*.

Puzzle of death

The *Kathopanishad* is a dialogue between the disciple Nachiketa and the preceptor Yama, the king of death. Yama explains that the "I", the self is not the body. The body is a vehicle of the rider, the *atma*. With the dissolution or the death of body, the self or *atma* does not die. The self is like the master of the chariot (body). The intellect or *buddhi* is the charioteer, the mind is reins that control the horses and the horses are the senses, which enjoy the objects. The self is that part of the cosmic program of information, knowledge, intelligence and wisdom, which is eternal and immortal. This self enters into new wombs and takes new forms. This intelligent information is preserved as the causal body to propagate creation. The seed therefore contains the causal body of a tree. It travels as genetic information through generations, propagating and sustaining this creation.

With the advancement of information technology, the whole idea of self or the soul can now be understood in terms of a software file for a processor, the mind. Loss of this mind file (software) is death. This mind file can in future be possibly inserted into a silicon chip and transplanted to create the transmigration of soul. Advance techniques in the field of assisted reproduction have already created clones of animals. And now the stage is set for cloning a human being, creating immortality.

Finally the *Kathopanishad* advises the student to arise, awake and learn the knowledge and wisdom, at the feet of real masters. Thus many seers who composed various *Upanishads* have provided different insights into the secrets of life and creation. This knowledge is the fundamental base of Hindu philosophy as well as for Ayurveda.

In summary, this discussion on Hindu metaphysics helps us to understand that the human body is an intelligent autonomous self-driving vehicle that can analyse its surroundings with a flawless auto-pilot software system called *atma*. Just as a car has sensors to warn of a collision, cameras to monitor blind spots, ultra sonic radar, light wave radar (LIDAR), *etc*., the body has the sense organs that help in the navigation of the body. Similar to self-driving cars, which use cloud computing to act on traffic data, weather, maps, adjacent cars, and surface conditions among others, the mind (hardware) processes all the data acquired by the sensors and helps monitor the surroundings better and make informed decisions. Judgemental errors are due to quality of processing of the information. The best quality of mind processing leading to right knowledge is termed as *satwik*. Poor quality of information processing is termed as *tamasik*. *Rajasik* is an intermediate quality. Processing faults lead to judgmental errors and accidents. Judgmental errors are called *pragnyaparadh*. *Pragnyaparadh* is an important cause of all diseases.

Chapter : 4

Religion, Science and Medicine

Religion is defined as a cultural system of designated behaviour, ethics, morals and practices, world views, sanctified places, texts and prophecies and organization that relates to humanity and to supernatural, transcendental or spiritual elements, (Wikipedia). Ayurveda is deeply connected to the Hindu or *Sanatana dharma*. It is the most ancient religion of antiquity. It has no prophet. The *Vedas* are the most revered texts of *Sanatana dharma*. *Veda* literally means knowledge. *Rig*, *Yajur*, *Sama* and *Atharva* are the four *Vedas*. Each of these *Vedas*, addresses different aspects of human life and society. The objectives of human life are called *purusharthas*. They are *dharma* (duty/code of conduct/order of nature's laws), *artha* (material wealth/achievements), *kama* (desires/ambitions/personal pleasures) and *moksha* (ultimate deliverance from all attachments and the cycle of death and rebirth). The *Rigveda* represents *dharma*. *Atharvaveda* stands for *artha*, *Sama* stands for *kama* and *Yajur* stands for *moksha*, (*Vedamoorthy taponishta pandit Shriram sharma acharya-Gayatri mahavignyan*). Ayurveda is believed to have originated from the *Atharvaveda*. It is replete with details of diseases of a spiritual, traumatic and organic nature. There is mention of a variety of drugs, herbs and surgical procedures apart from prayers, *mantras*, charms and amulets.

"O, life! When you are propitious, the drugs of *atharvan* (charms), the drugs of *angirasas* (juices of plants and animals) and divine therapies (prayers to the sun, water and other natural elements) and drugs of human artifice (intellect) all bear fruit, (*Atharvaveda 11.4.16. History of Medicine in India* – Dr Pranjivandas Mehta).

The *Atharvaveda* recognized the ability and intelligence of animals to invent healing herbs, "The boar knows the plant; mongoose knows the remedial herbs, what once the serpents, the *Gandharvas* know those I call to aid for him," (*Atharvaveda Kand 8. Su. 7. Verse 23. History of Medicine in India* - Dr Pranjivandas Mehta).

Modern medicine is no exception. It learnt the procedure of giving enemas from *ibis*. There is a long tradition of holy men of different religions healing people. Temples were the places of healing from time immemorial in all the cultures of the world. Priests, shamans, monks and diviners were the standard health providers. This practice continues even today in many remote areas of the world along with the use of *mantras*, incantations and amulets.

Even in the West there is a history of tradition that connected religion and medicine. For over a thousand years until the Renaissance period the church establishments built hospitals, provided medical training and licensed physicians to practice medicine. Philosophy, physics and physician all these three terms have one common origin. Philosophy literally means pursuit of knowledge and acquiring of wisdom. Investigation of the nature, knowledge of the causes and reasoning with the help of knowledge *etc*., are all part of philosophy. A physic is a person who practices the art of medicine. Physics is the science of matter and energy. Science according to Karl Pearson is a critical systemic nature of facts in their comprehensive entirety but not selected at random. The totality of knowledge with regards to man and his environment is the real essence of medicine. The holistic approach of Ayurveda correctly fits this definition. Charak says that the knowledge of the whole cannot accrue from the mere knowledge of a part.

Nahi gnyanavayena krutsne gneye gnyanamutpadyate l (Ch. Vi. 4.5)

Hindu thought appears to be a beautiful blend of all these three subjects, *viz*., philosophy, science and medicine. It is difficult to understand where philosophy ends and medicine begins. Ayurvedic philosophy is based on the *Sankhya* and *Vaisheshika darshanas*. Spirituality and science complement each other here. From '*Vid*' came the words *Veda* and *Vaidya* in India and in the West the words meta-physics and physician came from philosophy.

Let us see if the religious rituals and festivals have any link to the practice of medicine. Let us start with salutations to the sun (*surya namaskar*) in the morning. The sun is believed to be the soul of the universe, "*Surya atma jagatah*". To an intelligent person this prayer should be the proclamation of a great scientific truth. The sun gives us both light and heat, which energises the whole universe.

Shuchi, the practice of keeping oneself and the environment clean before performing any religious activity is compulsory for any Hindu.

A high level of hygiene is the most important single factor to ensure good health. It is the most important facet of preventive medicine of Ayurveda called *swasthavrittha*. An improvement in standards of hygiene has a major effect in reducing the incidence of communicable diseases. The Hindu way of greeting with folding hands is a 'touch me not' technique invented much before the appreciation of asepsis by modern science. This technique, which was at the root of evolution of the concept of asepsis, was traditionally practiced by Hindu Brahmins for millennia. The merit of this practice remained obscure and it was sometimes misunderstood. This very concept has now been put to use by modern medicine as surgical asepsis. It acted as an insurance against communicable infections. It is a Hindu custom not to mix freely with a family in which a death has occurred for a period of ten days. This custom probably came into practice with the knowledge that most infections have an incubation period of one week. The idea of quarantine in conjunction with the hygienic technique of 'touch me not' has been practiced from time immemorial in India. Modern medicine had no knowledge about this type of surgical asepsis practice before the 18th century, when for the first time an Austrian monk, Semmelweiss observed the benefits of washing one's hands. Today if modern surgery has scaled great heights it is because of this principle of asepsis. No wonder Semmelweiss is considered to be the father of modern surgical asepsis. But this very scientific idea got corrupted in the country of its origin as the practice of untouchability.

Another interesting practice is of cow worship and *pancha gavyaprashan*. Compared to the buffalo, the cow is a difficult animal to tend and maintain, and it is less economical. Yet the cow was worshipped and kept in the house and looked after with religious devotion. The cow was believed to mitigate the sins of a person. In the context of Ayurveda, sin (*papma*) is a synonym for disease. The cow was the key in preventive medicine. The term vaccination is derived from the word *vaca*, which in Latin means cow. A mixture of cow dung, urine, curd, milk and *ghee* mixed in a copper plate, is administered in small doses orally to people once a year. It is known as *pancha gavya prashan*. It is in fact a technique to deliver the attenuated intestinal microbes from the cow, which worked as an oral vaccination improving the general resistance or immunity of an individual against a number of monsoon specific diseases. It is administered normally once every year as a booster dose. Elsewhere in this book this topic is dealt with in greater details. Boiled and cooled water stored in copper or silver vessels is advised for drinking purposes. These two elements are ionizing and therefore are bactericidal. It was a unique method, which cleansed the water from the disease producing bacteria. It served the purpose of healthy drinking water very well.

All the medicinal plants that are used in the worship of various deities have suggestions to an intelligent vaidya for their use in therapy for various diseases. One objective of the worship was to save these plants, serving the purpose of ecology. *Amla*, *Tulsi*, *Bilwa* and *Panchvalkal* are but a few such examples. *Vata savitri poornima* is a festival for women. During this festival a married woman worships the ficus group of plants to ensure the longevity of her husband's life. While the worship of these plants helped the ecology, it also gave an indication to an intelligent vaidya that these plants are the choice remedy for infections of the female genital tract. Research conducted by the author has confirmed that the bark of these ficus plants has a wide spectrum of antimicrobial activity especially against all the pathogenic organisms in the female genital tract. *Tulsi* is the most revered plant. It is considered to be dear to Lord Vishnu. Lord Vishnu is said to reside in the chest of the human body. *Tulsi* is an effective remedy for most chest or respiratory disorders. The *Bilwa* tree is a must in all Shiva temples. Shiva's place in the human body is located in and around the umbilicus. *Bilwa* is a very effective remedy for hyper acidity and all types of diarrhoea and dysentery. Similarily, *Amla* is a plant which is worshipped religiously and is also a very useful rejuvenating medicinal plant. During the *Ugadi* festival, it is compulsory for every Hindu to consume a small quantity of *neem* leaf. *Neem's* medicinal properties as an antimicrobial are well known and need no emphasis. The ancient ritual practices appear to be based on the scientific insights of our ancestors, which are now verifiable by modern scientific tools.

Even Hindu gods and their idols were conceived on the basis of different ideals pursued by different people. *Vighnaharta* (destroyer of obstacles) Ganesh is indeed modelled on the basis of the steps necessary to ward off obstacles. The elephant head signifies a big head (brainy), the sharp piercing eyes, broad, wide open ears and closed mouth, characterize a successful person, who can succeed in overcoming all the obstacles in his path. All the gods of the Hindu pantheon *e.g.*, Rama, Krishna, Shiva and Hanuman *etc*., are worshipped for the ideals they stand for. Thus the idols stand for these ideals.

The role of psyche as the cause of disease was well understood by our ancient *acharyas*. Charak states that negative emotions, *e.g.*, fear, hate, anger, jealousy, greed, frustration and delusion are enemies and are the cause of diseases. Positive health resulted from positive emotions, such as love, hope, confidence, assurance, generosity, *etc*. Hence Charak advised *sadvritta* (good moral behaviour) and *swasthavritta* (code of healthy living) for a healthy life. The most popular Hindu text is the *Bhagavat Geeta*. It is an elegant manual for right code of conduct and a balanced way of life. It provides guidelines on mental, intellectual and physical well being. The spiritual (*bhakti*), intellectual (*gyan*) and code of conduct for action (*karma*) are addressed very practically. In the modern world of heightened stress, this text offers solutions and solace. In my opinion, every student of medicine should study the *Bhagavat Geeta* to become a true healer. There is a need to develop an interface between spirituality and the mental health of an individual for a better quality of life, especially for those patients afflicted with psychiatric problems. Modern medicine is increasingly realising the need for a holistic approach to religious beliefs and practices of patients undergoing treatment for chronic diseases, mental illnesses or terminal stages diseases.

Modern research has now established the anatomical sites of emotions. Cannon-Bard have demonstrated that the emotional flow occurs from the limbic system in the midbrain. The seat of aggressive behaviour of a person resides in the lower limbic system (*amygdala*). Animal experiments have demonstrated that the surgical excision of this part can make an aggressive animal docile. Emotions release chemicals into the circulation. The level of lactic acid is raised, when a person becomes extremely anxious. That heredity and genetics also play a part in social behavioural patterns was known to our ancestors. It is now proved that a person with a 47XYY chromosal setup has an anti social character.

Ayurveda lays great stress on environmental factors in relation to health. It was William James who, in 1884, first realized that environmental stimuli can affect emotions. Emotions in turn affect the internal organs producing different types of responses. Stress causing a peptic ulcer is one such example. Pavlov, the great Russian physiologist proved that the emotions resulted in organ responses through his brilliant experiments on dogs. He demonstrated that if a dog is conditioned to a particular stimulus, like putting on a light just before serving food, it salivated even when no food was served, when the light stimulus was given. This he termed as conditioned reflex.

Many of our modern scientific discoveries are the result of intuition. It was only later that all the intuitionally based discoveries were proved experimentally and established. Modern scientific tools and knowledge can now help to prove many such concepts hitherto thought to be empirical. Thus Hindu religion, science and Ayurveda are truly a beautiful blend and wonderful picture of synthesis.

Chapter : 5

Definition of Ayurveda

Ayurveda literally means the science of life. *Ayu* means life. *Veda* is *vidya*, the true knowledge. *Vidya* is like a road map for a traveller and Ayurveda is a road map of health for a life time. There are different varieties of Ayurveda addressing different forms of life, *e.g.*, *Vriksha* Ayurveda, *Ashwa* Ayurveda and Ayurveda for humans etc.

How is *vidya* or knowledge defined?

The word *Veda* has its origin in the root *vid* or *vidya* (true knowledge). *Vidya* is defined as follows:

Sa vidya ya vimuktaye l

Knowledge is the power that liberates man from confusion and ignorance. A man without knowledge is a confused person. Sensing, learning, gaining information and understanding a subject are at the root of knowledge. Knowledge is simply actionable information. No action is possible without knowledge.

Vidya or knowledge can be defined as ideas and inspiration that the mind gains from the processed information resulting in actions. Actions are performed through one's mind, speech and the organs of cognition and conation. Knowledge based actions result in wholesome outcomes. *Avidya* or ignorance ends in unwholesome outcomes.

Sushruta defines Ayurveda as follows:

Iha khalu Ayurveda prayojanam vyadhupasrushtanam
Vyadhi parimokshah swasthasya rakshanam cha l

Ayurasmin vidyati anena va aayur vindati iti Ayurvedaha ll
(Su. Su. 1/12, 13)

The objectives of this science are to enjoy life, protect it and promote its span, giving relief to a person suffering from disease and maintaining the health of healthy persons.

Let us now define life from the perspective of biomedicine. Defining life has been a great challenge to both philosophers and scientists from time immemorial. Life is a characteristic that distinguishes physical entities having biological processes. The chief biological or physiological processes of living organism are homeostasis, organization, metabolism, growth, adaptation, response to stimuli and reproduction. Survival and reproduction are the key purposes of biology. Life encompasses all living beings including microbes, plants, animals and man.

All living organisms have basic structural and functional units known as cells. They are well organized into various systems to allow them to perform different life functions. Cells multiply by mitosis. Reproductive cells are called male and female gametes. Formation of an embryo or the seed requires the union of male and femal gametes. It is the first step in reproduction. The living body is a very efficient combustible machine that works at a very low temperature. It converts ingested food to energy to help cells and tissues in their growth and sustanance. It is called anabolism. Organic matter is broken down through catabolic processes. Together this is called metabolism. The metabolic fire is called *agni* in Ayurveda. The body needs to maintain the temperature of its internal environment constant in relation to the external environment. For example, in the cold we shiver to generate more heat, whereas in the hot summer, we sweat to cool off. This regulation helps the state of equilibrium in a living organism. It is called homeostasis, or the *sama* state. This state of *sama* is fundamental to health from the Ayurvedic stand point.

Sama dosha samagnishcha sama dhatu malakriya

Health is a state when the *doshas*, *dhatus*, *agni* and *malas* (excretions) are in a state of *sama*. The concept of homeostasis in modern biomedicine was first described in 1865 by Claude Bernard, a French physiologist, who is considered the father of experimental medicine. He observed that the circulating body fluids, *viz.*, blood, serum, and intra organic fluids, *etc.* constitute the internal environment, which preserve the necessary relation of exchange in equilibrium with the external cosmic environment. However, the term homeostasis was coined later in 1962 by the American physiologist, Walter Bradford Cannon.

Growth occurs with the building of tissues. Life is cyclic in nature. The life cycle starts with the embryonic stage and progresses through successive stages comprising the foetus, child, adult and declines in old age and ends in death. Death is a certainty of all life. Death is a harbinger for a new life. Life, death and rebirth according to Hindu philosophy is a never ending cycle of events called *samsara*. Cellular replication, growth, senescence and death occur continuously all through life.

Life is a mixed bag of wholesome and unwholesome, happy and sorrowful experiences, which form the basis for health and disease in man. Ayurveda is that science which addresses the measures for maintaing the health of a healthy person and remedying the disease states in him.

Hitahitam sukham dukham ayuhtasya hitahitam l
Manam cha tacha yatroktamAyurveda sa uchyate ll

Swasthasya swathya rakshanam Aturasya roga nivaranam l

The whole idea of maintaining the health of a healthy individual is a highly interesting and a laudable positive health concept, which is different from disease management. From the point of view of Ayurveda, prevention of disease is more important than curing the disease. Susruta has defined health as follows:

Samadosha samagnischa samadhatu malakriyah l

Prasanna atmendriyamanah swasthamityabhideeyate l

A person is healthy, when his *doshas* (key regulators of all the systems, *viz.*, *vata*, *pitta* and *kapha*), *agni* (metabolic fire), *dhatus* (tissues) and *malas* (excretae) are in a balanced state; his soul, body, mind and organs of cognition and conation are in a perfect state of coordination and his mental disposition is happy and cheerful. It is the state of homeostasis of the milieu interior in Ayurveda. As per the current understanding ninety five percent of diseases have their origin in the mind and only five percent are organic in nature. The Ayurvedic definition of health, in my opinion, is the best and most appropriate. Mere absence of an organic disease is not equivalent to the health of a person. Thus the Ayurvedic approach is a holistic approach that considers the body, mind and soul in unision. The gross body or corporate body is called *sthoola deha*. The subtle body or the mind is called *sookshma deha*. There is yet a third body, the causal body or *karana deha,* which represents the soul. Inside the seed is the causal body of a tree. Within the seed is the blue print or genetic programme for the tree. How are *sukha* (happiness) and *dukkha* (sorrow) caused?

Hetustu sukha dukhascha yogo drushta chaturvidha l

Natmendriya manobuddhi gocharam karma va vina l
Sukham dukham yatha yacchya bodhvyam tattatochyate ll
(Cha. Sha. 1/131)

Excessive, inadequate and pervert indulgence of all the five senses and organs of action are responsible for unhappiness or *dukkha*. Proper and well coordinated actions by the quartet of the soul, mind, intellect and *indriyas* result in happiness, whereas improper and uncoordinated actions by the quartet lead to sorrow.

The scope of Ayurveda extends much beyond the biological boundaries. It defines life in more humane way as follows:

"*Ayuh Kamayamanena Dhrama Artha Sukhavaham*" (*Vagbhata Sutra Sthana.* 2)

अयु: कमायामानेन धर्म अर्थ सुखावहम

A long and happy life is essential for fulfilling the objectives of life. There are four objectives of life according to Hindu philosophy. These are called *purusharthas*. They are *dharma* (conforming to stipulated personal and social obligations and duties), *artha* (wealth and material achievements), *kama* (personal desires, ambitions, sex, reproduction *etc.*,) and *moksha* (liberation from ignorance/bondage). Achievement of these objectives is only possible if a person is healthy. Thus Ayurveda has a role that enables an individual to fulfill all the objectives of life. Ayurveda helps primarily to promote and maintain the health of the healthy and secondly to give relief from disease in a person.

Rene Descartes said, "I think therefore I am. *"Cogito ergo sum."* Life and consciousness are synonymous. The consciousness is also the primary property of the whole universe and the universe exists in the infinite consciousness in the form of the formless '*Brahmn*'. Intelligent cosmic consciousness is an independent entity and is at the root of life and the universe. It is the unique distinguishing feature of Hindu philosophy.

Sankhya philosophy believes that the creation is rooted in knowledge. The knower is the most powerful and is the efficient cause or creator. He is called *purush* or *kshetragnya* (knower of the field of action). Thus the creator, is not a physical entity or God, but supreme knowledge. The Creator, in my opinion is like a powerful software program. To illustrate this with an example, the creator of an earthen pot is neither the potter nor the mud and not even the potter's wheel, but it is the knowledge of pot making. The entire cosmic drama runs in a well- orchestrated program. The planets move in orbits with mathematical precision. The seasons come in programmed cycles. All systems in our body function in a well organized and orchestrated form like a program.

Thus a Hindu believes that the whole world is rooted in knowledge. This is called *pragnyanam* or perfect or supreme knowledge. It is a combination of consciousness and intelligence. "*Pragnyanam Brahmn.*"

The *Taittiriya Upanishad* defines *Brahmn* as "the infinite infallible, never altering and ever lasting supreme true knowledge, *"Satyam gyanam anantam Brahmn"*.

In the last chapter we discussed the sixteen characteristics or *kalas* of *pragnyanam*, namely, sentience (*sanjnanam* or *chetna*), ignorance *(ajnanam)*, knowledge (*vijnana*), electric response and presence of mind (*prajna*), ability to understand and memorise (*medha*), vision (*drishti*), fortitude (*dhriti*), intelligence (*mati*), ability of original thinking (*manisha*), sorrow (*juthi*), memory (*smrithi*), intent (*sankalp*), resolution (*kratu*), speedy action (*ashu*), desire (*kama*) and passion (*vasana*). This sixteen phase *pragnyanam* obviously represents the consciousness intelligence combine.

Consciousness is one. It is seen in man, in animals, in gods and *Brahmn*. Consciousness is self-illuminating; it has remained constant throughout the ages. It is unborn and deathless. This consciousness beholds the '*pranashakti*' (the life force) says Swami Vidyaranya in his treatise *Panchadasi*. It is like a canvas that is always ready for a new picture. It is awareness, an ability to perceive one's relationship with one's environment. Thus the consciousness provides the capacity to receive, process and store, recall, recognize and perceive information. It becomes actionable as knowledge. It will be useful for the reader to understand the definitions of a few terms that are commonly used.

Data: Data are raw facts and figures that have no meaning on their own.

Information: Data that have been interpreted within a context, so that it has meaning to the user. In other words it is the flow of messages.

Knowledge: It resides in the user. It is a combination of information, experience and insight that may benefit an individual or organization. In other words, it is information that can be acted upon.

***Gyata*:** Knower, ***Gyanam*:** Knowledge; ***Gyeyam*:** That which should be known.

Knowledge enables an individual to organize or program all activities. *Pragnyanam* or perfect knowledge is the essence of life. With knowledge a man perceives, imagines and dreams, experiences emotions of joy and sorrow *etc*., acts with resolve and performs with determination. The quality of knowledge determines the quality and class of the action.

Freeman Dyson defines life as a material system that can acquire, store, process and use information to organize the activities. It uses the energy from the various sources in this universe for the purpose of its activities.

Thus a living organism harnesses four chief types of forces in nature, *viz.*, nuclear force, electromagnetic force, electroweak force and gravitational force. The resonance of sound is also a powerful form of energy. It is the reason why the ancient civilizations called sounds like AUM or Amen as *mantras* generating new life (*pranava*). The living body is a combustive machine that generates energy through oxidative metabolism. The consciousness beholds these energy forms as life force or *prana shakti*. The holistic approach considers a human being as a part of the whole, meaning the universe. The environment around us is similar for all living organisms. All the organisms are interconnected through well organized, complicated net works of pulsating energy fields. The energy field that envelopes a man is called the aura. The *prana* concept in Ayurveda is this very pulsating energy field in and around the living human body.

The consciousness also flows freely in different channels of intelligent webs. The *Charaka Samhita* made a very important statement in the *Viman Sthana*, with regard to the relation between man and his environment. All the matters of perceptions that exist in the universe also exist in man *(Purushoyam lok sammita/yavanthohi loko murthimantho bhava visheshah tavantah purushe, yaavanthah purushe tavanthah loke).*

This echos the *Sankhya* perception of *pinda* (microcosm), *Brahmanda* (macrocosm) and *nyay* explained in earlier chapters.

Albert Einstein held a similar view when he said, the human being is a part of a whole called by us, the universe, a part limited in time and space. He experiences himself as something separate from the rest, a kind of optical delusion of his consciousness.Modern medicine also confirms this view. The human being is not just the product of his genes but equally, the result of his environment. Quality of life also plays a role in shaping ones abilities. Thus nature and nurture play complimentaery roles in ones life and its goals.

Another important statement, which is of the utmost significance is that Ayurveda accepted the twenty four constituents of creation described by the *Sankhya* philosophy. Creation is primarily the result of the union between the adynamic sentient self, *purusha* with the dynamic material and unmanifest *prakruti*. *Purusha* is the principle of sentience or consciousness (*chetna*). It is non potential. Yet it sets the *prakruti* into a dynamic mode to create life systems. This can be compared to the combination of software and hardware in a computer.

Chapter : 6

Purusha and Prakruti

So far we have dealt with *purusha* at length. Let us now understand *prakruti*.

Prakruti

In the beginning before creation manifested, only sentient *sat* or *Brahmn* or *Purusha* existed. It willed to become many. *Avyakta prakruti* initially was unmanifest. Union with *purush* transformed it into the expression of materially manifested *prakruti*. The word *prakruti* is derived from the roots *pra* and *karoti*. It signifies the forward progression and action, signifying its dynamism.

Karya karana kartrutve hetu prakruti hi utchyate l

The cause for any action and the necessary instruments together are collectively defined as *prakruti*. The combination of *prakruti* and *purush* results in life systems. Living human beings, whether, man or woman are called *purush*.

Shad dhatu purush
Panchamhabhhoota shareeri samavayah purusha iti utchyate l

Khaadaayah chetana shashta dhatavah purushah smruta ll
The combination of the five proto-elements and the sentient purush is known as shat (six) dhatu purush.

Bhoomi aapo analo vayu kham mano buddhih evacha l
Ahamkaram iteeyam me bhinna prakrutih ashtadhaa ll
(Bhagavat Geeta. 7/4)

The primordial *prakruti* is eight fold. There are five proto-elements, the mind, intellect and *ahamkar* (the power of self identification from non self).

The twenty four elements of life (*Sankhya* model of creation)

Mahabhootaani ahankaaro buddhi avyaktam evacha l
Indriyani dasha ekam cha pancha cha indriya gocharaah ll
(Bhagavat Geeta. 13/6)

The conglomeration of twenty four elements that include the subtle unmanifest *prakruti* along with the five proto elements, intellect, power of self identification and the eleven *indriyas* inclusive of the mind and five *tanmatras* together form the material *prakruti* comprising twenty four elements. Union of the *purush* with this conglomeration makes it the *purush*, comprising twenty five elements.

Itccha dvesha sukham dukham sanghaatah chetana dhrutih l
Etat kshetram samasena savikaram udahrutam ll (ibid 13/7)

Desire, hate, happiness and sorrow, life functions and resolute actions *etc*. are all outcomes (*vikaras*) of this combine. Such a combination is known as *kshetra*, the field of consciousness. This combine can sense its environment through the mind and sense organs. It enables all the physiological processes in the body to operate. An individual thus becomes the perceiver, thinker, achiever, seer and judge, visionary, *etc*., through the mind's action. Through the sense organs he sees, hears, feels, smells and tastes. Through the organs of action he performs all his routine activities. This combine is also called the *chikitsa purush*, the one who can be treated.

The union of purusha with prakruti is the beginning of life systems.

Mahat is the vast matrix of consciousness pervading the entire universe. Consciousness is the ocean of unidentified intelligence. From *mahat* the manas or mind systems are added to life systems.

Mind collectively refers to those aspects of the intellect and consciousness manifested as a combination of thought, perception, memory, emotion, will and imagination. A thought is the manifestation of memory. Memory is the power to recall processed and stored information. In simple terms, the mind is a memory bank. Many different types of memories are known, *viz*., elemental, atomic, evolutionary, karmic, articulate, inarticulate, conscious and unconscious memories. The intellect or power of judgement operates from the mind. Human mind systems are capable of gathering information and using it appropriately like any other semiotic agency. Andrade, in 1999, described semiotic agency as information gathering and using systems (IGUS). Zurek extended these properties to living entities. Semiotic agency merges and transforms the internal and external flows of energy.

Manas is mind in Ayurveda

Lakshanam manaso gyanasyabhavo bhava evacha l
Satih atmendriyaarthanam sannikarshena vartate ll (Cha. Sha. 1/17)

Vaidhrutyam manaso gyatam saanidhyat taccha vartate l

The mind functions in coordination with the soul, *indriyas* and their objects to obtain knowledge. In the absence of mind no knowledge is possible. Only when the mind is present can knowledge be acquired.

Subjects and actions of the mind

Chintyam vicharyam uhyam dhyeyam sankalpam evacha l
Yatkinchit manaso gyeyam tat sarvamhi artha samgyakam ll
(Cha. Sha. 1/19)

Thinking, enquiring, debating, contemplation, resolving, knowing and recalling what was known are the objectives of mind.

Indriyabhigrahah karma manasatwasya nigrahah l
Uho vicharscha tatah param buddhi pravartate ll (Cha. Sha. 1/20)

Receiving objects from the sense organs (receiving information), control of the sense organs by the mind, imagination and enquiry are the actions of the mind.

Ayurveda believes in oneness of the mind, characterized by the nature of enquiry, debate and doubt, *(mano vimarsha rupam)*. *Smruti* is the power of recalling information and knowledge, or memory. *Chintan* is the power of contemplation and thought processing. Whereas *buddhi* (intelligence) is the faculty of reasoning, decision making and judgment, *(buddhihi nishchayatmaka)*. *Dhee* is the power of emotional control and *dhruti* is that of volitional control. The *Bhagavat Geeta* defines *dhee* and *dhruti* as below.

Dukheshu anudvignamanaah sukheshu vigataspruhah l
Veeta raaga bhaya krodha sthitadhee muniruchyate ll

A person who can control and conquer emotions and desires, passion, fear and who is harmonious in both happiness and distress is called *sthita dhee* (rooted in a steady mind). He is also called a *muni* (saint).

Dhrutya yaya dharayate manah pranendriya kriyaah l
Yogena avyabhicharinya dhruti sa partha satwiki ll

Dhruti: This is the faculty that enables an individual to be steadfast, unfailingly righteous and resolute in all actions by controlling the mind, *indriyas* and life force.

Vivek: This is the experiential, discriminating intelligence or the wisdom, which enables a man to discriminate right from wrong, like separation of milk from water, (*ksheera neera viveka*).

Every living cell is conscious and intelligent. It plans its own growth, endows the hereditary characters, initiates and performs actions instinctively just as a man constructs his house, rail roads and other structures, (Nels Queli - 1916). In other words intelligence plays an important role in creation. Intelligence in the cell creates all its organelles, drives the regulators, functional and structural genes. A single celled embryo has a blue print capable of developing the human body comprising seventy two trillion cells.

Let us now try to understand the mechanisms of intelligence. The information is present in genes. We are aware that artificial intelligence is processed through digital and analogue coding in a computer. How exactly the information is processed in the brain is not known as yet. A third possibility could be quantum processing, though quantum computers have not yet been constructed. It is believed that information is coded in humans to be partly analogue and partly digital. In genes, the information is most likely coded in digital form. Advances in the neuro sciences have led to a tremendous revolution in understanding of the consciousness. What was once considered as junk DNA (ncRNA) or non coding RNA is currently taking centre space in the human genome. Studies now indicate that the function of the ncRNA is driven by a language that couples the analog and digital information, which helps information processing in the brain. Newer mechanisms are being hypothesized for the complex processing of information that occurs in cells in the body as well as in the brain. The evolutionary goal is to help gather greater amounts of information rapidly which is processed, stored and utilized and finally discarded when not required, by utilizing the free energy. ncRNAs allow a more efficient coupling of energy to information, wherein less energy is required to represent and process more information, condensed in analogue and digital form, into smaller spatial and temporal domains, ideal for the different environments found in neural tissues. They permit rapid acquisition of information from the environment, along with fast, flexible processing and elimination of that information, when it is no longer necessary. They facilitate accelerated evolution of an organism's information content and functional computational systems. The molecular computing system of RNA – protein interactions, a result of fine grained information encoded and accumulated over evolutionary time, interacts with sensory inputs and stress to produce "cellular intelligence." This emerging panorama opens entirely new dimensions of information processing in the brain (George St. Laurent III).

Ahankar: This is an important element of the self, it is the ID of the self. All biomolecules possess the property of self assembly. In terms of biology, self assembly is the organzation of molecules. A cell duplicates, multiplicates and perpetuates itself. It is this biological property, which has enabled billions of species to survive on this globe. Recognition and rejection of the non-self is also a form of *ahankar*. Thus it forms the basis of the power of immunity. The word, *ahankar*, is literally translated by many as ego.

Manas or mind: The mind systems operate through three levels of qualities of coding and processing of information, generating different classes in knowledge and resultant perceptions, experiences and actions. These are known as *trigunas* or three primal qualities, *viz*., *satva*, *rajas* and *tamas*. The different permutations and combinations of these three primal qualities result in infinite numbers of living beings with different levels of intellect and behaviours. At the time of embryogenesis, the imbalance in proportions of these primal qualities results in three main *prakrutis* or constitutions based on the predominance of one of the qualities. Thus the three main types of personalities are born out of *triguna*. The proportions of these qualities are also subject to change at different times resulting in varied moods, attitudes, behaviour and actions. A mythological (*Puranic*) story illustrates *triguna* personalities very succinctly. Sage Kashyapa, is believed to be the first human and therefore we are all known as his descendants. He had three wives. The offspring of the first wife are *devas*, those of the second wife are *danavas* and those of the third wife are *rakshasas*. The *devas* represent the *satwic*, *danavas* the *rajasik* and *rakshasas* the *tamasik* behavioural traits in man.

What are the characteristics of persons having different primal qualities?

Satwa

The perfect quantal or digital coding and processing of information in a *satwic* person's mind results in true and clear knowledge and perfect actions. *Satwa* signifies subtlety, clarity and luminosity of thought and judgment. It is the balancing quality for the two opposing modulators of qualities, *rajas* and *tamas*. It helps to regulate and organize these opposing forces in the right direction to achieve equilibrium. It is characterized by subtlety and luminosity. At a cellular level, it is the liquid crystal state of both the cell membrane and the protoplasm, enabling the highest and most balanced functionality.

Tatra satwam nirmalatwat prakashakam anamayam
Sukha sangena badhnati gnyana sangena dehinam l
(Bhagawat Geeta 14/6)

Satwa results in clarity, illumination of the mind and a state of positive health and absence of disease. A *satwic* person is a happy, faithful, healthy and strong person, who is loving in nature. They are persons of fortitude, duty bound and non-craving, with strong convictions and are fond of unctuous, tasty, sweet and hearty foods.

Rajas

Rajasic types are associated with a slightly inferior level of coding and processing system in the mind. This results in rather less than perfect knowledge and emotionally charged judgements associated with vigorous thoughts and emotions with motivated actions.

Rajo ragatmakam viddhi trishna sanga samudbhavam
Tannibadhnati kaunteya karma sangena dehinam l
(Bhagawat Geeta 14/7)

Rajas signifies passionate desire and motivated action. When this quality increases, it results in imbalance of the mind and man becomes selfish, greedy, develops an excessive craving for things and becomes ill, both physically and mentally. A *rajasic* person is highly emotional, proud, egoistic and boastful, gets angry easily and becomes violent. He is fond of hot, dry, spicy, sour and salty foods that promote disease and sorrow.

Tamas

Tamas signifies darkness and ignorance. This is due to a very poor quality of coding and processing of information in the mind that results in incorrect, inappropriate and perverse images and knowledge. This causes mental inertia that leads to perverted actions. Inertia is the result of Brownian motion of particles in motion without any particular direction and momentum. Inertia at the level of the mind dulls the thought process.

Tamastu agyanajam viddhi mohanam sarva dehinam

Pramada aalasya nidra bhi, tanni badhnati Bharata ll
(Bhagawat Geeta 14/8)

Tamas causes ignorance or false or illusive knowledge and confusion. Due to this a person becomes deluded, lazy and inactive and can become depressive, addictive and drowsy or comatose. The *tamasic* person is fond of stale, fermented, tasteless, spoilt left over food. Every man has all the three traits in him but in different proportions resulting in millions of different personalities, only three broad categories are described for practical purpose.

The primal qualities create different *manasik prakrutis*, meaning different mental and behavioural make up of a person. Depending on permutations and combinations of these three qualities of processing types of consciousness during embryogenesis soon after conception, millions of different types of psychic personalities are possible, Charak in *Sharira Sthana* describes fifteen psychic personalities, namely seven *satwic*, six *rajasic* and three *tamasic* types.

Satwic

1. ***Brahma***: Pure, truthful, self controlled, discriminative mind, knowledgeable, understanding, power of exposition, ready wit, excellent memory, free of passion, desire, anger, greed, conceit, infatuation, envy, dejection, intolerance and equanimous in nature.

2. ***Arsha***: Devoted to daily religious rituals of sacrifice, studies, vows, homa offerings, celibate, hospitable and free from pride, conceit, attachments, hatred, infatuation, greed and anger. Genius, eloquent, restraint, retentive are the characteristics of an *arsha*. He is like a rishi.

3. ***Aindra***: Like Indra, the lord of the *devas*. Leadership, authoritive in speech or commanding, ritualistic, energetic/powerful, splendour, without blemish, foresight, virtuous, wealthy, sensuous pleasure seeking.

4. ***Yamya***: Like Yama, who is commonly known as the god of death, he is the most righteous in his judgments. Propriety, righteousness, unassailable, upright and hard working, sharp memory, weilds authority and power, free from passion, attachment and envy, hate and infatuation are the hallmarks of this personality.

5. ***Varuna***: Valiant, courageous, clean, lives in good and clean environment and enforces hygiene, ritualistic, fond of aquatic sports and honourable persuits are such a person's qualities. They are equanimous in giving favours as well giving recriminations.

6. ***Kauvera***: Like Kubera, the lord of wealth, he commands status, honour, luxuries and attendants. Constant pusuit of virtue, wealth and pleasures, uprightness, interest in recreation are such a person's virtues. They can be moody at times.

7. ***Gandharva***: Fond of dancing, song and music and loves to be praised. Their hobbies are writing poetry, literature and history. Addicted to pleasures of aromas, flowers and recreation. Free from envy.

***Rajas*: (Character is tinged with passion)**

1. ***Asura***: Characterized by demonish behaviour. Valiant, despotic and envious, terrifying, pitiless and fond of self adulations.

2. ***Rakshasa***: Intolerant, full of hatred, vengenance and cruelty. They are gluttonous, fond of eating flesh, indolent, somnolent and envious.

3. ***Paisacha***: Ghost like in behaviour, voracious eaters and highly sexual, unhygienic, coward, a bully and indulges in abnormal types of recreation and diets.

4. ***Sarpa***: Like a serpent, they are touchy, respond strongly when excited, indolent, fearsome, fond of food and recreation.

5. ***Preta***: Like a wandering spirit they are envious, indiscriminate and vulgar in character and conduct. They are excessively fond of food, are lazy and covetous.

6. ***Sakuna***: Bird like in nature with strong attachments, delights in food and recreation, fickle minded, intolerant, non acquisitive are characteristics of the *sakuna* type.

***Tamasic*: (Directionless mental disposition/Inertia)**

1. ***Pasava***: Disgusting behaviour, somnolent with no intellect and forbidding disposition and diet. Indulges in abnormal sexual habits and pleasures.

2. ***Matsya***: Pussilanimous unstable mind, unintelligent, greedy for food with strong likes and dislikes. Fond of water, itinerant hobbies and habits.

3. ***Vanaspatya***: They lead a vegetable like life. Lazy, moronous and gluttonous eating habits are their nature.

How do these primal qualities cause creation?

Kanada (*vaisheshika darshan*) hypothesized that *anus* (atoms) and *paramanus* (sub atomic particles) of the material *prakruti* are organized into biomolecules that form the basic materials for creation. Various permutations and combinations under the influence of the three primal qualities create five subtle *tanmatras*.

The *tanmatras*:

1. ***Shabda:*** Sound perception.
2. ***Sparsh:*** Tactile or touch sensation.
3. ***Roopa:*** Visual sensation
4. ***Rasa:*** Taste sensation
5. ***Gandha:*** Olfactory function (smell sensation)/Aroma.

These senses (*tanmatras*) are believed to be the cause of the five proto elements, five organs of cognition and five organs of conation. This concept of genesis of substances from the non material quality is based on the G*unavat dravyam* principle.

James Jeans, a renowned physicist states something similar in his book, "*Mysterious Universe*". "Today there is wide measurement of agreement, which on the physical side of the knowledge is heading towards a non mechanical reality. The universe begins to look more like a great thought than like a great machine. Old dualism of mind and matter, which was mainly responsible for supposed hostility seems likely to disappear, not through matter becoming any more shadowy or unsubstantial than heretofore or through the mind becoming resolved into a function of working matter, but though substantially matter resolving itself into creation and manifestation of mind."

Modern scientific progress has made great strides in understanding the nature of life and as well the universe. Matter now is further reduced to subatomic particles *e.g.*, quarks and preons. Interchangeability of energy and matter is now an established fact, (Einstein's famous equation, $E=mc^2$). Forces are expressed in terms of frequencies and wavelengths of different magnitudes.

The five protoelements or *pancha mahabhootas*

1. ***Prithvi***: The earth. Its characteristic is *gandha* (aroma).
2. ***Aap*:** Water. Its characteristic is taste or *rasa*.
3. ***Tej*:** Solar power. Its charactetristic is vision.
4. ***Vayu***: The wind. Its characteristic is tactile sensation.
5. ***Akash*:** Sky? Space? Void?

Many people consider *akash* as either space or void. *Akash* cannot be space. Space is designated as an independent entity called the *dik*. Space is one of the nine substances, which are different from the *pancha mahabhoota*. The characteristic of *akash* is sound. Sound cannot propagate in a void. Hence *akash* as one the five *mahabhootas* should be equated to the principle of sound. Of the three primal qualities, the *sattwa* creates *akash*. The combination of *sattwa* and *tamas* results in the formation of water. The combination of *sattwa* and *rajas* forms *tejas*. Pure *rajas* causes the formation of *vayu*, and *tamas* the *prithvi*. Thus *pancha mahabhoota* are born out of *pancha tanmatra*.

Matter is always considered in the space and time frame work. The three dimensional space concept in terms of electromagnetism and gravity is now no more relevant. With the addition of the dimension of time to the three dimensions of space, it has become the four dimensional space time continuum. The whole creation can now be condensed into matter, energy, gravitation, space and time. The chronology of events that follow the interplay of matter and energy is time. Inter play of all these elements and forces leads to various events. This chronology of events represents time. Irreversibility is the fundamental property of time.

Ayurveda also considered both space (*dik*) and time (*kaal*) amongst the nine essential substances. These nine substances are the *pancha mahabhoota*, *purush* (*atma*), mind (*manas*), time and space. The concept of time in the orient is circular like a wheel, where past, present and future merge into each other. This is the basis for the cycles of birth and death (*kaala chakra*) leading to rebirth. Whereas the occidental concept is linear past, present and future and then fullstop. Space in biology is the biosphere. Biological time is that in which the phenomenon life is manifested over billions of years by its expression through evolution of the many species on earth. Chronobiology is all about the seasons and biological clocks. Ayurveda attaches great importance to chronobiology. *Dina* and *rutu charyas* (daily and seasonal life lifestyles and diets) are described for the maintenance and promotion of good health in Ayurveda.

Atma the principle of *chetana* represents the *purusha* of the *Sankhyas* and *Brahmn* of the *Vedantins*. It is probably the unified field of astro physicists. It is a non potential surveyor. It is a form of biocatalysis. It is the basis of life. All the living systems are the result of the combination or union of *purush* with *prakruti*. It is subtle, eternal and indestructible, and self born and it enjoys the material world bound to *prakruti*. It cannot be dissolved by death and it enters into new wombs to take on new forms of life. It carries with it the burden of past lives. *Charak Samhita* states that it is the principle of knowledge. It determines the life span, knowledge and capabilities, which are predetermined on the basis of its past births. The twenty characteristics of *atma* are as follows:

1. *Aayu* (life span), 2. *Atma gnyana* (knowledge of the self), 3. *Manas* (mind), 4. *Indriyas*, 5. *Praana*, 6. *Prerana* (inspiration), 7. *Dharma* (order of nature's laws), 8. *Aakruti* (the form), 9. *Swara* (voice), 10. *Varna* (colour and complexion), 11. *Sukha* (happiness), *dukkha* (sorrow), 12. *Icchaa* (desire), 13. *Dwesha* (envy), 14. *Chetana* (consciousness), 15. *Dhruti* (strong resolve), 16. *Buddhi* (intellect), 17. *Smruti* (memory), 18. *Ahankar* (self identification), 19. *Prayatna* (effort), 20. *Dehantara prapti* (rebirth).

We know that genes carry within them instructions in the form of chemical memory spun into the fragile thread of the DNA spiral and transmit them from one generation to the next since eternity. Does the transmigration of the soul or *atma* represent the biological (genetic) hereditary information transmitted from one generation to another over billions of years of existence in this universe? The genome dictates all the above twenty functions of *atma*.

Additional reading

Andrade E, Maxwel Demon's and Natural Selection: Semiotic Approach to Evolutionary Biology, Semiotica 127: (1/4):133-149.

From Dynamical to Semiotic Account of Emergence. Cybernetics and Human Knowing , Vol. 15 nos. 3-4pp.

Chapter : 7

Pancha Mahabhoota

The *pancha mahabhoota* are the five proto elements of the universe. All that exists in this world is essentially made up of five proto elements or *pancha mahabhoota*.

Prithvi: Earth

Parthivastu gandho gandhendriyam
sarva moorta samooho guruta cha iti l

The earth represents the quality of aroma, the nose that recognizes smells, all solid forms and those that possess the quality of heaviness. Another important quality is roughness or *kharatwa*. It is predominant in *tamas*. In the earlier chapter we have discussed how the sense of aroma creates both the sense of smell and the *prithvi mahabhoota*. The qualities of *prithvi* fit the description of the carbon atom.

Aap or *jala mahabhoota*: Water

Aapyastu raso rasanendriyam sarva drava
samooho guruta shaityam retascha l

Water *mahabhoota* is born out of the sensation of taste, it is the source of the taste buds of the tongue, all liquid forms, heaviness, coolness and semen. Water is the most important major constituent of all living beings. Indeed water is life. We know the chemical symbol of water as H_2O.

Tej mahabhoota: Light and heat

Taijasastu roopam roopendriyam varnah santapo bhrajishnuta
paktih amarshah taikhshanyam shauryam cha l

Tej mahabhoota is born out of the visual sense, it causes the organ of sense (eye), colour, heat, lustre, digestion of food, unease, acute symptoms and chivalry. The sun gives us both light and heat through radiations. It is the most important form of energy on which this universe survives.

Vayu mahabhoota: Air

Vayavyastu: sparshah sparshanendriyaam sarva cheshta
samoohah sarva shareera spandanam laghuta cha l

From the sense of touch *tanmatra* the skin is formed, all the bodily movements and all the pulsations and sense of feeling light (lightness) result. Air, as we have already noted, is composed chiefly of nitrogen and oxygen. Air is believed to be the cause of all actions. Nitric oxide gas is an important neuro transmitter, which will be discussed later.

Akash mahabhoota: Sky

Antarikshastu shabdah shabdendriyam
sarva chidra samooho viviktacha l

The sky is born out of sound *tanmatra* and it creates the organ of hearing (ear). It causes porosity and vividity. Sound is a very important form of energy. It has already been described in an earlier chapter.

Ayurveda considers that all existence is *panchabhautic*. Is it possible to verify this concept scientifically?

Chapter : 8

Chemistry of Life

Let us now understand *panchabhutas* from a scientific point of view. Is *akash* equivalent to space?

Space

Edwin Hubble is credited with the discovery of space. Space is a hard vacuum containing a low density of particles, predominantly it is a plasma of hydrogen and helium and electromagnetic radiation (light and heat *etc*.), magnetic fields, neutrinos, dust and cosmic rays (energy particles). The following diagram is self-explanatory. Since space is a vacuum, sound does not travel in space. Whereas sound is the characteristic of *akash* or the sky. Hence space cannot be equated with *akash*. The sky is like a blue canvas of different shades of scattered light. The sky or *akash* appears blue in colour due to the fact that blue light is scattered in all directions by tiny molecules of air in the earth's atmosphere. The different colours of the sky depend on the different colours scattered.

***Akashic* records:** Sylvia Brown who had predicted the advent of the devastating 2020 pandemic in 2006, described the *akashic* records as follows:

"The *Akashic* Records have been described in a number of ways by a number of different people and cultures. Edgar Cayce knew them as the collective memories and histories of every thought, sound, vibration, moment and event in eternity. The Hindus thought of them as every thought, word and action, recorded on a substance called "*akasha*," which they believed was the primary principle of nature from which earth, water, fire and air were created. Psychologist Carl Jung called them the Collective Unconscious, a powerful conceptual force but not necessarily a literally recorded one". (Page. 80. *Prophecy* – Sylvia Brown, published in 2006.)

In *Panchadashi* by Vidyaranya the consciousness is described as a canvas of infinite dimensions ever ready for a new picture to be painted. He called it *chitra deep*.

***Akash vani*:** The sounds from the sky. Sound is a form of energy produced by the vibrations of particles of matter. It requires a medium, *e.g*., air, water or other materials. It is a longitudinal mechanical wave, consisting of an oscillatory elastic compression and an oscillatory displacement of fluid. This is how it becomes audible to the human ear. Sound energy is imperishable. Earlier we have discussed the resonance of sound. Resonance of sound pervades all life forms.

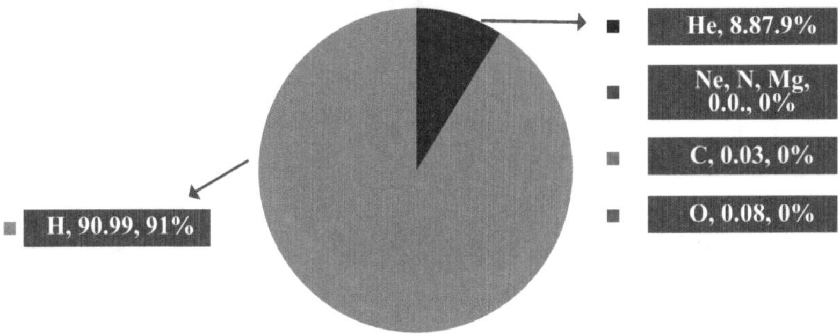

Composition of space

Earth's crust

The earth's crust is mainly compsed of oxygen, silicon, calcium and magnesium. Silicon and carbon have a similar chemistry.

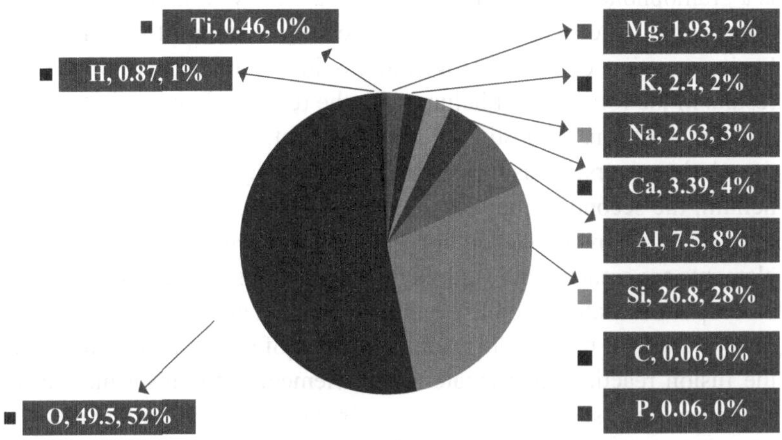

Composition of the human body

In the human body, silicon is replaced by carbon.

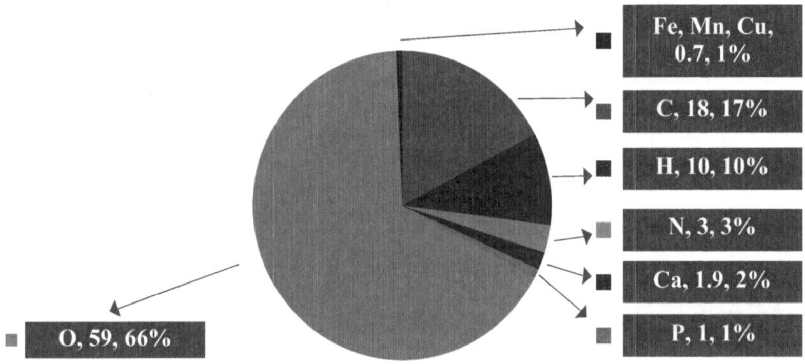

The basic chemistry of life depends only on four elements out of more than a hundred odd elements of the periodic table in chemistry and two powerful energy forms. The elements are carbon, hydrogen, oxygen and nitrogen. Two other elements of lesser importance are calcium and phosphorous. Together these six elements constitute 98% of the human body mass. We know today that there are two types of life. One is carbon based and the other silicon based. Silicon based life is found deep in the earth's crust at very high temperatures. Both carbon and silicon have similar atomic numbers and other chemical properties. Both have the capacity to store memory. An example of carbon memory is a gramophone record and silicon chips too are well known for storing information. The hydrogen atom is the corner stone of this universe. Fusion reaction of two hydrogen atoms in the atmosphere of the sun results in the formation of helium with the release of energy in the form of solar radiations consisting of light and heat. These radiations sustain the whole universe. This fusion reaction of two hydrogen atoms forming helium, the second element of the periodic table, ironically is the basis for making the hydrogen bomb. From the hydrogen atom, a hundred odd elements are created with various fusion reactions to make the elements of the periodic table. Fred Hoyle has shown that all the nucleo synthesis fusion reactions require the resonance factor of sound. At the root of all the fusion reactions that create a new element is the resonance factor of sound. Thus sound energy acquires great importance in the creation of new life. *Pranava mantra* (AUM) or amen are the resonant sounds that are believed to be responsible for the creation of new life by all the ancient cultures. Thus *akash mahabhoota* plays an important role in the formation of life. So also the light and fire from the sun are essential ingredients for life formation. The sun is considered to be the heart of the universe.

Nada Brahmn (Sound as the creator)

Asau adityo Brahmah (Sun is the creator)

A. Oparin (*Soviet Science*, 1980) states that a definite combination of physico-chemical factors of the environment lead to the formation of organic substances, the precursors of bio- molecules, under the effect of solar ultraviolet radiation, electric discharges, heat, cosmic rays, shockwaves and ultrasonication due to tidal waves *etc.* A mixture of carbon, hydrogen, nitrogen and water results in the synthesis of many low molecular weight biological substances and related organic compounds, the hydrocarbons, as well as aminoacids, nitrogen bases and their oligomeres. This hypothesis can be tested in the laboratory through an experiment.

It is believed that the first primitive life originated in the depths of the oceans. Saline water, simulating seawater is taken in a glass beaker. A petroleum hydrocarbon (12-14 carbon atom chain) is added to the saline water. If this solution is observed under a polar microscope one can visualize the particles in Brownian motion. Into this solution UV radiation, simulating the sun's rays, is passed in the presence of atmospheric air. It results into vigorous motion of the particles, resulting in the detachment of the H atom from the hydrocarbon molecule. Now ultrasound is introduced. Oxygen dissolved in the water now gets bound to the carbon atom yielding the polar group C=O. This is the simplest head of lipid molecules, which forms the basis for all the cell membranes. Further, the heads and tails of these lipid molecules organize forming into liquid crystalline aggregation visible under the polar microscope. The ultrasonication causes the formation of bilayer lipid forms penetrated by nitrogenous proteins. Now activity starts in the functional cell membrane. Self assembly, hierarchic orderly organization and self replicational processes are initiated. The liquid crystal form of the cell membrane ensures its molecular mobility and stability. This experiment explains the basis of the formation of a functional cell wall.

Ayurveda professed that the chemistry of life is based on the *pancha mahabhoota* or the five proto elements. Modern science belives that the four elements, *viz.*, carbon, hydrogen, oxygen and nitrogen are at the root of the chemistry of all things. Let us now try and compare and contrast these two concepts. The cell wall is the most functional part of a cell.

If we understand these proto elements on the basis of their characteristics described in our *shatras*, we reach the following conclusions. *Prithvi* is known by its characteristic aroma. Any student of chemistry will vouch that no aroma can exist without carbon. Hence it is common sense to equate *prithvi* with carbon.

In silicon based life, which exists at very high temperatures carbon is replaced with silicon. Both of them share similar chemistry and a very important attribute, the memory. *Aap* is water. It is the union of two hydrogen atoms with one oxygen atom (H_2O). *Tej* is solar radiations. We have already discussed this form of energy. *Vayu* is air. It is roughly 80% nitrogen, 20% oxygen and some other minor gases. *Akash* is characterized by sound. Sound is an energy. Ultrasound is that part of sound energy, which we cannot hear. We have earlier discussed the role of the resonance factor of sound, described by Fred Hoyle. This factor is required to obtain a carbon atom in an activated state. An activated state of carbon is essential for life. This is the most important step in the evolution of life and the universe.

Hindu scriptures have mentioned two *Brahmns*, *viz.*, *Aditya* (sun) and *Naada Brahmn* (sound) as the causes of creation. When two forces, *viz.*, *akash* and *tej* combine with the elements consisting of *prithvi* (carbon/silicon), *aap* (hydrogen + oxygen) and *vayu* (nitrogen + oxygen) it results in all life and the universe. Modern scientific developments have proved that carbon, hydogen, oxygen and nitrogen are the only four elements which form the basic chemistry of life. In order to create any life out of these elements, energy from the sun and sound are pre-requisites. Thus the Ayurvedic concept of a *panchabhautic jagat* stands validated.

Earlier in the experiment by the Russian scientist, A. Oparin, it was clearly demonstrated that the various motions of the particles resulted into the final organization of cell structure. Ayurveda explained the same phenomena through three primal qualities. The *tamas* quality is a non progressive hither and thither motion, called Brownian motion. *Rajas* signifies the vigorous forceful motion of the particles in the solution of the experiment. It is due to introduction of atmospheric air. Ayurveda describes *vayu* or air to be most rajasic. *Satwa* represents the balanced, organized, luminous and clear motion of particles that results in a liquid crystal state. *Tej* (solar energy) and *akash* or sound energy causes the organization of cell structures because of their *satwa* quality. Thus three different types of particle motions create all the solids, liquids and gaseous elements.

How does all this information prove the validity of the *panchbhautic* theory? Since every thing under the sun is declared to be *panchbhautic* even the living cell is also be *panchbhautic*. Carbon of *prithvi*, hydrogen and oxygen of *aap* contribute to the formation of fats (C=O) and carbohydrates (CHO). Addition of nitrogen from *vayu* to the carbon and water results in the formation of aminoacids and proteins. Proteins are of three types, *viz*., gene proteins, structural proteins and functional proteins. The cell wall is the most functional part of the cell. It is lipo-proteinous in nature. Carbohydrates are the fuel for intracellular combustion, which is the energy source that sustains all the activities in a cell. They are also important for the formation of a ground substance or matrix. The liquid-crystal form of the bilayer lipid cell wall and protoplasm is the result of the action of *satwic tej* (solar energy) and *akash* (sound energy). This liquid crystal state is responsible for the molecular mobility and the stability of the cell. Let us see how modern medicine represents the formation of various levels of composition of the human body. Wang, Pierson and Hemsfield have represented the organization of the human body beautifully as shown in the diagram below. The first level starts at the atomic level of hydrogen, carbon, oxygen and other elements like nitrogen and phosphorus *etc*., leading to molecules of water, proteins, lipids and carbohydrates which lead to cells and then to all the seven tissues needed to compose the whole body. The basic structure of the living body, the DNA mainly requires four atoms of the elements, *viz*., carbon, hydrogen, oxygen and nitrogen. The diagramatic presentation below is self explanatory.

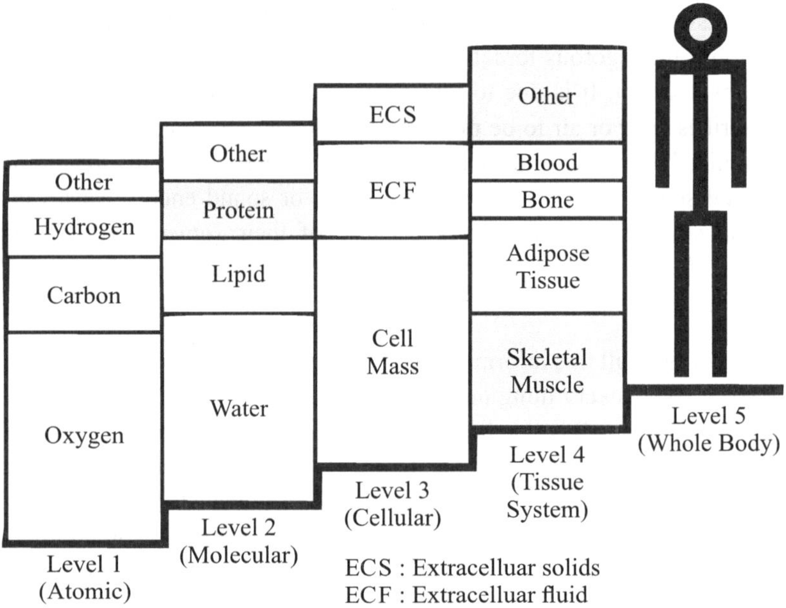

Five levels of human body composition

After Wang, Pierson & Heymsfeld, 1992

(Source: Five Level Model - New Approach to Organising Body Composition Research. Z H Wang *et al,* Am. J. Clin Nutr. 1992, July.)

Thus modern scientific knowledge helps in validating the *pancha mahabhoota* theory of evolution. Bereft of this background knowledge a student in an Ayurvedic college, who is taught that his body is made of earth, water, fire, air and sky, gets totally confused and lost. He starts wondering how these elements form the chemistry of his body. Unless he gets a satisfactory answer, which is convincing, he remains in a perpetual state of confusion. Hence in this chapter an effort was made to explain the *pancha mahabhoota* concept in terms of modern physics, chemistry and biology.

Chapter : 9

Embryogenesis

Sushruta established a parallel between crop cultivation and human conception or embryogenesis.

Dhruvam chaturnam sannidhyad garbhah syad vidhipurvakam l
Ritukshetrambubijanam samagryadamkuro yatha ll
(Susrhuta – Shareer, 2:33)

For crop cultivation one requires four factors, *viz.*, the proper season, field for cultivation, nourshing water and good quality seeds. In human reproduction also, four definite factors are required. In the context of human reproduction, the *ritu* (season) is the fertile period of the menstrual cycle, which is between 12-16 days from the onset of the menstruation. *Kshetra* (field) is *garbha-shayya* or the uterus, where the embryo gets embedded. Nourshing *rasa dhatu* or the blood plasma (feto placental circulation) represents *ambu* or the water. The word *bijanam* represents the male and female gamates.

In the *Charak Samhita* interesting questions are asked with regards to embryogenesis. How is it that the embryo is formed out of the congujal union of male with female? How does the embryo take the shape of a human being? How do congenital deformities occur? If the all-knowing *atma* is a part of the conglomeration of that which forms an embryo, why is that some are borm un-intelligent?

It is fascinating to see how our ancient seers tried to stretch their imagination to explain all the factors involved in fertilization and embryo formation in the absence of any knowledge of the *micro-anatomy* of the gamates and proper anatomy and physiology of the genital tract. Charak enumerated six entities or *bhavaas* that are required to form an embryo. They are *matrija* (maternal), *pitrija* (paternal), *atmaja* (soul), *satmyaja* (congeniality), *satwaja* (mind) and finally *rasaja* (placental nutrition to the foetus). The embryo has tissues, organs, attributes and functions derived from each of them. The soft tissues, *e.g.*, flesh, lipoid tissue, skin *etc.*, and organs, *e.g.*, the heart, liver, spleen, pancreas, umbilicus, kidneys, bladder and intestine (large and small), stomach, mesentery and omentum *etc.*, are of maternal origin (*matrija*). Hard and strong structures in the body are derived from the father (*pitrija*). These comprise all the body hair, nails, teeth, bones, veins, arteries, tendons and semen. It is interesting to note that modern medicine also identifies even individual cell structures as of maternal or paternal origin, mitchondria are of maternal origin whereas the centiole is of paternal origin.

Ayurveda conceptualises a role for *atma*, which is known as the transcendal self, which is the all knowing principle of knowledge and is a universal architect. It is also described as omniform (which can take any form), ageless, immortal and indivisible. When *atma* enters into the union of gamates it causes the beginning of living systems in the embryo. This transcendal *atma* after entering the embryo becomes *jiva* (embodied *atma*). *Jiva* signifies the beginning of life. This *jiva* carries with it the capability for action, and it also enjoys the fruits of action. Thus from the unmanifest stage, the *atma* enters the stage of manifestation called *jiva*, heralding life. In him the fruit of action, *ahanka*r (sense of self hood), reincarnation and memory are established. He becomes the subject of pain, pleasure, passion, delusion, life and death. Charak affirms that even in the absence of the physical body *ahankar*, fruit of action, reincarnation and memory exist in an unmanifest stage as part of the cosmic intelligence.

Atma can be compared to the knowledge of a potter who knows the technique of making pots of different shapes. It is like the architectutral blue print of a house. The knowledge of making things exists even in the absence of mud, a pot or a house. It casts a dye to get a human form in the embryo, just as a statue is formed out of metal. If there are any defects in the pot or the house it could be due to failure on the part of the instruments and materials and/or their organization. It is like software. There can be errors in its programming or there can be failure of the hardware. Therefore birth of unintelligent people or congenitally deformed people is not due to any lack of knowledge on the part of the transcendal *atma,* but is due to failure of the instruments, in other words brain development or gene mutations (hardware failure). The mind and body are the instruments (*upakarana*/hard ware) for the soul. This explantion clearly shows that our ancient seers understood that embryogenesis is a genetic program.

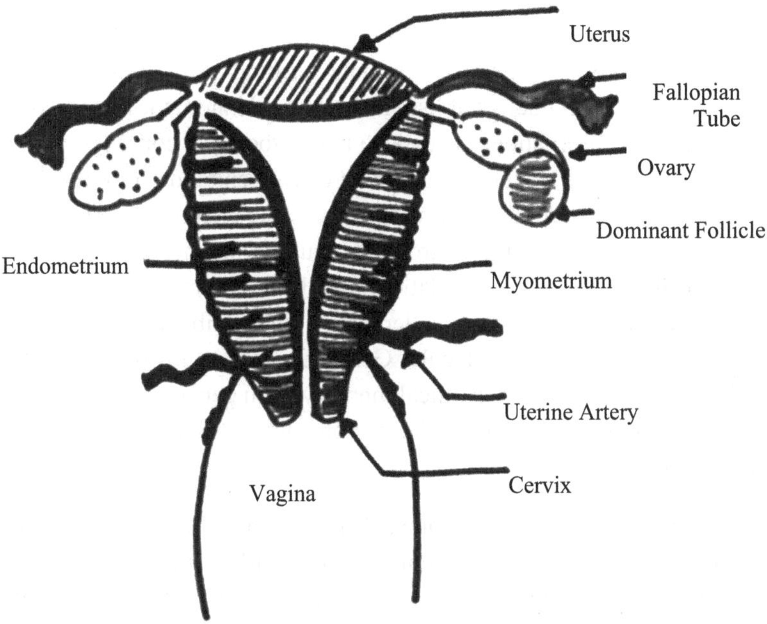

Female Genital Tract

(Garbhashaya, Aartav Vahini, Antah Phal)

Illustration of uterus and adnexae

Let us try to understand the modern conceptualization of human fertilization. After ovulation, the oviduct grabs the ovum into it, where the spermatozoa are waiting for it. Only one of the millions of sperms succeeds in penetrating into the oocyte after dissolving its proteinous outer covering, called the zone pellucida, by an enzyme, acrosin, located in its head. The centriole in the sperm forms an aster and it organizes the mitotic spindle. The spindle is formed through the fusion of both maternal and paternal chromosomes. In the chromosomes reside the genes, which carry the memory of inheritance. The centriole is a self-reproducing entity and it is the principal organizer of mitotic apparatus. Any defect in the centriole can end in failure of fertilization or chromosomal aberrations, resulting into genetic abnormalities. Sushruta talked of *beej* and *beej bhaga dushti*. *Beej dushti* is related to defects in the sperm or the ovum. *Beeja bhaga* means some part of the gametes suggesting chromosomal aberrations. Much before Darwin, Hindu seers established that man shares a common ancestry with all other living beings in this universe by establishing *pancha mahabhoota* based chemistry of life. They also knew the units of genetic inheritance residing in the gametes, much before Gregor Mendel established the law of inheritance based on his independent observations. They also understood that consanguinity was one of the factors for the development of congenital deformities. Hence they strictly forbade the marriages in the same clan or *gotra* for at least seven generations. Genes control and regulate enzymes, metabolism and protein formation and degradation. The basic structure of the genome is the double helix structure called DNA (deoxy-ribonucleic acid). This DNA is an intelligent molecule. Genes are the groups of amino acids, which carry in them the chemical memory from generation to generation from time immemorial. The inherited characteristics develop because of this memory.

Let us now see all the attributes that develop in the embryo from *atma (atmaja).* They are destination of one's birth, lifespan, knowledge of the self, mind, all the organs of cognition and conation, respiration, excretory function, comprehension, body structure and figure, voice, colour and complexion, health and happiness, disease and misery, envy, desire, consciousness, courage or resolution, intellect, memory and capacity to make an effort. When one compares and contrasts this description of *atma* one can easily correlate it with the modern concept of genomic programming. Genetic imprinting occurs within the first week after conception. Another important player in embryogenesis is the *manas* or the mind. Mind connects the *indriyas* to the *atma.* The mind has five important functions. They are *dhee (*reception*), dhriti* (retention)*, smriti* (recall or memory)*, chintan* (thinking), and *buddhi* (intellect). Thus when the mind gets yoked to the *atma* the thinking systems start to function. The sentient *atma* expresses through the mind, which acts like an instrument. The brain is the hardware for the functioning of the mind. When the embryo is endowed with a pure mind, which is not afflicted by passion (*rajas*) and inertia (*tamas*) one can recollect past births. This person is known as *jatismara.*

In the embryo, the mind contributes devotion, character, purity, envy, memory, delusion, sense of sacrifice, jealousy, valour, fear, anger, torpor, zest, ferociousness, softness, fore-bearing nature and fickle mindedness *etc*. These attributes are expressed in the proportion of *satwa* (purity or clarity), *rajas* (passion) and *tamas* (inertia or delusion). All the above features born out of the mind are termed as *satvaja.*

Brain development is very important in intrauterine growth programming. This fact was well appreciated by our ancient seers, which led them to advise the use of milk, fresh butter and *ghee* in early pregnancy and till the end of the first trimester. Omega-3 fatty acids are essential for neuronal, retinal and brain development. Maximum fetal brain growth occurs during 4-14 weeks of gestation.

According to Charak the *rasadhatu* also contributes to embryogenesis. *Rasadhatu,* essentially refers to mother's nutrition and her body composition. If the body composition is affected by the poor quality of nutrition, the genomic programming for the intrauterine growth is affected. Good nutrition contributes to proper embryo formation and growth of the foetal body structures, the life force in the embryo, strength, zest and satiety. Modern research has proved that poor nutrition affects the maternal body composition, which leads to hyperglycemia, hypoprotenemia and deficiency of omega-3 fatty acids. This adversely affects the growth program and also brain development in the foetus. *Rasa* also signifies the optimal feto-placental blood flow. Therefore Charak has described *rasadhatu* as an important element.

Lastly, *satmya* or congeniality of the environment, diet and concordance of all the other factors involved in embryogenesis are equally important. The *satmya* results in the following attributes in embryogenesis; namely, health, zest, optimal functions of all the organs of cognition and conation, voice, complexion, happy mental state and charitable nature. Thus the embryo is born out of *satmya* too.

Chapter : 10

Dravya and Gunas

Properties of *dravya*

Yathaashritah karmagunaah kaaranam samavaayi yat l
(Cha. Su. 1/50)

A substance is that in which the action (*karma*) and quality (*guna*) exist in an inherent inseparable combination.

Samavaya

Samavayah apruthakbhaavo bhoomyadeenaam gunaih matah l
Sa nityo yatra hi dravyam na tatraaniyato gunah ll (Cha. Su. 1/50)

Samavaya is the inherent inseparable combination of qualities of substances like earth *etc*.

Wherever there is a substance the quality exists in it eternally.

***Guna*:** It is the quality of a substance. Every substance acts as per its quality.

Definition of quality (*guna*)

Samavyee tu nishchestah kaaranam gunah ll (Cha. Su. 1/51)

Quality exits in an inseparable combination in a substance and it is inactive. Action is rooted substance (*dravya*).

An interesting idea of Ayurveda is that two mirror image qualities exist in nature. Temperature is an example, wherein hot and cold are two opposite ends of the same entity. Matter always exists in two opposite mirror image forms. According to physics, if there is matter there has to be antimatter. Interestingly therefore *Sankhya* and Ayurveda have rejected the idea of non-existence of matter. Even in modern medicine a similar concepts exist, *e.g.*, substances that cause thickening and others thinning of the blood. There are ten pairs of opposite *gunas* or characteristic properties. These are described a little later and are important for the action of any food substance.

Definition of *karma* (action)

Samyoge cha vibhage cha kaaranam drvyam ashrayam l
Kartavyasya kriya karma karma naa anyad apekshate ll
(Cha. Su. 1/ 52)

Action is performing the work that is to be accomplished. It is done either by combining or dividing. Action exists in a substance alone.

Ten pairs of opposite or mirror image qualities that can be identified clinically. Substances exert their actions and they can be identified by the ten opposite qualities. The predominance or deficiecency of each *dosha* is identified based on qualities. Thus understanding these *gunas* is important for all Ayurvedic practitioners.

1. ***Guru*** (heavy): These substances are heavy to digest and can cause an increase in weight, *guru* also means the substances that cause hypertrophy of cells and tissues. *Laghu* (light) is the opposite *guna*. These substances are light and easy to digest. They are slimming or thinning agents.

2. ***Sheeta*** (cold): They are cold and they undermine the metabolic fire on one hand and prevent the generation of free radicals on the other hand. In other words *sheeta dravyas* (substances) possess anti oxidant and anti inflammatory properties. *Ushna* (hot) is the opposite *guna*. Such substances are hot and increase oxidative damage, cause a rise in temperature. They cause burning. In other words *ushna* quality is the harbinger of inflammation.

3. ***Manda*** (slow): These are slow in action or slow metabolisers. *Teekshna* (acute or fast acting) is the opposite guna.

4. ***Snigdha*** (unctuous): They usually are oily or lipoid substances that are unctuous and nourishing, they can cause excessive fat deposition in the body. Lipoid substances form important constituents of the lipoproteinous cell wall. *Ruksha* (dry) substances are usually depleting and thinners. They cause dehydration and wasting or atrophy in the tissues.

5. ***Shlakshna*** (amorphous): They produce finess, softness and smoothness in the body structures. *Khara* (rough): These substances cause roughness and are granular in appearance and feel.

6. ***Sandra*** (solid/viscous): It signifies compactness and sturdiness. *Drava* (liquid) substances have a flowing quality. Our body is more liquid than solid. The various types of fluids include, blood, plasma, intra cellular and extra cellular fluids.

7. ***Mrudu*** (soft/mild)/*kathina* (hardness/prolonged).

8. ***Sthir*** (steady): Long standing action. *Chala* (mobile): Short lived action.

9. ***Sukshma*** (subtle): Usually these substances act very subtly. They enter into minute spaces and produce the effects. *Sthula* (gross) is the opposite, example is macromolecules.

10. ***Vishada*** (transparent). Its opposite is *pitchila* (sticky/greasy).

Pancha bhoota and their qualities

Substances which are predominantly made up of *prithvi* are heavy, hard and steady. Whereas those that are made predominantly from water or *aap* are cold, oily, soft and liquid in nature. *Taijasa* substances are normally hot and acute in action and are light, subtle and dry in quality. Those that are *vayaveeya* possess the characteristic *gunas*, *viz*., lightness, subtleness, dryness and coolness. *Akasheeya dravya* are soft, transparent, light and subtle.

Of these twenty *gunas* there are eight that are most important. These are *mrudu* or *manda, teekshna, guru, laghu, snigdha, ruksha, ushna* and *sheeta.* These are the ones, which cause eight fold *veeryas*. *Veerya* is the pharmaco dynamic potential action of a substance. The drugs act through their *veerya*. Of these eight *gunas*, *sheeta* and *ushna* are the most important because they represent *soma* and *agni*. It is through these *gunas* that food and drugs act in the body. It is a method of appreciating the clinical results based on the physical changes after the usage of food or a drug.

Another parameter is *rasa* or taste. The *rasa* of a substance is its taste. It is appreciated by the chemical receptors on the taste buds of the tongue. *Rasa* is the basis of all the biochemical actions on the body, be it food or drugs. Drugs act by *virya* and *prabhava*. All food substances act on the body tissues through the medium of *rasa* and *vipaka*. Modern medicine recognizes only four tastes, *viz*., sweet, sour, salty and bitter. Umami (Japanese) is a new taste added as the fifth taste. Ayurveda recognizes two additional tastes namely pungent and astringent. These two tastes are not recognized by the specialized chemo-receptors on the tongue, but by neuronal stimulation of nerve endings.

Madhura rasa: This is the sweet taste. All those substances, which taste sweet, *e.g*., sugar, honey, rice and *yashtimadhu* (glycerrhiza glabra) *etc*., are considered to possess *madhur rasa*. It pleases the senses and coats

the mouth. It is nourishing in its quality, therefore the majority of food items possess this *rasa*. Most sweet tasting substances are predominently carbohydrates. The basic chemistry of carbohydrates is CHO. Bio-chemistry of sweetness is related to the release of OH ions. *Madhura rasa* has *gunas* that are *guru*, *snigdha* and *sheeta*. It is formed through the combination of *prithvi* (carbon) and *aap* (H_2O). The flesh of most animals is *madhura* in taste, as it should be by the rule of *sheeta*. The exception to this rule is *anoop mamsa* (meat of water dwelling animals), which is *ushna*. *Madhur rasa* is the best *vatanulomak* (facilitates the smooth excretion of stool and urine). It increases *kapha*. The exception to this rule is honey, old *shali* or rice, barley, wheat and *moong etc.* It is *vata shamak* (alleviation of *vata*) and moderately *pitta shamak.* Therefore traditionally in India, sweets are served first, because the hungry stomach signifies *vata prakop* (increase in *vata*). *Madhur rasa* is the best for alleviating *vata* (*vata shaman*).

Properties of the sweet taste when consumed in normal prportions

Sharira satmyat sapta dhatu abhivardhanam (because of its congeniality or homologation it promotes all the seven *dhatus*), *ayushyah* (increases life span), *shashtendriyani prasadanam* (improves acuity of all the six *indriyas* including the mind), *bala varna kara* (improves the strength and colour complexion), *pitta visha marutaghna* (it destroys *pitta*, poison and *vata*), *trushna daaha prashamana* (alleviates thirst and burning sensation), *twachya keshya, kanthyo balyah* (promotes skin, hair, voice and strength), *preenana, jeevana, tarpana brumhana sthairyakarah* (promotes happiness, life, nutrition, hypertrophy and sturdiness), *ksheena kshata sandhaana karo* (improves the condition of the wasted and injured), *ghraana mukha kantha oshta jivha prahladano* (pleasing to the nose, mouth, throat, lips, and tongue), *daaha moorcha prashamana* (relieves burning sensation and giddiness), (*Charak. Su.* 28/43).

What happens when sweet tasting substances are consumed in excess

Sthaulyam (obesity/corpulence), *maardavam* (softness), *aalasyam* (laziness or lethargy), *ati swapnam* (hypersomnia) *gauravam* (heavy feeling), *anannanabhivesham* (loss of appetite), *agni daurbalyam* (weak digestive fire), *aasya kanthayor mamsaabhivruddhi* (hypertrophy of flesh in mouth and throat), *shwaasa kaasa, pratishyaya, alasaka, sheeta jwara, aanaaha, aasya madhurya,* (dyspnoea, cough, cold, constipation, fever with rigors, intestinal torpor, sweet taste in the mouth), *vamathu* (vomiting), *samgyahara pranaasha* (loss of consciousness and voice), *galagandamala, shleepada, galashopha,* (multiple enlarged lymph nodes in the neck, elephantiasis, swelling in the neck), *basti dhamani, gale upalepa* (increased mucous discharge from the urinary bladder, vessels and throat), *akshai aamaya abhishyandaani* (eye diseases and conjunctivitis *etc*.), (*Cha. Su.* 26/43).

Amla rasa: This is the sour taste. It is the result of the union of *aap mahabhoota* (H_2O) with *tej* (solar radiations). The taste buds peceive a sour taste through the release of H^+ ions from a substance. Tamarind, *amla*, buttermilk, curd, *matulunga etc*., are examples of substances with *amla rasa*. The moment it is placed on the tongue the teeth become sensative, and it also causes an increase in salivation. Because of its pleasing nature, it is called *hridya*. It enhances *pitta*. Its characteristic qualities are *snigdha*, *ushna* and *laghu*. It is mildly *vata shamak*, moderately *pitta prakopak* and *kapha prakopak*. Normally, a sour taste increases the *pitta*, but pomegranate and *amlaki* are exceptions. Ayurveda advises that a*mla* and *lavan rasas* be consumed in the middle portion of a meal.

Amla rasa rochayati agnim deepayati, deham brumhati, oorjayati. It causes improvement in taste and relish, stimulates digestive fire, causes hypertrophy (increase in bulk) of tissues and increases vigour. *Mano bodhayati* (enlightens the mind), *indriyani dhrudeekaroti* (strengthens the sense organs), *balam vardhayati* (increases the strength), *vaatam anulomayati* (prevents formation of gas), *hrudayam tarpayati* (provides satisfaction to one's heart), *aasyam aasraavayati* (increases salivation), *bhuktam apakarshayati, kledayati, jarayati, preenayati* (it propels the ingested food downwards, moistens and digests and provides a pleasant satisfaction or gratification), *laghu, ushnah snigdhascha* (it is light, hot and unctuous in character), (*Cha. Su.* 26/43).

When used in excess the following complications occur

Dantan harshayati, tarshayati, (teeth get on edge and thirst is provoked), *sambheelyati aksheeni* (flinching of the eyes), *samvejayati lomaani* (causes horripilations), *kapham vilapayati* (liquifies cough), *pittam abhivardhayati* (stimulates *pitta*), *raktam dooshayati* (vitiates *rakta*), *mamsam vidahati* (sloughing of flesh), *kaayam shithileekaroti* (dilapidates the body), *ksheena kshat durbalanaam shwayatu mupaadayati* (wasted, chachectic and debilitated persons become edematic). It causes suppurations in inflammations due to its fiery nature.

Lavana rasa: This is salty in taste. It is due to the combination of *prithvi* (carbon) and *tej* (solar radiation) *mahabhootas*. Ref. *Susrut Su*. 42/4. A salty taste is perceived by the receptors on the tongue due to the release of sodium ions. The atomic number of carbon is six, that of sodium is eleven and silicon fourteen. Many different substances taste salty. Common salt is an example. It dissolves immediately in the mouth, causes watering and is an appetiser. It is the most dominating of all tastes. Its characteristic gunas are *guru*, *snigdha* and *ushna*. It also possesses the *teekshna guna*. Though all salts should be *ushna* in nature, the exception to this rule is *saindhava* salt, which is *sheeta* in nature. *Lavna rasa* is the best *vata shamak*, *pitta prakopak* and *kapha prakopak*.

Properties of *lavana rasa* (common salt)

Pachana (digestive), *kledana* (liquefier), *deepana* (stimulator of digestive fire), *chyaavana* (defluxive), *chedana* (incisive), *bhedana* (breaks/disruptive), *teekshana* (acute), *sara* (flowing in nature), *vikasya* (diffusive or expansive), *adhasamsravyakashakaro* (causing downward flow or laxative), *vata haro* (destroyer of *vata*), *stambha bandha sanghaatavidhamanah* (relieves stiffness, obstruction and accumulations), *sarva rasa pratyaneekabhoota* (it masks all other tastes), *aasyam aasraavati* (it causes increased salivation), *kapham vishyandayati* (it liquefies mucous), *maargaan vishodhayati* (it removes obstructions and clears all passages), *sarva shareersavayavaan mrudu karoti* (softens all organs and parts of the body), *rochayat aaharam* (increases the taste of food), *aahara yogi* (congenial to food), *naati atyartham guru, snigdha, ushnascha* (moderately heavy, unctuous and hot), (*Cha.Su*. 26/43).

Effects of excessive consumption of salt

Pittam kopayati (aggravates *pitta*), *raktam vardhayati* (increases the flow of blood and its pressure), *tarshayati* (aggravates thirst), *moorchayati* (causes fainting), *tapayati* (increases heat of the body), *darayati* (breaks the tissues), *kushnati mamsaani* (causes ulcerations), *pragalayati kushtani* (it dissipates dermatosis), *visham vardhayati* (increases toxicity), *shophan sphotayati* (it breaks open inflamed boils and abscesses), *dantaan chyaavayati* (loosens the teeth), *pumstwam upahanti* (causes sexual dysfunction in men or impotence), *indriyaani uparnaddhi* (it impairs the function of the sense organs), *vali palita khaalityam aapaadayati* (induces premature wrinkles, grey hair and baldness), (*Cha. Su.* 26/43). It predisposes a person to varous diseases, *viz.*, *rakta pitta* (hemothermia/bleeding disorders/hemophilia), *amlapitta* (acid peptic disorders), *visarpa* (acute spreading infections), *vata rakta* (rheumatic disease), *vicharchika* (bulbous eruptions), *indralupta* (alopecia) *etc.*

Tikta rasa: This is bitter taste. Most alkaloids taste bitter. It is made from a combination of *vayu* (N & O) and *akash* (sound energy). As of today, no uniform structural chemistry of bitterness is understood, but it is assumed to be due to release of cations (*Ganong – Physiology*). Bitter gourd (*karela*) tastes bitter. The structure of bitter taste receptors has been identified recently. Apart from the tongue, these receptors have been identified on the bronchial muscles. *Neem* and coffee are examples of *tikta rasa*. This shows that tastes receptors exist in many tissues of the body apart from the tongue. Bitter coffee can cause bronchial relaxation in an acute asthmatic attack. Thus it is very clear that tastes indeed produce pharmaco dynamic actions. That most anti microbial drugs taste bitter is a common observation.

Properties of bitter taste

Swayam arochishnuh api arochakaghnam (itself being unappetising it improves the appetite in persons with loss of appetite), *vishaghna* (antidote to poison), *krumighno* (wormicide), *moorcha daaha kandu kushta trushna prashamana* (alleviates fainting, thirst, itching and dermatoses), *mamsayo sthirakaranaam* (imparts firmness, compactness and tone to muscles), *jwaraghnah* (febrifuge/anti-pyretic), *deepana* (stimulator of digestive fire), *paachana* (digestive), *stanya shodhana* (purifies breast milk), *lekhana* (depletive) of *kleda meda vasa majja lasika puya sweda mootra pureesha* (moisture, fat, flesh marrow, bonemarrow, lymph, pus, sweat, urine and faeces). It is *rukshya* (dry), *sheeta* (cold) and *laghu* (light), (*Cha. Su.* 26/43).

Complications of over consumption of substances with a bitter taste

Ruksha khara vishada swabhavat (because of the dry, rough and clear qualities) it dries up (*shoshayati*) all the seven *dhatus*. *Srotasaam kharatvam upadayati* (all the channels in the body become rough), *balam aadatte karshayati glapayati mohayati bhramayati vadanam upashoshati* (by depleting the strength of a person it causes emaciation, weakeness, fainting, giddiness and gives a dehydrated look to the face. *Aparan cha vata vikaraan upajanayati* (it causes many other *vata* based diseases).

Kashaaya: This is astringent taste. It is due to the combination of *prithvi* and *vayu*. This taste is basically perceived through nerve stimulation, not through chemical receptors on the taste buds. *Jambool* is an example of *kashaaya rasa*.

Properties of *kashaaya rasa*

Samshamanah (pacifier), *sangrahi* (astringent), *sandhaanakar* (binding the broken parts), *peedana* (compressor), *ropana* (healing), *shoshanah* (dessicant), *stambhana* (styptic), *shleshma rakta pitta prashamana* (it alleviates kapha and hemothermia), *shareera kledasyopayoktaa* (it dehydrates the body fluids). Its qualities are *sheeta* (cold), *ruksha* (dry) and *laghu* (light).

Complications due to excess consumption of astringent substances

Aasyam shoshayati (mouth dries up), *hrudayam peedayati* (heart attack, angina pectoris), *udaram aadhmapayati* (abdominal distension), *vaacham nighrunnati* (loss of speech), *srotasya avabadhnati* (obstruction to channels), *shyavatwam aapadayati* (complexion becomes dark), *pumstwam upahanti* (impotency), *vishtabhyam jaraam gacchati* (food gets digested slowly), *vaata mootra pureesha retamsya avagruhnati* (scanty flatus, urine, faeces, and semen), *karshyati glapayati tarshayati stambhayati* (induces emaciation, weariness, thirst, stiffness), *khara vishada rukshaat pakshavadhagraha, apataanaka, ardita prabrutinam vata vikara janayati* (due to its qualities of roughness, clearness and dryness, many *vata* diseases like hemiplegia, spasms, convulsions and paralysis may occur due to its over use.

Katu rasa: This is the pungent taste. It is due to the combination of *tej* and *vayu*. *Sunthi*, *marich*, *pippali*, *hing*, red peppers and bile are pungent. It is irritating and causes watering of the eyes. It irritates all the membranes and is excreted through urine and faeces causing severe burning micturition and defecation. Its *gunas* are *laghu*, *ruksha* and *ushna*, but *pippali* and *lasun* are exceptions and are *snigdha* and *guru* in nature. It increases *vata* but exceptions are *sunthi*, *pippali* and *lasun*. It increases *pitta*. It is *kapha shamak*. In anorexia use of *katu* and *lavan* substances like ginger and salt will help by their *kapha shaman* property. *Tikta*, *katu* and *kashaya rasas* should be consumed at the end of a meal.

Properties of *katu rasa*

Vaktram shodhayati (cleanses the mouth), *agnim deepayati* (it kindles the digestive fire), *bhuktam shoshayati* (desiccates the ingested food), *ghraanam aasraavayati* (causes running of the nose), *chakshur virechayati* (causes watering of the eyes), *sphuteekaroti indriyani* (it sharpens the sense organs), *alasaka shwayathu upachaya udard abhishyanda sneha sweda kleda malaan upahanti* (it relieves intestinal torpor, oedema, obesity, urticaria, fluid accumulation, unctuousness, sweat, moisture, excretions), *rochatyashanam* (increases the taste of a meal), *kandoor vinaashayati* (it destroys pruritus), *vranaan avasaadayati* (it heals abscesses), *krimeen hinasti* (vermicide), *mamsam vilayati* (it breaks down the muscle), *shonita sanghaatam bhinatti* (it breaks down clots), *bandhaan chinatti* (clears barriers), *margaan vivrunoti* (dilates the passages), *shleshmaanam shamayati* (alleviates kapha). Its qualities are *laghu* (light), *ushna* (hot) and *ruksha* (dry).

Complications when pungent substances are consumed excessively

Vipaka prabhavat (on account of the effect of *katu vipaka*) it causes *punstwam upahanti* (impotency), *mohayati* (fainting), *glapayati* (weariness), *saadayati* (weakness), *karshayati* (wasting), *moorchayati* (unconsciousness), *namayati* (bending down), *bhramayati* (confusion), *kantham paridahayati* (burning in the throat), *shareera taapam upajanayati* (raises the body heat), *balam ksheenoti* (diminishes strength) and *trushnaam janayati* (increases thirst), (*Cha. Su*. 26/43).

All food substances act by their *rasas*. That tastes exert pharmacodynamic action is now confirmed by modern science. There are specific receptors for each taste. Bitter taste receptors are now found in bronchii. A bitter taste can relax bronchial musculature. A drink of bitter coffee can avert an acute attack of bronchial asthma. The wisdom of Ayurveda could differentiate the quality of sweetness of cane sugar from that of honey. Honey was advised for diabetic persons, whereas cane products were contraindicated. We know now that honey is mainly composed of fructose, which does not require insulin action to enter into a cell like glucose. Once inside the cell, it is converted into glucose. Therefore about 10 gms of honey a day can be consumed by a diabetic person without any harm. Modern medicine was not willing to believe the beneficial effects of cow's *ghee* till recent times. But now, it is accepted to be beneficial in reducing atherogenic lipids, due to its content of omega 3 fatty acids. Omega 3 fatty acids are believed to be essential for brain development, again proving the the old aphorism, '*Ghrutam buddhi vardhakam'*. As modern scientific research progresses many of the Ayurvedic aphorisms will become more meaningful.

Vipaka

Katu tikta kashayaanaam vipakah praayashah katuh l
Amlo amlam pachyate swadurmadhuram lavanasthathaa ll
(Cha. Su. 26/58)

Madhuro amlo cha snigdha bhavaat trayo rasaah l
Vaata mootra pureeshaanaam prayo moksha sukhaabhava ll 59

Katu tikta kashayastu rukshabhaavaat trayo rasaah l
Dukkhaaya moksha drushyante vaata vin mootra retasaam ll 60

Shukrahaa baddha vinmootro vipako vatala katuh l
Madhurah srushta vinmootro vipakah kapha shukrala ll 61

Pitta krut srushta vinmootrah pako amlah shukra nashanah l
Teshaam guruh syanmadhurah katukaamlaavato anyatha ll 62

Three *vipakas* are described. Pungent, bitter, astringent tastes are converted post digestion into *katu vipaka*. *Amla rasa* results into *amla vipaka* and *madhur*, *lavana rasas* produce *madhur vipaka*.

Katu vipaka is *ruksha* and *laghu* in nature and causes an increase in *vata*. It causes constipation and is detrimental to *shukra dhatu*.

Amla vipaka is *snigdha* and *laghu* in nature. It increases *pitta*. It causes easy and profuse passage of urine and faeces and is detrimental to *shukra*.

Madhur vipaka is *guru* and *snigdha*, increases *kapha* and *shukra* and causes easy passage of flatus, urine and faeces.

Rasa therefore is superceded in effect by *vipaka* depending upon the changes in *gunas* of the substance during the process of *vipaka*.

Raso nipaate dravyaanam, vipakah karma nishtayaa l
Veeryam yaavat adheevasa sannipaataam cha upalabhyate ll
(Cha. Su. 26/66)

The action of *rasa* is limited to the initial stage of digestion, whereas *vipaka* lasts till the end of digestion. The effect of *veerya* lasts from the beginning of ingestion of a substance or drug till it is completely removed from the body.

In *vipaka*, the food or drug with six different tastes undergoes total conversion through two stages, *viz.*, *prapak* or *awasthapak* and *nishtapak*. *Awasthapak* refers to GI digestion with the help of various digestive juices containing enzymes, hormones, *etc. Nishtapak* refers to metabolism at the cellular level. Ayurveda conceived thirteen different types of *agnis*, *viz.*, five *bhutagnis* (one each concerned with each proto element), *jatharagni* (one that is located in the stomach, duodenum and intestines) and seven *dhawagnis* (one for each of the prime body tissues). *Rasa* and *vipaka* of the food substances are guiding principles for understanding the way they act in the body and give desired or undesired effects.

Vipaka relates to the various conversions that foods undergo in gastro intestinal digestion. The six types of tastes are converted into three final pathways of post digestion into intermediate changed tastes called *vipakas*. Food substances either end up in acidic or alkaline forms. Human biochemistry states that food substances are digested by acidic and alkaline juices in the gastro intestinal tract and assumes one of the three types of pH, *viz.*, neutral, acidic or alkaline. Ayurvedic *vipaka* is also of three types. *Madhura vipaka* is usually neutral in pH, *amla vipaka* is acidic and *katu vipaka* is alkaline in nature. In the body, ash left by metabolism need not have the same earlier reaction it possessed before digestion and metabolism, since it is modified by many other factors. Proteins, phospholipids and nucleoproteins yield a lot of H^+ ions (acid), which are neutralized by alkaline elements before they are finally excreted. Fruits and vegetables have lots of positive ions *e.g.*,

Ca^{++}, Mg^{++}, Na^{+}, K^{+}, to neutralize the acid produced from proteins. They contain organic acids like citric, malic, tartaric and lactic acids, which are oxidized to CO_2 and excreted through the lungs. Potassium salts of these acids are oxidized into potassium bicarbonate, which is excreted through urine. Thus vegetables and acid fruits have alkaline effects. There are exceptions *e.g.*, benzoic acid in cranberries is excreted as hippuric acid. Examples of dietary substances having a neutral effect are butter, butter milk, honey, olive oil, onions, apples and sugar, (Ref. *Human Biochemistry* – James Orten, Pg. 795). All these substances are described in Ayurveda as substances with *madhur rasa*. Hence equating *madhur vipaka* to neutral pH, *amla vipaka* to acidic and *katu vipaka* to alkaline appears logical.

Veerya or potency

Mrudu teekshna guru laghu snigdha ruksha ushna sheetalam l
Veeryam ashtavidham kechit, kechit dwividham aasthitaah ll

Sheetoshnam iti, veeryam tu kriyate yena yaa kriyaa l
Naa veeryam kurute kinchit sarvaa veerya krutaa kriyaa ll
(Cha. Su. 26/65)

Soft (mild), acute, heavy, light, unctuous, dry, hot and cool are the eight potencies of substances according to some, whereas others believe in only two of the eight. These are cool (*sheeta*) and hot (*ushna*). All the actions of substances are based on the potencies. Without potency, no action is accomplished. All drug action is based on potency, whereas the dietary agents accomplish action mostly through *rasa* and *vipaka*. In short *veerya* is the pharmaco dynamic action potential of any drug. *Vata*, *pitta* and *kapha doshas* are the substances produced at different sites and different levels of digestion of food substances in the gastro intestinal tract. The relationship between *doshas*, *rasa*, *vipaka* and *veerya* will be discussed in detail in later chapters.

Prabhava: Selective potency

Rasa veerya vipakaanaam saamanyam yatra lakshyate l
Visheshah karmanaam chaiva prabhava tasya sa smrutah ll

Katukah katukah paakam veerya ushnah chitrako matah l
Tadvat danti prabhavaattu virechayati maanavam ll
(Cha. Su. 26/67-68)

Inspite of the similarity in *rasa vipaka* and *virya*, if a substance acts differently on a specific target, it is called *prabhava*. Examples are *chitrak* and *danti*. Both of them have *katu rasa*, *katu vipaka* and *ushna veerya* properties, but *danti* is purgative. Thus purgation is due to *prabhava* or specific action. We know that certain substance act on specific organs, *e.g.*, utertonic action of methergin and certain drugs act on specific receptors, *e.g.*, alpha and beta receptors on blood vessels.

Part - II

Longing for a Long and Healthy Life

Chapter : 11

Ayush Kaameeyata

Ayush kaameeyata: How to achieve a long and healthy life

The purpose of Ayurveda is to achieve a long and healthy life in order to be happy, and also to achieve the four *purusharthas* (objectives of human life), *viz.*, *dharma* (social & personal duties), *artha* (professional life/providing meaning to one's life through work), *kama* (achieving personal desires) and *moksha* (detachment from all objects of the senses/ the final deliverance).

Ayuh kamayamanena dharma artha sukha sadhanam l
(Asht.hr. Su.1/2)

From the point of view of Ayurveda, *sukh* or happiness is health and sorrow is disease.

Sukha sangyakam arogyam vikaro dukkha evacha l (Charak)

Food, regular rest and sleep, and controlled sexual practice are the three foundation columns for a long life, (*Traya upasthambha: ahara, nidra, brahmacharyam iti* l *Charak. Brahmachryam Ayushkaranam*). *Brahmacharyam* is not complete abstinence for a house holder, but it is controlled sexual practice. Complete celibacy is prescribed for a *brahmachari* and *sanyasi*.

Ahara or *anna* being the source of life and energy, it occupies the prime position for all living beings. Food sustains life, and nourishes the body and its cellular structure in its proliferation and growth. Food, air and water are the basis of life, without them life cannot be sustained.

Ahara shayayana abrahmacharyaih yuktya prayojitaih l
Shareeram dharyate nityam aagaramiva dhaaranaih ll
(Asht. Hru. 7/52)

Food is defined as what people and animals eat to survive. Food usually originates from animals or plants. Food, which is eaten by living beings, contains the nutrition that makes people and animals healthy and provides them with energy. The consumption of food should be enjoyable to humans. Edible or potable substances (usually of animal or plant origin), consist of nutritive components such as carbohydrates, fats, proteins, essential minerals and vitamins. These (when ingested and assimilated after digestion) sustain life, generate energy, and lead to growth and maintain the health.

Can life be enjoyed without disease?

Yuktaahara viharasya yukta cheshtasya karmasu l
Yukta swapnavabodhasya yogo bhavati dukkhah ll
(Bhagavat Geeta Ch. 6)

Freedom from the sorrow of disease can only be obtained by regular intake of a properly balanced diet, and daily practice of the prescribed right lifestyle, appropriate movements and actions associated with the right cycles of sleep and wakeful periods.

Nityam hita ahara vihara sevee sameekshakari vishayeshu asaktah l
Data samah satyaparah kshamavan aaptopasevi cha bhavati arogah ll
(Asht. Hr. *Su.* ***5/36)***

Regular daily intake of wholesome food, and practicing appropriate life styles are essential for the prevention of disease. One's life style should take into account certain special behavioural and attitudinal qualities that include spiritual, moral and social practices. A person should possess the following characteristics: One should be contemplative or studious about things, disinterested in enjoying the objects of the senses, generous, judicious, truthful, forgiving and ever ready to serve the learned and elderly. These qualities of one's psyche and physical actions in a person qualify for what is called *sadvritta* or the appropriate moral code of conduct and a good life style. *Sadvritta* is an essential pathway to achieve a long, healthy and happy life of a hundred years. We should realise that the mind rules the body. Mental stress causes many psychosomatic diseases. These spiritual qualities result in good health by preventing stress and thus enhance longevity of life, whereas the opposite qualities cause the health to deteriorate and shorten the life span.

Food must be consumed in moderate and measured quantities. There are three golden principles, which are most important with regards to consumption of food, (Charak).

Hitashee syat l Eat only that which is wholesome.

Matrashee syat I Eat in measured quantities.

Jeerne ashneeyat l Eat only after the previously consumed food is digested.

If you practice these three golden rules no disease can affect you. Today, we talk of various diets that are measured in calories, because food is converted into energy, which is calculated in calories. Excessive calorie intake with less expenditure of energy, due to sedentary life styles leads to metabolic syndrome, obesity and cardiovascular diseases. Whenever the food intake is deficient both in quality and quantity it causes malnutrition leading to wasting disorders.

Qualities of food chosen by people of different personality types

We have so far learnt about the different personality types of people. Different types of personalities have different preferences in food. The different types of foods exert different benefits or ill effects in the body.

Ayuh satwam balam arogyam sukha preeti vivardhanam l
Rasya snigdha sthira hrudya aharam satwika priya ll
(Bhagawat Geeta Cha. 17)

All enlightened people (*satwik*) by choice enjoy tasty (sweet in taste), unctuous, satiating hearty meals. These foods result in long term health benefits, lead to an increase in life span, and enhance mental prowess, immunity and health. They provide self-satisfaction and happiness.

Katu amla lavana atyushna teekshna ruksha vidahinah
(Bhagawat Geeta Cha. 17)

Foods that are pungent, sour and salty in taste, extremely hot, acute and dry in nature and cause a burning sensation in the body, produce distress and varieties of diseases. These types of food are preferred by people, who are highly motivated, ambitious and arrogant *rajasi* types.

Similarly left over, stale and exposed foods not only cause diseases but also cause depression. These foods are consumed by ignorant and perverted *tamasi* people.

The Ayurvedic concept of mechanisms of actions of food substances is based on its *panchabhautic* content, *i.e.*, the attributes of a substance *viz.*, *gunas* (ten pairs of opposite or mirror image attributes), *rasas* (perception of taste by the chemical receptors on the tongue), *vipaka* (intestinal digestion and tissue metabolism). Knowing these different aspects, helps us to understand the actions of the substances on the body. Today we talk of food items in terms of proteins, fats and carbohydrates and the calories they generate. An Ayurvedic physician depends on the tastes and qualities of food substances for all the dietetic advice, he is required to give to his patients. It is commonly seen that a modern medical practitioner is not well equipped to advise on the benefits or complications of different types of articles of diet. Ayurvedic dietetics in my opinion should be promoted universally.

Chapter : 12

Alimentary Digestion

Yat annam deha dhatu oja bala varna aadi poshakam l
Tatra agnih hetuh ahaara anna hyapakvaad rasaadayah ll
(Cha. Chi.15/5)

All the body tissues, resistance power, strength and complexion, *etc.*, are dependent on the nutrition provided by food. It is the digestive fire, which digests the food and converts it into the nutrients and the waste material to be excreted. The nutrient part of food is converted into seven different tissues of the body starting from *rasa dhatu*.

Annam aadaana karma tu praanah koshtam prakarshati l
Tat dravaih bhinnasanghaatam snehena mrudutaam gatam ll

Samaanenaavadooto agnirudaryah pavanodvahah l
Kale bhuktam samam samyak pachati aayuh vivardhate ll
(Cha. Chi. 15/6-7)

The *praana vayu* propels the ingested food into the stomach. The fluids in the stomach moisten and break it down into small particles due to the effects of unctuous elements. Now the digestive fire secreted with *paachakagni* or *pitta* along with *samaana vayu* digest the food eaten in the proper quantity and at the appropriate times. This way the body is nourished leading to a long and healthy life. Just as the fire cooks food, food is similarly cooked or digested in the lower part of the stomach. After ingesting the food comprising six tastes it gets digested (cooked up) sequentially. In the first phase of digestion, as the result of digestive substances of the sweet taste (carbohydrates) frothy *kapha* is secreted. In the next phase, digestion of acidified food results in liquid secretion of pure *pitta* (bile), which results in the digestion of fats and proteins. Once it reaches the *pakwashaya* (large bowel) the food is dehydrated. With the absorption of water, substances with pungent and astringent tastes are digested with the production of *vata*. The digestion process starts right in the buccal cavity, with the salivary enzymes. The second phase of digestion is in the stomach by hydrochloric acid and the enzymes, pepsin, trypsin, *etc.*, followed by bile released from the liver and gall bladder, pancreatic secretions and the enzymes and secretions in the small bowel. The third phase of microbial digestion and fermentation occurs in the large intestine along with the production of gases. Food not only nourishes the body, but its taste and fragrance also please the senses, and provides satiation.

Mechanism of digestion

Bhauma aapya aagneya vaayavyah pancha ushmanaah sanaabhasa l
Pancha aahaara gunaan swaan paarthivaadeen pachanti hi ll
(Cha. Chi. 15/13)

Each of the five elements, starting from *prithvi* to *akash* in the food substances are digested or cooked by their own respective type of fire. These are the five *bhootagnis*, which nourish all the tissues made up of different elements.

Saptabhih deha dhataro dhatavo dwividham punah l
Yathasvam agnibhih paakam yaanti kitta prasadavat ll
(Cha. Chi. 15/15)

The seven tissue elements (*dhatus*) also undergo combustion by their respective fires called *dhatwagnis*. They divide food into two parts; that which is nourishing and waste matter.

Rasat raktam tato mamsam maamsaat medah tato asthi cha l
Astho majja tatah shukram shukraat garbhah prasaadaja ll
(Cha. Chi. 15/16)

From *rasa* to *shukra* all the seven *dhatus* are formed one after the other. From the *shukra* embrogenesis occurs. Thus *agni* is the most important element apart from *tridoshas*. In effect the body is a very efficient combustion machine.

Ayurvarno balam swathyam utsaho upachayau prabhaa l
Ojah tejo agnayah praanaaschokta dehaagni hetukaah ll
(Cha. Chi. 15/3)

If the digestive fire is normal it promotes a long life span, a glowing complexion. strength, health, the zeal to work, proper nourishment, glow, immune power, radiance and life force.

Chapter : 13

Mechanisms of Dhatu Formation

Different mechanisms and processes of *dhatu* formation

Ayurveda postulated three laws to explain the mechanisms for the bio-conversion of various *dhatus*. These mechanisms were hypothesized through timeless experiential wisdom based on intuition, the sound observation of natural phenomena, logic and intellectual brilliance. There were no experimental laboratories to prove all these theories, but common sense examples were used to explain the different physiological mechanisms.

The three laws for the bioconversion and formation of various *dhatus*

1. *Kedari kulya nyaya,* the law of sequential watering of the squares in a rice field.
2. *Ksheera Dadhi nyaya,* the law of conversion of milk to curd.
3. *Khale Kapota nyaya,* law of the way the pigeons pick the grains of their choice.

Kedarikulya nyaya

It is proposed that all the *dhatus* are formed sequentially from one another, starting from *rasadhtu* to *shukradhatu* in serial order. This mechanism is compared to the method of watering a rice field. In this method the water flows serially into all the squares of the field from one to the next. In this fashion *rakta* from *rasa*, *mamsa* from *rakta*, *meda* from *mamsa*, *asthi* from *meda*, *majja* from *asthi* and finally *shukra* from *majja* are formed serially. *Rasa dhatu*, the first *dhatu*, has all the different types of nutrient substrates that build all the tissues. These substrates are serially supplied to the seven *dhatus*. Thus some *dhatus* form in a few days, whereas some take months.

On the face of it, the idea of the *kedarikulya* law of conversion of various *dhatus* may appear very simplistic to some and even ridiculous to others. But a deeper understanding of the biochemistry with regards to the formation of different tissues shows the scientific validity of these ancient insights. The logic behind the mechanisms of Ayurveda can now be explained by modern bio-chemistry more scientifically. *Kedarikulya nyaya* explains the mechanism of conversion of the nutritional constituents of *rasa dhatu*. *Rasa dhatu* is the substrate from which all the *dhatus* form serially. *Shukra*, the final *dhatu* fits the description of gamete production and steroid hormone function. It is stated that *majja* (bone marrow) is the source for the formation of *shukra*. Do sperms really originate from the bone marrow? How do we understand this statement?

On the face of it *majja*, the bone marrow contributing to the formation of *shukra* might sound absurd. Fortunately modern endocrinology now explains the important role of bone marrow in triggering the gonadal function. The final *dhatu*, *shukra*, is formed only after the full development of *majja dhatu* in adolescence and signals the arrival of menarche. Sushruta called this state as *samarthagata veeryatwa*. What causes this sudden dramatic development? Before the teenage years, the hypothalamo-pituitary gonadal axis is inactive as though in slumber, and it is activated only at puberty. As adolescence approaches, the red marrow in the long bones of a child is converted into yellow fatty marrow, which is an important source for extra gonadal steroidogenesis. The extragonadal steroid hormone (estradiol) is secreted in the yellow fatty bone marrow. This estradiol triggers the positive feedback to the hypothalamus and activates the hypo-thalamo pituitary gonadal axis. The concept of Ayurveda with regards to the role played by the bone marrow in the generation of *shukra dhatu* thus stands validated, thanks to modern research.

Similarly, the fact that the origin of hard *asthi* is the soft, liquefied *meda dhatu* (lipoid tissue) may also appear strange and difficult to explain. Let us see if we can try and understand the basis of this hypothesis. *Meda* is lipoid tissue. The bone is formed from the periosteum, which is in intimate contact with fat or *meda*. At first the cartilage gets ossified to form the bone, which requires the action of vitamin D. Vitamin D (Ergestrol) is lipoid in origin. If Vitamin D is deficient, the calcification of the bones fails and this result in rickets. Thus the lipoid origin of the *asthi dhatu* hypothesis stands vindicated with a proper understanding of modern biochemistry.

***Kshira dadhi nyay*: Law of conversion of milk into the curd**

The scientific explanation of biochemical reactions in living cells was not possible in ancient times. Ayurveda tried to explain these transformations in the body on the basis of common sense examples, experiences and observations in day to day life. Thus they tried to explain the bio-conversions of tissues on the basis of the daily observation of the conversion of milk into curd. Though the actual mechanism of the conversion process could not be explained, the result was obvious. Milk did change into curd. So also some similar mechanisms caused the conversions and formation of different tissues or *dhatus*.

Discovery of enzymes by Edward Buchner in the year 1897 revolutionised the understanding of the mechanisms of conversions in the living body. It is interesting and also useful to know the story of this invention. Edward was experimenting with yeast with the objective of improving the quality of wine. Till then it was believed that yeast transformed the grape juice into wine, but he wondered whether the yeast was really responsible for the conversion into wine. He took yeast, mixed it with some sand, in a muslin cloth and squeezed the mixture to obtain the filtrate without any living yeast organisms in it. This filtrate, when added to grape juice resulted in wine. He thus discovered that it was not the yeast, which transformed the grape juice in to wine, but some substance inside the yeast. This substance got its name, the enzyme, which literally means something inside the yeast. He thus laid the foundations of modern biochemistry and enzymatology. *Kshira dadhi* logic can now easily be explained on the basis of enzymatic conversions. Milk is converted in to curd due the enzymatic action of lacto bacilli. Thus Ayurveda explained all the bioconversions in the body in simple language using common sense examples.

Khale kapota nyaya: Law of selection

This law is based on the method by which the pigeons pick up grains scattered on the ground through choice and selection. Every *dhatu* or tissue requires a specific substrate for its formation. This substrate is provided by the *rasa dhatu*. Thus only such substrate is selected that will be required to form the concerned *dhatu*. This is how some substances reach their specific target tissue bypassing other tissues. Examples are iron for *rakta dhatu* and zinc for *shukra dhatu*. Thus a knowledge of modern science helps in understanding Ayurveda and its mechanisms better.

Chapter : 14

Vitiated Agni

The causes for abnormal digestive fire

Abhojanat ajeernaathibhojanat vishama bhojanaat l
Asaatmya guru sheeta ati ruksha samdushta bhojanaat ll

Vireka vamana sneha vibhramah, vyadhikarshanaat l
Desha kaalartu vaishamyad vegaanaam cha vidhaaranat ll

Dushyati agnih, sa dushtognam na tat pachati laghvapi l
Apachyamaanam shuktatwam yaatiannam visha roopatam ll
(Cha. Chi. 15/44)

Abstaining from food, indigestion, over eating, irregular eating, eating of unwholesome, heavy to digest, cold, stale and putrid food, improperly conducted procedures of emesis, purgation, oleation, loss of weight following a disease, incompatible clime and country, and the suppression of natural urges cause vitiated or abnormal *agni*. This leads to failure to digest even small quantities of food. This undigested food turns sour or ferments and behaves like a poison in the body.

The signs of food poisoning (*anna vishasya lingaani*)

Tasya lingam ajeernasya vishtambham sadanam tatha l
Shiraso ruk cha moorchaa cha brhamah prushta katigrahah ll

Jrumbha angamardah trushnaa cha jwara chardihih pravaahanam l
Arochako avipakamscha ll (Cha. Chi. 15/45)

Food poisoning causes the following complications.

1. Indigestion. 2. Intestinal stasis causing abdominal distension. 3. A feeling of extreme weakness. 4. Head ache. 5. Fainting attacks. 6. Giddiness. 7. Stiffness of the waist and the back. 8. Yawning. 9. Body ache. 10. Thirst. 11. Fever. 12. Vomiting. 13. Dysentery. 14. Anorexia. 15. Irritable bowel causing mis-digestion and mal-absorption.

Grahani: Location and actions

Agni adhishtaanam annasya grahnaat grahanee mataa l

It is called *grahani* because it receives and absorbs the digested food. Indeed it is the seat of digestive fire, the *agni*.

Nabhe uparih agni balena upashtabdho upabrumhitaa ll

Apakvam dharatyannam pakwam srujati parshvatah l
Durbalaagni balah dushtatwam eva vimunchati ll
(Cha. Chi. 15/ 56-57)

It is located in the umbilical region (small bowel). It holds the undigested food till it is properly digested and absorbed. The remaining unabsorbed food is expelled. If the digestive fire is weak or vitiated it expels undigested food.

Four functional states of *agni*

If the digestion of food occurs improperly, it will result into *aama dosha*. For the normal state of *agni*, the normality of *saman vayu*, *kledak kapha* and *pachak pitta* are essential. Following the proper digestion of food the *saara* (useful essence) is retained and absorbed as the chyle and waste matter is excreted as *mala* by *apana vayu*.

Agni exists in four functional states.

***Mandagni* (Low grade metabolic fire)**

Durbalo vidhati annam tad yaati urdhwam adhopi va ll
(Cha. Chi. 15/51)

Weak digestive fire does not digest the food properly and may expel this undigested food either upwards (vomiting) or downwards (diarrhoea). It is due to *kapha* affliction of *agni*. It manifests as hypochlorhydria. This leads to poor digestion. A poor metabolic state as in the case of hypothyroidism is another manifestation of *mandagni*.

***Tikshnagni* (Excess of metabolic fire)**

Teeksno manda indhano dhaatoon vishoshyayati pavakah ll
(Cha. Chi. 15/50)

When this fire is powerful and food supply is deficient, it consumes the body tissues. It is due to vitiation of *pitta*. It leads to excessive hunger and voracious eating habits, it may be comparable to thyrotoxicosis (*bhasmak*).

***Vishamagni* (Vicarious metabolic fire)**

Vishamo dhatu vaishamyam karoti vishamam pachan ll
(Cha. Chi. 15/50)

Disturbed and irregularly stimulated digestive fire causes imbalance in the *dhatus* and disturbs homeostasis. It is due to vitiation of *vata*. Irregular and erratic eating habits can result in abnormal digestion, which leads to poor absorption. Stress related acid peptic disease may also fall in this category.

Samagni

Yuktam bhuktavatah yukto dhatu saamyam samam pachet ll
(Cha. Chi. 15/51)

When *agni* is well balanced and healthy food is eaten, digestion occurs properly and all the body elements will be in a state of homeostasis. This is the normal state of metabolic fire, which results in normal digestion and formation of proper chyle or *annarasa*.

Adhastu pakwam aamam va pravruttam grahaneegadah l
Uchyate sarvam evaannam prayo hyasya vidahyate ll
(Cha. Chi. 15/52)

Grahanigada is essentially disease due to improper digestion, absorption and assimilation of food, resulting in a mixture of digested and undigested food.

Ati srushtam vibaddham va dravam tad upaveshyate l
Trushna arochaka vairasya praseka tamakaavitah ll
(Cha. Chi. 15/53)

A person who suffers from improper absorption experiences thirst, loss of appetite, dysgeusia, excessive salivation (ptyalism), asthma and sometimes passes large, hard stools and at other times liquid stools.

Shoona paadakarah sa asthi parvaruk chardanam jwarah l
Loha aamagandhi tikta amla udgaraashcha jaayate ll
(Cha. Chi. 15/54)

If the condition progresses this person develops oedema on both the feet and hands, pains in the bones and joints, vomiting and fever. He exudes a foul smell of metal or raw meat and gets bitter and sour (acid) eructations.

Ingested food when not digested properly due to the three abnormal states of *agni* as stated above, will result in *annarasa,* which is abnormal in quality. This abnormal *annarasa* is toxic in nature and acts like a poison. This is called *aama* in Ayurveda. All the pathologies in the body have their roots in the generation of this *aama*. According to modern medicine, it is usually believed that many of the GI disturbances are caused by various infections and/or irregular eating habits. *Srotodushti* occurs due to accumulation of *doshas* at the site of the disease process. *Srotas* are channels of varying sizes, from microtubular channels, capillaries and blood vessels to the large tubular structures of the GI tract. Obstruction to these channels is the cause for stagnation of *doshas* and it is the beginning of the disease process. Micro-organisms are ubiquitous. Why a particular infection begins at a particular site is still not answered by modern medicine. Ayurvedic conceptualization of *sroto avarodh* (obstruction to the channels) appears to be reasonably sound. *Aama* formation leads to *saama* state of *doshas*, *dhatus* and *malas* causing a disturbance to the homeostasis in the body, which results in innumerable diseases. The entire process of Ayurvedic diagnosis of a disease depends on identifying the *saamata* of different *doshas*, *dhatus* and *malas*. Thus understanding the function of *agni* is vital for all the treating physicians.

Agni sankalpana: Concept of *agni* in Ayurveda

Sama dosha samagnishscha sama dhatu mala kriyah

The four basic and fundamental requirements for health (*swasthya*) are the three *doshas* (*vata*, *pitta* and *kapha*) and *agni*. We now study *agni* and its important role in metabolism.

Agni in the human body is the metabolic fire. The Latin equivalent of fire is *ignis* and its English equivalent is ignite. *Agni Suktam* (*Rigveda*) describes it as *purohitam*, meaning the saviour of the city of nine gates (*nava dwara puri*) or the living body. The human body is a most efficient combustion machine that works at very low temperatures. In the body the metabolic fire digests food and transforms it into the different tissues of the body. In the course of digestion of food, the three *doshas*, *viz.*, *kapha*, *pitta* and *vata* are also generated. All physiological processes generate heat. One example is thermogenesis of ovulation that causes a subtle rise of half a degree Fahrenheit. Ayurveda therefore has described *aartavam* as *aagneyam* (heat producing). Mitochondria, which are the power house of all living cells is other example. Mitochondria are of maternal origin. Metabolism in tissues generate free radicals. Free radicles cause the inflammation process in the body. Any inflamed part of the body is hot and in fever the temperature rises. Inflammation is a complex biological and protective response of the body's immune system involving molecular mediators to remove the irritant causes, harmful agents and causes healing and homeostasis.

According to Ayurveda, *agni* bestows nourishment, energy, power, wealth, intelligence, knowledge and good health and it also maintains the thermal balance of the body.

The Bhagavat Geeta describes it as a fire that digests four types of ingested foods, in association with *prana* and *apana vayus.*

Aham vaishwanaro bhootwa praninaam dehamaashritah l
Pranaapana samahitwa pachamyannam chaturvidham ll
(Bhagavat Geeta, Chp. XV)

The Upanishads have described two forms of fire. The first is the *garhyapatya vahni*, which burns constantly. The other one is *aavaahaniya*, which is dependent on *garhyapatya vahni* for its subsistence. It bestows *prana*, the vital force.

Sa esham eva vaishwanaro vishwa roopah pranah agni udayate l
(Prasnopanishad)

Pranaagni, that resides in *jathara* (gut) is *vaishwanar*, consisting of infinitely different hues of life fire. *Jathara* and *koshta* are two terms used for the abdominal cavity.

Of the three *doshas*, *pitta* is a form of *agni* due to its *ushna teekshna gunas*. *Pachaka pitta* aids digestion and absorption of food to give nourishment. *Ranjaka pitta* helps in the transformation of *rasa dhatu* to *rakta dhatu*. *Alochak pitta* illumines the mind through processing of information to create true knowledge. *Sadhaka pitta* is instrumental in successfully achieving the goals of various actions. *Bhrajaka pitta* causes a shiny, glowing complexion. All the *pittas* are forms of heat that cause a number of transformation processes in the body.

The human body is a combustion machine that constantly requires fuel in the form of carbohydrates, which are burnt by oxidation processes to provide energy to enable it to perform all the bodily actions. The entire body's metabolic processes are thus dependent on *agni*. It maintains the thermal balance in the body. A thermostat that creates a set point temperature is located in the dorsomedial hypothalamus, which is the part of the lower brain. Any disturbance to this central thermostat causes a rise in the temperature level above the set point resulting in fever.

Normal set point levels of temperature: 37.5°C (99.5°F) - 38.3°C (100.9°F). The locations where temperature is normally recorded are otic, rectal, oral and axillary. Of all the places the most accurate is otic (ear). Fever level: Maximum: 41°C (105.4°F) – 42°C (107.6°F).

Pyrogens are the agents that trigger a pyrexial response. These are of two types, *viz*., exogenous (*aagantuka*) and endogenous (*aabhyantara*). Common exogenous pyrogens are the lipopolysaccharides that are derived from the cell walls of infection producing bacteria. These activate the arachidonic acid (AA) pathway and cause the release of prostaglandins (PGE2). PGE2 disturb the hypothalamic thermostat and cause the temperature to rise above the set point to produce fever. Endogenous pyrogens: Any invasion by a foreign substance leads to inflammation and the activation of the immune system, which is associated with the release of cytokines, *viz*., IL-1 and IL-6. These in turn activate the arachidonic acid (AA) pathway to trigger the release of PGE2. Thus release of prostaglandins (PG) are at the root of pyrexial response in the body.

When the set point of the body temperature is raised, shivering occurs due to muscular contractions as a result of activation of the autonomous nervous system, along with the release of acetyl-choline and adrenaline. This causes peripheral vasoconstriction and prevention of sweat formation in the skin resulting in prevention of heat loss from the body. The fever subsides as the temperature returns to the set point resulting in a reversal of the process. This results in vasodilation and with the beginning of sweating, the body begins to cool. Rarely seizures occur in children during fever.

At the onset of death the heat totally departs from the body and the body becomes cold. It is a Hindu belief that at the time of death Lord Shiva departs from the body and therefore the dead body is known as *shava*. Shiva's location in the body, according to Hindu mythology, is *shikha*, the part corresponding to the hypothalamus. Shiva's anger or disturbance results in fever.

The primary site of *agni* that constantly burns is *jathar* or *koshta* or the abdominal cavity. *Jatharagni* is the chief of the fires that maintains twelve other types of fires described by Ayurveda. There are five *bhutagnis*, which act at the levels of the *tanmatras* of the *panchbhootas*. It simply means that they act at the molecular level and bring about transcription to form various *dhatus* or tissues. The other *agni* are the seven *dhatwagni*. They are responsible for tissue metabolism and other transformation processes. Therefore, *jatharagni* should not simply be equated to gastric juices or the hydrochloric acid contained in it.

The other site of *agni* is the tongue. Speech is believed to be ruled by the fire god. Thus speech is described as fiery speech. The speech centre (Broca's area) is located in the frontal lobe of the dominant hemisphere of the brain, usually the left. Thus *agni* function is also inclusive of all the neurohormonal transmission and enzymatic transcription systems. The hypothalamus has a temperature regulation centre. The hypothalamus also releases thyrotropin/thyroid stimulating (TSH). The thyroid hormone plays a major role in the metabolism of the entire body. It is dependent on the nutrition of the body. "The role of thyroid hormone," which is given below is a direct quote from a publication from Precision Clinical Medicine (PCM).

Thyroid hormone regulation of metabolism

Thyroid hormone (TH) is required for normal development in a child, as well as for regulating metabolism in the adult. The thyroid hormone receptor (TR) isoforms, α and β, are differentially expressed in tissues and have distinct roles in TH signalling. Local activation of thyroxine (T_4), to the active form, triiodothyronine (T_3), by 5′-deiodinase type 2 (D2) is a key mechanism of TH regulation of metabolism. D2 is expressed in the hypothalamus, white fat, brown adipose tissue (BAT), and skeletal muscle and is required for adaptive thermogenesis. The thyroid gland is regulated by thyrotropin releasing hormone (TRH) and thyroid stimulating hormone (TSH). In addition to TRH/TSH regulation by TH feedback, there is central modulation by nutritional signals (*jathara agni* connection), such as leptin, as well as peptides regulating appetite. The nutrient status of the cell provides feedback on TH signalling pathways through epigenetic modification of histones. Integration of TH signalling with the adrenergic nervous system occurs peripherally, in the liver, white fat, and BAT, but also centrally, in the hypothalamus. TR regulates cholesterol and carbohydrate metabolism through direct actions on gene expression as well as cross-talk with other nuclear receptors, including peroxisome proliferator-activated receptor (PPAR), liver X receptor

(LXR), and bile acid signalling pathways. TH modulates hepatic insulin sensitivity, especially important for the suppression of hepatic gluconeogenesis. The role of TH in regulating metabolic pathways has led to several new therapeutic targets for metabolic disorders. Understanding the mechanisms and interactions of the various TH signalling pathways in metabolism will improve our likelihood of identifying effective and selective targets. (Rashmi Mullur, Yan-Yun Liu, and Gregory A. Brent).

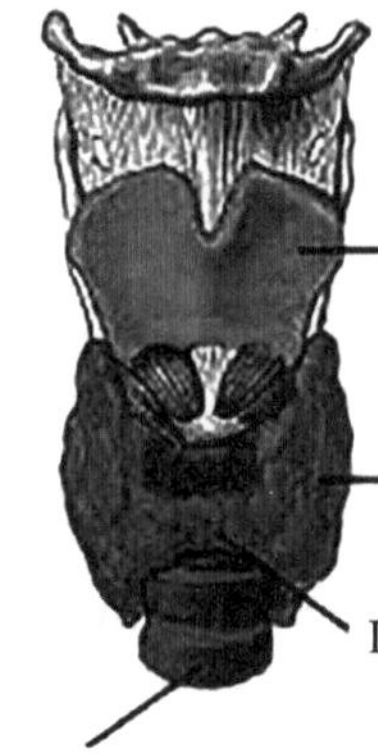

Illustration of thyroid

Koshta and gut microbiome

The origin of the word *koshta* is rooted in the ritual of *yagna* and has very interesting religious, philosophical and physiological connotations. It actually means a *yagna vedi* or sacrificial platform, where fire wood is burnt. The purpose of a *yagna* is meant to nourish the organs of cognition and conation. The gastro intestinal tract is the main seat of digestion and absorption of food. It nourishes all the body tissues. Apart from gastric acid, enzymes and hormones in the stomach and small intestine, the role of the large gut in relation to digestion of food has only been recognized recently. Digestion of food in the large gut is dependent on its microflora or gut microbiome. Modern scientific research on microflora revolutionized the understanding of the structure and function of gut microbiome with reference to digestive, neuro immune and biological processes in the gut, creating a paradigm shift in understanding the host microbiome symbiosis.

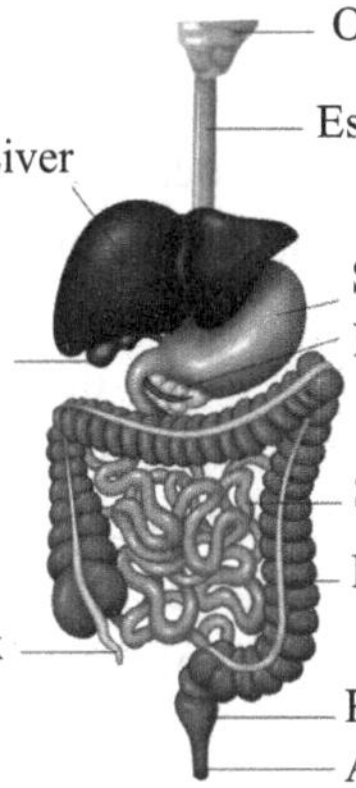

Illustration of digestive tract

What is gut microbiome?

It comprises 3,000-10,000 species of microbes numbering almost 100 trillion that reside in the gut with about 60% within the colon. They are not just mere harmless commensals, but are now recognized as symbiotic and mutualistic, making the human body a meta-organism. Entero types are mostly anaerobic. Only the cecum has a good density of aerobic colonies.

Common genera

- **Bacteroides (30%):** Clostridiae, Fusobacteria, Eubactereciae, Ruminococcus, Peptococcus, Bifido bacteria.
- **Fungii:** Candida, Saccharomyces, Asperilligus, Penicillium.
- **Arachea**: Important for metabolizing bacterial products of fermentation.

Bacteroides: Ferment and breakdown proteins, fats, enzymes, dead host bacterial cells, collagen, elastin, etc.

Prevotelle: These are the bacteroids that digest the indigestible substrate of carbohydrates by saccharolytic fermentation and generate energy. They help in the production of essential vitamins of the B group and Vitamin K *etc.*, they aid in the absorption of short chain fatty acids, produce hormones for the storage of fats and also metabolize bile salts, sterols and xenobiotics. Colonic epithelium metabolizes fats, particularly butyrates, whereas the liver metabolizes propionates. Muscle cells generate ATP and energy by metabolizing acetates. They also induce the development of lymphoid structures (payer's patches), assist in the development and differentiation of host intestinal epithelium and produce mucosal based immunity (IGA) providing protection against opportune pathogens. They are now considered a key to the development of bone, brain and behaviour. They help in maintaining homeostasis. It is no wonder then, that in the light of current information, gut microbiome appeared to be a forgotten organ. It is now believed that the metabolic power of gut microbiome is almost equal to that of the liver.

Diet and gut microbiome

Different types of diets are believed to be associated with colonies of different types of genera of microbes in gut flora. Thus food borne microbes colonize the gut. These include bacteria, fungi and even viruses. Long term dietary habits influence the structure or composition of colonies, as well as the activity of trillions of gut microflora.

A non vegetarian diet promotes bile tolerant microbes, *viz*., alistipes, and bacteroides *etc*. It enhances the expression of genes that biosynthesise vitamins, carcinogenic compounds & beta lactamase genes. An animal origin diet and western diets with high protein, fat and sugar content have a predominant presence of Bilophila wadworthins. They also alter the genetic composition and metabolic profile of gut microbiome leading to genesis of inflammatory bowel disease and metabolic syndromes (obesity and cardio vascular disease) as well cancer. Gut microbial metabolic products are known to cause many pathological conditions including heart disease. The gut bacterial metabolic by-product trimethyline N-Oxide (TMAO) is now considered as a marker for myocardial infarction. Recent research on autism has shown its association with Sutterella wadworthens in the gut.

Fermicutes are more prevalent in the gut of those consuming a vegetarian diet. These, *viz*., Roseburia, eubacterium and Ruminococcus bromi, *etc*., metabolize indigestible plant poly saccharides.

Dysbiosis is state of imbalance that disturbs the homeostasis of normal gut microbiota composition leading to a large number of diseases. Malnutrition also promotes disease producing rogue bacteria.

Gene studies of gut microbiome

The total DNA of the gut microbial ecosystem consists of about five million genes, almost ten times the number of the human host genes. Gut microbes in normal condition of health are no mere non self-antigen producing agents thus causing a new paradigm shift in immune-biology of the gut. In response to stressful situations the microbial genome undergoes changes far more rapidly as compared to the host genome, and thus responds promptly. Gene products of microbiota compliment host physiology through biochemical and metabolic actions. The enteric nervous system is a new discovery that functions through non-cholinergic and non-adrenergic mechanisms coupled now with new intelligence systems of gut microbiome.

Is this what we understand commonly as gut instinct or gut brain?

Path breaking research by Felix Somers and others published in *Nature* (2003) have shown that germ free rats failed to develop a lymphoid system, Payer's patches and a mucosal immune system and thereby failed to produce a number of soluble IgA & anti-microbial peptides. This resulted in failure to provide a physical and chemical barrier to pathogenic bacteria.

A human being is not a single entity, but meta-organism, being a host to multitudes of organisms. The intestine is thus a dynamic habitat, where modifications in transcription, generation of new protein and metabolic profiles occur due to microbes. Life style issues (*pragnyaparadh, srotovarodh*), diet (*junk food*), poor hygiene, antibiotics and steroids *etc*., constantly affect microbial composition in the gut leading to many diseases. Gut motility and sphincter control mechanisms also play a major role in the digestive system. H. pylori is a pathogenic bacteria and is considered to be a cause of gastro-oesophageal reflux disorder (GERD). Normally the stomach produces so much hydrochloric acid that even an iron nail can be dissolved. Therefore it is a wonder that H. pylori thrives in the stomach. When the acid pH weakens because of dilution by alkaline bile reflux into the stomach due to pyloric sphincter incontinence, H. pylori gets an appropriate habitat to thrive and multiply and produce pathology. Repression of sphincters or *vegavarodh* is an obvious cause of incompetence of the sphincter, resulting in disease production. Thus *vegavarodh* becomes an important cause of many pathological conditions. Now let us see the ways in which the gut microbiome can be altered.

Role of prebiotics & probiotics

Prebiotics: Non digestible food ingredients stimulate growth and activity of a variety of gut bacteria. Their fermentation selectively allows specific changes in proliferation, composition and/or activity in gut microflora that confers benefits to the host's wellbeing and health, *e.g.*, galactopolysaccharide, inulin, fructooligosaccharide (FOS), lactulose and mannan oligosaccharide (MOS). "There is now compelling evidence that links enteric microbiota & brain function (Li, *et al.*, & Rao, *et al.*, 2009). Proliferation of bifido bacteria & lactobacillus strains in the colon have anxiolytic and mneumonic effects through action on the hippocampus & amygdala by altering glutamate transferase in the brain. Prebiotic feeding elevates NMDAR (N-Methyl-D aspartate receptor sub units) and D-Serine, neurotrophic factor – (Helen M. Savignae *et al.*, *Neuro Chemistry International*). Many *deepana* and *pachana* herbs may be acting as prebiotics.

Probiotics: These are live organisms, that when consumed orally are known to give health benefits. Metcknikoff first suggested in the early 19th century that the seeding of the human gut with harmless lactobacilli from curd, will cause a decrease in the intestinal pH and inhibit proteolytic bacteria. Similarly *takra* (butter milk) treatment in *grahani* is a technique of introducing live yeast organisms into the gut. Below we give an ingenious ancient technique with oral use of live microbes for the purpose of enhancement of general immunity, known as fresh *pancha gavya prashan*.

Hindu religious rituals and Ayurveda used this technique of seeding beneficial colonies through use of a combination of cow dung, urine, milk, curd and *ghee*, called *panchagavya* from time immemorial. In *pancha karma* and other medicinal uses animal products are used.

Preparation of fresh *pancha gavya* (*Dharma Sindhu*)

Mix 12.5 gms. fresh cow dung and 25 ml of fresh cow's urine in a copper vessel and stir properly and filter through a clean muslin cloth. Now add to 25 ml each of milk and curd to the filtrate, mix properly and then add 5 ml of *ghee*. The suspension should be stored for half an hour and then dispensed on the day of *Shravani* in a small single dose of 2 ml, orally.

Why on *Shravani* day?

During the months of July & August, there is a large incidence of cowpox infection in cows. Cowpox and other viruses and bacteria are expressed in all the products from the cow. The *Shravani* festival is celebrated during this period. The acidic pH of the urine coupled with the ionizing property of copper help kill or attenuate microbes (both harmful and helpful), therefore a copper vessel is used for making *panchgavya*. Our recent research studies (16s RDNA) have confirmed that the concentration of pathogenic organisms in *panchagavya* are reduced and beneficial probiotic lactobacilli concentration enhanced after half an hour of exposure in a copper container.

Organisms in cow dung

Intestinal organisms in cow dung

- **Anerobic organisms:** E .Coli, tetanus, aerobic typhoid, and tuberculosis etc.
- Eupencillium, Borifimosum produce strongly antifungal agents, CK2108A/Ck2801B, They inhibit the growth of Corprophyllus fungi.
- **Viruses:** Cow pox, poliomyelitis etc.

Cow's urine

- Acidic pH attenuates and detoxifies the microbes. It is a powerful bio-fungicide and contains quinolones & flavoquinolones.
- Susceptible fungal strains: Fusarium oxysporum, claviceps purpuria, Asperligus orizae

Crystalline cow urine distillate fractions are now patented. CSIR patent 6410059. Anti-fungal, antimicrobial, anti-cancer activities have been claimed but not yet proved.

Curd and milk provide a neutral nutrient medium, lacto bacilli and lactoferin B, a powerful antimicrobial protein.

Ghee helps in the enteric coating of the suspended attenuated microbes in *panchagavya* suspension, so that it helps to bypass hydrochloric acid in the stomach by lipophylisation.

Additional benefits of *panchagavya*

It contains N, S, PO_4, Na, Mn, carbolic acid, iron, silicon, Cl, Mg, citric, succinic Ca salts, the vitamins A, B, C, D, E, erythropoietin, *etc*. By introducing it into the small and large gut, cultures of live attenuated microorganisms in small doses stimulate the lymphoid system (Payer's patches) and produce immunity. Repeating it every year acts a booster dose.

Is this an ancient technique of immunization?

Vaccination is derived from the word *vacca*, meaning cow in Latin. Transplanting organisms from the cow into humans is a novel method of improving immunity. The powerful antioxidant activity of *panchagavya* has been established by many studies. Because of the capacity to scavenge free radicals, it is used by many traditional practitioners in cancer therapy. Ayurveda has used cow's urine as *bhavana dravya* in many medicinal preparations consisting of herbs and minerals. All these new developments in gut microbiota should open our minds with regards to the traditional use of animal products and provide us with a new direction for research and development in terms of probiotics and prebiotics from Ayurveda.

Chapter : 15

Nidra

Regular sleeping habits are an important part of the lifestyle of a person desirous of a long, healthy and happy life. The earliest sign of anxiety and mental depression is the inability to sleep well or sleep deprivation or insomnia. From the view point of Ayurveda, sleep is one of the three foundation pillars of life, the other two being nutrition and controlled sexual activity.

Sleep is a naturally recurring state of mind and body, characterized by an altered state of consciousness, relatively inhibited sensory activity, near total inhibition of voluntary muscles associated with poor interaction with one's surroundings. Shakespeare described sleep as death of the day's life cycle. But the fact is that the brain works furiously, while we sleep. There are two stages of sleep. REM (rapid eye moments) sleep during which the eyes are shut, but the eye balls are roving with movement. Most dreams occur in this stage. The second is a stage of deep sleep, which is non REM. There is little body movement. Snoring is another feature. During this phase, there is intense electrical activity in the brain that can be seen on an electro- encephalogram (EEG). This phase of sleep has a great restorative power. Capacity of the mind in terms of memory, will power *etc.*, and the immune system are boosted by good sleep. Sleep deprivation causes paranoid behaviour and leads to a decline in skills.

What causes sleep?

Yadaatu manasi klante karmatmanah klamanvitah l
Vishayebhyo nivartante tada swapiti manavah ll (Cha. Su. 21/34)

As the organs of action get exhausted due to work, the mind also gets tired and fails to connect with objects of the senses and thus a person falls asleep. Usually, at night, a person goes to sleep happily after a hard day's work. Sleep rejuvenates a person. When one wakes up in the morning after a good night's sleep, a person feels fresh and relaxed. Therefore Ayurveda describes sleep as *bhoota dhatri*, meaning the foster mother of all living beings. It is now established that in the darkness of night, a number of hormones, *e.g.*, melatonin, the growth hormone, *etc.*, are secreted. These help in healing the wear and tear that occurs throughout the day and helps in growth. A child who sleeps well, grows well. There are body clocks (chrono- biology) that vary with day and night and with every changing season. *Vata*, *pitta* and *kapha* are regulated in accordance with the Circadian rhythm.

Regular, good sleep leads to happiness (*sukh*), strength (*bala*), immune power (*pushti*), potency (*vrushata*), knowledge (*gnyan*) and a long life (*ayuh*). Loss of sleep or insomnia causes grief or sorrow (*dukh*), lean body or cachexia (*krushata*), weakness (*durbalata*), impotency (*kleebata*), ignorance and a short life span or death (*mrutyu*). Sleeping in the day time causes unctuousness (*snigdhata*) leading to excessive accumulation of *kapha*, the only exception being in the *greeshma rutu* (summer), when sleeping for a short time in the day time is advisable. Staying awake very late at night causes dryness and accumulation of *vata*. Hence early to bed at night is most beneficial for maintaining good health.

Swapna: Dreams

A dream is a succession of images, ideas, emotions and sensations that usually occur involuntarily in the mind during certain stages of sleep. Dreams mainly occur in the rapid-eye movement (REM) stage of sleep - when brain activity is high and resembles that of being awake. According to Dr J. Allan Hobson, the major function of rapid eye movement (REM) sleep associated with dreams is physiological rather than psychological. During REM sleep the brain is activated and warming its circuits and is anticipating the sights, sounds and emotions of the waking state.

Manovah srotansi dosha poornam athava na
atiprasupta purushah swapnam pashyati l

Poorvadehanubhutanstu bhootatma swapatah prabhuh l
Rajoyuktena manasa gruhnat arthaan shubhashubham ll
(Su. Sha. 4/36)

A person, who is not in deep sleep (*i.e.*, who is in the REM phase) sub consciously experiences, one's good or bad experiences of his or her past and current life through a disturbed mind, due to excessive *rajas* quality. What is the right time to wake up after a good night's sleep?

Brahme muhoorte uttishttet swasthyo rakshaartham aayushah l
(Ashtang. Hr. Su. 2/1)

A healthy person should wake up early, before sun rise, in order to protect and enhance one's life span, for this is best time, when the mind is peaceful and memory is excellent. This principle does not apply to a person who is sick.

Chapter : 16

Vyayam

Vyayam: Excercise

Ayurveda advises a code of conduct for both day and night, based on different seasons in order to safe guard one's good health. It is called *swastha vritta*. One should follow the prescribed *dinacharya* (daily chores of activities). Exercise or *vyayam* is a very important part of *dinacharya*.

Laghavam karma samarthyam deepto agnih medasah kshayah l
Vibhakta ghana gatratwam vyayamat upajayate ll
(Asht. Hr. Su. 2/10)

Exercise results in lightness of the body, betters activities and skills, it kindles the *jatharagni* (metabolic fire), reduces the fat and enables the body to become muscular and strong. Exercise should be performed followed by a proper oil massage. One should not do more exercise than one can tolerate.

Vata pitta aamayee baalo vruddho ajeernam cha tam tyajet l

A person suffering from *vata* and *pitta* related diseases and indigestion, children and old people should not do heavy exercise.

Ardha shaktya niveshyastu balibhih snigdha bhojibhih i
Sheeta kale vasante cha mandameva tato anyada l
(Asht. Hri. 2/11)

Those who are strong and eat rich food should exercise regularly. How much one should exercise depends upon his or her capacity to tolerate exercise. One should not overdo exercise and tire oneself. Cold winters and spring are the best seasons for exercise. In other seasons moderate exercise is prescribed. Regular exercise is a promoter of good health.

Tam krutwa anusukham deham mardayeccha samantatah l
(Asht. Hri. 2/12)

After good exercise one should get a stimulating body massage.

Complications of over exercising

Trushna kshayah pratamako rakta pittam shramh klamahh l
Ativyayamatah kaso jwara chardhishcha jayate ll
(Asht. Hri. 2/14)

Excessive exertion can cause thirst, consumption, asthma, bleeding disorders, and breathlessness and tiredness, it can also cause cough, fever and vomiting.

Vyayam jaagaradhwa stree hasya bhashyadi sahasam l
Gajam simham ivakarshan bhajannati vinashyati ll
(Asht. Hri. 2/16)

Just as a lion is harmed by pulling a heavy weight elephant, exercise beyond one's endurance capacity is harmful. Similarly, staying awake late in the night, long distance walks, excessive indulgence in sex and false bravado are harmful and should be avoided.

Chapter : 17

Sadvritta

***Sadvritta*: Good code of conduct for a long and healthy life**

The word *sat* means good or virtuous or moral and *vritta* means a code of conduct or a prescribed regimen with regards to one's personal and social behaviour. It involves a life style in which both mind and body control take centre stage and guide the spiritual, mental and social conduct of a person. To be happy is to be healthy. The modern world is cursed by stress. Stress is the cause of many psychosomatic disorders. Mind control and spirituality result in well balanced actions. A person acts in three ways, *viz.*, mental, verbal and physical. Controlled actions are called *tapsya* or *tapas*.

***Manasik tapas*: Actions performed with a controlled mind**

Manaprasadah saumyatwam maunam atma vinigrahah l
Bhava samshuddhih ityeti tapo manasamuchyate ll
(Bhagavat Geeta 17/16)

A pleasant and contended state of mind, gentleness, silence and self-control associated with pure thoughts are the characteristics of *manasik tapas*.

***Vangmaya tapas*: Good verbal control**

Anudvegakaram vakyam satyam priyam hitam cha yat l
Swadhyaya abhyasanam chaiva vangmayam tapa utchyate ll
(Bhagavat Geeta 17/15)

Words that do not result in an emotional outburst, which are truthful, pleasing and wholesome and are aimed at overall welfare are at the root of verbal control. Studying scriptures and self- introspection are important ingredients of literary or verbal tapas. The *Upanishads* have prescribed a strict practice of speaking the truth as the most important ingredient of a good code of conduct.

Satyam bruyat, priyam bruyat, satyam apriyam na bruyat,
asatyam priyam api na bruyat ll (Taittireeya Upanishad)

(Speak the truth, speak pleasing words, do not speak a truth which is unpleasant, do not speak an untruth even if it is pleasing.)

Sharirik tapas: Good physical code of conduct

Deva dwija guru praagya poojanam shaucham arjavam l
Brahmacharyam ahimsa cha shareeram tapa utchyate ll
(Bhagavat Geeta 17/14)

Respecting and worshiping gods, learned brahmins, teachers, the elderly, scholars and revered persons, practising personal hygiene, sexual control/celibacy (depending on one's status of house holder or *sanyasi*) and non-violence, and being straight forward are the virtues of a person performing bodily *tapas*.

Nityam hita ahara vihara sevee sameekshakari vishayeshu asaktah l
Data samah satyaparah kshamavan aaptopasevi cha bhavati arogah ll

Vagbhata gives a very concise, two line *sutra* for a disease free life and positive health. Regular daily intake of wholesome food and an appropriate life style are essential features that prevent disease. The life style includes certain moral, behavioural and attitudinal qualities that a person should possess. One should be contemplative or studious, disinterested in objects of the senses, generous, judicious, truthful, forgiving and ever ready to serve the elderly. These qualities of psyche in a person are called *sadvritta* or the appropriate and good moral or spiritual life style that is an essential ingredient of a long, healthy and happy life. We should realise that mind rules the body. Mental stress causes many psycho-somatic diseases. These spiritual qualities enhance longevity by preventing the stress that shortens life spans. Thus *sadvritta* is a very important ingredient of one's life style. It is a great stress buster. Modern medicine in my opinion should include *sadvritta* in the medical education curriculum.

Chapter : 18

Healthy Lifestyle Regimen

(Swastha Vrutta)

Swastha denotes self (*atma*) as seated in oneself. *Atma* is the state of joy (*ananda*). This state denotes health or *arogya*. It is different from *aroga* the disease free state. *Swastha vritta* is a regimen prescribed for keeping oneself healthy and happy.

Earlier we had discussed *sadvritta*. The key to success of *sadvritta* is to master the control of *dharaneeya vegas*. Controlling the negative emotional urges of *kama* (unjustified desire), *krodha* (anger), *lobha* (greed), *moha* (delusion), *mada* (arrogance) and *matsara* (jealousy). These six qualities are said to be enemies within you (*arishad varga*). Fear is yet another important emotion that causes stress. It needs to be conquered if one wants to be happy and healthy.

Not controlling these natural urges will lead to verbal misconduct of abuse, hurt and lying. It is the main cause of quarrels, violence, thefts and adultery *etc*., which end up in loss of peace of mind, health, wealth and happiness.

Heath involves all three, *viz*., self, mind and body. *Sadvritta* addresses both the self and mind. Yoga, pranayama and meditation are additional aids to the goal of positive health.

Let us now learn about the daily regimen of *swastha vritta*.

Dina Charya (Day time regimen)

Time to wake up and get out of bed

Early risers may have observed that birds start singing, almost one and a half hours before dawn breaks. This is the best time to get out of bed and start one's day. This is called the most auspicious *Brahme muhoorat*, when the whole atmosphere is purest, with least pollution, purer air and the least noise. It is a good practice to recite a small prayer, as this is the time when the mind is most calm and receptive.

***Danta dhavan* (cleaning of teeth) and *mukha shuddhi* (cleaning of the oral cavity)**

Dental health is most important to safeguard good health. Dental cavities and gum disease are some of the most common causes of ill health. Teeth, many times, act as septic foci creating diseases in different areas of body. Consumption of too many sugary items results in gum disease and dental caries. Teeth act as a septic focus leading to many chronic diseases in the body.

Ayurveda prescribes the following bitter and astringent herbs to be used as dental brushes: *Neem* (Azdirachta indica), *babul* (Acacia Arabica) and *karanja* (Pongamia pinnata).

These bitter herbs possess antimicrobial activity, and also improve the activity of the taste buds on the tongue. The tongue should be checked to see if it has any coating and should be cleansed daily. The coating contains a lot of disease producing microbes. The gums should be gently massaged with the fingers. This is very important to improve the health of the gums. A fine powder made up of *triphala*, *trikatu*, *lavang*, *twak* (*tej patra*) and *elaichi* could be used to massage the gums and improve oral health. Gargling with warm water mixed with a little sesame oil (*kaval* and *gandoosha*) is also very good to maintain effective oral health. All mucous secretions should be removed when you wash the face and eyes. Tickle the pharynx to stimulate the vagus nerve.

***Usha paana* (Drinking water)**

Drink at least 500 ml of warm water stored in a copper vessel to stimulate bowel action. Copper being an ionising metal has antimicrobial properties.

Cleansing the bowels

Sukha mala pravrutti (easy passage of stools) is a very important criteria for good health. Stool must be well formed. Any abnormality is suggestive of indigestion.

***Surya namaskar* (Sun prostrations) and other yogic exercises**

Performing *surya namaskar* in the morning sun is good exercise and gives one an opportunity to expose ones body to the morning sun rays that help generation of vitamin D in the skin.

Udwartana (Application of paste to the body and lightly rubbed into the body parts)

This procedure is carried out in order to improve the complexion, and lustre of the skin. It improves the tactile perception of the skin and also the firmness of the muscles. A fine powder of *chana* (Bengal gram) is used along with sesame oil.

Abhyanga (Oil massage)

This is usually carried out with oils or medicated oils to restore the shape and texture of the body and the tone of the muscles. All parts of the body are massaged to restore health in a number of musculoskeletal problems.

Snana (Bath)

It is a most exhilarating and energising practice aimed at cleansing the body of all the dirt accumulated over the previous day and night. It removes fatigue and tiredness of the body. It is thus a most important procedure of *dinacharya*. It prepares a person for their spiritual journey of the day, which includes meditation and prayers *etc*. After completion of these rituals the action for the day begins.

Application of oil to the hair

Oleation of the hair and head massage is essential for good and healthy hair growth. It prevents alopecia and greying and improves the eye sight.

Pratimarsha nasya (Instilling two drops of oil in the nose)

This prevents many nasal conditions, *e.g*., colds, sinusitis etc.

Dhooma pana (Inhaling medicated smoke)

Aromatic herbs like *chandan*, *twak*, *ela*, and *yashtimdhu* are burnt to produce smoke for the purpose of *nasya*, which is inhaled alternately through each of the nostrils. This prevents a lot of ear, nose and throat diseases.

Anjana (Application of collyrium)

It is both a cosmetic as well as a preventive for number of eye pathologies. Application of *anjana* is expected to improve sharpness of vision.

Diet regimen

This has already been described in an earlier chapter.

Sleep

Sleeping in the day time is strictly avoidable, except for a short nap during the hot summer months.

***Ratri charya* (Night regimen)**

The time from dusk to dawn constitutes the night. A whole day's hard work causes a lot of wear and tear of the body machinery. A good night's rest is desirable to heal this wear and tear. Once a person returns home they are expected to carry out certain acts of personal hygiene to prevent the entry of outside microbes. Foot wear is prohibited inside the home. Washing the hands and feet, and if necessary taking a bath are essential ingredients of the aseptic practice of any Hindu house hold.

***Sayam sandhya* (Evening prayers)**

Evening prayers are said as darkness begins to set in. An early, light dinner is advised. Before going to bed it is good to say a small prayer to ward off anxiety and stress. A glass of milk before going to bed is useful from the point of view of nutrition and getting a sound sleep, as milk induces sleep. A comfortable bed is advised.

Sleep and sexual activity have already been described earlier.

***Rutu charya* (Seasonal regimens)**

Ayurveda recognises the importance of chronobiology in maintaining human health. The whole year is divided into six *rutus*, each of two months duration. It is necessary for human beings to adapt and acclimatize to the changing weather of each changing season. Accordingly Ayurveda advises a planned regimen for each *rutu* in terms of diet, exercise, clothing, lifestyle and sex.

***Vasanta rutu* (Mid March to mid May)**

The cold season ends with the arrival of the warmth of *vasanta*. Green leaves, blooming flowers and the sweet song of the Cuckoo welcome *vasanta rutu*. It is the season of *kapha dosha dusti*, causing many disorders, e.g. colds, flu like symptoms, conjunctivitis and some minor infections.

Kaphakara heavy foods, with sweet, salty and sour taste are to be avoided. Light and easily digestible food is advised. Examples are old rice, wheat, honey, and pomegranate. Avoid sleeping in the day time. Light exercise, sparing sex are advised. Bitter herbs to counter *kapha*, *e.g.*, *neem* are advised. Prophylactic emesis (*vamana* - one of the *panchakarma*) is advised to prevent diseases which have a *kapha* origin.

Greeshma rutu (Mid May to mid July)

As opposed to *vasanta*, in *greeshma rutu*, heavy foods, with a sweet, salty and sour taste are advised. Rice, lentils, *ghee*, *sattu*, cool water, fresh fruit juices, meat soups and curd mixed with pepper are recommended. A short nap at midday is advised. Cool surroundings around one's dwelling place are ideally suited in this season. Fragrant flowers and light cotton clothes are desirable. Late nights and indulgence in sex should be avoided.

Varsha rutu (Mid July to mid September)

With the rains the atmosphere cools, which aids *vata prakop*. Water becomes impure. Boiled, cooled water should always be used for drinking. Hot and easily digestible light food is desirable. Old grains of rice, wheat, meat soups are examples. Butter milk with *trikatu* (ginger, piper longum and black pepper) is advisable to fight gastro intestinal infections and raise immunity. Day time sleep is prohibited. Indulgence in sex should be avoided.

Sharad rutu (Mid September to mid November)

During Autumn, trees start shedding their leaves, rains abate, the heat increases and at this time *pitta* is aggravated. Sweet and bitter tastes are beneficial to health for they off set the aggravation of *pitta*. Light and easily digestible foods are preferred in this season, such as old rice, wheat, green gram and *ghee*, which are healthy. Honey and grapes, *amlaki* and *patola* are also very good.

Two *pancha karma* procedures are advised.

- *Virechan* (Laxation): This is good for relieving *pitta* (*shaman*).
- *Rakta mokshana* (Blood letting): Once in a year blood letting is believed to promote good health. Modern researches have shown that donating blood, twice a year prevents ferroptotic damage to body. This confirms the role of *rakta mokshan*.

Hemantha rutu (Mid November to mid January)

When the winter season begins the cool air becomes invigorating. Physical stamina and strength of the body, along with digestive power, increase. Heavy foods that are sweet, unctuous, sour and salty are preferable in this season. Some examples are lentils *e.g.*, green gram, horse gram, rice, jaggery and wheat, meat, fish and milk products. In this season, light, cold and dry foods are preferable. Sesame seeds, dry fruits and nuts are recommended. Fermented drinks and wines *etc.*, are enjoyable in this period along with sexual indulgence. Warm clothes are essential in this season.

Shishira rutu (Mid January to mid March)

The weather is still cold in this season, warranting the use of warm clothes. The regimen for this *rutu* is similar to that of *Hemanta rutu*. Heavy, sweet and unctuous foods are the foods of choice.

Part - III

Molecular Mechanisms that Govern Body Functions

Chapter : 19

Tridosha Vignyan

Dosha dhatu malamoolamhi shareeram l

Dosha, *dhatu* and *mala* are the very foundation of life.

Let us now unfold the meaning of this *sutra*. We have so far studied the body composition at different levels. At the sub-atomic level the *tanmatras*, at the atomic level, the *panchabhootas* and at the molecular level, the bio-molecules (proteins, lipids and carbohydrates) forming tissues (*dhatus*) and the respective excretory elements that uphold the body through various energy based metabolic molecular mechanisms. All biological processes depend on three key molecular mechanisms, *viz*., regulatory, transcriptional and structural. *Vata*, *pitta* and *kapha* are the main or key players that are responsible for all molecular mechanisms that control biological processes, both physiological and pathological in the body, according to Ayurveda.

Proper functioning of the human body requires well-coordinated, intelligent information and knowledge systems that orchestrate molecular biological mechanisms. We have already described *trigunas* and their role in operation of intelligent information and knowledge systems, in detail in Chapter VI of Part I. *Tridoshas* are the pivot around which all the biological processes of the body are centred. Ayurveda has described their origin from the five proto- elements. It means they are subtle physical molecular entities. Thus nonphysical *trigunas* and physical *tridoshas* complement each other in organization of structure and functions of the body.

How does Ayurveda work?

Kaaryam dhatu saamyam l (Cha. Su. 1/53)

The process of bringing the body's key elements into equilibrium is the whole theme of Ayurveda.

Pathogenic factors in the body and mind

Vayuh pittam kaphah cheti shareero dosha samgrahah l
Manasah punaruddishto rajascha tama evacha ll

Prashamyatih aushadhau poorve daiva yukti vyapashrayah l
Manaso gyana vigyana dhairya smruti samadhibhih ll
(Cha. Su. 1/57-58)

Vata, *pitta* and *kapha* are the morbid factors that cause bodily diseases. They need to be controlled by drugs, by proper reasoning and application procedures and finally spiritual practices.

Rajas (passion) and *tamas* (delusion) need to be controlled by means of knowledge, specialized knowledge, fortitude and memory, and by improving concentration.

Qualities of *vata*

Ruksha sheeto laghu sookshma chalo atha vishadah kharah l
Vipareeta gunaihi dravyai maruta samprashaamyati ll
(Cha. Su. 1/59)

Dry, cold, light, subtle, mobile (unstable), clear (transparent), rough in texture are the qualities of *vata*. When increased, these qualities cause an upward regulation of *vata*. The opposite qualities, *viz*., unctuous (*snigdha*), hot (*ushna*), heavy (*guru*), gross (*sthoola*), steady (*sthira*), viscous (*pitchila*), and smooth (*slakshna*), pacify or regulate *vata* downward.

Qualities of *pitta*

Sasneham ushnam teekshnam cha dravam amlam saram katu l
Vipareeta gunaihi pittam drvyayai aashu prashaamyati ll
(Cha. Su. 1/60)

The qualities of *pitta* are unctuous, hot, acute, liquid and flowing, and pungent in taste. The opposite qualities, *viz*., dry (*ruksha*), cold (*sheeta*), mild (*manda*), stable (*sandra*) and sweet and bitter tastes pacify the pitta.

Qualities of *kapha*

Guru sheeta mrudu snigdha madhura sthira pitchilaah l
Shleshmana prashamanam yaanti vipareeta gunai gunah ll
(Cha. Su. 1/61)

Qualities of *kapha* are heavy, cool, soft, unctuous, and sticky or slimy and the taste is sweet. It is opposed by light (*laghu*), hot (*ushna*), dry (*ruksha*), mobile (*chala*) and clear (*vishada*) qualities: pungent, bitter and astringent tastes pacify *kapha*.

Sarvadaa sarva bhavanaam saamanyam vruddhi kaaranam l
Hraasa hetuh vishesashcha pravruttih ubhayasyacha ll
(Cha. Su. 1/44)

The general principle that applies to all things, is that similar qualities of substances increase similar ones and dissimilar ones decrease the opposite qualities. This is the most important principle which is applied to increase or decrease the body elements in most Ayurvedic therapeutics.

Dosha, guna and karma		
Vata (Vayu + Akash)	***Pitta (Tej + Jal)***	***Kapha (Prithvi + Jal)***
Ruksha – it depletes	*Alpa snigdha* – somewhat unctuous dehydrating	*Guru* – causes hypertrophy, heaviness or obesity
Sheeta – cooling - good clotting agents	*Ushna* - hot. Causes perspiration, dehydration	*Sheeta* – cooling - clotting agent
Laghu – lightening or thinning	*Teekshna* – acute - fast acting or evacuating and detoxicating (*shodhan karta*)	*Mrudu* - softness and poor tone
Sukshma - subtle - easy penetrability into deeper tissues	*Drava* – liquid – liquefier	*Snigdha* - unctuous – oily - *kledan*
Chala – increases motility	*Sara* - flowing – liquid quality inspirational or stimulant of bowel motion and laxative action	*Sthira* – steady – *dharana* or retention
Vishada – transparent - it cleanses, removes *aama* or all that is sticky and harmful discharge like pus		*Pitchila* – *lepana* - sticky – like an ointment
Khara – coarse and rough – *lekhana* – debriding agent		*Slakshna* - *ropan* – healing

continued...

		Manda - slow to act, *shaman* agents that pacify irritants and pain
		Sandra – moistening and cooling pleasing – *prasadan karta*

Before we begin any further discussion on *tridoshas* let us understand the basics of modern molecular biology.

Molecular biology or biochemistry of life

Biochemistry of life is the study of biomolecules with regards to the various biological processes they perform, in order to organize the structure and functions within living cells and between cells, tissues and organs of an organism. The foundation for modern biochemistry was laid with the discovery of the enzyme by Edward Buchner in 1897. The story of his discovery of the enzyme has already been given in Part II, Chapt 3.

Biomolecules are comprised of carbohydrates, lipids, proteins and nucleoproteins. In earlier chapters we have discussed biomolecules (monomers and polymers *etc.*,) in detail along with their role in cell formation. It is now necessary for us to understand the mechanism of information transfer in a cell, which is necessary for all biological actions. This is the field of molecular biology. Molecular biology currently covers three disciplines, *viz.*, molecular genetics, protein science and metabolism.

The sugars, starches and fibres found in fruits, grains, vegetables and milk products are Carbohydrates. They provide energy, storage of energy and structural stability of DNA and genetic information transfer. All sugars are carbohydrates, but all the carbohydrates are not sugars. Lipids (phospholipids) are the most important constituent of the cell wall. Lipids are commonly present in all oily substances and are non-polar, meaning water insoluble. Lipids are broken down into molecules of glycerol and fatty acids. Proteins, called structural proteins, are most important for building cell structures and repairing all tissues. There are also gene proteins and enzyme proteins, which are involved in making antibodies, hormones and other chemicals in the body. They are made up of amino acids. Nuclear proteins are made up of nucleic acids. The nucleic acids, DNA or deoxyribonucleic acid and RNA or ribonucleic acid are present respectively in the nucleus and cytoplasm of the cell. They carry the genetic information. In an earlier chapter the role of junk DNA was discussed in regards to information processing and transfer. Molecular genetics is all about biological information transfer and the consequent functions that occur in the cell. The foundation for this discipline was laid with the discovery of the DNA helix by James Watson, Francis Crick, Rosalind Franklin and Maurice Wilkins in 1958. The central theme of molecular biology is to convert or transcribe the genetic material into an RNA copy, which is then translated into various proteins (regulatory, functional or transcriptional and structural), which are responsible for all the biological actions in the body.

Let us now turn to Ayurveda and understand the evolution of *tridoshas* that are the key functions of controlling the body structure and function.

Visrgadana vikshepaihi soma surya anila yatha l
Dharayanti jagaddeham kaphapittanilaastada ll (Su. Su. 12/8)

Ayurveda, in its holistic appreciation of man and his environment, ventured to find common mechanisms that operate in both of them. The sun, moon and the wind are three key players that uphold our outside world through all the seasons, in the same vein the inner world of the living body is upheld by three comparable key players, the *tridoshas*, *viz.*, *pitta*, *kapha* and *vata*. They are *pancha mahabhootic* in origin and are formed as by-products of digestion of food substances.

Shakte dravyadhishtatavena swatantraavasthitatwabhavaat
vataadeenam na shaktitwam kintu dravyatwameva l

Energy or power is substance based. Therefore energy is not independent. Whereas *tridoshas* exert powerful actions, they are physical substances. They are both subtle (*kala*) in form and powerful in action. Their existence can be perceived and evidenced by certain gross features (*kaleeya*) of the outcomes of their actions. For example a nerve is a gross structure, but the nerve impulse is very subtle. But action on muscle causing contraction can be seen as due to the nerve impulse.

Vayuh pittam kapham cheti trayo dosha samasatah l
Vikruta avikrutam deham ghnanti te vartatanticha ll (Vag.Su. 1/7)

When any of the three *doshas*, *vata*, *pitta* and *kapha* are abnormal they cause disease and damage to the body and when they are normal they uphold the structure and functions of the body.

Rasasrung mamsa medo asthi majja shukrani dhatavah l
Sapta dushya mala mutra shakrut sveda adayo api cha ll

Rasa (chyle & plasma), *rakta* (blood), *mamsa* (muscle), *meda* (lipoid tissue), *asthi* (bone), *majja* (bone marrow) and *shukra* (sex hormones and gametes) are *dhatus* and as well *dushyas* meaning alterable or afflicted by *doshas*. Urine, stool, sweat, *etc*., are *malas*.

The three different pathways by which *tridoshas* travel in the body are:

Kshaya sthanamcha vriddhischa doshanam trividha gati l
Urdvam cha adhashcha tiryak cha vigyeya trividha para ll

Trividhacha apara koshta, shakha marma asthi sandhishu l
Chaya prakopa prashamah pittadeenam yathakramam ll

Gatishcha dwividha drushta prakruti vaikruti cha ya ll
(Cha. Su. 17/ 111-114)

Deficient or hypo, normal and hyper activity are the three pathways through which the *doshas* affect the body. The action of the *doshas* also depends upon their mobility, location and direction. This could be upwards, downwards or in any direction. *Doshas* can develop pathogenesis in the abdominal cavity, peripheral extremities, bones and joints. Their normality or abnormality determine whether a person is healthy or unhealthy.

Unfortunately many try to equate *tridoshas* with the four humours or fluids of the Greek humours theory. The four humours are blood, phlegm, yellow bile and melancholy (black bile). They certainly are not comparable.

The *panchmahbhootas* are the building blocks of both man and the universe. Regulation of the structure and function is controlled by the *tridoshas*. The *vayu* and *akash mahabhootas* combine to form *vata dosha*. *Tej* and *aap mahabhootas* combine to form *pitta dosha*. *Prithvi* and *aap doshas* combine to form the *kapha dosha*. *Doshas* are the tripod on which life rests. The *tridoshas* form the basic biochemistry of all living beings. They also represent basic molecular mechanisms, *e.g.*, the regulation, functional bio-conversion or transformation or transcription and structural mechanisms respectively in the body. *Kapha* and *pitta*, are both described as lame *(pangu)*. *Vata* regulates both *pitta* and *kapha*. The life force or *prana* is dependent on these *doshas*. The biochemical integrity of the body thus rests on them. Normality is the balance of these *doshas* that maintain the whole body physiology and thereby the health of a healthy person is maintained. These *doshas* can be vitiated by *atiyoga* (excessive indulgence), *ayoga* (poor or absent interaction) and *mithya yoga* (perverse interaction) of various factors, *viz.*, *kaal* (season or time), *artha* (indulgence in sensual pleasures) and *karma* (actions) resulting in disease. These factors include the environment, lifestyle, psyche, stress, age, food, nutrition and trauma *etc*. Once these *doshas* get vitiated, they adversely affect the *dhatus* and *malas* resulting in diseases.

Shukra shonita samyoge yo bhavet dosha utkatah l
Prakrutih jayate tena tasya me lakshanam shrunu ll
(Su. Sha. 4/73)

Prakrutim iha naranam bhautikeem kechit ahuh l
Pavan dahantoyaih keertitastu tisrah ll
(Su. Sha. 4/80)

Conception occurs with the union of *shukra* with *shonita*. The *tridoshas* participate during this process. Every individual is born with a combination of all these three *doshas*, with one or the other being preponderant at the time of conception. The preponderance of a particular *dosha* at the time of conception remains throughout life and is called *prakruti* or constitution. In other words *prakruti* represents one's genome that directs the intrauterine foetal growth program. This program determines the life span and genetic potential of an individual. Constitution determines one's psyche, his/her capabilities, body structure, vulnerability to disease, and also life span. Depending on their constitution, everybody reacts differently to various stresses that affect them, both in states of health and ill health. Today we know that cell surface receptors also are characterized genetically. Hence the study of *doshas* is very important for a student of Ayurveda. It is necessary to understand everything about the *doshas*, their signs and symptoms and manifestations, both when they are normal and abnormal.

Chapter : 20

Vata Dosha

Vata is the principal dynamic regulatory agent or force of the body. The word *vata* is derived from *va*, meaning motion. There is no life without motion. It is described as *rajasic* signifying a force with qualities of dynamism, motion and propulsion. It is derived from the combination of *akash* (resonance factor of sound that enables nucleo synthesis) and *vayu* (chiefly nitrogen and oxygen). In the words of C. Dwarkanath, "it is biological *vayu*". It is a regulatory principle that is self generated and self propagating. It is responsible for conduction, regulation and propagation of all impulses. It integrates all vital structures and functions of the body by regulating the actions of the other two important principles, *viz.*, *kapha* (structural) and *pitta* (transforming or transcriptional). Its physical qualities are *ruksha* (dry), *laghu* (light), *sheeta* (cold), *daruna* (hard), *chala* (motile), *vishada* (non-sticky), *khara* (rough or granular), *sukshma* (subtle). When we see an increase in any of these qualities, an excess of *vata* can be inferred. Thus a physician examining a patient can diagnose the predominance of *vata* through observing these *gunas* or physical qualities. The opposite qualities or *gunas* alleviate *vata*. These are *snigdha* (unctuous), *guru* (heavy), *ushna* (hot), *slakshna* (smooth or amorphous), *mrudu* (soft), *pitchila* (sticky) and *ghana* (solid). Identification of these *gunas* in the signs and symptoms make it easy for a physician to make a diagnosis. This helps to plan therapy to increase or decrease *vayu*, as the case may be, through diet, drugs and life styles changes. What an ingenious idea for diagnosis and therapy, when no advanced investigational facilities were available!

The main locations or the sites of *vayu* are *pakwashaya* (large bowel), lumbar back region, anal canal, ear, *asthi dhatu* (bone) and skin (organ of touch sensation), the most important site of *vayu* being the large bowel.

Pakwashaya kati sakthi shrotra asthi sparshanendriyam l
Sthanam vatasya tatrapi pakwadhanam visheshatah ll (Vag. Su. 12/1)

The *Kashyap Samhita* additionally quotes the *majja* (neural tissue and marrow) as yet another site. There yet is another dimension to the site of the *pakwashaya* that merits consideration here. The gut has the largest concentration of microbes. The DNA of this microbiota is ten times larger than that of the human specific DNA in the human body. It is now believed that these microbes not only play a major role in digestion of food, but also play a major role in gene based informational feedback. Gut brain axis, gut feeling or gut instinct are examples of this system. *Pakwashaya*, or the large bowel, thus constitutes the main site of *vata dosha*. Pain anywhere in body, and especially in the bones, is attributed to an increase in vitiated *vayu*. We will discuss the relationship of NO and pain related to prostaglandin generation. Bone marrow and the central nervous system are encased in *asthi dhatu*. The relationship between neurotransmission and *vayu dosha* will be described in due course.

Functions of *vayu*

Dosha dhatu malamoolam sada dehascha tam chala l
Utsahochvasanishwasa cheshta vega pravartanah ll

Samyaggatyaa cha dhatunam akshanam patavenacha l
Anugrahat avikrutah ll (Vag. Su. 11/12)

Dosha dhatu and *malas* are regulated only by *vayu* when it is normal, for it is the most powerful of all the three *doshas*. Enthusiasm, inspiration, expiration and all voluntary and involuntary actions of the body are regulated by *vayu*. It causes the circulation of *dhatus e.g.*, *rasa*, *rakta, etc*., throughout the body. It is also responsible for the excretion of *malas* (excreta). *Vayu* is responsible for all the sensory and motor functions of the nervous system. It stimulates *agni* (metabolic fire). It is also responsible for the organogenesis in the embryo. There are five types of *vayus*.

Prana vayu

Sthaanam pranasya sheersho urah karna jivhasya nasikah l
Urah kantah charo buddhi hrudaya indriya chittadhruk ll
(Vag. Su. 12/5)

Shteevanam kshavathu udgara nishwasa anna pravesha krut l

The locations of *prana vayu* are the head, chest, heart, ears, tongue, nose, throat, intelligence, *indriyas* and vision. Spitting, coughing, breathing, eating and deglutition of food are its functions. It impels all the senses, and is a carrier of all the perceptions by the mind. It is responsible for respiration. According to Sushruta it nourishes the whole body.

Udana vayu

Urasthaanamudansya nasa nabhi galanscharet l
Vakpravrutti prayatna oja bala varna smruti kriyah ll
(Vag. Su. 12/1)

Its locations are the chest, nose, umbilicus and throat. Speech, expiration of air, effort, immune power, strength, colour and complexion and memory are controlled by *udana vayu.* It is located in the tracheo-laryngeal region of the neck. According to Sushruta it is responsible for inspiration, expiration, speech and control of all the organs of sense. Charak has stated that it maintains the cohesive unity of the whole body. It is the cause of buyoyancy in a living person.

Samana vayu

Samaano agni sameepastha koshte charati sarvatah l
Anne ghruhnaati pachati vivechayati munchati ll
(Vag. Su. 12/8)

It is always in close proximity to the metabolic fire. It resides in the *koshta* (GI tract), and moves all over causing peristalsis of the bowel. It receives, digests and separates food into the nutritious, useful portion and waste materials. It causes absorption of nourishing chyle and excretes the waste. It is the stimulator of *agni* (metabolic fire). It aids digestive processes and causes absorption of the digested food. Its main location is in the umbilical region.

Vyana vayu

Vyaano hrudisthitah krutsna dehachaari mahajava l

Gatyapakshepana utkshepa nimesha unmeshanadikah l
Prayah sarva kriyah tasmin pratibaddhah sharirinam ll
(Vag. 12/ 6,7)

It is located in the heart and moves all over the body through the circulation. It causes circulation of all the fluids in the body. It is present everywhere in the body, and is responsible for all the movements of the body, even the minutest movements, *e.g.*, closing and opening of the eyes. It is the most powerful and fastest of all the *vayus.*

Apana vayu

Apaano panagah shroni basti meddhra uru gochara l
Shukra aartava shakrun mootra garbha nishkramana kriyah ll
(Vag. Su. 12/8)

It is located in the anal region, pelvis, bladder, penis and thighs. It is responsible for the excretion of all the waste (*malas*), *viz*., semen, urine, sweat, faeces and menstruation in females. Organo-genesis in the embryo and the delivery of the foetus *etc*., are also functions of *apana vayu*.

Vayuh tantra yantra dharah , praana udaana samaan
vyaana apaana, atma pravartaka iveshtana l.

Unccha vachanam, niyanta pranetacha manasah, sarvendriyarthanam udyojakah sarvendriyarthanamabhivodha, sarva shareer dhatu vyuhakarah, shrotra sparshanayo moolam, harshotsahyo yonih, samirano agnih dosha sasoshanah, kshepta bahi malanam, sthoolanam srotasam bheta, karta garbhakritinam, ayusho anuvritt pratya bhooto bhavati akupita l (Charak Su. 12/8-1)

In the above verse, Acharya Charaka describes in detail the functions of *vata* when it is in a state of harmony. Let us now learn all about *vayu*.

Unvitiated, normal *vayu* is described as both the *yantra* and the *tantra*, (*Yantra tantra dharah). Yantra* is a machine that accomplishes a process. *Tantra* is the knowhow of the process on which the mechanisms operate. It is both the software and hardware. *Vayu* controls whole body organization, comprising seventy trillion cells. There are five types of *vayus*, *viz*., *prana*, *apana*, *udana*, *vyana* and *samana*.

Prana vayu signifies the very life force. It also means a powerful force and associated motion. It is responsible for inspiration and expiration.

Udana refers to its location in the upper part of the body. It is an upward flow against gravity. Expiratory part of respiration control is the function of *udana vayu*.

Samana vayu (*samam anayati iti*) is the one that homogenizes food in the gastrointestinal (GI) tract. It is responsible for all the peristaltic actions of the gut and aids digestion and absorption in association with *pachaka pitta*.

Vyan vayu (vi + anspandate) or *visheshena* spandate. It means a progressive, powerful, pulsatile motion, *e.g.*, pulse in the blood vessels and neural transmission. It is also described as *maha java*, meaning very powerful and moving at a very high speed. It is responsible for all vascular, neuronal and endocrine functions in the body. It pervades the whole body.

Apana vayu (*apanayati, apasarati*) signifies downwards flow. It throws out or excretes all metabolic waste such as sweat, urine and faeces *etc*. It controls menstrual and seminal flow. It is also responsible for uterine contractions and delivery of the foetus from the uterus, and for the organogenesis in the foetus and the form and features of the foetus, (*karta garbha akritinam*). From conception to the time of delivery, intrauterine foetal growth occurs in four stages. The first stage is of gene imprinting, following mixing and matching of the maternal and paternal chromosomes. This results in the formation of the unique genome of the foetus. This process is completed in the first six days post conception. The genome controls and directs foetal growth and determines its genetic potential throughout the entire life span.

Functions of *vayu* in general in its physiological state

Vayu impels the upward and downward movements in the body, conducts and controls the mind, initiates and invigorates all the senses, receives all the sensory stimuli, propels all the *dhatus* (transportation), organizes all the *dhatus* or body elements, plans all the bodily organization and all biological processes (*vyuhakar*), impels speech, hearing ability and tactile sensation, is the source of all emotional excitement and animation, stimulates the digestive fire, desiccates morbid doshas, eliminates the excreta (*malas*), removes the obstruction to *srotasas* (subtle, as well as gross), and organizes the foetal body structure.

It is described as *atma pravartakah*. What is *atma*? How does *vayu* regulate all the bodily functions? *Atma* denotes "I" or the self, my self-awareness and awareness of my environment. *Purush*/the conscious element/agent/a dynamic witness or observer/soul are also synonyms for it. It is like a software that needs a hardware processor for its actions. Atma expresses through the action of *vayu*. It controls and inspires the mind, (*niyantah pranetecha manasah*). *Atma* experiences the pleasures and pains of this world through the physical instruments derived from the *prakruti* (mind).

It organizes all the tissues of the body in a planned way (*sarva shreera dhatu vyuhakara*). It integrates the whole body, (*sandhana karah sharirasya*). It is responsible for metabolic fire (*sameeraner agneer dosha samsoshanah*). It is also the basis for one's life span, when in the physiological state, (*ayusho pratyabhuto bhavati akupita*).

Vayu thus regulates and integrates all the sensory and motor functions of the body. A gaseous element regulating all the biological functions in the body was unthinkable for any modern scientist before the discovery of nitric oxide (NO). Until that time only chemical neuro-transmitters, *e.g.*, adrenaline, acetyl choline, *etc.*, were known. The Nobel Prize was awarded to Furschgot and Zawadski in 1980, for their discovery of NO gas. It has revolutionised the understanding of the role of neuro-transmitters and also the mechanisms of maintaining normal vascular tone. Nitric oxide is a gas produced by the endothelial cells of the vascular system and many other tissues of the body, *viz.*, the brain, CNS and the nerves. It is a bi-atomic gas produced by the action of the enzyme nitric oxide synthase on the amino acid L-arginine. The by-product of this reaction is another amino acid, L-citrulline, whose presence in tissues can be measured as a marker of nitric oxide synthase activity. Nitric oxide synthase is found in the endothelium, brain and central nervous system. Nitric oxide itself has a lifetime of only milliseconds in the circulation; it is rapidly degraded to nitrite and nitrate and then excreted. L-arginine, a semi-essential amino acid is a substrate for the generation of NO. It is synthesized by the action of different nitric oxide synthases in different tissues of the body. In the nervous system it is nNOS. It is called Geneproduct-1. It generates NO in neurons and glial tissues. It regulates the cerebro-vascular tone and regulates learning and memory (*prana* and *udana vayu* functions). The second nitric oxide synthase is inducible iNOS which is called Gene product –2. It generates NO in monocytes, macrophages, smooth muscle cells, cardiomyocytes, hepatocytes, mega-karyocytes, *etc*. It plays a major role in maintaining the general immunity and inflammatory reactions of the body (*vyana* and *samana vayu* functions). eNOS, the third gene product, is responsible for generation of NO in the vascular endothelial cells (*vyana vayu*). It determines the cerebral blood flow. NO reacts with guanyl cyclase resulting in cGMP, which is the relaxant of all the smooth muscles, including the sphincters in the GI tract (*samana vayu* function). It causes vaso-dilatation. This action of NO is responsible for penile erection, which is the basis for the action of sildenafil (Viagra) – *apana vayu* function. NO also functions as a neurotransmitter in non-adrenergic and non-cholinergic pathways of myocardial contractility and GI tract motility. It prevents adhesion and aggregation of leucocytes and platelets, thus maintaining the integrity of the vascular system. NO is different from other neuro-transmitters since it has two-way actions on both afferent and efferent nerves, as well as on pre- and post-synaptic neurons.

Pathological effects of NO

NO is a diffusible universal messenger that mediates cell to cell communication all over the body. Constitutive and inducible NO regulates numerous essential functions, *e.g.*, adequate perfusion of mucous membranes and immune response *etc*. Deficiency and depletion or excess of NO can lead to a number of pathological conditions, *e.g.*, inflammatory bowel diseases, endothelial dysfunction, hypertension, athero-sclerosis, and diabetes. Free radicals and advanced glycosylation end products inactivate NOS resulting in various pathologies. Similarly, depreciated *vayu* (*vata kshaya*) is known to cause a number of different types of diseases as we will see. Vitiated *vata* is associated with aches and pains in the body. Similarly, prostaglandins are chiefly responsible for inflammation and the pain sensation. NO is a vasodilator. It supports male libido.

There is emerging evidence of close association between NO and prostaglandins (PG). Prostaglandins are local hormones produced in almost all the tissues and body fluids in response to diverse stimuli, such as, mechanical, thermal, chemical, bacterial, hormonal, *etc*. Synthesis and metabolism of prostaglandins are dependent on NO. Just as with *vayu*, the spectrum of actions of NO and prostaglandins encompass a wide range of biological processes. NO can activate cyclooxygenase (COX) enzyme (Selvemini D, Misko *et al* – 1990). Arachidonic acid (AA) is the precursor for all the different prostaglandins (PGs). AA is produced from the metabolism of dietary linoleic acid. The action of the enzyme cyclooxygenase (COX) on AA results in PGs. Lipooxygenase (LOX) action on AA results in leukotriene. Cyclooxygenase (COX) and leukotriene are also the mediators of inflammation. They have a profound effect on microvasculature causing exudation of plasma. They cause release of histamine from basophils, also cause chemotaxis of leucocytes. PGs (PGE and PGA) release erythropoietin from the renal cortex, which is an essential factor for erythropoiesis.

Prostaglandins have a wide range of actions on all systems of the body. Some PGs *e.g.*, PGE, PGI and PGA act as vasodilators, whereas PGF and TXA (Thromboxane) are vasoconstrictors. They exert a major effect on the blood cells. TXA causes platelet aggregation. PGE causes smooth muscle relaxation in the bronchial tree, uterus and GI tract etc. Gastric hydrochloric acid and other secretions are reduced, whereas the secretion of mucin is increased by PGA, PGI2 and PGE. PGs cause luteolysis (lysis of corpus luteum). In pyrogenic induced fever PGs are released. They also amplify the pain sensation in the inflammatory processes and exert a profound influence on carbohydrate metabolism by an insulin like action and cause inhibition of lipolysis. PGs regulate synthesis of cAMP by activating or inhibiting adenylate cyclase in the membrane bound receptors. Thus the function of PGs can be compared to the action of various *vayus* in health as well as in disease. (Adapted from *Ayurveda & Modern Medicine* - Dr R. D. Lele)

If we limit the functions of *vayu* only to neurotransmission and hormonal functions, we only partially explain the whole idea of *tantra yantra dhara*, described by Charak. It cannot explain all the functions or actions envisaged for *vata dosha* in the normal state. Neuro-hormonal basis only explains the *yantra* part of the whole *tantra yantra dhara*. *Tantra* relates to the concept of biological information transfer and its control by hormones over the seventy trillion cells of the body under one unified command. Therefore the concept of *vata* probably also relates to regulation of genes and gene products. The brilliant discovery, in 1953, of the double helix structure of deoxyribo nucleic acid (DNA) as the basic structure of the gene laid the foundation for molecular biology. The description of *vata* given by Charak makes it imperative to rediscover *vata*, *pitta* and *kapha* as the concepts of molecular biology. Nucleic acids are proteins by nature. All the proteins have nitrogen as a benchmark. *Vayu* is predominantly nitrogen. Various biomolecules, that include gene proteins and small gas molecules *e.g.*, NO and CO act on surface receptors of the cells to form a ligand receptor complex resulting in a specified action depending on the type of cell. The ligand receptor complex results into a series of intracellular events. They include the formation of messenger RNA (mRNA) and a copy of DNA in cytoplasm (transcription). Formation of new protein (translation) occurs in ribosomes. This newly formed protein builds cells and also repairs its damaged DNA. One of the most important regulatory genes discovered is P53 which controls cell replication. It regulates repair and programmed cell death (apoptosis). Gene mutation can cause cancer. Therefore it is also known as a molecular policeman. The regulatory type of gene proteins act through endocrine, paracrine and autocrine mechanisms. (Dr R. D. Lele). Therefore the functions of regulatory gene proteins are similar to those of vayu satisfying Charak's description of *vayu* as *tantra yantra dhara*.

Another interesting description of vayu is, it being *rajo pradhan*. Raja is signified by fast, powerful and motivated motion and action. In the previous chapter in the experiment by A. Oparin with a solution made of hydrocarbon polymer in sea water, it was seen that in the beginning, the particles in the solution moved in Brownian motion. When this solution was exposed to ultraviolet irradiation in the presence of atmospheric air, these particle started moving rapidly. This change in the type of particle motion can be compared to *rajas*. When ultrasound waves were introduced into this solution the particles were observed to organize themselves into cell layers. This organizational ability is derived from the *satwa* quality of *akash*. Sound is the quality of *akash mahabhoota*. The biological *vayu* (*vata dosha*) is the result of a combination of both *vayu* and *akash*. *Vata* thus regulates both the structure and function of the body correctly fitting into the theme of *tantra yantra* description of Charak.

Excessive (*ati yoga*), deficient (*hina yoga*) and perverse (*mithya yoga*) interactions with the objects of the senses occur due to *pradnyaparadh*. *Pradnyaparadh* is committing irrational actions or volitional aggression due to failure of intelligence. Venturing outdoors unprotected when the weather is rainy and chilly is bound to invite fever and cold. This is a simple example of *pradnyaparadh*. Irrational, perverse behaviour, abnormal life styles, hostile environment and irregular eating habits, eating junk foods *etc*., adversely affect the *dosha* equilibrium resulting in disease. With this background let us learn more about *vata* from the point of view of Ayurveda.

Qualities of *vata dosha*

Tatra ruksho laghuh sheetah kharah sookshmah chalah anilah l

Vata dosha can be recognized by its qualities, *viz*., dryness, lightness, coolness, roughness, subtleness and mobility.

Vayu, when normal, performs a multitude of physiological functions. But if it becomes abnormal it is responsible for various types of pathologies in the body. Today we appreciate that free radicals in the form of singlet oxygen, H_2O_2, NO, peroxynitrite, *etc*., are the cause of a variety of pathologies in the body. *Vayu* thus plays a very important role in both the healthy and disease states of the body.

Symptoms of *vata vriddhi*

Vruddhastu kurute anilah l

Kaarshya kaarshnya ushnakamatwa kampa anaah shakrutghan l
Bala nidra indriyabhramsha pralaapa bhrama deenataah ll
(Ashtanga Hru. 11/5.6.)

An increase in *vayu* activity in the body causes harsh speech or stuttering (*vakparushya*), emaciation (*kaarshya*), darkening of the skin (*kaarshnya*), tingling of the body (*gatra sphuran*), liking for hot objects (*ushnakamatwa*), insomnia (*nidra nash*), debility (*alpabalatwa*), hard stools (*gadhavaryastwam*) and constipation. *Vata* in excess can cause loss of the senses, confusion, irrelevant speech and severe weakness.

Symptoms of *vata kshaya*

Lingam ksheeno anile angasyasaado alpam bhashite hitam l
Sangyamohah tatha sleshma vruddhi yukta aamaya sambhava ll
(Asht. Hru. Su.11/5)

When *vata dosha* is deficient, it causes debility of the body, loss of physical activity, speech, awareness and consciousness. *Vata kshaya* is usually associated with the symptoms of an increase in *kapha*, (*Ashtang Hr.Su*. 11-15).

Symptoms of *vata dushti*

When we refer to increased (up) or decreased (down) regulation of *vata*, we are talking of normal *vata*. When we use word *dushti* (vitiated), it means the change in its original character, akin to a mutated gene or abnormal gene product.

Excessive physical exercise *(vyayam)* or exertion, fasting *(anashan)*, anxiety *(chinta)*, stress, fear, grief, dry and stale food, food in smaller than the required quantity, leading to under nourishment *(rukshalpa pramita ashanam)*, exposure to chilly winds and extreme low temperatures, and staying awake late at night, result first in its increase and at a later stage to vitiation of *vayu* (*Cha.Su.*,17-76). Trauma, fractures, excessive indulgence in sex, sex within three hours after the intake of food (in the post digestion state) or in the evening, carrying heavy weights, horse riding and incorrect therapy are the other causes for the vitiation of *vata*. Certain foods also increase *vata*, *e.g.*, *moong dal*, *masoor*, *vatana* (green peas), *chana* (Bengal gram), *rajmasha* (beans), *etc.*

Chronobiology also affects *vayu*. It is up regulated in the interval from post midnight to pre- dawn, in the evening and in old age. It accumumulates in *greeshma ritu* (summer), gets vitiated in *varsha ritu* (rainy season) and resolves in *sharad ritu* (autumn). Coolness and dryness of *vata* associated with the heat of *greeshma ritu* help in accumulation of *vayu* in this period. Hot and unctuous qualities decrease *vata dosha*.

Chapter : 21

Pitta Dosha

Pitta
Aushnam taikshnam laaghavam anatisneho varnascha shukla aruna varja visrau rasaucha katuka amlo pittasya atma roopani l
(Cha. Su. 20/16)

Pittam tikshnam dravam pooti neelam peetam tathaivacha l
Ushnam katurasam chaiva vidagdham cha amlam evacha ll
(Su. Su. 21/11)

Pittam sasneha teekshna ushnam laghum visram sara dravam l
(Vag. Su. 1/11)

Pitta is characterized by the various qualities as described below:

Hot, acute, light, and moderately unctuous, other than white and red in colour (*charak*), yellow or blue in colour (*sushruta*), liquid in consistency, malodourous, pungent and sour in taste are the features of *pitta.*

Locations of *pitta*

Pakwamashaya madhyastam pittasya l (Su.Su. 21/6)
Pittasya yakrut pleehanau hridayam drushti twak cha ll
(Su. Su. 21/7)

Naabhih amashayah swedo laseeka rudhira rasah l
Druk sparshanam cha pittasya naabhih atra visheshata ll
(Vag. Su. 12/2)

The umbilical area, situated between the upper and lower gastro intestinal tract, is the special location of *pitta*. Other locations are the liver, spleen, heart, eyes, skin along with touch sensation, blood, plasma, sweat and sebum.

Functions of *pitta*

Darshanam pakti ushma cha kshuth trushna deha maardavam l
Prabha prasado medha cha pitta karma avikarajam ll
(Cha. Su. 18/54)

Pittam pakti ushma darshanaih ll (Vag. Su. 12/2)

Kshutrung ruchi prabha medha dhee shauryam tanu aardavam l
(Vag. Su. 11/3)

Vision, digestion, temperature, hunger, thirst, taste, softness and suppleness of the body, lustre, a pleasing disposition, intelligence, steadfastness and chivalry are all functions of *pitta*. The taste buds are chemical receptors. For all mental functions it is basically neuro-hormone chemistry at work. *Pitta* is thus all about transformation chemistry. *Pitta* and *agni* are one and the same in the opinion of Sushruta.

The characteristic of *pitta* is heat, because of which it causes burning and digestion, *etc*. When it is deficient, it can be increased with hot substances, and when it is increased it is pacified by cold substances or applications. Thus there is no other internal body *agni* apart from *pitta*.

After digestion, the second most important principal function of *pitta* is on *rasa dhatu*, the formation and thereafter the transformation functions that help in the formation of different *dhatus* of the body from *rasa dhatu*. It is formed by the combination of *tejas mahabhoota* and *aap mahabhoota*. The word *pitta* is derived from the word *aatap* or fire. Its main function is *pak* or cooking through combustion, which causes various bio-transformations in the body. Kanad first described this concept of transformation as *pilupak* in *Vaisheshika* philosophy. *Pitta* is chiefly *teja pradhan*, whose quality is *satwa*. *Satwa* is characterized by subtlety and luminosity, and it is derived from solar radiations. It is a great force of organization. The liquid crystal form of cell protoplasm is due to the liquid property of *aap* (water) *mahabhoot*, which is also a constituent of *pitta*. Vision (being a visionary or wise) and also visual perception, intelligence and lucidity of mind, digestion and assimilation of food, maintenance of the thermal balance of the body, hunger, thirst, softness, suppleness, radiance, lustre, cheerfulness, courage and valour are all functions of *pitta*. *Agni* (the fire) of the body is located in *pitta*. In essence, the concept of *pitta* is a functional mechanism of biotransformation in the body. Its consistency is *sara* (flowing), *drava* (liquid) and *ishat sneha* (slightly unctuous). Its physical characteristics are *laghu* (light), *katu* (pungent), *amla* (acid), *ushna* (hot) and *teekshna* (penetrating). It smells fleshy and putrid. Vagbhata described the umbilical region (*nabhi*) as its main location. *Nabhi*, the umbilical area signifies the organs, *viz*., the stomach, duodenum, small intestine, liver and spleen (*amashaya* including *pachyamanashaya*). Plasma (*rasa dhatu*), blood (*rudhir*), sweat (*lasika*), eyes and skin are additional locations of *pitta*. When *pitta* is normal, it performs a multitude of functions in the body of the nature of transformations and when it is abnormal it produces specific pathological conditions that can be identified by its various attributes or *gunas* as described earlier. There are five types of *pittas*.

Paachak pitta: The digestive fire

Pakwa aamaashaya madhyastam pittam chaturvidham annapaanam pachati, vivechayati cha dosha rasa mutra pureeshaani tatrasthameva cha atma shaktya sheshanam sharirasya agni karmana anugraham karoti, Tasmin pitte pachaka agnih iti sangya l (Su. Su. 22/10)

Tyakta dravatwam paakaadi karmana analashadvidam l
Pachati annam vibhajate saara kittau pruthak tatha ll
(Vag. Su. 12/11)

Tatrasthameva pittanam sheshanam api anugraham l
(Vag. Su. 12/12)

It is located between the upper (*amashaya*) and lower (*pakwashaya*) GI tract. Its character is of fire. It digests four varieties of food and drink, differentiates the nutrient from the waste (urine and faeces) and assimilates the nutrients into the body. Because of predominance of *tej mahaboot*, *pitta* loses its fluidity and acts like fire (*anala*). It causes *paka* (cooking/combustion/ digestion). It divides the digested food into *sara* (essence) and *kitta* (waste matter) with the help of *saman vayu*. The *sara* part is absorbed as *anna rasa* (chyle), which is further transformed into *rasa dhatu*. *Kitta* is excreted from the body as faeces through the anal canal and as urine through the urinary tract with the help of *apana vayu*. *Pachaka pitta* supports all other forms of *pitta* and *agnis*.

All gastrointestinal secretions, including hydrochloric acid and the various hormones and enzymes in different digestive secretions in different parts of the GI tract are all under the control of several genes, gene products, neuronal, hormonal and chemo-transmitters. In my opinion *pachak pitta* represents all these digestive mechanisms of biological transformations. The process of digestion is supported by *kledak kapha* and *saman vayu*.

Ranjak pitta

Yattu yakrut pleeho pittam tasmin ranjako agnih itisangyal Sa rasasya raaga krut ll Su.Su. 21/10

Amashayashrayam pittam ranjakam rasa ranjanat l Vag. Su. 12/12

It is located in *amashaya* (stomach, duodenum, spleen and liver). The liver and spleen play a major role in the formation of blood, haemoglobinization of red blood cells (RBCs) and also destruction of aged red cells. The red colour of *rakta* is the result of the action of *ranjakpitta*. Haemoglobinization of erythrocytes gives blood its red colour. Erythropoiesis requires the intrinsic factor in the stomach. The duodenum is the site for the absoption of iron. The role played by the liver is vital for the production of globin and haem (iron pigment). The destruction or break down of RBCs occurs in the spleen. Overall, Ayurveda related various organs like the liver and spleen as sources for blood formation but there is no mention of bone marrow. However there is mention of *rakta majja* (red bone marrow) as the origin of *rakta dhatu*. *Pitta* as a cause of vision in the eye is dependent on the colour pigment of rods and cones in the retina, (C.Dwarakanth).

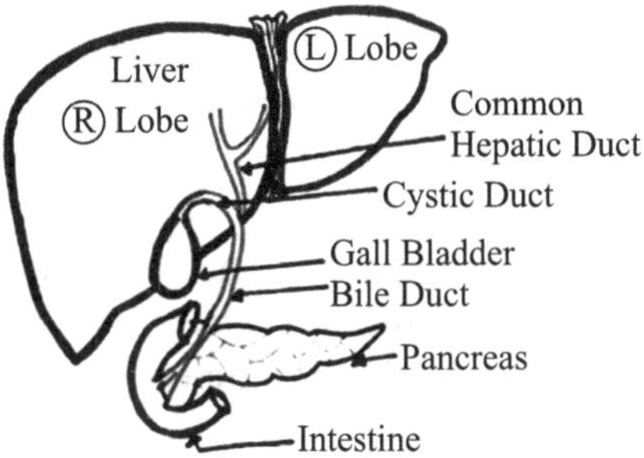

Liver / Gall Bladder / Pancreas
(Yakrit, Pittashay, Pleeha)

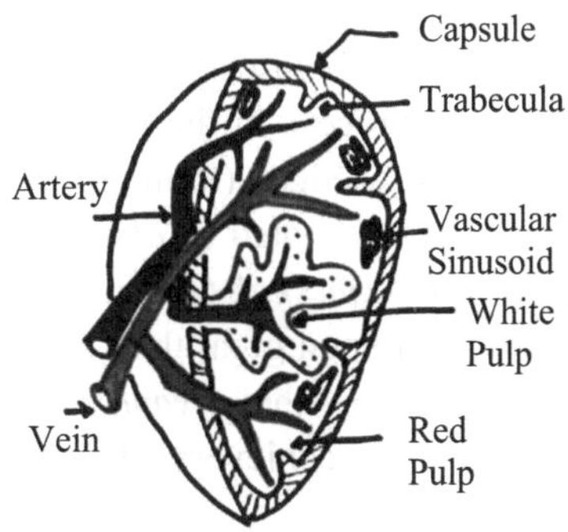

Spleen
(Pleeha)

Diagram of liver and spleen

Sadhaka pitta

Buddhi medha abhimanadyaih abhipretartha saadhanaat l
Saadhakam hrudgatam pittam ll
(Vag. Su. 12/13)

Yat pittam hrudaya samstham tasmin sadhako agniriti sangya l
So abhiprarthita manoratha sadhanakrut uktah ll
(Su. Su. 21/10)

Sadhaka pitta is located in *hridaya* (heart/brain). It is also responsible for *medha* (memory), *buddhi* (intelligence) and *abhiman* (self esteem). These are the functions of the higher brain. Achieving the desired objective needs fire in one's heart. Predominant *sadhak pitta* is the quality of achievers. Its other functions are *shourya* (valour), *abhaya* (fearlessness), *krodha* (anger), *harsh* (joy), *moha* (delusion). These are the basic behavioural instincts of man that are controlled by the hippocampus and amygdala regions of the brain. Therefore this *pitta* is intimately related to brain metabolism.

Alochaka pitta

Yat drushtya pittam tasmin alochako agnih iti sangyaa l
Sa roopa grahanadhikrutah ll (Su. Su. 21/10)

Roopalochantah smrutam l drukstham alochakam ll
(Vag. Su. 12/14)

Alochaka pitta is the fire that gives the power of insight. It causes the thought process in the mind, provides power to processes information into knowledge (thinking and contemplation). The vision of a visionary is rooted in *alochaka pitta*. It resides in the eye of a seer. It is *buddhivisheshak* (a requisite quality for intelligence) and is a quality bestowed upon great thinkers. In other words, *alochak pitta*, represents the third eye, the *gnyana chakshu*. Ayurveda clearly differentiates the thinkers and achievers into two different categories.

Braajaka pitta

Yattu twachi pittam tasmin bhraajako agnih iti sangya l
(Su. Su. 21/10)

It is the fire that is located in the skin. Good blood circulation, proper nutrition and metabolism in the skin bestows a characteristic glow, colour, complexion, radiance and lustre to the skin.

Abnormal *pitta functions*

Symptoms of increased *pitta* activity

Peeta vita mootra netra twak kshut trush daaha alpanidratah l
(Asht. Hru. 11/6)

Increased yellow colouration of the skin (jaundice), eyes, urine and faeces. It also causes excess hunger, thirst, a burning sensation and insomnia (difficulty in sleeping), (*Ashtang Hr.* 11-7). It leads to a bitter and sour taste, symptoms of toxicity, fainting attacks and debility. It is also responsible for all the signs of inflammation *e.g.*, exudation, pus formation and putrefaction. Predominance of *pitta* occurs at midday and in the middle of the night. Seasonal accumulation of *pitta* occurs in *varsha ritu* (the rainy season). Its provocation occurs in *sharad ritu* (autumn) and normalization in *hemanta ritu* (winter).

Decrease in *pitta*

Mando analah sheetam prabhahaani l

A decrease in the levels of *pitta* results in poor digestion, causes cold and clammy feet, and loss of radiance, lustre and complexion of the skin leading to pallor, (*Ashtang*).

Causes for vitiating *pitta*

Grief, fear, anger and jealousy, exposure to excessive heat, hot season (*sharad* and *greeshma ritus*), midday and the middle of the night, the sexual act soon after a meal are factors that vitiate *pitta*. Repression of natural urges for thirst and hunger also vitiate it. Hot, pungent, sour and salty foods, sesame seeds, linseed, horse gram, mustard, curd, fermented drinks, wine, oil, smoking, *etc.*, increase *pitta*.

Let us understand how the thermal balance and energy generation in the body is sustained from the modern biomedicine perspective. The body is the product of food (*aahara sambham vastu - Cha. Su.* 28-45). Under the principle that everything under the sun is *pancha bhautic*, the four types of food, *i.e.*, those which are eaten, drunk, licked and masticated, are converted into small *parmanus* (subatomic particles) to form the constituents of *panch bhautic* tissues in the human body. *Tanmatras* are the minutest particles, forming different elements. Kanad in his *Vaisheshik Siddhant*, talked of the chemical changes following cooking, resulting in irreversible union of *paramanus*, resulting in newer elements of the body. To this process he gave the name *pilupak*. *Pilu* means subtle subatomic particles of atoms. Through various functions, *dahana* and *pachana*, the macromolecules in food are broken down into small particles and transformed into different elements of the body.

Agni or *anala* (fire) are the two synonyms of *pitta*. Apart from the *tejas* element, the water element is responsible for the fluidity, liquidity and viscosity characteristics of many of the digestive juices containing different enzymes that are secreted from different organs forming the gastro intestinal tract. Examples are gastric hydrochloric acid secretion, bile and pancreatic secretions.

Agneyatwat pitte dahana pachanadishu abhipravartamaneshu agnivat upacharah kriyante antagniriti; ksheenehi agni gune tat samana dravyopagayat ati vruddhe sheeta kriyopayogaadagamascha pashyamo na khalu pittavyatirekaat anyo agniriti ll (Su. Su. 21/9)

Because of its functions of combustion or oxidation (*dahana*), digestion (*pachana*), conversion (*parinama*), transformation (*paravritti*), illumination and visualization (*prakashana*), colouring (*ranjana*), lustre (*prabhakaram*) and generation of heat (*tapana*), *pitta* is treated as *agni*. It is responsible for the function of combustion resulting in various biotransformations in the body. With the use of substances which are of dissimilar or similar qualities it can be decreased or increased.

Solar radiation is the prime source of energy of this universe. *Tej mahabhoot* represents this very energy. Chlorophyll is the green pigment in the chloroplasts of plants. This absorbs energy from the rays of the sun and converts it into chemical energy. Water and atmospheric CO_2 are converted into oxygen and carbohydrates. This process is called photosynthesis. These carbohydrates are now stored as food in plants, which are consumed as food by both animals and human beings. A living cell, through a special form of combustion at very low levels of temperature, efficiently breaks down all gross food substances into simple forms, *viz.*, amino acids, fatty acids, glucose *etc.* Carbohydrates form the fuel that generates energy for all the body functions. Energy is required for immediate utilization for all the physiological functions in the body and it is stored for future utility in the form of glycogen from glucose and fat from lipid fatty acids. This process is called metabolism, which involves the processes of degradation, conversion and synthesis. To represent these three aspects of human physiology, Ayurveda uses three specific terms, *deha, sharir* and *kaya*. *Deha* represents anabolism (synthesis), *shairir* represents catabolism (degradation) and *kaya* is *agni* that represents both these facets in combination called metabolism. The food substances consist of carbohydrates (CHO), proteins (CHON) and fats (C=O). The energy is locked in the bonds between the atoms of the molecules of these fuels. Energy of 690 Kcal can be liberated by combustion of one mole carbohydrate (180 gm) with the release of H_2O and CO_2 molecules. Cell respiration is a special form of oxidation. It is through the process of oxidation that the cell generates energy in the form of chemical energy and not as heat.

Enzymes are natural biological catalysts that help all biochemical reactions to take place very rapidly with a high degree of specificity, through well-defined pathways in the body. Biochemical reactions of can be of two types, *viz.*, *samyoga* (addition and substitution reactions) and *vibhaga* (reduction, oxidation, decomposition and displacement reactions). Various enzymes and hormones (functional proteins) catalyse this oxidative process, and finally liberate chemical energy, called adenosine triphosphate (ATP), which is termed as the energy currency of the body. Every cellular function requires ATP, cytokines, growth factors and hormones.

As explained in an earlier chapter, *vata* in conjunction with *pitta* performs different intra cellular events, such as signalling molecules resulting into signal transduction. These transduction mechanisms cause either an increase or decrease of cAMP/cGMP or IP3/DAG or Ca_2 or other ionic channels. The cAMP in the presence Ca_2 calmodulin complex activates protein kinase A (PKA). IP3 regulates intracellular Ca_2 and in the presence of cAMP, it activates protein kinase C (PKC). Some receptors are protein tyrosine kinases themselves. Activation of these kinases causes catalysation of oxidative phosphorylation in the cell leading to either activation or inhibition of various intracellular mechanisms and events. All these intra cellular mechanisms of various transformations are indeed representations of *pitta* function, (*Ayurveda and Modern Medicine* - R. D. Lele).

Paktim apaktim darshanam adarshanam
matrabhavatvam ushnam prakruti

vikruti varnau shauryam bhayam krodham
harsham moham prasaadam

ityevam aadeeni cha aparani dwandwan iti ll
(Cha. Su. 12/11)

Digestion, indigestion, vision or its impairment, variations in body heat, normality or abnormality of body colour and complexion, valour or fear, anger and joy, confusion or a lucid, pleasant mind are all the opposing characteristics of *pitta*. Emotions, higher functions of the brain such as *buddhi* (intelligence) and *medha* (memory power) depend on *pitta* function (brain metabolism). *Sadhaka* and *alochaka pitta* have already been described.

Thus *pitta* is an important player for all molecular mechanisms responsible for all the bodily functions of transformation involving functional enzyme proteins, cytokines, hormones, *etc*.

Chapter : 22

Kapha Dosha

Kapha or sleshma

This is the third primal constituent of the body, whose structure is formed by the combination of *aap* and *prithvi mahabhootas* (H_2O + C in the excited state). Its quality is *tamas*, which means inertia or Brownian motion. In Brownian motion the particles cannot move over large distances. Hence, *prithvi* and *aap* are the cause for all the solid and semi liquid components of the body. *Sleshma* is also used as a synonym for *kapha*. *Sleshma* is derived from *slisha dhatu*, *slisha aalingane*, meaning embracing. Thus *kapha* signifies cohesion or binding. It is akin to the function of connective tissue along with the ground substance (muco-polysacharide), which binds all the cells and tissues together. All cellular structure of the body is *kapha* in origin.

Carbohydrates and lipids are formed by the combination of carbon and water. Proteins are formed through the penetration of nitrogen from *vayu* into a combination of *prithvi* and *aap*. Proteins are of three types, *viz*., regulating proteins, structural proteins and functional proteins. Proteins and fats represent the structural mechanism of the body. Undoubtedly *kapha* represents the structural organization of the body. It represents the cyto-skeleton of the cell, lipoid and protein structural organization of the cell wall and protoplasm, ground substance, connective tissue, *etc*. The cell wall is made up of lipoproteins. The tissue proteins are made up of structural proteins, *e.g*., collagen, actin, myosin, haemoglobin, myoglobin, *etc*. Collagen is the main content of all the connective tissues of the body including the skin, muscle, cartilage, bones, *etc*. It is the bone collagen matrix that binds the calcium to make bones hard and strong. Loss of collagen in old age leads to osteoporosis in the bones and wrinkles in the skin. Interestingly, Ayurveda depicts all changes related to old age to be a result of a decline in *kapha* and an increase in *vata*.

Locations of kapha

Amashayah shleshmanah l (Su. Su. 21/6)

Shleshmanah urah shira kantha sandhayah l (Su. Su. 21/7)

Urah kanthah shirah kloma parvanyamashayo rasah l
Medo ghraanam cha jivha cha kaphasya sutaram urah ll (Vag. Su. 12/3)

Kapha is mainly located in the chest. Its origin is in *amashaya*. It is present in the head, nose, throat, tongue, joints, lungs, *rasa dhatu* and fat tissue.

Functions of *kapha dosha*

Sneho bandha sthiratwam cha gauravam vrushata balam l
Kshama dhrutih alobhascha kapha karma avikarajam ll
(Cha. Su. 18/51)

Kapha causes *brimhana* (hypertrophy), *poorana* (replenishment) and *gaurava* (heaviness or obesity). Its functions are *vrishya* (increased potential for libido), *sthairya* (steadfast mind), *vyayamshakti* (good tolerance for exercise), *vyadhi kshamatwa* (high resistance to disease), *ropan* (healing) and *sandhi bandhanam* (stable joints). Its physical characteristics are *snigdha* (unctuous), *sneha* (oily), *slakshna* (viscous), *saandra* (solid/compact), *pitchil* (slimy), *sthir* (steady), *sheeta* (cold) and *guru* (heavy).

Forgiveness, courage, forebearance, zest, virility, knowledge, understanding, generous, stable structures in the body, good strength and smooth joints are the features of normal *kapha dosha*, (Charak). There are five types of *kaphas*.

Kledak kapha

Amashayastha shleshma swa shaktya sheshanam shleshmasthanam shareeasya chodaka karmana anugraham karoti l (Su. Su. 21/14)

It is located in the upper gastro intestinal tract or *aamashay*. It moistens food, aids its digestion and nourishes other *kaphas* and the whole body. It is produced during the early phase of digestion of food that starts with salivary secretion and non-acid secretions in the stomach that include mucin. *Kledaka kapha* moistens and processes the food and presents it in a form that is suitable for *pachak pitta* and *samanavayu* to properly digest it. It nourishes all different types of *kapha* in the body.

Avalambak kapha

Urasthah satrikasya swaveeryatah l

Hrudayasyaana veeryat cha tat stha eva ambu karmana l
Kaphaadhmanam cha sheshanam yat karoti avalambanam ll

Ato avalambakah shleshma ll (Vag. Su. 12/15)

Urasthah trika samdharanam aatma veeryena anna rasa hitena hridayavalambanam karoti l (Su. Su. 21/14)

It is located in the chest. By its inherent strength it supports the *trika sandhis* (joints) at the neck, shoulder, as well as at the sacro iliac and hip joints. These two joints are very important from the point of the stability of the body to maintain the right posture. The *kapha pradhana rasa dhatu* is formed after digestion of food. It provides strength and nourishment to *hridaya* and the whole body by circulation. It nourishes the rest of the *kaphas*, through hydration.

Bodhaka kapha

Jivha mool kanthasto jivhendriya saumyatwat samyak rasa gyane vartate l (Su. Su. 21/14)

It is located in the base of the tongue and the throat. It is responsible for the salivary secretions (the very initial phase of carbohydrate digestion) and appreciation of taste through the taste buds.

Sleshaka kapha

Sandhi samshleshat shleshakah sandhishu sthitah l (Vag. Su. 12/18)

It is located in the joints and lubricates and nourishes them. Synovium and synovial fluid in the joint capsules are part of *sleshaka kapha*.

Tarpaka kapha

Shirasthah sneha santarpana adhikrutatvat indriyanam atmatvam samveeryena anugraham karoti l (Su. Su. 21/14)

It is located in the head. Due to its unctuous character the *tarpaka kapha* nourishes the brain and all the organs of cognition. Cerebro spinal fluid (CSF) is a part of *tarpak kapha*.

Daardhyam shaithilyam upachayam karshyam utsaaham aalasyam vrushataam kleebataam gyaanam agyaanam buddhim moham evaani chaapraani dwandwaaneeti ll (Cha. Su. 12/12)

Muscularity, well nourished, energetic, potent, knowledgeable, intelligent *etc*., are characteristics of the normal state of *kapha*, whilst flabby muscles, a wasted body, laziness, impotence, ignorance, stupidity, *etc*., are characteristics of abnormal states of *kapha*.

Symptoms of increase in *kapha*

Agni sadana praseka aalasya gauravam l
Svaitya shaitya shlatha angatwam shwasa kaasa atinidrata ll

It causes depletion of *agni* resulting in dyspepsia, excessive salivation, lassitude, a feeling of heaviness, pallor, clay coloured faeces, cold clammy limbs, looseness of the body parts, dyspnoea, cough with expectoration and excessive sleep with drowsiness, (*Ashtang Hr. Su.* 11-7).

Symptoms of decrease in *kapha*

Kaphe bhramah l shleshmashayanam shoonyatwam
hrut dravah shlatha sandhitaa ll

Symptoms of kapha depletion are confusion and dizziness, emptiness of all the organs of *kapha*, a weakened heart with palpitations, and looseness of joints, (*Asht. Hr. Su.* 11-16).

Shleshma kshaye rukshata antardaaha aamashayetara
shleshmaashaya shoonyata sandhi shaithilyam trushna
daurbalyam prajaagaranam cha l (Su. Su. 15/11)

Sushruta has added dryness, internal thirst or dehydration, excessive thirst, weakness and insomnia.

Kapha also signifies *udaka karma* or maintaining the fluid balance of the body in both the intra and extra cellular spaces. It nourishes, protects, lubricates and supports all the tissues of the body. Barring red blood cells (*rakta*) and bone (*asthi*), all the tissues of the body are made up of *kapha*. *Asthi dhatu*, which is more solid and gives structural stability to the body is not a part of *kapha* organization. The exclusion of *asthi dhatu*, in my opinion, requires more clarity. Porosity and hardness being attributes of *vayu*, bone might have probably been considered as a location of *vayu*. The overall description of *kapha* broadly conforms to the structural mechanism of the body. Body cells and tissues require new protein formation for their growth and maintenance. The structural proteins are actin and myosin, myoglobin of muscle, haemoglobin of RBCs, collagen, elastin of the skin, transport proteins *etc*. Since the five main tissue elements, *viz*., *rasa*, *mamsa*, *meda*, *majja*, *shukra* and *ojus* are all *kapha* elements, it signifies that the body is verily *kapha* in origin. All the solid and liquid constituents are *kapha* in nature due to the *prithvi* and *aap mahabhoot* origin of *kapha*. Why *rakta* and *asthi* are not included as *kapha* elements is really perplexing. A probable reason could be due to the fact that, the red colour of *rakta* is specific for *pitta* and hardness is a special feature of *vayu*. *Majja dhatu* forms the main composition of the brain as per the Ayurvedic concept. The neuro and psychological attributes of *kapha* are related to *majja dhatu*.

Causes that provoke *kapha*

Kapha gets provoked by cold substances, in winter and especially in the spring (*hemant & shishir ritus*), in the early morning soon after sunset, and soon after a meal. Sleeping during the day, not exercising, laziness, foods which are slimy, unctuous and heavy to digest and which have a sweet, sour or salty taste, increase this *dosha*. Foods that are heavy in quality cause obstruction in the body channels (*abhishyandi*), *e.g.*, food grains (barley, black gram, wheat, beans, sesame seeds, *etc.*), curds, milk and its preparations, by products of cane, meat of domesticated animals and water dwelling beings, fats and sweet fruits (bananas, dates, coconuts *etc.*,) lotus stems and Indian water chestnuts are but a few examples of the foods that increase *kapha dosha*. *Kapha* is white in colour, heavy, unctuous and sweet in taste when it is in its normal state. When it gets vitiated, it turns salty.

Chapter : 23

Concept of Prakruti

Constitution

Shukra asrug garbhini bhojya cheshta garbhashayah rutushu l
Yasyad dosho adhikoh tena prakrutih saptadhoditaa ll
(Ashta. Hru. Sharir. 3/83)

The diet and life style of a pregnant mother, the state of her uterus and ovulatory cycles at the time of conception (union of male and female gametes), affect the proportional strengths and balance of the three *doshas* causing the predominance of one or another *dosha.* The preponderant *dosha* determines the *prakruti* of the new-born. There are seven *prakrutis*.

Vibhutvat ashukaritvat balitvat anya kopanat l
Swatantryat bahurogitwat doshanam prabalo anilah ll
(Ashta. Hru. Sharir. 3/84)

Being all pervasive, quick, powerful and independent, and also being capable of vitiating others, *vata* is the most powerful of all *prakrutis* and is the cause of many diseases.

All individuals are unique in the makeup of their body, mind, character and behaviour. Everybody responds differently to different types of stresses, be they physical, mental or due to disease or to a therapy. It is said that one man's meat is another man's poison. This uniqueness of an individual is called *prakruti*. Hence, Ayurveda insists on a customised therapeutic approach to each individual based on their *prakruti* or constitution. It has been observed that the more two individuals resemble each other, the greater are their chances of developing the same diseases. Clusters of people with similar characteristics based on psyche and morphology (genetic or hereditary) are grouped into different types of *prakruti* to enable an Ayurvedic physician to type an individual into seven dosha based *prakrutis* or constitutions.

Earlier we had described the differentiation of clusters of human beings depending on their psyche. Three main psyches were differentiated in terms of their volitional and emotional behavioural patterns, *viz.*, *satwa*, *rajas* and *tamas*. A further differentiation of clusters based on *doshas*, into seven types of constitutions, is made based on various parameters, such as the build, physical potential, psychic nature, emotional responses, *etc.*, of people. *Prakruti* is determined at the time of fertilization due to the predominance of one or the other *dosha*. We now know that an individual's potential is genetically determined through gene imprinting. At the two cell stage in the first six days after fertilization the unique genome is expressed. This process of genome formation is achieved through gene imprinting. Ayurveda called it *brahmalekh* or *vidhi vidhan*, which means destiny. This determines the habitus or the constitution of a person and is permanent throughout one's life. Only at the time of death of a person does it undergo any change. The advantage of knowing the *prakruti* is that we can identify persons prone to certain diseases or disabilities. Thus *prakruti* is one of the most important and useful tools, both for prevention and treatment of diseases.

At the time of fertilization of the oocyte by the sperm, the *doshas*, either singly or in a combination of two, or rarely all three are predominant. The predominant *dosha* or *doshas* determine the habitus or constitution of an individual. They form the innate nature of a person and this is designated as *prakruti*, which remains unchanged till the end of the life span. There are an innumerable number of prakrutis. Based on certain physical, psychosexual, metabolic, and other attributes, *e.g.*, predisposition or vulnerability towards certain disease conditions and their response to therapy, the individuals are typed into seven common clinically recognisable *prakrutis*. Our ancient people understood that there is a close relation between the build, symmetry of the body and psyche of an individual. The capabilities of a person and their life span are also determined by the *prakruti*. Ayurveda tried to use simple clinical parameters to identify an individual's *prakruti* on the basis of the signs for identification of various *doshas*. *Vata* relates to all that is concerned with neurohormonal regulatory mechanisms. In a person whose predominant *dosha* is *vata prakruti*, these mechanisms dominate over others. Thus such a person is thin, more active mentally and physically weak. *Pitta* relates to thermal and enzyme biotransformation mechanisms. Hence a person with dominant *pitta prakruti* suffers from an excess of these mechanisms. Their thermal balance or metabolic rate is always on the higher side of normal and their build is medium. They are more likely to suffer from inflammatory conditions. *Kapha* is related to structural mechanisms. Such a person is strong, well-built and slow. Thus Ayurveda pioneered a simple clinical technique useful in identifying a person's proclivities to a pathology and this helped a physician to plan both prevention and therapy.

Many others also similarly tried to classify people on the basis of physic and temperament. Hippocrates called it habitus. Type A and type B individuals were classified on the basis of their temperament. In the recent past a new method of classification based on the dominance of the structures derived from the embryonic germinal plate, *viz*., ecto, endo and mesoderms has become popular, because of good clinical correlation. It is called Somato-typing.

In endomorphs, the gut and viscera dominate. Such persons have a large trunk and abdomen with tapering limbs and small hands and feet. They have soft, delicate skin. By temperament they are viscerotonic. They are fond of eating, are lazy, always craving comfort and support of others, complacent and tolerant.

In a mesomorphic person, tissues developed from the mesoderm, *viz*., muscles and bones *etc*., dominate. They are strong and well built, with broad shoulders and large hands and feet. On the basis of psyche, they are classified as somatotonics. They are assertive, energetic, forthright and unrestrained.

Ectomorphs are thin, fragile, and flat chested with long thin limbs. These are also by temperament known as cerebrotonics. They are introverts, sociophobic and love solitude. From a common clinical point of view ten types of somato-types are recognized. They are endomorph, ectomorph, mesomorph, ectomorphic endomorph, ectomorphic mesomorph, endomorphic ectomorph, endomorphic mesomorph, mesomorphic ectomorph, mesomorphic endomorph and midrange wherein all the three are present in near identical proportions.

Somato-typing has been found to be effective in clinically correlating many pathological conditions, *e.g*., myocardial infarction is found to be more common amongst endomorphic mesomorphs. From the foregoing one can easily see a striking similarity between the concept of *prakruti* and somato-typing. The relevance of examining the *prakruti* in clinical practice should be given greater stress in all medical and Ayurvedic curricula, as it helps a person to plan their lifestyle and diet such that they balance the dominant *dosha* and thereby prevent a likely disease. The uniqueness of Ayurveda is its greater stress on preservation of normal health and prevention of disease rather than the therapy of diseases. Thus Ayurveda is more a preventative and health maintenance science that helps in increasing longevity of life without disability. In my opinion health education and lifestyle management in Ayurveda can be made a subject for universal education, not only for the medical students.

Let us now try to understand the gene, genome and genetics and also epigenetics in detail. In 1860 Gregor Mendel postulated that discreet individual packets or units of inherited traits are transmitted to the progeny of the next generation. It was only in 1909 that this unit of inheritance was named as the gene. The gene is an irreducible unit of heredity and biological informational systems. It is comparable to an atom in reference to matter and a bit or byte in reference to digital informational systems, (*The Gene* - Siddhartha Mukherji). Genes reside in the chromosomes located in the nucleus of a cell. Chromosomes are thread like filaments that are stained blue with aniline dyes. In humans each cell normally contains 23 pairs of chromosomes. There are 22 pairs of autosomes and one pair of sex chromosomes, which differ in males and females. Females have two copies of the X chromosome whilst males have one X and one Y chromosome. Genes carry information and instructions from one generation to the next in the form of chemical memory in DNA. Genes are thus the carriers of genetic information and are the basis of heredity. In 1910 Thomas Morgan identified the location of the genes to be on the chromosomes. Chromosomes are stained by coloured dyes, hence the name. The chemical composition of a gene consists of DNA. In 1926 Avery showed that genes can even be transmitted from heat killed, dead bacteria into living bacteria, proving that the gene is an inert chemical protein (DNA). The function of the gene is to carry a message or instructions to make proteins (complex multi-dimensional macromolecules). Proteins are the true work horses of the cell. These proteins perform multiple cell functions. They act as receptors for other proteins. They are involved in signal transduction from cell to cell. They are also involved in enzyme activities. The latter are called transformational proteins, and structural proteins create structural components of molecular scaffolding in a cell. Regulatory proteins regulate other proteins in a well-coordinated way to properly orchestrate the life cycle of a cell. In short genes provide the blue prints to build or form regulatory, functional and structural proteins in a cell.

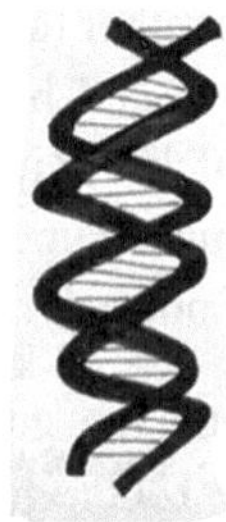

Double Helix DNA

Illustration of DNA

Deoxyribonucleic acid, more commonly known as DNA, is a complex molecule that contains all of the information necessary to build and maintain an organism. All living organisms have DNA within their cells. Whenever organisms reproduce, a portion of their DNA is passed on to their offspring. Most DNA is located in the cell nucleus (called nuclear DNA), but a small amount of DNA can also be found in the mitochondria (called mitochondrial DNA or mtDNA). RNA or ribonucleic acid is the molecular cousin of DNA and it is located in the cytoplasm of the cell.

The genetic code is the set of rules by which information encoded in genetic material (DNA or RNA sequences) is translated into proteins (amino acid sequences) by living cells. The genome of an organism is inscribed in DNA, and in some viruses in RNA. The backbone of DNA is made up of a chain of sugars and phosphates strung together. In RNA, the sugar is ribose, hence it is called ribonucleic acid. In the case of DNA it is deoxyribose.

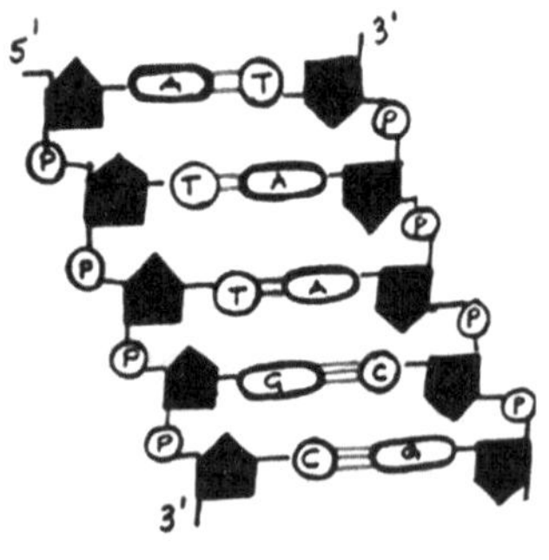

DNA

- ⬟ - Deoxyribose Sugar
- P - Phosphate
- A - Adenine
- T - Thymine
- G - Guanine
- C - Cytosine

Illustration of DNA molecule

The four amino acid bases that protrude out from the backbone, are adenine (A), guanine (G), cytosine (C) and thymine (T). In the case of RNA thymine is replaced with uracil (U).

DNA = AGCT

RNA = AGCU

The human genome is an encyclopaedia of all the genes with all foot note annotations, instructions and references. It is a library of total information. The human genome consists of roughly between 21000 – 25000 genes. They provide master instructions to build, repair and also program cell death to maintain the human organism. It is the genome that rules the body organization as the constitution does for the governance of a nation.

Protein formation

How are proteins built? What are the mechanisms that operate in protein building?

Proteins are the key molecules and building blocks of a cell. Protein formation is a two-step process. Genes carry the messages or information to build proteins.

The DNA of a gene encoding the ruby coloured eye of a fruit fly copies into RNA, as a message called messenger RNA (mRNA). It provides the blue print for producing a red colour pigment in the eye of its progeny. Creating mRNA (molecular message) is an intermediate mechanism. This process is called transcription. Proteins are synthesized in ribosomes located in endoplasmic reticulum in cytoplasm. The mRNA molecule provides instructions through a genetic code (codon) to synthesize proteins. This mechanism is called translation.

DNA ----> RNA------>Protein

It is known as the central dogma of molecular biology.

Some viruses are capable of transferring RNA to DNA. This is called a reverse transcription mechanism. This process is orchestrated by the reverse transcriptase enzyme. These viruses are called retroviruses, *e.g.*, the human immune deficiency virus (HIV).

Cell division

Normal cells have a number of enzyme proteins that attach to phosphate groups. These are called kinases. These are molecular master switches that switch on to activate the functions of proteins. The Src gene is one proto-typical kinase in a normal cell, which tightly regulates cell division using on and off switches. Thus cellular division is controlled. A normal proto oncogene gets activated by a carcinogen through mutation and becomes an oncogene. An example is the mutated viral Src gene. An abnormal Src gene after mutation is permanently over activated and is always on over drive and causes cancer. It turns on other signals, and amplifies them to make it a powerful internal signal that causes abnormal mitosis at a great speed, which causes cancer. Proto oncogenes (ras, myc, neu) and the retinoblastoma gene (Rb) are molecular pivots of the cell. They are gate keepers of cell division and are tumour suppressors. They are responsible for apoptosis or programmed cell death. Thus normal cell division is controlled. When these tumour suppressor genes are down regulated it causes abnormal cell division or mitosis leading to cancer.

Mechanisms of biological information transfer

Transmission of genetically inherited traits to progeny from generation to generation in terms of colour, texture of hair, colour of the eyes, life span and potential of an individual *etc*., was known to Hindu culture from time immemorial. Biological information transfer from generation to generation was explained in terms of the succession of seed to plant and plant to seed. Ayurveda explained congenital disorders and deformities based on *beeja dusti* (defect in embryo) or *beeja bhaga dushti* (defective chromosomes and genes). To a great extent *karma siddhant* (theory of past life deeds) were also sought to be explained on this basis.

Genotype and phenotype

Genotype: This is the set of genes in our DNA, which are responsible for a particular trait. For example, two organisms that have even the minutest difference in their genes are said to have different genotypes.

Phenotype: The physical expression in terms of the morphology (appearance or trait) or biochemical characteristic of an organism as a result of the interaction of its genotype and the environment, for example, skin colour, height, behaviour, *etc*., according to the individual's genetic makeup and environment.

Let us now understand *vata*, *pitta* and *kapha* of Ayurveda in the light of genetics. *Vata*, *pitta* and *kapha* are described as *panchabhautic* (physical entities) in origin, and are at the root of morphological, behavioural and the controlling mechanisms of all biological processes in the body, *viz*., regulatory, transformational and also structural activities. Both pathology and physiology in the body are orchestrated by them, Hence *doshas* are also considered as *dhatus*. When vitiated they cause disease in a similar way as the mutated genes do. *Dosha* imbalance is the cause of all diseases. In earlier chapters we have learnt that the function of *vata* is regulatory, *pitta* is about transformational functions and *kapha* is related to structural formation mechanisms in the body. We have also seen that all the three *doshas*, when in excess, deficient or abnormal, cause diseases similar to the way amplified, deficient and mutated genes cause different clinical pictures of disease states.

Compare this information with *vata*, *pitta* and kapha, which uphold the homeostasis of the body when normal. When disturbed (over expressed, hyper activated, down regulated or defective) they cause disease as do different gene proteins. *Desha* (geographical location & environment), *kala* (age, season, time of the day), *vegavarodha* (repression or holding of natural urges), trauma and *pragnyaparadh* (intelligence failure leading to judgmental errors), *aahar* (food), life style, *etc*., are the factors that affect the *doshas* and create imbalance in a manner very similar to epigenetic factors that modify or affect gene expression.

Epigenetics is new development in genetics, which developed after the successful decoding of the human genome. That environmental changes affect gene function is now well demonstrated. Epigenetics is the study of inherited changes in gene expression (active versus inactive genes). These changes do not involve the underlying DNA sequence. The change is limited to the phenotype without any change in the genotype. It affects the capacity of the cells in the way they read the genes. Epigenetic change is a regular and natural occurrence but can also be influenced by several factors including age, the environment/lifestyle, and disease state. Epigenetic modifications can manifest as commonly as the manner in which cells terminally differentiate to end up as skin cells, liver cells, brain cells, *etc*. The toti potent cells can differentiate into different types of body cells based on the medium they are grown in, in the laboratory. Epigenetic change can have more damaging effects that can result in diseases like cancer. At least three systems, including DNA methylation, histone modification and non-coding RNA (ncRNA) associated gene silencing are currently considered to initiate and sustain epigenetic change.

Let us compare and contrast epigenetic modification to what Ayurveda says about the factors that affect the *doshas*. *Pragnyaparadh* is considered as the single most important cause of disease genesis. It is all related to perceptions of the mind. The same event can cause different types of perceptions in the mind. For example, railway accidents are daily events in one's life. They hardly evoke any emotions. But if someone near and dear is lost in this accident, then this very accident can cause great mental trauma and stress. Perceptions, beliefs thoughts are the result of the epigenetic signals from the environment on the mind. Mind in turn interprets these signals as positive or negative and passes them to DNA. In turn genes read these perceptions, accordingly blue prints are made for making the different proteins, which alter the biological processes in the body and also in the immune system. One gene can create 30,000 proteins. Thus positive perceptions and beliefs produce healthy signals and negative ones cause disease. The placebo effect is due to positive beliefs. Nocibo is the opposite of placebo. Thus *sadvrutta* has an epigenetic basis.

It will not be out of place to now learn the basics of circadian rhythms and chronobiology, and their relationship to *dosha* molecular mechanisms.

In Latin *circa* means around and *diem* means day. There are rhythmic day and night or wake and sleep cycles which are regulated by nature. These rhythms are synchronised with the revolutions of the earth. Many biological processes are regulated by the circadian clock. *Dosha* predominance varies with the time of day and night too. Chronobiology is the formal study of daily, tidal, and seasonal rhythms in which biological processes are altered. Ayurveda gives great importance to these events and has described the remedial actions depending upon diurnal or seasonal alterations.

Dr Hall, Dr Rosbash and Dr.Young have demonstrated, using the fruit fly, Drosophila melanogaster that these biological clocks help organisms to adapt to the changing day and night oscillations and rhythms. They isolated a gene called the Period (PER) gene. Mutations in the PER gene can shorten, lengthen and even abolish the period of the circadian rhythm. The period gene is located on the X chromosome. PER is the protein encoded by the period gene. It accumulates during the night and is degraded during the day. These clocks influence alertness, hunger, metabolism, fertility, mood and other physiological functions. Circadian clock dysfunction can lead to disorders, *e.g.*, insomnia, depression, diabetes *etc.* In 2017 these researchers received the Nobel Prize for their work on circadian rhythms.

Dina charya and *Rutu charya* are based on these Circadian rhythms and biological clocks of the human physiology.

Chapter : 24

Individual Prakrutis

Vata prakruti

Sphutita dhusara kesha gatra l
Sheeta dvesha chala dhruti smruti, buddhi chesta
sauhardra drushti gatayo ati bahu pralapaah ll

Alpa vitta bala jivita nidrah sannasakta chala jarjara vaachah l
Nastika bahubhoja savilasa geeta haasa mrugayakalila lolaah ll

Madhura amla katu ushna satmyakangah
krusha adeergha aakrutayah sashabda vataah l
Na drudha na jitendriya na cha aaryaa na cha
kaantaadayita bahuprajaa va ll

Netraninchaisham khara dhoosarani mrutopamani l
Unmilitaneeva bhavanti supte shaila
drumanste gaganam cha yaanti ll

Adhanya matsaraadhmatah stenah prodwandwa pindikah l
Shrugala ushtra grudhra aakhru kakaanookascha vatika ll
(Asht. Hru. Shar. 85-89)

At the time of fertilization of an egg by the sperm (*shukra shonita samyoga*), if there is a preponderance of *vayu dosha* over the other *doshas*, *vata prakruti* develops.

Description of an individual with a preponderance of *vata prakruti*

Physical characteristics

The person is of small build, with a thin frame and has poor physical strength. He is not fair in complexion or handsome. He has coarse and rough hair on the head and face, and coarse nails and skin. He is prone to develop new growths.

Mental functions

Such persons dislike cold things; love sweet, sour and salty taste; have a short term memory with poor retention and recall; are very talkative; have poor concentration; sleep only for a short time and usually stay awake till late at night; in dreams they fly high in the sky; they are accomplished in the arts of dance and music.

Nature

They are generally timid; jealous, prone to thievery; selfish; unfriendly; ungrateful; habituated to biting their nails and grinding their teeth; lack self-control; less fortunate and usually not wealthy. Such men are not attractive to women; they have limited progeny. They hate cold and like hot things and like travelling. They have irregular food habits and are normally constipated with scanty urine and sweat secretions. Their nature is likened to that of animals such as the dog, fox, camel, rat, vulture and crow.

Pitta prakruti

Teekshna trushnaa bubhukshuh l
Gaura ushna angah tamra hastanghri vaktrah
shooro maani pingakesho alpa romaa ll

Dayita maalya vilepanamandanah sucharitah shuchishrita vatsalah l
Vibhava saahasa buddhi balaanvito bhavati bheeshu
gatirdvishamtam api ll

Medhaavi prashithila sandhibandhanamso
nareenam anabhimato alpa shukra kamaah l
aavaasah palita taranga neelikaanam bhunkte
annam madhura Kashaya tikta sheetam ll

dharma dweshi swedanah pooti gandhir
bhooryucchara krodha paana ashashane eershyah l
suptah pashyet karnikaramplaashaan
digdaholkaavidyudarkaanilamscha ll

Tanooni pingaani chalaanichaisham tan
alpapkshmani hima priyani l
Krodhena madyena raveshcha bhasa
ragm vrajantyashu vilochanai ll

Madhyayusho Madhya balaah panditah kleshabheeravah l
Vyaghra arshakapi marjara yakshaanukaashcha ll
(Asht. Hru. Sharir. 3/90-95)

Persons with such a constitution have a medium build with a reasonably good life span; they experience acute hunger and thirst; are voracious eaters and hate hot food; fond of cold, sweet, bitter and astringent tastes; their skin has a slightly yellowish tinge; they are moderately muscular with poor tone; possess only moderate strength; their joints are not well knit; their nails, eyes, palate, tongue, lips, palms and soles are coppery red; their hair turns grey at a young age; they sweat profusely giving out a bad odour; the opposite sex are attracted to them; their sexual urges are limited. They get angry very fast and can be pacified equally fast. They exude an aura; are intelligent, learned, sagacious, good debaters and valiant fighters. In dreams they see lightening, meteors, fire, and the Bustard tree (*Palash*), *etc*. Their character is comparable to that of animals such as the cat, monkey, tiger and bear.

Kapha prakruti

Shleshmaa somah shleshmslashtena saumyo goodha
snigdha shlishta sandhi asthi mamsah l
Kshut trut dukkha klesha gharmair tapto
buddhya yuktah satyasandhah ll

Because of its origin from water, the individual with *kapha prakruti* is gentle, deeply rooted, soft in nature with strong well-built musculature, bones and joints. They can tolerate hunger, thirst, heat, hardships and difficulties with ease. They are intelligent, skilful and truthful.

Priyangu doorva sharkarakaand Shastra
gorochana Padma suvarna varnah l
Pralamba baahuh pruthupeenavakshaa
mahalalato ghananeelikeshah ll

Their skin colour shines like some plants, *e.g.*, *priyangu*, *doorva,* and sugarcane, *gorochana* weapon, lotus and gold. Their body is well crafted with long arms, a broad chest, wide forehead, and tufted black hair.

Mrudvanga samavibhaktacharu deho bahu ojo
rati rasa shukra putra bhrutyah l
Dharmatma vadati na nishturam cha jatu
pracchannam vahati dhrudham chiram cha vairam ll

Individuals with *kapha prakruti* have a well-crafted, symmetrical, delicate body structure, with abundant immune strength, sex drive, *shukradhatu*, and tend to have many progeny and servants. They are generous, soft spoken and hold a grudge for a long time.

Samadadviradendra tulya yato jaladambhodi
mrudanga simhaghoshah l
Smruti manabhiyogavan vineeto na cha balye
api ati rodano n lolah ll

They move like a powerful elephant, their voice resonates like a drum-like musical instrument (*mrudanga*), roars like a lion, and bursts like the clouds. They are polite, have a good memory and are venerated. They are not greedy, and were happy babies.

Tiktam kashayam katuka ushnam alpam sa
bhunkte balavaan tathaapi l
Raktanta susnigdha vishaala deerghah
suvyakta shuklasitapakshmalaksha ll

They are strong despite the fact that they consume food in small quantities; fond of hot, bitter, astringent and spicy tastes. They have pleasant, wide, expressive eyes.

Alpa vyvahara krodha paana ashanehah
prajyayurvito deerghdarshee vadaanya l
Shraddho gambheerah sthoola lakshyah kshamaavaan
aaryo nidralu deerghasutra krutagyah ll

They indulge only briefly in talking, drinking, eating and business. Their anger is short lived; their life span is long and they are far sighted; they are silent, faithful and thankful; strive for higher objectives; forgiving and polite. They love to sleep and are habituated to procrastination.

Swapne sa padmaan savihangamalaamstoyashayan
pashyati toyadamscha l

Brahma rudra indra varunataksharya hamsa gaja adhipaihi l
Shleshma prakrutayah tulyah tarkshya simha ashwa go vrushaih ll
(Asht. Hr. Sharir. 3/ 96-103)

In dreams they see lakes full of blooming lotuses and flocks of swans and birds flying in group formations. Their character is like that of the gods, *viz*., Brahma, Rudra, Indra, Varuna and the sun and they are likened to animals such as the lion, horse, cow and bull.

In short a person of this constitution is fair complexioned, muscular, strongly built, good-looking, with a pleasant personality. They have expressive eyes and a forceful voice. They are brave, forbearing, and have good physical endurance. They are not greedy, have a good grasp of subjects and a good memory. They are fond of hot, bitter, astringent and spicy foods and are bestowed with good fortune, wealth and friends. They are steadfast, grateful and reliable. They dream of swans and lakes etc. Their nature is comparable to that of the gods and a king and they are compared to animals such as the lion, elephant, and swan.

What happens when two, or all the three *doshas* are up-regulated in a *prakruti*? If two are predominant it is called *dwandwa* and if all three are in an excited state it is called *sannipata prakruti.*

Prakruteeh dwaya sarvottha dwandwa sarva gunodaye l
(Asht. Hr. 3/103)

The characteristics of the respective *doshas* predominate, leading to different disease states.

Sama doshah samastastu shrestaa nindya dwidoshaja l (Charak)

When all the *doshas* are in a balanced state, it is best for health. When in imbalance they are harmful.

Tatha vataladyah sada aaturah l

Vatadi dosha prakrutis are always the cause of some disease or the other.

Tatradyastrayo nityaturaa doshanushayita
shareeratwat visheshatah dwandwa prakrutayah l

Teshu hi guna mishrita vikara karishu kshut
pipasadishviva arogya vyapadeshah l (Ashtanga Sangrah)

Trayastu prusha bhavanti aaturah l (Charak)

If all the three *doshas* are in a state of up-regulation, the person is permanently diseased. If two *doshas* are in preponderance there will be mixed symptoms and signs pertaining to the two *doshas*. Symptoms like hunger, thirst and disease have to be identified on the basis of *doshas*. The state of mind, based on the predominance of *satwa*, *rajas* and *tamas* is equally important functioning of the *doshas*. Based on these qualities of the mind there are seven *prakrutis*, namely: 1. *Vata*; 2. *Pitta*; 3. *Kapha*; 4. *Vata pitta*; 5. *Vata kapha;* 6. *Kapha pitta*; 7. *Sanni paata;* which are affected.

Jati kula desha kala vayaaptyaya aatma niyataa hi tesham
purushanam te bhava visheshaa bhavanti l (Cha. Sha. /1)

Different environmental factors, including race, caste (profession), geographical regions, the weather, time (day, night, and season) and age, send signals to the mind. The mind perceives and reads these signals through coding and other processes. The way these processes operate have been discussed in earlier chapters in relation to the qualities described as *trigunas*. These qualities dictate the state of mind or *satwa*. We have already learnt that the mind is yoked to the conscious self. The self creates the blue print, and based on its reading of the external signals, gives instructions for all the regulatory, transcriptional and structural biological processes that occur in intelligent body cells. Thus the *satwa*, *raja* and *tama prakrutis* direct and propel the *dosha* functions. Thus the quality status of the mind, based on *satwa*, *raja* and *tama prakrutis* creates the precise *dosha* imbalance to produce different signs and symptoms of disease. Thus the epigenetic factors of the environment modify the *satwa*, *raja* and *tama* qualities first, and thereafter affect the *dosha* (gene protein) functions, which cause alterations in biological processes, leading to the majority of psychosomatic diseases.

Chapter : 25

Charts of Doshas and Prakrutis

Self identification charts for *doshas* and *prakrutis*

Method of self-identification of *vata prakruti*
1. Inability to sleep well. 2. Instability of gait and exessive body movements. 3. Prominently visible veins all over the body. 4. Prone to irritation and anger. 5. Dislikes cold things. Prefers warm things. 6. Coarse, dry and sparse body hair. 7. Such a person is unstable, both physically and mentally and is always on the move. 8. Preference for unctuous, hot, sweet, sour and salty foods. 9. Thin body build. 10. Very talkative. 11. Flash memory and poor retention. **Advice:** Avoid *vatakar* objects (substances or activities that increase *vata*).

Method of self-identification of *pitta prakruti*
1. Dislikes eating hot food. 2. Excessive thirst. 3. Prone to excessive inflammatory swellings on the skin. 4. High craving for food. 5. Excessive perspiration or sweating. 6. Malodourous sweat. 7. Learn and understand easily. 8. Is easily provoked to anger. 9. Haughty nature. 10. Loves eating sweet, bitter, astringent and cold food. **Advice:** Avoid all substances and activities that promote *pitta*.

Method of self-identification of *kapha prakruti*
1. Stable and well built. 2. Does not sweat much. 3. Well nourished body. 4. Does not require too much food and water. 5. Calm nature. 6. Feel less thirst. 7. Good retentive memory. 8. Does not get provoked easily. 9. Humble, disciplined, strong and forgiving nature. 10. Loves to eat spicy, bitter, sour and hot food. Usually persons with *kapha prakruti* have better immunity, rarely fall sick. As a preventive measure they should avoid substances which are *kaphakara.*

Identifying the different physical characteristics of a *dosha* clinically, is the first step to prescribing diets and drugs, which have opposite characteristics, to balance the *dosha,* in therapeutics.

Relationship between *dosha* and *rasa* (taste)		
Vata kar **(Increasing *vata*) Up regulation**	***Pitta kar*** **(Increasing *pitta*)**	***Kapha kar*** **(Increasing *kapha*)**
Katu – Pungent	*Katu* – Pungent	*Madhur* – Sweet
Tikta – Bitter	*Amla* – Sour	*Amla* – Sour
Kashaya – Astringent	*Lavana* – Salty	*Lavana* – Salty
Vatanashak **Down regulation**	***Pittanashak***	***Kaphanashak***
Madhur - Sweet	*Madhur* – Sweet	*Katu* – Pungent
Amla - Sour	*Tikta* – Bitter	*Tikta* – Bitter
Lavana - Salty	*Kashaya* - Astringent	Kashaya – Astringent

Tridosha* and *ashta vidha virya sambandh		
Vatanashak	***Pittanashak***	***Kaphnashak***
Ushna	*Sheeta*	*Ushna*
Snigdha	*Mrudu*	*Tikshna*
Mrudu	*Guru*	*Ruksha*
Guru		*Laghu*
Vatakar	***Pittakar***	***Kaphkar***
Sheeta	*Tikshna*	*Sheeta*
Tikshna	*Ushna*	*Snigdha*
Ruksha	*Laghu*	*Mrudu*
Laghu	*Ruksha*	*Guru*
Ashtavidhavirya: Guru, snigdha, hima, mrudu, laghu, ruksha, ushna, tikshna. ***Dwividhavirya: Ushna and sheeta.***		

Relationship between *tridosha* and *vipak*		
Vatanashan	***Pittanashan***	***Kaphanashan***
Guru	*Guru*	*Laghu*
Madhura		*Katu*
Amla	*Madhura*	
Vatakar	***Pittakar***	***Kaphakar***
Laghu	*Laghu*	*Guru*
Katu	*Amla*	*Madhura*
	Katu	*Amla*
Shushruta*, two *vipakas* : *Guru and laghu ***Charak*, three *vipakas: Madhura, amla, katu***		

***Tridoshas* and the mind (*mann*)**		
Vata	***Pitta***	***Kapha***
Mana prerna - Inspiring mind	*Mana prasada* - Pleasant mind	*Sneha* - Affectionate
Rajapradhan - Predominantly *rajas.* Fast thought process	*Satwpradhan* - Predominantly *satwa*	*Tamapradhan* - Predominantly *tamas* - lazy
Manoniyaman - Mind control	*Harsh* – Happiness	*Mansikstirata* - Stable mind
Sarvendriya udyojag - Initiator of all sensory and motor impulses	*Krodh* – Anger	*Manobalakar* - Strengthening resolve
Cheshtha pravartak - Promulgator of action	*Medhajanana* - Source of intelligence	*Kshamavan* - Forgiving nature
Utsahadayak - Enthusiastic in action	*Shaurya* – Valour or valiant	*Dhairyawan* - Brave
Bhayashoka - Fear and grief	*Kshipra prakop prasad* - Easily angered and easily pleased	*Alobh* – Charitable
Chanchalta - Fickle minded	*Parakrami* - Valiant, successful, winner	*Utsah* – Enthusiastic
Sheegraskhobh - Easily depressed	*Abhiman* - Egoistic, proud	*Gyanvan* - Knowledgeable
Sheeghravismarnashelata - Easily forgets	*Nipunamati* - Sharp memory and intelligent	*Budhiwan* - Intelligent
It is essential to understand the mental qualities of a person, in order to identify the predominant *dosha* while treating any mental diseases.		

***Tridosha and kaal* (Chronobiology of *doshas*) [*Prakop kaal*]**		
***Vata vridhi / Prakop* (up regulation and vitiation)**	***Pitta vridhi / Prakop***	***Kapha vridhi / Prakop***
1. *Sheetakaala* - Winter	*Sharad rutu* & summer	*Sheetakaala* - Winter & *vasanta rutu*
2. *Abrahkal* - Rainy season	*Madhyan* - Mid-day	*Suryodaypashchat* - Morning after sun rise
3. *Pradoshkal* - Time of high tide	*Ardharatri* - Midnight	*Pradoshkal* - High tide
4. *Ushakal* - Before sunrise	*Anna Paachan kal* - During digestion	*Bhuktamatrakal* - Immediately after having food
5. *Aparaahanna* - Post mid-day	*Sharad rutu*	*Vasant rutu*
6. *Anna parinama kala* - Post digestive period in the evening around 4 p.m		
7. *Grishma & varsha rutu* May, June, July, August		
It is important to know the time of the aggravation of the symptoms associated with *doshas*. This will help to identify *dosha* imbalance.		

Chapter : 26

Dosha Dhatu Mala Samanvaya Chikitsa

General therapeutic principles

Vayor anyatra tajjanstu tairovotkrama yojitai l

With the exception of *vayu*, fasting (*langhan*) is advised in all other *dosha vruddhi* conditions.

In case of *kshaya* or deficiency or depletion of any *dosha* other than *vayu, brumhan* (nourishing) therapy is advised as a choice. *Langhan* is depletion. *Brumhan* is supplementation therapy. In case of *vayu* the opposite line of therapy is advised.

Rasa vruddhi*: Excess formation of *rasa dhatu

Depletion therapy should be initiated.

Rasa kshaya*: Depletion or loss of *rasa dhatu

Svayoni (substances with similar qualities) cause an increase in (*vardhan*) in similar qualities.

In case of *rakta vruddhi*: Venesection and bloodletting and laxation are the therapies of choice.

***Mamsa vruddhi*:** Surgical, caustic application and thermal treatments are advised.

***Meda vruddhi*:** *Apatarpan* (depletion), fasting, use of thinners are recommended.

***Meda kshaya*:** Supplementation therapy.

***Asthi kshaya*:** In conditions of *kshaya* of *asthi dhatu*, milk and ghee prepared with bitter tasting herbs is advised.

***Shukra vruddhi*:** Intercourse.

***Shukra kshaya*:** Abstain from bitter and spicy foods. Sweet and tasty nutritious foods are advised.

***Ojakshaya*:** *Jeevaneeya* herbs, *e.g.*, *Jivanti*, *etc*., milk and meat soups are advised.

Mala kshaya resulting from diarrhoea**:** Masha (*urad dal)*.

***Mootra kruchra* (dysuria)** and other urinary problems: *Prameha* therapy to be followed.

Why *dhatu vruddhi* and *kshaya* occur

There is a specific *dhwatagni* present in all *dhatus*. If such *agni* becomes weak the dynamic part of the previous *dhatu* fails to transform into the next *dhatu* leading to depletion or *kshaya*.

Vruddhi or increase of a *dhatu* occurs if there is excessive substrate of a particular *dhatu*, which undergoes transformation.

How the disease process sets in

The *rasa dhatu* first gets vitiated by *doshas*. Various irregularities in diet, life style and environment, alter *dosha* balance, impacting *rasadhatu* and other *dhatus* and *malas* as well as the *srotasas,* with the manifestation of different diseases.

Pathogenesis of disease occurs in six phases of *kriya kalas* called:

1. *Chhaya* (Accumulation of *doshas*)
2. *Prokapa* (Excited state of *doshas*)
3. *Prasar* (Spread)
4. *Sthana samshraya* (Localisation of doshas)
5. *Vyakti* (Clinical expression of disease)
6. *Bheda* (Termination)

Vayu

Ushnena yukta rukshaadya vaayo kurvanti sanchayam l

Accumulation of *vayu* is caused by qualities of dryness, *etc*., getting associated with heat.

Sheetena kopam

It is excited and vitiated by coldness.

Ushnena shamam snigdhadayo guna ll

Hot and unctuous qualities pacify vitiated *vayu.* This is called *prasham* or *shaman.*

Pitta

Chhaya or *sanchaya* or accumulation, means increase and accumulation of *doshas* in their own location or site. Qualities that increase *pitta*, described earlier, in conjunction with coolness cause accumulation of *pitta.*

Kopa or *prakop* or aggression, excitement or a vitiated state occurs, due to hot quality, when the *doshas* leave their normal location and spread into the body or enter into circulation (*prasara*) and when these excited *doshas* localise in different *srotasas*, they cause diseases to manifest. *Pitta* becomes vitiated due to hot qualities.

The opposite qualities, *e.g.*, coolness and slowness, etc., correct *pitta*.

Kapha

Qualities of coolness and unctuousness cause accumulation of *kapha*. The hot quality excites the accumulated *kapha*. Dry and hot qualities pacify *kapha*.

Seasons

***Vayu*:** *Greeshma* : **Chaya**. *Varsha* : **Prakop**. *Sharad* : **Prasham**
***Pitta*:** *Varsha* : **Chaya**. *Sharad* : **Prakop**. *Hemant* : **Prasham**
***Kapha*:** *Shishir* : **Chaya**. *Vasanta* : **Prakop**. *Greeshma* : **Prasham**
Apart from the season, the geography, environment, diet, life style, emotions and stress play their role in vitiating the *doshas*.

Pathogenesis of vitiating *doshas*

Asatmya indriyartha samyoga: Improper use of *indriyas* or organs of cognition and conation (organs of action).

There are three types of interactions, namely

Heena: Poor use or disuse.

Ati: Excessive use.

Mithya: Perverse use or misuse.

Time (*kaala*) or the season (*heena*, *ati*, *mithya*) and age.

Karmacha dushkrutam: Bad deeds of the current life or previous lives, (*heena*, *ati*, *mithya*).

Pragnyaparadh: Failure of intellect to decide between right and wrong, which leads to wrong judgments. Wrong judgements lead to wrong actions.

Types of locations of disease production due to *dosha* imbalance

1. *Shakha* (Extremities) 2. *Koshta* (Abdominal cavity) 3. *Asthi* (Bones) 4. *Sandhi* (Joints)

***Shakha gata vyadhis*:** *Rakta*, *mamsa*, *meda* to *shukra* and skin related diseases.

***Koshta marg*:** *Maha srotas* extending from *amaashaya* to *pakwaashaya* based diseases.

Examples are vomiting, diarrhoea, cough, asthma, ascites, fever, oedema, piles, internal tumours, abscess, *etc*.

***Madhyama marga*:** *Marmas* including head, heart, *basti*, *etc*., and joints along with nerves, vessels, tendons, and related diseases. Examples: Tuberculosis, hemiplegia.

How to treat vitiated *doshas*

Vayu

Procedures: Application of oil (*snehan*), oil massage (*abhyagam*), application of dry heat (*seka*), sudation (*svedan*), mild detox (*mrudu samshodhan*), warm, gentle oil, unctuous enemata.

Diet: Cereals with *gur*, sweet, sour, salty, mixed, nutritious foods. Substances that stimulate the appetite (*deepana*), aid digestion (*pachana*) and herbs like those of the *mustadi* group, along with unctuous substances like sesame seed oil, flax seed oil, cow's *ghee* or milk, meat soups and wine.

Lifestyle: Comfortable and restful.

Pitta

***Pancha karma*:** Laxatives with cool and sweet herbs (*swadu sheeta virechanam*).

Oral administration of *ghee* (*pittasya sarpisha paanam*).

Diet: Sweet, bitter, astringent tastes and also herbs of same tastes. Sweet and pleasant perfumes with *karpura*, *chandana* and *usheer* for application on the skin.

Lifestyle: Cool and pleasant environment, acceptable friends sharing joyful moments.

Kapha

Systematically performed strong and acute emesis and purgation (*vidhina yuktam teekshnam vamana rechanam*).

Diet: Small quantities of dry, hot, moderately acute, with spicy, bitter and astringent substances, old wine.

Lifestyle: Excessive interest in sex, staying awake late at night are beneficial to pacify abnormally increased and vitiated *kapha*. Dry massage, anxiety can pacify hyper activity.

The most important therapy for *kapha* is emesis, liquid gruel diet, honey, drugs that are anti *meda dhatu*, hard manual work, medicated smoke and gargling.

Visheshat vamanam yusha kshaudram medoghna aushadhaml dhoomopaseva gandoosha nihsukham sukhayacha ll

Imbalance of more than two *doshas*

In case of *vayu* + *pitta*, the protocol for *greeshma rutu* should be followed, (*greeshme marut pitta*).

In case of *kapha* + *vayu*, the protocol for *vasantha rutu* should be followed, (*vasantha kapha maruta*)

In case of *kapha* + *pitta*, the protocol for *sharad rutu* should be followed, (*kapha pitte tu sharadah*).

Vayu is described as *yoga vaahi* (it affects both *kapha* and *pitta*).

To win over disturbed *doshas*

Stage of accumulation is the right time to act to get results, (*chaya evam jayeddosha*).

When they get vitiated pacification is the only way to act without disturbing the other *doshas*.

When all the *doshas* are vitiated one should try and pacify the most powerful one, without disturbing the others, (*sarva kope baleeyamsam shesha dosha avirodhita*).

Clarifications

If *vata*, *pitta* and *kapha* are equally in a disturbed state, first pacify *vata*.

On the basis of location of the *doshas*, the order of treatment is first *kapha*, then *pitta* and finally *vayu*.

In the case of fever and diarrhoea, the order is first *pitta*, then *kapha* and finally *vayu*.

The *dosha*, which is increased in its *ashay* (organ) should be treated first.

If any treatment gives rise to another disease, it means the treatment is the wrong one.

Difference between *saama* and *niraama doshas*

When the digestive fire is mild in *amashaya*, the very first *dhatu*, *rasa* is improperly formed due to improper digestion and is vitiated by the abnormal doshas. *Aama* is created, which is like poison.

This *aama* further vitiates other *doshas* and causes the vitiation of the other *dhatus* and produces disease.

The right time for detoxification

In month of *Shravan* (July and August, rainy season) *vayu*, *pitta* in *Sharad* (September and October) and *kapha* in the month of *Chaitra* (March and April, *vasanta rutu*).

Swastha vrutta describes in detail the methods to maintain a positive state of health in an individual.

When to administer medicine

1. In case of strong *kapha dosha* the medicine should be administered on an empty stomach.
2. If *apaana vayu* is disturbed drugs should be administered before food.
3. If *samaana vayu* is vitiated drugs should be administered half way through meals.
4. If *udaana vayu* is aggressive, drugs are to be administered post dinner.
5. If *vyaana vayu* is affected the medicine should be administered post breakfast.
6. If *praana vayu* is affected the drug should be mixed with a portion of the food at each meal.
7. In the case of poisoning, vomiting, hiccups, thirst, breathlessness and cough repeated administration of the drug is indicated.
8. In loss of appetite, the drug should be administered, mixed with the food.
9. In case of *kampa*, (tremors), *aakshepa* (epilepsy or convulsions), and hiccups, light (easy to digest) foods such as *moong dal* gruel should be given.
10. In the case of diseases of the head and neck, medication should be given at bedtime.

(Ref. *Ashtanga Hriday Su.* Chapters 11- 14).

Part - IV

Physiopathology of Body Tissues

Chapter : 27

Saptadhatus or Seven Prime Tissue Elements of the Body

Charak has described the human body as being made up of a very large number of microscopic and sub atomic sized (*paramanu*) units. Probably this microscopic biological unit of the body described by Charak represents the smallest living unit of the body, the cell. It is estimated that there are seventy two trillion cells in the human body. Each cell is intelligent and is a complete unit comparable to body. The functions of the different cells, *e.g.*, nerve cells (neurones), liver cells (hepatocytes), heart muscle cells (cardiomyocytes), *etc.*, vary. The cell has all the organs of the body (organelles), which are well defined for various functions. The nucleus is the reproductive organ of the cell. It transmits hereditary information through genes. The cell has a cytoskeleton. The different organs in the cell are called organelles. The cell wall functions like the brain. It is the most functional unit or mind of the cell. Cells communicate with each other and are also capable of locomotion.

The different types of cells form seven important tissue elements that make up the whole structure of the living body (*deha*). The word *deha* is derived from the word *dih*, which means to grow. The term *deha* used for the body signifies anabolism. There is yet another word which is used as synonym to *deha*, *viz.*, *sharir*. *Sharir* is derived from the word *shiryate*, which signifies the action of breaking down into pieces. It signifies ketabolism. A third synonym for the body in Sanskrit is *kaya*. *Kaya* refers to *agni*, it represents the combination of both anabolism and ketabolism, or in other words the entire process of metabolism (C. Dwarkanath). The body is the product of nutrition (*ahara sambhavam vastu*). The function of a *dhatu* is to support (*deha dharanath*) and nourish (*poshanath*) the body. Thus *dhatus* not only form the structure of the body, but also support all the functions in the body. They are seven in number, *viz.*, *rasa*, *rakta*, *mamsa*, *meda*, *asthi*, *majja* and *shukra*.

Dadhaati dhatte vaa shareera mana praanaan iti dhatu l

Dhatu is that, which nourishes and supports the body, mind and life.

Dhadhati dhatte vaa rasa rakta mamsa
medo asthi majja shukra dhaatun iti l

Dhatu is the one that nourishes all the seven *dhatus*.

The ingested food is digested by the *pachakagni* (digestive fire) in the stomach (*jathar*) and intestines. *Pachakagni* is the chief metabolic fire of the body, which is referred to in the *Upanishads* as *garhyapathya vahni*, which constantly and relentlessly keeps on burning. It is the source for all the other types of *agnis*, and all of them are sustained by it. It maintains the body temperature with a set point that is located in the hypothalamus. It splits the complex food substances (starches, fats and proteins) into simple components (glucose, fatty acids and glycerol and amino acids). *Kayaagni*, *dehagni* and *pachaka pitta* are the terms used for this metabolic fire or *agni* that digests food and transforms it into small, simple, absorbable and assimilable unit molecules. Energy in the form of heat is generated through the breakdown of molecular bonds. The body thus, very efficiently produces energy through a combustive mechanism. *Agni* also separates the *kitta* or waste substances from the nutrient part of the ingested food. The seat of *pachakagni* is *agnidhara kala* that is located in *grahani*. This refers to the mucosal layer covering *amashaya*, *pachyamanashaya* and *pakwashaya*. This *kala* secretes all the enzymes, hormones and other secretions for digestion and absorption of food and retains it in the GI tract until the time that the processes of digestion, absorption and assimilation are complete, (*At. Hru. Sha*. 3/49-54).

There are thirteen *agnis* in all in the body. *Agnis* perform different functions. They are located in the five proto-elements and the seven *dhatus*. Those which cause the fragmentation of food substances into basic atoms or particles or *tanmatras* of the proto-elements are called *bhutagnis*. They also help in converting the atoms into molecules that aid in the formation of cells and tissues, help growth and reproduction and thus sustain the tissues or *dhatus*. Thus the concept of *agni* forms the basic molecular biochemistry of the body. In other words this metabolic fire, through the process of combustion, breaks the atomic bonds in food and releases the energy necessary for forming the substrate for development of different tissues. These tissues are constantly formed to replace the degenerated, senile and dead tissues in continuous metabolic processes. Therefore *dhatus* are found in two states. The first state is called *poshak*, that which constantly nourishes the *dhatu* to help its formation and sustenance. The other is *poshya*, that which helps to maintain or sustain the form and function of the *dhatu*. The seven *dhatwagnis*, representing each of the *dhatus* help in the bio-conversion of *dhatus* from one into the other as will be described later. Thus all the *dhatus* are maintained in a state of dynamic equilibrium in a healthy individual. Equilibrium or homeostasis of all the *doshas*, *dhatus*, *agni* and *malas* is a requisite for a healthy person as per Ayurvedic conceptualization.

Sushruta states that, the *dehaagni* causes *ayu* (life span), *varna* (colour and complexion), *bala* (strength), *swasthya* (health), *utsaha* (zeal), *upachaya* (nourishment), *prabha* (radiance), *ojus* (immune strength), *teja* (brilliance) and *agni* (fire). Following the digestion of four different types of foods, the nutritious portion is absorbed in the intestine and is assimilated into the *rasa* and *rudhira* (blood) as *anna rasa* or chyle. From this *anna rasa* the *rasa dhatu* is formed, which is the first of the seven *dhatus*. *Rasadhatu* is the substrate for all the following six *dhatus*. *Rasa*, *rakta*, *mamsa*, *meda*, *asthi*, *majja* and *shukra* are the *sapta* (seven) *dhatus*. What is not absorbed is thrown out of the GI tract as waste (*kitta*) or faeces (*mala shakrut*) and urine (*mootra*). Vitiated *agnis* affect the *doshas*, *dhatus* and *malas* adversely and cause diseases.

The four functional states of *agni*

Mandagni

Durbalo vidahtyatrannam tadyat urdhwam adhopi vaa
(l Cha.Chi. 51)

Weak digestive fire causes acid peptic disorder, vomiting and/or diarrhoea. Due to the dominance of *kapha*, *pachakagni* is inhibited, leading to very poor digestion.

Teekshnagni

Teekshnam manda indhano dhatoon vishoshayati l
(Cha. Chi. 35/50)

Unduly excited digestive fire causes wasting of tissues in cases of poor nourishment. It is a condition, where the *agni* is highly excited due to *pitta* affliction, in which a person has excessive hunger without satiety. Such a person has frequent meals, has a parched mouth and feels thirsty. It results in a condition called *bhasmaka*.

Vishamagni

Vishamo dhatu vaishamyam karoti vishamam pachan l
(Cha. Chi. 35/50)

Erratic digestive fire afflicts and vitiates the *dhatus*. Fitful and erratic *agni* is due to affliction of *vata*. It causes intestinal colic, abdominal distension, constipation, diarrhoea, dysentery, ascites, and heaviness in the limbs.

Sama agni

Yuktam bhuktavato yukto samyam samam pachan l
(Cha. Chi. 35/51)

Normally functioning *agni* ensures proper digestion of the ingested food and brings about a state of equilibrium of all the three doshas resulting in homeostasis.

Ama and *saama*

Due to poor strength of *agni*, *annarasa* (digested chyle) undergoes fermentation and putrefaction, resulting in stasis of the *rasa* in the *amashaya*. Such a *rasa dhatu* is called *aama*. The formation of *rasa dhatu* in itself is primarily abnormal, (*Ashtang. Hru. Su.* 13/25). Impaired *vata*, *pitta* and *kapha* also result in *ama dosha*. *Ama* is described to be like poison or a toxic substance (*visha*) similar to spoilt *kodrava*.

Causes of *ama* formation (*Charaka* in *Chi.* 15/42-44)

In all the following conditions, *viz*., starvation (*abhojan*), indigestion (*ajeernam*), excessive eating (*atibhojan*), irregular eating habits (*vishamaashana*), eating incompatible foods (*vishamaashan*), consumption of heavy to digest food articles, cold, dry spoilt foods (*guru sheeta atiruksha dushta bhojanat*), following emesis (*vamana*), purgation (*virechana*), oleation (*snehana*), excessive weight loss or wasting (*vyadhi karshanath*) diseases, abnormal environments and climates (*desha kala rutu vaishamyam*) and suppression of natural bodily urges (*vega vidharana*), a person is unable to digest even easily digestible foods. The result is improperly digested food, which gets fermented (*shuktatwa*) and acts like a poison or toxic substance (*visha roopatam*). This is how *aama* is generated resulting in a number of diseases (*saama vyaadhi*).

Many are of the opinion that in the first stage of inflammation (*kriyakala*), the *dosha dushti* is due to *aama dosha*. *Dosha* vitiated *aama* afflicts *dhatus* and *malas*, resulting in diseases. These diseases are called *saama*, (*Asht. Hru. Su.* 8/13-14).

Saama rogas*: Diseases due to *aama rasa dosha

Fever (*Jwara*), loose motions (*atisara*) and dysentery (*pravahika*) are some acute conditions of *saama dosha*. Chronic disease conditions caused by *aama* are irritable bowels (*grahani*), hepatitis, cirrhosis and ascites (*udara*), generalized oedema (*shotha*), anaemia (*pandu*), urinary diseases and diabetes (*prameha* and *madhumeha*), rheumatoid conditions (*aamavata*). Most of the fore mentioned diseases are considered to be bacterial in origin according to current medicine. Are the microbes the true cause of the diseases? Maybe not.

We now know that the human body is a meta-organism, where microbes are equal partners. Gut microbiome is currently a hot new research subject, which is developing new dimensions in modern medicine. The gut is host to billions of microbes, whose volume of DNA is far in excess of human specific DNA, providing another additional information transfer system of signalling. Many of the gut bacteria function as benefactors to humans in terms of digestion of food substances, producing beneficial and vital vitamins, *e.g.*, Vitamin B-complex and Vitamin K, *etc.* It is observed that characteristics of bacteria vary with different diets. Microbiome of a vegetarian person is different from that of a non-vegetarian. Thus eating habits have an important bearing on disease. *Mandagni* or *vishamagni* probably represent the altered character of microbiome, wherein normal bacteria mutate and become pathogenic, setting up infection with formation of toxic matter generated by bacteria aiding fermentation and putrefaction (*aama*), creating inflammatory processes. We can now see that the primary cause of many infectious diseases is due to normal, non-pathogenic bacteria becoming pathogenic in character. Thus the character of digestive fire is important in the causation of disease.

Chapter : 28

Different Body Tissues and Kalas

How different tissues of the body are formed according to Sushruta

The outer most layer of the body is the skin, which has seven layers.

Agni soma vayuh satwam rajastamah pancha indriyaani bhootaatma iti praanah l

Tatra khalu esham pravruttasya shukrashonitasya abhipachyamaanasya kshirasyeva santaanikak sapta twacho bhavanti l (Su. Sha. 4/3-4)

We have already seen that *prana* is a combination of the soul, *agni*, water, air and mind and its three qualities, coding and processing of information and five senses. When it enters into the union of male and female gametes, the skin (*twacho*) with seven layers develops just like a thick crust (layer of butter) develops after boiling milk. Each of the layers is of a thickness less than the size of a grain of rice. Different diseases originate from the different layers. Interestingly, modern medicine also describes seven microscopic layers of the skin.

1. ***Avabhaasini*:** It gives the skin a glow and imparts different shades of colour. *Sidhma* (cloasma) and *padmakantak* are the diseases associated with this layer.
2. ***Lohita*:** Diseases such as *tila*, *kaalaka*, *nyaccha* and *vyanga* originate from this layer.
3. ***Shweta*:** *Charma dal*, *ajagallika* and *mashak* originate from this layer.
4. ***Taamra*:** *Kilaasa* (leucoderma) and *kushta* are the diseases associated with this layer.
5. ***Vedini*:** *Kushta* (skin diseases including leprosy) and *visarpa* (erysipelas) are the diseases associated with this layer.
6. ***Rohini*:** *Granthi*, *apachi* and *arbuda* are the diseases associated with this layer.
7. ***Mamsa dhara*:** Fistula, abscesses and piles originate from here.

Sushruta describes seven *kalas* or membranous layers that define the limits of several *dhatus* or organs.

Kalaah khalu api sapta bhavanti dhatu aashayaantara maryaada l

(Su. Sha. 4/5)

Yathaa hi saarah kaashteshu chidyamaaneshu drushyate l
Tathahi dhatur mamseshu chidyamaaneshu drushyate ll

Snayubhishcha praticchannan santatamshcha jarayunaa l
Shleshmanaa veshtitaamcha api kalabhagaamstu taam vidu ll
(Su. Sha. 4/6-7)

When wood is cut, its inner core is visualized. In the same way when the muscle is cut the *dhatus* (*rasa* and *rakta*) become visible. The unctuous membranous structures covered by muscles and tendons are defined as *kalas*.

***Mamsa dhara kala*:** In this *kala*, *shira*, *snayu*, *dhamani* and *srotasas* and their extensions are present. (*Shira snayu dhamanee srotasam prataana bhavanti*).

***Rakta dhara*:** It is within the muscle tissue. It is mainly blood and veins or vessels and also the liver and spleen. (S*honitam visheshashcha shirasu yakrut pleehoshcha*).

***Meda dhara*:** It is present in the abdomen and small bones all over the body. The fat in the long bones is called *majja*. (*Medo hi udarastham manwasthishu, mahatsu cha majja bhavati*). The small bones contain red marrow or *sarakta meda*. The lipoid content of the muscle is called *vasa*.

***Shleshma dhara*:** This is present in all the joints. It lubricates and helps the mobility of the joints.

***Purisha dhara*:** The fifth *kala* is the one that is present in *pakwashaya*. It holds the faeces formed after absorption of the digested food. It is placed below the liver in the abdominal cavity where the division between the absorbed and waste matter for excretion occurs.

***Pitta dhara*:** Four types of ingested food are digested in the stomach and intestine, from *aamashaya* to *pakwashaya*. On account of it being the location of *pitta*, the food is digested by its fire and absorbs the nutrition from the food. This layer that holds the *pitta* is called *pittadhara kala*.

***Shukra dhara*:** It pervades the whole body. Just as *ghee* is an integral part of milk and *gur* is an integral part of sugarcane, so is *shukra dhatu* present all over the body.

Chapter : 29

Srotas

Sravanat srotamsi l (Cha. Sutra. 30/12)

Sravana literally means secreting, oozing and transuding.

Srotas are the channels or spaces that transudate, secrete, exude and store the various secretions. They circulate and transport the substances that participate in a number of biological processes, nourish and sustain all the body elements. They have different sizes and shapes, varying from subtle and small (even microscopic), to intermediate and large in size and are tubular or reticular. Usually they are of the same colour as the substance they carry. The human body is indeed a bundle of circulating channels. They carry all the *dhatus*, *malas* and *doshas*. The *manovaha srotas* circulate consciousness, intelligence and perceptions of all sensory and motor types. Health of the *srotas* is very important. Any obstruction or abnormality in them leads to causation of disease, (*Cha. Vim.* 5). Therefore all the biological and metabolic processes are dependent on the health of the *srotas*. Thus man is a bundle circulatory channels.

Swadhatu sama varnani vrutta sthoola anooni cha l
Srotamsi deerghani aakrutyaa prataana sadrushani cha ll
(Cha. Vim. 5/25)

Channels (*srotamsi*), veins (*sira*), arteries (*dhamani*), ducts (*rasayanya*), capillaries (*rasa vahini*), tubes *(naadi)*, passages (*panthaanah*), tracts (*marga*), pores (*chidra*), glands (*samvruta samvrutani*), cystic cavities (*aashaya*), organs of storage (*niketa*), storage spaces for different *dhatus* *(dhatwavakaasha)* are all varieties of *srotas*.

Some of the important organ systems are enumerated as *srotas*. These organ systems do not strictly fit into the anatomical descriptions of organs. Ayurvedic anatomy is more functional.

The thirteen types of *srotas*

Praana udaka anna rasa rudhira mamsa meda asthi
majja shukra mootra pureesha sweda vahaan iti; vata pitta
shleshmanaam punah sarva shareera charaanaam sarvaani
srotamsi ayanabhootaani, tadvat ateendriyaanaam punah
satwaadeenam kewalam chetanavat shareeram
ayanabhootam adhishtana bhootam cha l
(Cha. Vim. 5/6-2)

Prana (life force), *udaka* (water), *anna* (food), *rasa* (plasma), *rudhira* (blood), *mamsa (muscle), meda (adipose tissue), asthi (bone)*, *majja* (marrow), *shukra* (semen), *mootra* (urine), *pureesha* (faeces), *sweda* (sweat) flow through different and specific channels or *srotas*. Whereas *vata*, *pitta* and *kapha* circulate all over the body and along every channel. The intellect and mind, being supra-sensorial traverse throughout a sentient individual.

Prana vaha srotas

Tatra praanavahanam srotasaam hrudayam moolam mahasrotascha l

Pradushtanaam tu khalu esham idam vishesha vigyanam bhavati l Ati srushtam ati baddham kupitam alpaalpam abheekshanam va sashabda shoolam uchwasantam drushtwa praanavahanyasya srotamsi pradushtaani iti vidyaat ll (Cha. Vim. 5/7)

The central thoracic cavity encloses the heart and the roots of all the main channels that carry the life breath (*prana*). When this *srotas* gets dilated, afflicted or obstructed, it can cause severe pain and difficult, prolonged, torturous and noisy respiration.

Tatra praana vahe dwe, tayor moolam hrudayam rasa vaahinyascha (praana vahinyascha) dhamnyah, Tatra viddhasya aakroshana vinamana mohana brhamana vepanaaani maranam va bhavati l (Su. Sha. 9/12)

According to Sushruta the two main roots of *prana vaha srotas* are the heart and the arteries, or pulsating vessels that carry nutrient plasma. Injury to them cause unbearable pain (to such an extent that a person may cry out and shout), syncope (falling unconscious), confusion, giddiness, tremors and even death.

In earlier chapters we have discussed in detail about how *prana* is the force that sustains life. It is the result of multiple biological processes conducted by the various systems of the body. This includes the respiratory, cardiovascular and alimentary systems. Respiration is thoracico-abdominal in nature, where the diaphragm plays a very important part. Nutrition provided through the porto-caval system is very important for sustaining *prana*. Thus *pranavaha srotas* is not limited to the respiratory system alone as is normally understood by Ayurveda practitioners.

Udaka vaha srotas

Udaka vahanaam srotasaam taalu moolam klomam cha, pradushtanaam tu khalu eshaam idam vishesha vigyaanam bhavati; tad yatha – jivha talu oshta kantha kloma shosham pipaasa cha atipravruddhaam drushtwodaka vahaanyasya srotaamsi pradushtaaneeti vidyat l (Cha. Vim. 5/8-1)

This *srotas* that carries the aqueous element in the body extends from the palate to kloma. When afflicted it gives rise to the following signs and symptoms: Unquenchable thirst with drying of the tongue, palate, lips, throat and kloma. The location of the kloma is yet undetermined. It is probably an organ or location connected with fluid balance in the body. It could be the lungs, as the lungs are important in relation to the fluid balance in the body.

Udaka vahe dwe, tayor moolam taalu klomam cha, tatra viddhasya pipaasa syavaangata sadyo maranam cha l (Su. Su. 9/12)

The two sources of the channels carrying water in the body are the palate and kloma (? lungs). If any injury occurs to these parts, it will lead to excessive, insatiable thirst, cyanosis of the body and instant death, (Sushruta). Dehydration and hypovolemia are the result.

Anna vaha srotas

Aamashayo moolam vaamam cha parshwam, pradushtaanaam tu khalvesham idam vishesha vigyaanam bhavati; anannaabhilashanam arochakam avipakau chardim cha l (Cha. Vim. 5/8-2)

The channels that carry ingested food present in the regions of *aamaashaya* (stomach) and the left side of the abdomen are known as *anna vaha srotas*. Any morbidity afflicting this channel leads to loss of appetite (anorexia), loss of taste for food articles, indigestion or dyspepsia and vomiting.

Anna vahe dwe, tayor moolam amashayo anna vahinyashcha dhamanya, tatra viddhasya aadhmaanam shoolo annadwesha chardhih pipaasa aandhyam and maranam cha l (Su. Su. 9/12)

The two sources of the channels carrying food are *aamashaya* and the channels and vessels that carry nutrition in the body. Injury to either of them causes distension of the abdomen and colicky pain, anorexia, vomiting, thirst, syncope and even death.

Rasa vaha srotas

Rasa vahaanaam srotasaam hrudayam moolam dasha cha dhamanyah l (Cha. Vim. 5/8-3)

The heart and the ten large, pulsating vessels *(dhamani)* comprise *rasavaha srotas.*

Rasa vahe dwe, tayor moolam hrudayam rasa vahinyashcha dhamanyah. Tatra viddhasya shoshah praana vaha viddhavachya maranaani l (Su. Su. 9/12)

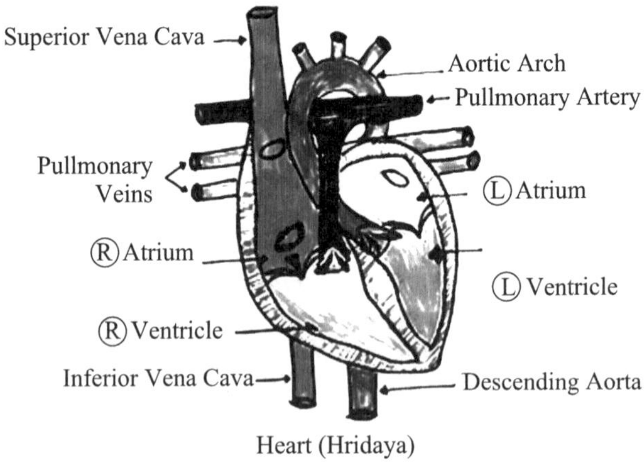

Illustration of heart with main vessels

The heart and vessels that carry nutrient fluid are the roots of this *srotas*. When injured it causes wasting and all the signs of injury seen in the *prana vaha srotas*, *i.e.*, severe pain and difficult, prolonged, torturous and noisy respiration, and even death.

Rakta vaha srotas circulate the blood all over the body through arteries, and the organs that form this *srotas* are the liver and spleen.

Shonita vahanaam srotasaam yakrut moolam pleehaa cha l
(Cha. Vim. 5/8-3)

Rakta vahe dwe, tayor moolam yakrut pleehaanau rakta vahinyashcha dhamnyah, tatra viddhasya shyavangata jwaro dahah paanduta shonita gamanam rakta netrata l
(Su. Su. 9/12)

The liver, spleen and blood vessels are the roots of this *srotas*. Injury to them cause cyanosis, anaemia, fever, thirst, and bleeding from different sites in the body, including the eye.

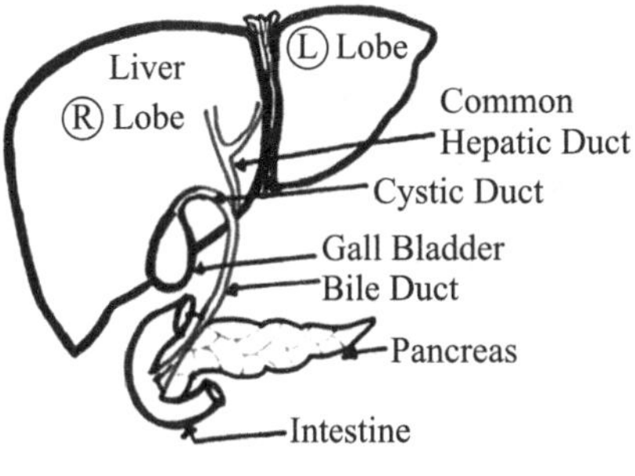

Liver / Gall Bladder / Pancreas
(Yakrit, Pittashay, Pleeha)

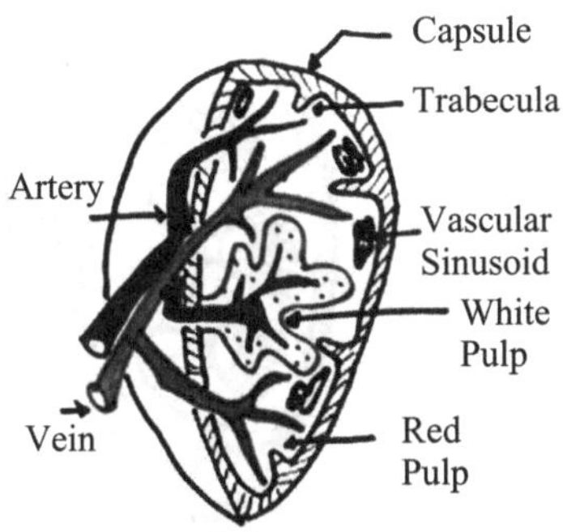

Spleen
(Pleeha)

Mamsa vaha srotas

Illustration of liver and spleen

These consist of muscles and skin.

Mamsa vahaanaam cha srotasaam snayurmoolam twak cha l
(Cha. Vim. 5/8-3)

Mamsa vahe dwe, tayor moolam snayu twacham rakta vahashcha dhamnyah, tatra viddhasya shwayathu maamsa soshah sira granthayo maranam cha l (Su. Su. 9/12)

The fibrous membrane covering the muscle and the channels that flow into muscle cells are the two roots of this *srotas*. When injured it can cause generalized oedema of the body, wasting of muscles, swelling or varicosity of the veins and even death, (Sushruta).

Medo vaha srotas

These consist of the kidneys (*vrukka*) and omentum (*vapa vaha*).

Medo vahaanaam srotasaam vrukkau moolam vapavhanam cha l (Cha. Vim. 5/8-3)

Medo vahe dwe, tayor moolam kati vrukkau cha, tatra viddhasya swedaagamanam snigdhangata talu soshah sthoolata shophah pipaasasaa cha l (Su. Su. 9/12)

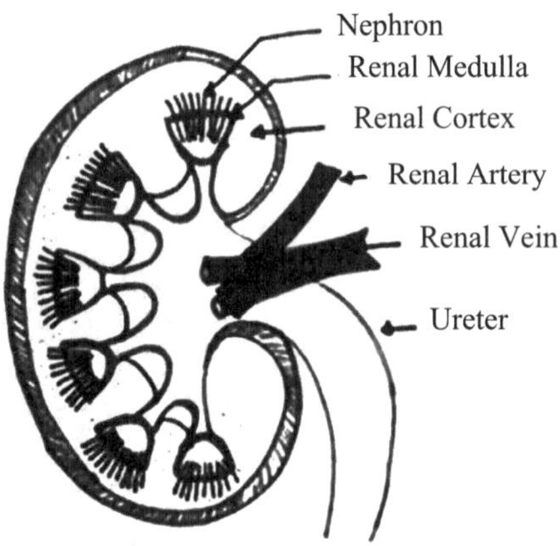

KIDNEY (Mootravaha Srotas)

Illustration of kidney

Both the kidneys and the omentum are the roots of *medo vaha srotas*. When injured they can cause excessive sweating, soft body parts, dryness of the palate, obesity, oedema and thirst. The suprarenal (adrenal) glands are probably part of *vrukka*, and should be considered.

Asthi vaha srotas

These consist of fat, the buttocks and thighs.

Asthi vahaanaam srotasaam medo moolam jaghanam cha l (Cha. Vim. 5/8-3)

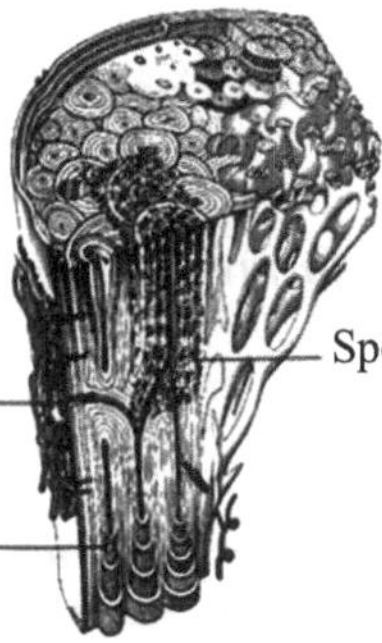

Structure of Bone

Majja vaha srotas

Illustration of bone

These comprise the bones and joints.

Majja vahaanaam srotasaam astheeni moolam sandhayascha l
(Cha. Vim. 5/8-3)

Shukra vaha srotus

These comprise the testes and penis.

Shukra vahanaam srotasaam vrushanau moolam shophascha l
(Cha. Vim. 5/8-3)

Another version from *Sushruta*, is:

Shukra vahe dwe, tayor moolam stanau vrushanau, tatra viddhasya kleebata, chira praseko rakta shukrata cha l (Su. Su. 9/12)

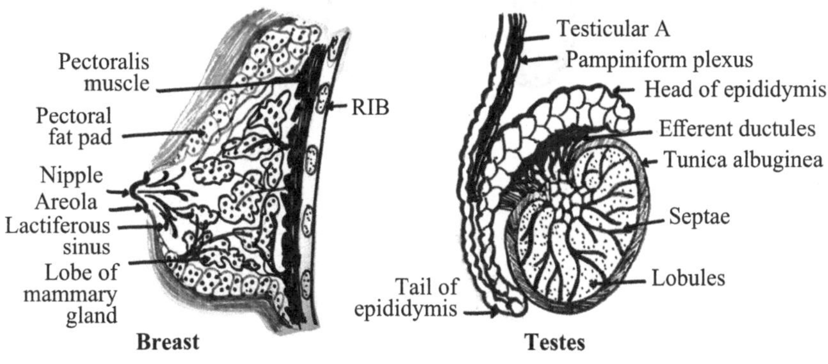

Illustration of breasts and testes

The breasts and testes are the two roots of this *srotas*. Injury to them can cause impotency, delayed ejaculation or total ejaculation failure and hemospermia.

Aartava vaha srotas

This is not described by *Charaka*. *Sushruta* gives the following description.

Aatrava vahe dwe, tayor moolam garbhaashaya aartava vaahinyashcha dhamanyah, tatra viddhayaam vandhyatwàm maithuna asahishnutwam aartava naashashascha l (Su. Su. 9/12)

The two main sites of *aartav* are the uterus and the channels that transport the female gametes. If they sustain injury, it will lead to sterility or infertility, dyspareunia and menopause.

Mootra vaha srotas

These comprise both the loins and the bladder. If it is afflicted, it gives rise to symptoms of polyuria, frequency of micturition and dysuria, incontinence, turbid urine, *etc*.

Mootra vahaanaam srotasaam bastirmoolam vankshnaucha l (Cha. Vim. 5/8-3)

Mootra vahe dwe, tayor moolam basti medhram cha, tatra viddhasya baddha vastita mootra nirodhah stabda medhrataa cha l (Su. Su. 9/12)

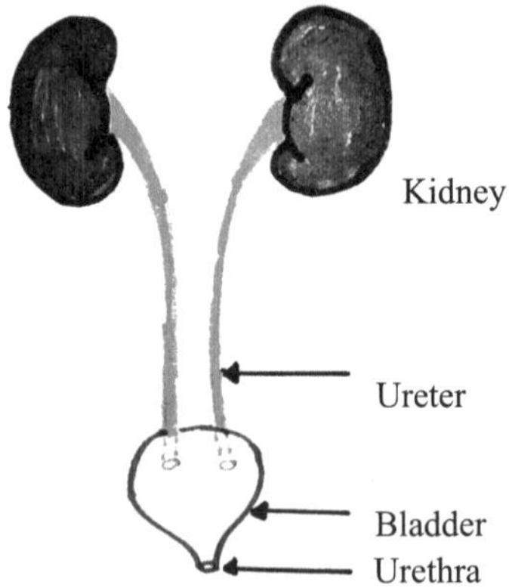

Illustration of urinary tract

The bladder and penis are the two main sites of *mootra vaha srotas*. Injury to them causes retention of urine with bladder distension and loss of sensation for micturition leading to incontinence.

Pureesha vaha srotas

This comprises *pakwashaya* (colon) and *guda* (rectum and anal canal). Any affliction to it causes pain and difficulty in passing stools, constipation, hard or watery stools with passage of noisy wind, *etc*.

Pureesha vahaanam srotasaam pakwashayo moolam sthoola gudam cha, pradushtaanam –kruchrena alpaalpam sa shabda shoolam ati drava atigrathitam atibahu cha upavishantam l (Cha. Vim. 5/8-3)

Pureesha vahe dwe, tayor moolam pakwashayo gudam cha, tatra viddhasya aanaho durgandhata grathitantrata l (Su. Su. 9/12)

Injury to this *srotas* causes abdominal distension, a foul odour and hard impacted stools in the colon.

Sweda vaha srotas

The channels carrying sweat or perspiration comprise fat and hair follicles (*loma koopa*). When afflicted it causes anhydrosis, hyper hydrosis, rough skin or excess soft skin, a burning sensation and horripilation.

Sweda vahaanam srotasaam medo moolam loma koopashcha l

Pradushtaanam ---- aswedam atiswedanam paarushyam atishlashnatam angasya paridaham loma harsham ll (Cha. Vim. 5/8)

How the *srotas* get afflicted and vitiated

Teshaam prakopaat sthanaasthaschaiva margaascha shareera dhaatavah prakopam aapadyante, itareshaam prakopaaditaraani cha l

Srotaamsi srotaamsyeva, dhaatavashcha dhaatunaiva pradushayanti pradushtah l teshaam sarveshaameva vata pitta shleshmanah pradushta dooshayitaaro bhavanti, dosha swabhavat iti ll (Cha. Vim. 5/9)

On account of their natural behaviour, when the *doshas* get vitiated, they afflict and vitiate the *srotas* that are obstructed or disturbed and also the *dhatus* while in their original site or even while being transported. The vitiated *strotas* and *dhatus* further vitiate other *srotas* and *dhatus* to establish the disease. In an earlier chapter we have shown that any obstruction to the flow of substances in channels aids accumulation and vitiation of *doshas*. Infections can take hold only if the *srotas* (spaces) are devitalised, either due to obstruction or vitiation, not otherwise. Thus *srotodushti* is the first phase in causing any infection or inflammation.

Common signs of *stroto dushti*

Ati pravrutta sango va siraanaam granthiyo api vaa l
Vimarga gamanam chaapi srotasam dusti lakshanam ll
(Cha. Vim. 5/24)

Signs of vitiated *srotas* are excessive secretion or flow, obstruction to the passage of secretions forming a mass or a cyst, or reverse flow of the secretions.

Chapter : 30

Pranayatanan and Marma

We have earlier described *prana* (life force) in detail. We now learn about its chief locations in the body. These locations are called *pranayatanas* (resorts of life force). The attributes or characteristics of *prana* are *agni*, *soma*, *vayu*, *satwa*, *rajas*, *tamas*, the five sense organs, *bhoota* (*pancha mahabhoota*) and *atma* (soul). It circulates all over the body through *naadis*. *Agni* represents *pitta*, *soma* represents *kapha* and *vayu* represents *vata dosha*. It has been discussed earlier that *prana* is life.

Dasha praanaayatanaani; Tad yathaa Moordhaa, kantha, hrudayam, naabhih, gudam, Basti, ojah, shukram, shonitam, Mamsam iti l teshu shat poorvani marma samkhyatani ll (Cha. Shar. 7/9)

There are ten vital locations or centres of the life force.

Moordha (Head) 2. *Kantha* (Throat) 3. *Hrudaya* (Heart) 4. *Naabhi* (Umbilicus) 5. *Gudam* (Anal region) 6. *Basti* (Bladder & urinary system) 7. *Ojah* (Vital essence or immune potential) 8. *Shukram* (Semen) 9. *Shonitam* (Blood), 10. *Mamsam* (Muscle tissue). Of these the first six are called *marmas*. *Marmas* when injured can end up in death.

Shankhau marma trayam kantho raktam shukram ojasi guadm ll (Cha. Su. 29/7)

Charaka in *Sutra Sthana* defines the head as the temporal region (*shankham*). The three *marmas*, mean, *hruday*, *basti* and *nabhi* are described as *marmatrayam*.

Dasha jeevita dhaamaani shiro, rasana bandhanam l kantho, asram, hrudayam, nabhi, bastih, shukra, ojasi, gudam ll (Ashtang Hru. Sha. 3/13)

Vagbhata also describes ten resorts of life. He defines the throat as being of two parts, one at the root of the tongue, and the other simply the throat. *Mamsa dhatu* is missing in the ten *pranayatanas*. The ten main arteries and veins are also considered as *pranayatanas*.

Marma

Sushruta defines *marma* as a junction where *mamsa* (muscles), *sira* (blood vessels), *snayu* (tendons), bones and joints meet. Since any injury to this location, which is very vital and leads to death (*maran*), it is called *marma*. There are one hundred seven *marmas* in number.

Maranaat marma l

Causative factors of disease

Arthanam (indriyartha) karmanah kaalasya cha atiyoga ayoga mithya yogah l (Cha. Su. 11/36)

Over indulgence, disuse and misuse of the senses and their objects and activities performed at the wrong time, are the three causes for all diseases.

Definition of health

Sama doshah sama agnishcha sama dhatu mala kriyah l
Prasanna aatma indriya manaah swastha ityabhi dheeyate ll
(Su. Su. 15/48)

A person is said to be healthy when *dosha*, *agni*, the seven *dhatus* and excreta are in functional homeostasis and *atma*, mind and the organs of sense and action are calm and peaceful together.

In my opinion this is the best definition of health. Thus it is seen that if there is harmony, it results in happiness and good health is happiness.

Disease

Rogastu dosha vaishamyam roga samyam arogata l
Vikaro dhatu vaishamyam l sukhanaam karanam samah ll

Roga (diseases) are due to disharmony or imbalance of *doshas*. Health and happiness are when the *doshas* are in equilibrium. Even the affliction of *dhatus* cause diseases.

Swasthasya rakshanam kuryat

Aswasthsyatu buddhiman l kshayet brumhyet
chapi dosha dhatu malaan bhishak l
Tavat yaavat rogah syat evat saatmasya lakshanam ll
(Su.Su. 15/47)

It is necessary to protect a healthy person from disease. An intelligent Vaidya should increase depleted *dosha*, *dhatu* and *mala* in a diseased person and *vice versa*, in all cases until a proper balance is achieved, which will lead to the person becoming healthy again.

Chapter : 31

Rasa Dhatu

Rasa dhatu

Rasa dhatu is formed by the action of *jatharagni*, which forms *annaras* or the chyle. *Rasa dhatu* is metabolized by its own *agni*. It takes about one day to form. It circulates throughout the whole body through vessels called *rasa vahinis*, *srotasas* (capillaries) and *siras*. It is located in the heart and vasculature, and it circulates throughout the entire body through blood vessels, capillaries and the lymphatic system. Its volume is nine *anjalies* (1 *anjali* = half a litre), (Ref. *Charak Sh.* 7/15).

Yat drava sara manda snigdha pitchilam rasa rudhira tadaapyam l (Charak)

Preenanam, snehanam, dharanam, rakta pushti l (Sushruta)

Its functions are to provide *preenanam* (a sense of satisfaction or happiness), *snehan* (oleation), *dharan* (up holding or preservation), *tarpan* (nutrition), *jivan* (life promotion/haemopoetic), *tushti* (satiation), *dhatu poshan* (nourishing all the *dhatus*). Erythropoiesis or generation of *rakta dhatu* and providing a sense of gratification are the two most important functions of *rasa*. Its physical qualities are *drava* (liquidity), *sara* (flowing nature or fluidity), and *manda* (flowing slowly), *snigdha* (unctuous) and *pitchila* (viscous). The word *rasa* is derived from *sara*, which signifies the flowing motion, (Ref. *Suhrut Su.* 14/13).

Kapha dosha is believed to be the by-product of the metabolism of *rasa dhatu*. It is also described as *mala* of *rasa dhatu*. Many persons equate this *mala kapha* to the mucus secretions from the various tissues of the body, probably because of the fact that secretions from the organs or tissues flow out. *Kapha dosha* is the outcome of digestion at the level of *aamashaya*. *Rasa* and *kapha dosha* have many similar properties and functions.

Twak saara

Saara of any dhatu refers to its robust and vibrant state. Ayurveda describes the signs of each *dhatu saara*. But there is no description of *rasa saara*. The condition of the skin mirrors the health or robustness of *rasa dhatu*. Thus *rasa saara* is called *twak saara*. Persons with *twak saara* are very pleasant and have a radiant complexion, and soft and luxuriant hair. According to Dalhana, the health of the skin and its thickness are indicators of the nutrition and quality of *rasa dhatu*. Therefore examination of the skin is essential to infer the health of *rasa dhatu*. The skin is the largest tissue of the body. *Twak saara* signifies a perfect state of skin health. Clinical features of a *twak saara purush* are unctuousness, smoothness, softness, radiance and appropriate skin thickness, covered with short, deep rooted and delicate hair, full of lustre. (*Charak Viman Sthan.* 8.113). A *twak saara* person is happy, fortunate, powerful, pleasant, intelligent, knowledgeable, healthy, and cheerful with a long life span.

Rasa vriddhi

Rasopi shleshma vat l (Asht. Hr. Su. 11/7)

Rasa is similar to *kapha* in all its qualities or attributes. Therefore, excess of *rasa* produces the same symptoms as increased *kapha dosha*. It causes poor digestion, excess salivation, lassitude, and a feeling of heaviness, white decolouration of faeces, cold and slack body parts, dyspnoea, cough and excess sleep, (*Asht. Hr. Su.*11/7). *Rasa vriddhi* is associated with excessive fluid retention, both intra and extra cellular, lymphedema and localized or generalized oedema.

Rasa kshaya

Ghattate sahate shabdam noschairdravati shoolyate l

Hrudayam taamyati swalpa chestasya rasakshaye ll (Cha. Su. 17/64)

Excessive loss of nutrient body fluids (deficient *rasa dhatu*) results in hypovolemic shock, *e.g.*, severe diarrhoea or vomiting. *Rasa kshaya* can also occur due to severe under or mal nourishment. The symptoms of *rasa kshaya* are restlessness, intolerance to loud sounds, dryness, fatigue, emaciation, exhaustion, a fast pulse, and pain and distress even on the slightest exertion, (*Cha. Su.*17/64, *As. Hr. Su.* 11/17).

Rasa dushti: Vitiation of rasa dhatu

Whenever we use the term *dushti*, it means there is a qualitative change, which is abnormal in form and function. In *rasa dushti*, the following symptoms are seen: Disinclination for food, anorexia, disguesia, aguesia (loss of taste), nausea, heaviness, torpor, fever with body ache, anaemia (pallor), obstruction of the channels, impotency, asthenia, wasting of the body, poor gastric fire, and premature ageing (wrinkles and greying of hair), (*Cha. Su.* 28/9 & 10). Examples are acute infections, bacteraemia, toxaemia and chronic inflammatory conditions. Let us see how this knowledge from Ayurveda compares to the various body fluids that circulate in the body.

Blood plasma: This is a light yellow fluid. It is obtained after removing all the solid elements from the blood. Its specific gravity is 1.015 - 1.035. The water content of plasma is approximately 90%. Its constituents are both water soluble and water dispersible. The chief functions of plasma, apart from providing nutrition are maintaining water regulation, heat regulation, blood pressure and osmotic regulation. Because of its high specific heat as well as conductivity and latent evaporation properties, by evaporation through the skin and lungs, it helps the body to lose a lot of heat. Proteins, *viz.*, albumin (55%), globulin (40%), fibrinogen (5%) form the solid constituents of plasma. The liver (*amaashay*) is the site where albumin, fibrinogen, prothrombin, and 80% of the globulins are formed. Plasma albumins are important in the transport of fatty acids, bilirubin and certain drugs, *e.g.*, sulphonamides. They also possess great buffering property, as well as having a nutritive effect. The plasma globulins also share these functions as well as the immune function. Gamma globulins are formed in the cells of the lymphatic tissue. The antibodies are modified gamma globulins. Therefore they are also called immunoglobulins. It is for this reason that Ayurveda considers that vitiation of *rasa dhatu* results in fever, (*Sush. Su.* 28/9). The plasma proteins are continuously catabolised or broken down, and simultaneously the rebuilding process keeps pace through anabolism, to maintain constant levels of plasma proteins and achieve a dynamic equilibrium. Many proteins are globulin in nature. They play a very important role in physiology, *viz.*, erythropoietin, ceruloplasmin, transferrin, HDL, LDL. These are mainly glycoproteins or lipoproteins. Amino acids in the diet are very important for the rapid regeneration of plasma proteins. A low protein diet, fasting, haemorrhage, plasma depletion due to any other cause results in decreased levels of plasma proteins. The site of degradation of plasma proteins is also probably the lumen of the intestine. The half-life of plasma proteins is about 10 days. At least 7-14 days are required for their complete regeneration. Other constituents of plasma are amino acids, smaller peptides, glucose, lipids, lactic acid, citric and other organic acids, ketone bodies, nitrogen waste products, pigments, inorganic salts and a small amount of enzymes, vitamins and hormones. The concentration of glucose is approximately 0.1%. Amino acids, lipids and glucose vary in amounts with the state of digestion and nutrition. All the three components increase after meals, reach a high point, later level off and then fall. Lipids of plasma are fatty acids, phospholipids, cholesterol and its esters. Most lipids are bound as beta-lipoproteins. Lactic acid and ketone bodies are also present in small amounts. Nitrogen waste products result from the breakdown of proteins, purines and other organic substances including urea and uric acid. Creatinine is also present in minute quantities. Carotene, bile pigments are present in traces. The positive inorganic ions in plasma are Na^+, K^+, CA^{++}, and Mg^{++}. The negative ions are Cl^-, HCO_3^-, $SO_4^=$ and $HPO_4^=$. All the body fluids contain more Na^+ whereas the fluid inside the cell contains more K^+. Bicarbonates and phosphates play an important role as buffers. Chloride ions have a definite role in electrolyte balance. Electrolyte balance is very important for homeostasis.

Body fluids: There are mainly two fluid compartments, intracellular (70%) and extracellular, *viz.*, interstitial fluid or the lymph (20%) and blood plasma (7%). The remaining 3% is the fluid in the intestinal lumen, C.S.F., and other compartments. As with other body constituents, there is a continuous turnover of the body water. There is a fairly constant level of water balance maintained between intra cellular and extra cellular fluids. Water balance is regulated by thirst and excretion through four channels, *viz.*, the skin, lungs, kidneys and the intestine. Of all these organs, the kidneys play the most vital role in water excretion. The skin and lungs are also important channels of water excretion, whose chief purpose is heat regulation of the body. Sushruta also refers to the importance of vitiated *rasa dhatu* in genesis of fever (*Su.* 28/9). Perspiration from the skin represents a significant means of water loss. Water loss in expired air is quite appreciable. Sweating, vomiting and diarrhoea with excessive fluid loss result in dehydration. Along with loss of water there is also loss of electrolytes. Sodium is a major cation of plasma and the interstitial fluid, whereas potassium and magnesium predominate in the intracellular fluid. Chlorides and bicarbonates predominate in the extracellular fluid. Phosphates, sulphates, organic acids and proteins predominate in the intracellular fluid. Various mechanisms operate to maintain the normal electrolyte balance in body fluids. Selective mechanisms like the sodium pump are very important. A balanced diet and water intake therefore are essential to maintain the electrolyte balance. The kidneys play an important role in the maintenance of electrolyte balance depending on dietary intake and the physiological needs of the body. The total osmotic effects of the plasma depend on the inorganic ions. Consequently, gains or losses of electrolytes, especially sodium and potassium ions cause shifts in the fluids in compartments to restore the osmotic equilibrium. The volume of blood in an adult is about five litres, of which the plasma is three litres. All the secretions of the body as well the interstitial fluid are derived from the plasma. Dehydration and loss of extracellular electrolytes cause shrinkage of the plasma volume, and the serum protein concentration and blood urea levels rise. The resultant negative balance of nitrogen and potassium lead to generalized tissue disintegration and eventually death. Dehydration causes the loss of plasma and interstitial fluid. Loss of potassium due to dehydration can cause heart block. The adrenal cortex has a profound influence on the electrolyte balance, due to the fact that it controls the level of Na^+ ions.

Lymph: The word lymph, literally means clear spring water. It has the same composition as the interstitial or tissue fluid. It is formed as a result of diffusion, filtration and osmosis from the capillaries. Lymphatic capillaries are very minute vessels. It contains less amounts of serum proteins and leucocytes. Circulation of lymph is an essential mechanism for tissue nutrition. Lymphatic capillaries draining the gut end in the thoracic duct, which in turn ends in the jugular vein in the neck.

Upa dhatus of *rasa*

***Stanya* or breast milk:** *Stanya* is *upadhatu* of *rasa*. Lactation, or secretion of breast milk (through the mammary glands) is due to the action of the posterior pituitary hormone, prolactin. In the post-partum period, another posterior pituitary hormone, oxytocin is secreted. It contracts the duct system to express the secreted milk. Once it reaches the threshold, dopamine is released, which causes a negative feedback to stop prolactin secretion. To establish milk secretion, suckling by the new born baby is essential. It is necessary that the baby is put to the mother's breast early after delivery, preferably within the first six hours.

Breast milk is the food that nourishes new born infants. According to Charaka, breast milk is the best nutrition for a new born baby. It provides *bala* (immunity and strength) and ensures good health to the new born, (*Charak Sh.* 8-54). In the immediate post-partum period, the secretion from the mammary glands, called colostrum, differs a great deal in character from the true milk, which usually begins from day three. Colostrum is a yellowish, alkaline and slightly viscid fluid. It has a higher content of total solids and all the components are not exactly the same as those of normal breast milk. Colostrum coagulates on heating, whereas milk does not. The lipids present in colostrum have a higher content of cholesterol, lecithin and fat. This fat has a higher degree of unsaturation. Colostrum seems to have a laxative action and may thus aid easy evacuation of meconium. It also provides immunoglobulins to the baby raising its immunity. The amount of colostrum secreted by the human female is rather small, about 150 – 300 ml. in 24 hours. Around the third or fourth day, true milk begins to be secreted, and the quantity of colostrum diminishes steadily. For one or two weeks thereafter, human milk continues to retain some of the characteristics of colostrum. This is reflected in the changing composition of the milk.

Milk forms an emulsion in water, stabilized by a complex of phospholipids and proteins absorbed on the surface of fat globules. It contains proteins in colloidal dispersion, lactose in true solution, and a number of minerals, particularly calcium and phosphorous. Some organic acids or their salts, vitamins, enzymes, and some undetermined constituents, including anti bodies and substances that possibly have anti-bacterial properties are also present. Human milk contains one or more bifidus factors (bifidogenic substances), which aid the growth of certain microorganisms found in the intestines of breast fed infants, (James Orten & Otto W. Neuhaus - *Human Biochemistry*, Ch.17, 553).

Sushruta has stated the following requisite qualities of good, healthy breast milk (*Sh.*10-32). It should be as white as a conch shell in colour, thin in consistency and should be uniformly miscible in water. After mixing in water it should not foam or form into threads. It should not float on water nor sink to the bottom. It should be sweet in taste and should not emanate any odour.

Stanya kshaya

Stanya kshaye sthanayormlaanata stanyaa sambhavo alpataa vaa l Tatra shleshma vardhana dravya upayogah l (Su. Su. 15/16)

When the breasts are not well developed and/or there is poor secretion of milk in the breasts, it is called *stanya kshaya*. In this condition the treatment with substances that increase *kapha* is advised.

Stanya vriddhi

Stanyam stanayor apeenatwam muhur muhur pravruttim, todam cha l (Su. Su. 15/21)

If there is excessive milk secretion, the milk collects in the breasts, causing engorgement of the breasts. This leads to repeated over flowing of breast milk, and it is associated with pain. If the accumulated breast milk is not expressed out and the congestion is not relieved, it can get infected, inflamed and develop into a breast abscess. This is a common occurance in the post partum period, usually in primipara. In order to prevent this complication, the new born should be put to the breast within six hours of delivery. The practice of early breast feeding needs to be encouraged.

Raja (Menstruation)

Raja is also an *upadhatu* of *rasa*, along with breast milk.

Rasath stanyam tatho raktam (Charak Ch. 15 –17)

Aartava kshaye yathochitakala adarshanam alpata va yoni vedana cha l

Tatra samshodhanam aagneyaanam cha dravyanaam vidhivat upayogah l

Once a month (usually every 28-30 days) there occurs cyclic bleeding along with the shedding of the endometrium. The bleeding usually lasts for three to four days and then stops. This is called *rajasrav* or *rajaswala* (menstruation). Modern medicine defines menstruation as the cyclical shedding of the secretory endometrium along with some amount of blood loss. These cycles cease with the onset of menopause. When there is depletion of *raja*, the menstrual cycle becomes scanty and irregular or there may even be amenorrhea. It may be associated with dysmenorrhea. This condition needs detox treatment and drugs that raise *agni.* Menstruation usually begins around the age of twelve. The first menstruation (menarche) occurs when the state of *samarthagata virytwa* (sexually competent state) is achieved. Women continue to menstruate cyclically till about the age of forty-five to fifty-five years. Thereafter the menstruation ceases. The cessation of menstruation is called *nashtartav* (menopause).

We will now learn about the mechanism of *raja* formation and its shedding during menstruation. Eggs or ova are released from the ovaries every month (14 – 16 days), during the reproductive age. The uterus prepares itself to receive the embryo in order to embed it. If the embryo fails to arrive and pregnancy does not happen, all the preparations for embedding are disrupted and expelled out as menstruation. The cuboidal epithelium covering the interior of the uterus regenerates and grows in multiple layers after every cycle. It is called the endometrium. Layers of the endometrium proliferate in the first half of the menstrual cycle and its glands begin to secrete in the second phase of the menstrual cycle to facilitate the embedding of the embryo and also to provide nutrition to it. If the embryo does not arrive, the superficial layers of the endometrium are shed. This leads to breakage of the blood vessels and there is concomitant bleeding. The basal layer of endometrium starts regenerating with the onset of a new cycle. Thus menstruation is not simply the method of ejecting a waste product, but an important biological function of reproduction. Hence *raia* is described as an *upadhatu*.

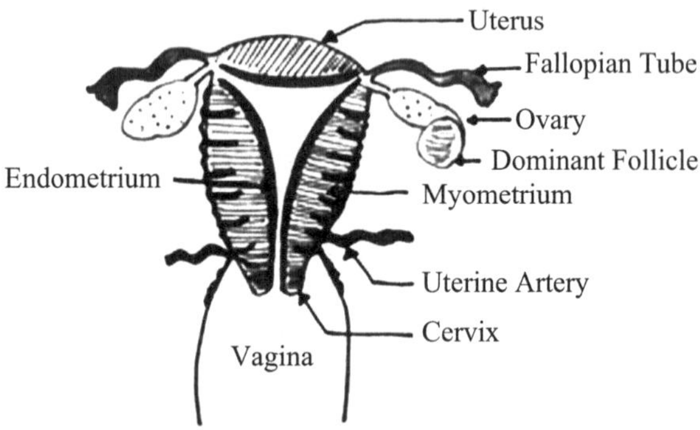

Female Genital Tract
(Garbhashaya, Aartav Vahini, Antah Phal)

Illustration of uterus and ovaries

There is yet another term *aartvam*, which needs to be properly defined. Bhavaprakash has equated *aartav* to *shukra dhatu* in females (*Aartavam api Shukravat - Bh. Pr. 29-221*).

Sushruta has described *aartava vaha srotas* that carry female gametes. He also states that any injury to this *srotas* or to its passages causes sterility (*vandhyatwa*). Obviously the term *aartava* should represent the female gametes and ovaries, and the fallopian tubes should be equated with *aartava vaha srotas*.

There appears to be a lot of confusion about the terms with relation to *stree shukra*, *aartav* and *raja*. They are used interchangeably by different authors. There is no agreement so far about the use of these terms amongst the Ayurvedic scholars. I feel that there is an urgent need for them to develop a consensus amongst themselves and once and for all properly define these three terms. In my opinion based on descriptions by Sushruta and Bhava Mishra, *aartav* needs to be equated to the ovarian functions, of both ovulation and ovarian hormone generation, since it is equated to *stree shukra*. *Stree shukra* is responsible for conception, strength and complexion of women. More details about *shukra dhatu* will be seen in a later chapter. Use of the term *raja* should be limited to menstruating endometrium.

Adolescence

It is the state of transformation from the childhood to adulthood.

Adolescence to puberty (*Samarthagata veeryatva*)

Adolescence is the period, during which a carefree child becomes a responsible adult. The age range of adolescence is from about thirteen to eighteen years. The physical and psychological changes begin before thirteen years and continue till after the age of eighteen years, (O. Sheil M. Turner, *Progress*, Vol. 12).

Puberty is defined as the state of being functionally capable of procreation (O. Sheil M. Turner, *Progress*, Vol. 12). It is also the time of development of the five main physical features or secondary sexual characteristics, *viz*., development of breasts; development of pubic hair; axiliary hair growth; increase in height; menstruation.

The state of reproductive competence associated with full development of all *dhatus* is described in all the Ayurvedic texts as *samarthagata veeryatva. Sushrut Samhita* gives the age for reproductive competence in males as 25 years and in females as 16 years, (*Su.Su.* 35-13).

Physical features	Age
Breast development	9-13 yrs
Pubic hair	9-13 yrs
Axillary hair	10-14 yrs
Increase in height	10-14 yrs
Menstruation	11-15 yrs

Onset of menstruation has a definite relationship with skeletal maturity. It usually commences after the maximum growth rate is achieved (6 – 11 cm/yr). When a girl reaches the maturity of bone age of 13-14 years, menarche occurs. Regular menstrual cycles are established only after 1-2 years following menarche.

Osler & Crawford in 1973, and Warren in 1983 have observed that menarche and reproductive competence correlate with the achievement of characteristic body composition with a critical degree of fatness rather than a critical weight. After the age of 8.5 years, there occurs a gradual increase in the size of the ovaries with the appearance of follicles. Sonographic visualization of more than 6 follicles of 4 mm diameter signals the arrival of puberty in girls. When testicular volume, in boys, reaches 10 ml or more, a spontaneous pubertal growth spurt begins. Malnutrition delays puberty. Loss in weight can occur due to lack of food, starvation, excessive exercise, chronic illness *etc*. It leads to a catabolic state, which favours the formation of 2-hydroxy oestrone instead of estradiol. Oestrone inhibits gonadotropins. Moreover with malnutrition, there is poor availability of oestrogen precursors. Weight loss of 10-15% of the normal weight for height delays menarche. Restoration of optimal nutrition leads to characteristic body composition, which is required for the onset of menarche.

During adolescence the circulating steroid hormones stimulate the proliferation of circulating red blood corpuscles. Frisch & Revelle (1970 – 1971) postulated a relationship between body weight and the age of onset of pubertal events. They showed, by analysis of body components, that the lean body weight to fat ratio is altered from the pre-menarche to post-menarche state from 5:1 to 3:1. During this period of adolescence, muscles, fat, bones and marrow all grow rapidly. But the most important of all these tissues is the bone marrow. From infancy to adolescence, there is an increase in the fatty yellow marrow. In adolescence the red marrow of the long bones is converted to yellow marrow. At puberty, the fatty, yellow marrow of the long bones forms 6% of the total body weight. This significantly contributes to extra gonadal oestrogen production. Other extra gonadal sites of production of oestrogen are fat and adrenal cortex. Androgens are aromatized to oestrogen by the fat tissue. By their positive feedback to the hypothalamus, these steroids from the marrow activate the hypothalamic pituitary and gonadal axis. This leads to establishing the events of the menstrual cycle.

With this background let us examine the concepts on genesis of *shukra dhatu* in Ayurveda. Sushruta states that menarche occurs at the age of twelve. This follows full development of all the first six *dhatus*, *viz.*, *rasa* (plasma), *rakta* (RBCs), *mamsa* (muscle), *meda* (fat), *asthi* (bone), and *majja* (marrow). When *majja* completes its development in the adolescent age, *shukra dhatu* begins to form. The question is whether *shukra* is directly derived from *majja*. Evidence shows that toti potent cells in the marrow can be changed into sperms. The testes and ovaries are both soft tissues, which are like marrow. The third piece of evidence is the role of fatty bone marrow in activating the hypothalamic-pituitary and ovarian axis, which in turn activates the dormant ovarian function. In Ayurveda, substances that improve the quality of *majja* (bone marrow) are recommended in the treatment of male infertility. All this evidence confirms the *majja shukra* relationship.

Stree shukra dhatu is of two forms. One is responsible for *beejotpatti* or *aartav* (gamete production) and the other is *sarva dehika stree shukra* (sex or ovarian hormones), that pervade the whole body. It circulates all over the body within *rasa dhatu* (circulating hormones in plasma). *Rasa dhatu* is believed to produce two *upa dhatus* (by-products) *viz.*, *raja* (menstruation) and *stanya* (breast milk). As described earlier, the endometrium progresses in layers to support the incoming embryo. This is possibly the reason to attribute the status of *upadhatu* of *rasa* to *raja*. Full development of blood, muscle, fat, bones and marrow are pre-requisites for the development of *shukra dhatu*.

Modern understanding of the important role of fatty bone marrow in activating hypothalamic- pituitary and ovarian axis vindicates the apparently simplistic hypothesis of Ayurveda with regards to the process of *shukra* formation from *majja*.

Menopause: *Nashtartav*

Natural menopause is an age related decline in endocrine function of the ovaries, associated with cessation of menstruation. Every girl child is born with a limited pool of follicles at birth. Exhaustion of this follicular pool results in the loss of ovarian endocrine (estradiol) function, resulting in menopause Menopausal age in women is between 45-55 years, Perimenopausal age is usually around 40 to 47 years. Because the life expectancy of women has increased to around 78 years on an average, currently there is a great increase in post-menopausal population, which needs medical care for various symptoms and complications.

Menopause is also part of larger age related phenomenon called climacteric. The ageing process is associated with a decline in potential for replication of all the cell systems in the body. This is due to alteration in the sequence of protein synthesis, shortening of telomeres and increased degradation in the cells. Menopause, is thus the result of defects in the genetic apparatus of cells, age related accumulation of free radicals, and the failure of regulating factors affecting the cells, *e.g.*, neurotransmitters, endocrines (*e.g.*, ovarian function), the immune system, *etc*. Ageing also adversely affects the homeostatic efficiency of the body. From the point of Ayurveda there is predominance of *vata dosha* in old age associated with significant depletion of *kapha*.

Therefore to consider that natural menopause is simply an oestrogen deficiency state is not correct. The surgical removal of ovaries causes an acute oestrogen deficiency state, which is amenable to oestrogen replacement therapy. Therefore, surgical menopause is different and should not be equated to natural menopause.

Climacteric also occurs in males, but the difference lies in the fact that the ageing process progresses much more rapidly following menopause in women, as compared to men. There are scant references to menopause in classical Ayurvedic texts. Shushruta attributed it to old age and stated that it occurs around the age of about 50 years, (*jara, pakva shariranam, yati, pancha shatah kshayam Su.Sh.* 3-11).

Daily consumption of *ghee*, milk and articles which increase *kapha* can delay the onset of menopause. Nutrition is a very important factor. It was observed during long wars, that the age of menarche was delayed. Post war with improved nourishment the age of menarche was reduced, (*ghruta kshiradi nityasu mudati kaphatmasu aartavam tishtathi chiram, viparitah svatho anyatha - Ashtang Sangrah,* S.1-69).

With ageing, *vayu dosha* increases significantly and there occurs a considerable decline in *pitta* and *kapha*. There is also a decline in all the seven *dhatus* starting from *rasa* and also of *ojus*. The Ayurvedic texts have described rejuvenation and virilification therapies specifically for the prevention of ageing in men. But there is no reason why the same principles of these therapies cannot be applied in women also.

Menopausal symptoms

They are of two types; immediate and late. Immediate symptoms relate to vasomotor, psychological, sexual and urogenital systems.

Vasomotor symptoms: Hot flushes, night sweats, palpitations and head ache form the most distressing symptoms of menopause. These are more severe after surgical menopause, especially in thin patients. These are attributed to disturbances of *pitta* and *vata*. Oestrogen replacement most effectively controls these symptoms.

Psychological symptoms: Twenty percent of women are affected with mood swings, anxiety, depression, decrease in libido and dementia of Alzheimer's variety. It is assumed to be due to amyloid deposition in the brain. Ayurveda attributes this to excessive *vata* causing *dosha* imbalance.

Urogenital symptoms: Urinary incontinence (stress & urge), vaginal dryness and prolapse of the uterus are very common. Ayurveda described *shushka yoni* (dry vagina with atrophy of the urogenital tract) and *maha yoni* (uterovaginal prolapse), and their increased association with menopause.

Long term effects of menopause

The skeletal and cardiovascular systems are affected.

Skeletal system: Osteoporosis occurs rapidly in women after menopause. It is responsible for the greater incidence of fractures of the spine (32%), proximal femur (16%), and distal radius (15%). There is greater susceptibility to osteoporosis in the Caucasian race, whereas incidence of this condition is very low in the Afro-Caribbean races. In India, the incidence is somewhere in between the two. Sedentary lifestyles, high protein meat diets, aluminium containing antacids, smoking and alcohol greatly predispose to osteoporosis. Bone reforming units (BRU) are responsible for skeletal growth, repair and replacement. They are under the influence of a variety of regulatory factors, *viz*., parathormone, calcitonin, vitamin D, growth factors, gonadal steroids, calcium, phosphates, *etc*. Oestrogen replacement therapy (ERT) therefore only partially helps the re-mineralization of bones and prevention of fractures. From the point of view of Ayurveda osteoporosis can be explained on the basis of excessive *vata* formation in *pakvashaya* (the lower GI tract) and *asthi dhatu* (bones). The GI tract has received the greatest attention in this ancient system of medicine. Correction of maladies in the GI tract is imperative in the treatment of all ailments concerning all systems of the body.

Cardiovascular disease: The decline of *ojus* (*ashta bindu para ojus*) and *avalambaka kapha*, due to excess of *vata* is the cause of cardiovascular disease, (*Hridayantu visheshena sleshmana sthanamuchyate* – meaning that the heart is the chief location of *kapha* (*Kashyap Pr.* 27)). A greater incidence of death is observed in postmenopausal women due to cardiac diseases. Atherogenic lipids are also increased in the serum in menopause.

Malignancy: *Apara ojus* also declines in the post-menopausal state. *Apara ojus* probably represents the white cell mass including those of T & B cells, which measure about half an *anjali* in volume. Due to the decline in the immune system, the incidence of malignant diseases increases.

Risk benefit ratio of hormone replacement therapy

The modern gynaecologist's approach to menopause therapy is simplistic and flawed, for it is based on the concept that menopause is simply an oestrogen deficient state. Many other hormones, *e.g.*, DHEA, melatonin *etc.*, are also deficient and many other systems in the body are affected. Moreover menopause is a natural process of transition to a new phase of life for a woman. Currently, hormone replacement therapy (HRT) is advocated right from perimenopausal age. Long term exposure to estrogens are known to predispose women to cancer. Oestrogens, the newer SERMS and tibolone, *etc.*, carry with them dangerous complications, *e.g.*, adverse cardiovascular states, thromboembolic disease and malignancy. A study published in *The Lancet* by Tungstal, *et. al*, in 1998 clearly established that there are no beneficial effects accrued by HRT on cardiovascular disease. Moreover there are reports suggesting an increased incidence of malignancy and thromboembolic disease. HRT can be at best used for a short time to overcome troublesome hot flushes. Again, not all patients are benefited by HRT, because of genetic characterization of E2 receptors. This finding supports the concept of individualization and customisation of therapy in Ayurveda based on individual constitution (*prakruti*).

Phytoestrogens

Modern science is therefore looking for very mild estrogenic substances of plant origin. These are known as phytoestrogens, which possess just 2% activity of estradiol. They are coumestans, lignans and isoflavines. The sources of these phytoestrogens are peas, chick peas, soya beans and lentils. Genisten and daidzein are two effective flavones with estrogenic activity.

Basis of Ayurvedic therapy in menopause

It is a holistic approach, considering the body, mind, and soul. Urbanization, improper sedentary lifestyles, mental and physical stress were recognized as factors responsible for early ageing and shortening of lifespans. The *Charak Samhita* states that those rishis, who left their forest dwellings and settled in urban surroundings became prone to various environmental diseases and aged rapidly leading to short life spans. Therefore Charaka advocated *rasayana* therapy to improve their vigour and vitality, along with improvement in their life spans. The other benefits of the therapy were improved mental abilities (memory and intelligence), health, youthfulness, colour, complexion, voice, generosity, strength and efficiency of both the organs of cognition and conation (*indriyas*).

Deergham ayuh smrutir medha, aarogyam
tarunam vayah prabha varnam swaraudarya dehendriya balodayam l
(Ast. Hr. Su. 39-12)

Rasayan is supposed to improve the quality of all the dhatus of the body, beginning from that of rasa.

Labhopeyam hi shastanam rasaadeenam rasayanam l
(Ast. Hr. Su. 39)

Rasayana is of three types, viz., achara rasayana; ahara rasayana; and dravya rasayana.

Achara rasayana: Improvement of life style

It is basically related to lifestyle management. It consists of the practice of *sadvritta* (good moral behaviour) and *swasthavritta* (healthy living). Fortitude, justness, unselfishness, truthfulness, a charitable nature, forgiveness, service mindedness, are all qualities of *sadvritta*. A study of 1700 women over a period 35 years, published in the April edition of *JAMA* (*Journal of the American Medical Association*), concluded that women who consumed a balanced diet and had good habits lived longer and with less disabilities, (*Atreya-Ayurvedic* healing for women).

Swastha vritta deals with the day to day conduct and life styles of a person, *dina* (day time) *charya*, *ratra* (night) *charya* and *rutu* (according to the season) *charya*. It is all about one's various activities, beginning right from the time a person wakes up in the morning. It prescribes a hygienic mode of living, eating and clothing, based on the time and season. Daily, systematic exercises, *e.g.*, *surya namaskars* (prostrations to the sun), and the practice of yoga and meditation, form an important part of *swastha vritta*. Exercising the muscles is most important to maintain the strength and proper mineralization of the bones. Strength of the bone essentially depends on the integrity of its collagen matrix. It is the collagen matrix that holds the minerals of calcium, magnesium and phosphates *etc*., in the bones. Osteoporosis in menopause is related to a decrease in *kappa* and *pitta* and an increase *vata dosha*. Deficiency of *kapha* signifies a decline in collagen, resulting in osteoporosis (manifestation of excess *vata*). A sedentary life styles enhance osteoporosis. Daily *surya namaskars*, exercises, yoga and meditation, therefore should form part of a preventive, therapeutic approach to menopausal syndrome.

Ahara rasayana (Food as drugs)

Shukra dhatu kshaya or depletion in *shukra* causes depletion of *ojus*. In *oja kshaya*, black gram, which contain alpha lipoic acid, milk, *ghee* and meat soups of forest dwelling animals are advised. *Ghee* has a special role in improving *shukra dhatu*. Currently opinions about *ghee* and its benefits have changed radically. Cow's *ghee* is now considered to be a good source of omega-3 fatty acids. It also reduces atherogenic lipids in the serum.

Til (sesame seeds) and its oil are very good in promoting *raja*. *Gur* in combination with *til* is advised for improvement of *raja*. Vegetarian diets help mineralization of bone, whereas non-vegetarian diets, especially those containing red meat are known to cause demineralization of bones. During metabolism of animal proteins, singlet H^+ ions are released in excess into the blood, making its pH acidic. In order to offset this acidity, calcium hydroxide from the bones is drawn into circulation to balance the acid base equilibrium. This is an important mechanism for development of osteoporosis in persons who eat meat. A balanced vegetarian diet, is thus most important in the preventive management of menopause. Chickpeas, Bengal gram and black gram are good sources of phytoestrogens similar to soya beans. Therefore I see no reason to replace them by soya beans in our country. Soybean is not native to India and does not offer any special benefits.

Dravya rasayana (Drug therapy)

In contrast to modern medicine, Ayurveda pays great attention to GI tract function. It is the site of continuous regeneration of all the three *doshas*. Correction of all three *doshas* can be done with *Triphala*. *Haritaki* (Terminalia chebula) is *ushna virya* and *vata nashak*. *Amlaki* (Emblica officianle) is *sheeta virya* and *pitta nashak*. *Vibhitaki* (Terminalia belerica) is *ushna virya* and *kapha nashak*. Stress releases free radicals. "The tiniest killer is not a virus, but it is a promiscuously reactive molecular fragment, free radical," (William Pryor). Ageing is due to accumulation of free radicals. Herbal *rasayanas* are excellent anti-oxidants and free radical scavengers. They act at five different levels, *viz*., prevention of formation of radicals by enhancing SOD, scavenging primary radicals, *e.g*., singlet O, hydroxyl ions, inhibition of lipid peroxidation, repair of lipid cell membranes, and repair of intracellular elements. *Tulsi* (Occimum sanctum), *amlaki, ardrak* (gingiber officianale), *guduchi* (Tinospora cordifolia), *katuki* (Piccrorrhiza kurroa), *shatavari* (Asparagus racemosus), *ashvagandha* (Withania somnifera) are all acknowledged herbal anti-oxidants. *Shilajatu*, an exudate from the selective Himalayan rock is described as an excellent *rasayana*. It has reversible NO captodactor activity, capability to increase SOD, glutathione peroxidase. It is mildly cytotoxic and reduces the carcinogenic potential. It contains valuable micronutrients *e.g.,* Fe, Cu, Zn, P and S.

Role of micronutrients

One of the most important negative results of the green revolution in agriculture is the introduction of oestrogens into the food chain through fertilizers and pesticides. Oestrogens are carcinogenic and are the leading cause for the increase in the incidence of malignancy.

Another important concern of nitrogen based fertilizers is the depletion of essential micronutrients, *e.g*., Zn in food grains. Additionally, preservation techniques also cause the loss of these very essential metallic and non-metallic micronutrients. A leading cause of high rates of male factor in infertility currently is zinc deficiency. Nearly two hundred enzymatic actions in the body are dependent on zinc. A child born with zinc deficiency can transmit immune deficiency to the next three generations.

Ayurveda introduced a novel way of supplying micronutrients through herb roots in the most bioavailable fashion. Asparagus racemosus, Ipomoea digitata, Embelica officianale contain betacarotene, Vit. A and Vit. C. Glycerrhiza glabra, Sida cordifolia, Ipomoea digitata, and Trapa bispinosa contain calcium, potassium, magnesium and manganese respectively. Withania somnifera and Ipomoea digitata, contain Zn, Fe and iodine.

Immunomodulation

There is a good evidence to show that many of the rasayana herbs are capable of strengthening the immune system *e.g.*, Tinospora cordifolia, Piper longum, Allium sativam, Withania somnifera, Achorus calamus, C. mukul, Occimum sanctum, *etc.* In menopause there is a decline in immunity. Hence rasayana therapy plays an important role in prevention and treatment of menopausal syndrome.

One of the most crucial complications of menopause is cardiac disease. *Terminalia Arjuna* is rated as the best cardiac tonic to protect women from cardiac disease. It is *hridya*, *varnya* (improves capillary circulation), *pramehaghna* (relieves diabetes), *shonita sthapana* (arrests blood loss or prevents early onset of menopause). It prevents collagen loss and also has a high content of bio-available calcium to prevent osteoporosis. It heals fractures (*sandhaniya*) and the phytochemical Bicalein it contains makes it a very good anti-oxidant. *Arjuna* therefore is one drug that can address both the problems of osteoporosis and cardiac failure.

Based on this premise, the author formulated *Collasyn* to prevent ageing, cardiac disease and menopausal syndrome. The content of *Collasyn* tablets are as follows:

Terminalia arjuna, Terminalia chebula, Trapa bispinosa, Embelia officianale, Sida cordifolia, Withania somnifera, Glycerrhiza glabra, Hemidesmus indicus, Tribulis terrestris, Terminalia belerica, Commiphora mukul, Tinospora cordifolia and *Shilajatu*.

Trapa bispinosa is *tridosha shamak* and *sheetavirya*, diuretic, rejuvenating and aphrodiasic. Sida cordifolia is *vaata pitta shamak* and enhances *rakta, mansa, shukra* and *oja*. Withania somnifera nourishes *majja*, and induces sleep. It also enhances *mamsa*, *meda* and *shukra*. Glycerrhiza glabra is a *rasayana*. It improves *rakta*, *majja* and *shukra dhatus*. Hemidesmus indicus purifies *rasa* and improves all the *dhatus* including *shukra*. Tribulis terrestris improves the quality of *meda* and is a good diuretic and aphrodisiac. It is *tridosha shamak. Triphala* is the best *vayosthapan* (anti-ageing) remedy. C. mukul is an excellent anti-atherogenic, *artav janak* and also heals fractures. Tinospora cordifolia is an established immunomodulator and *rasayan*. *Shilajatu* is again a much acclaimed anti-ageing agent due to its content of essential metallic micronutrients and its action of NO captivator.

The mechanism of action of *Collasyn* formulation is based on cardio-tonic, anti-lipidemic action, anti-atherogenic action, down regulation of beta receptors, anti-oxidant and immuno-modulatory action.

Is there any experimental evidence to prove the validity of *rasayana* therapy of rejuvenation?

There is convincing experimental proof that anti-oxidants prolong the life span of animals. Studies on *Chyavanprash* and *Brahmarasayan* confirm this fact. *Bhallatak* is yet another *rasayan*, which has been shown to inhibit cancer cell lines in tissue cultures, (Dr R. D. Lele, *Ayurveda and Modern Medicine*).

Studies on the cardio protective activity of *Terminalia arjuna* and *Collasyn* conducted by Dr Palep's Medical Research Foundation

Study conducted at

AU-KBC Research Centre

MIT Campus of Anna University

Chromepet, Chennai

Tamilnadu, India

Objective

To assess the extent of cardiac protection offered by the herbal formulations, *T. arjuna* bark extract & *Collasyn*, on chick embryonic cardiomyocytes against cardio-toxicity induced by Doxorubicin (adriamycin), a popular chemotherapeutic drug.

Principle

Different quantities of the given formulation in concentration of 10 mg/ml, steeped in autoclaved phosphate buffered saline (PBS) will be tested for its efficacy on a primary culture of chick cardiomyocytes. The analysis will be estimated by cell viability assay using the trypan blue dye exclusion method and microscopic monitoring of the morphology of the cells. The percentage viability will be plotted against the quantity of formulation used.

A study of the efficacy of the formulations against Doxorubicin induced cardio-toxicity on live chick embryonic hearts will be done by a careful dissection of a live embryo and monitoring the contractility in presence of the formulations and drug.

Materials

Primary culture of chick embryonic cardiomyocytes in M199 medium

Foetal bovine serum (FBS)

Phosphate buffered saline (PBS)

Standard drugs: Doxorubicin 10 μL of 10 mM (Incubation time: 10 minutes) Quinidine

Herbal formula: (a) *T. arjuna* and (b) Tab *Collasyn*: 10 mg/ml concentration (drug)

Live chicken embryonic cardiomyocytes in culture

Preparation of *T. arjuna* & *Collasyn*

Powder extract of *Terminalia arjuna* bark and powdered Tab. *Collasyn* was steeped in sterile PBS in the ratio 16:1 at a concentration of 10 mg/ml. 0.16 grams of both *T. arjuna* and *Collasyn* powder was accurately weighed and 16 ml of sterile, hot PBS was added to it, and allowed to cool. After cooling down, the mixture was centrifuged to separate the suspended particles. The solvent was carefully transferred to another container. The formulation of *T. arjuna* and *Collasyn* was filter sterilized before every use.

Method

1. Chick embryonic cardiomyocytes were isolated from an 8-10 day old chick embryo and cultured in M199 medium with 5% FBS.
2. The culture was incubated at 370°C for 24 hours in a CO_2 incubator to obtain a primary culture.
3. The 24 hour primary culture was pre-conditioned with different quantities of formulations (10, 20, 25, 50, 100 μL) for 2 hours.
4. Appropriate control experiments were performed. They included: (a) Standard negative control (No drug/formula). (b) Control exposed to Doxorubicin. (c) Controls pre-treated with the anti-arrhythmia drug (Quinidine) before exposure to Doxorubicin.

5. After the period of pre-conditioning with either *T. arjuna* or *Collasyn*, the cells were exposed to Doxorubicin for 1 hour to test the cardio-protective activity of the herbal formulation.
6. The cardiomyocytes were then observed microscopically for morphological changes and then trypsinised to analyse their viability using the trypan blue dye exclusion method.

Trypan blue dye exclusion method

1. An aliquot of cell suspension is suspended in 100 µl PBS and then diluted again by mixing it with 0.04% trypan blue solution.
2. The suspension with the dye is incubated for 2 mins and 10µL of this suspension is immediately loaded onto a Neubauer chamber/ hemocytometer for counting the cells.
3. The unstained (viable) and stained (non-viable) cells are counted separately in the hemocytometer.
4. The percentage of viable cells is calculated as follows: Percentage viability = No of viable cells/Total No. of cells x 100.

Statistical analysis

Each experiment was conducted thrice and the mean value obtained was plotted along with the standard deviation.

Cardioprotective activity of formulations on Doxorubicin induced cardiotoxicity in live chicken embryonic heart

A careful dissection of chick embryos with an intact beating heart was done and the heart transferred to a sterile Petri dish with PBS. The frequency of heart beat was monitored before the treatment with formulations for each embryo.

Preconditioning of the embryo with either *T. arjuna* or *Collasyn* (100 µl of 10 mg/ml formulation) was done as described above for 30 minutes before exposure to 10 µl of 10 mM Doxorubicin for 60 minutes. Pre-conditioning with 10 µl of 10 mM stock of *Quinidine* was used as a positive control.

The frequency of the heart beat was recorded and the percentage change in frequency calculated and plotted as a graph.

Results

Morphological analysis

There seemed to be no visible morphological changes on the cardiomyocytes treated with the formulation with the cardiomyocytes depicting the regular structure as in control cultures.

Cardioprotective activity: Primary culture of embryonic cardiomyocytes, (Figure 1).

Both *T. arjuna* bark as well as *Collasyn* seem to offer protection against *in-vitro* exposure to 10 mM Doxorubicin. The viability of the cells was higher in cells pre-conditioned with either formulation and then stressed with Doxorubicin, as compared to those treated with Doxorubicin alone. There was an increase in viability on increase in the concentration of the herbal formulation in both cases with the maximum viability seen when the cells are pre-conditioned with 100 μl of formulation (of a 10 mg/ml stock). The viability seen at the maximum concentration used was comparable to that obtained from cells pre-treated with Quinidine (standard anti arrhythmia drug [10 μl of 10 mM stock was used]).

It was also seen that the cardioprotective effect of *T arjuna* showed a slightly increased effect compared to that of *Collasyn* at concentrations greater than 50 μl of stock solution (10 mg/ml).

Analysis of cardioprotective effect of formulations against Doxorubicin induced cardiotoxicity in live chicken embryonic heart: Figure 2

The percent change in contractility of intact embryonic chick heart was plotted. The change observed seemed to be less when pre-treated with *T. arjuna* or *Collasyn* with *T. arjuna* offering a better cardiotonic activity against the cardiotoxic effect exerted by Doxorubicin. Doxorubicin by itself elicited a 37.5+/-3.52% change in cardiac contractility. When pre-treated with Quinidine and then exposed to Doxorubicin, the rate of change of the frequency of the heart beat was maximum with a 75+/-2.4% change observed. This could hint at an increased cardiotoxic effect of Doxorubicin in the presence of Quinidine.

However pre-treatment with both *T. arjuna* and *Collasyn* seems to offer pronounced protection against changes in contractility induced due to exposure to Doxorubicin.

Study 2: Study of the cardiotonic effect of *T. Arjuna* and *Collasyn* on chick embryonic cardiomyocytes in the presence of arrhythmia and ischemia inducers

Objective

To assess the efficiency of the herbal formulations *T. arjuna* & *Collasyn* on chick embryonic cardiomyocytes against *in-vitro* induced arrhythmia & ischaemia.

Principle

Different quantities of the given formulation in concentration of 10 mg/ml, steeped in autoclaved phosphate buffered saline (PBS) will be tested for their efficacy on a primary culture of chick cardiomyocytes. The analysis will be estimated by cell viability assay using the trypan blue dye exclusion method and a microscopic monitoring of the morphology of the cells. The percentage viability will be plotted against the quantity of formulation used.

Material

1. Primary culture of chick embryonic cardiomyocytes in M199 medium
2. Fetal bovine serum (FBS)
3. Phosphate buffered saline (PBS)
4. Standard drugs: Isoproterenol; Nifedipine; Ouabain 10 µL of 10 mM (incubation time: 10 minutes); Quinidine
5. Herbal formula: *T. arjuna*; *Collasyn* 10 mg/ml concentration
6. Live chicken embryos

Method

1. Chick embryonic cardiomyocytes were isolated from an 8-10 day old chick embryo and cultured in M199 medium with 5% FBS.
2. The cells were incubated in a CO_2 incubator for 24 hours at 37°C for the primary culture.
3. The 24 hour primary culture was pre-conditioned with different quantities of formulae (10, 20, 25, 50, 100 µL) for 2 hours.

4. Appropriate control experiments were performed. They included: (a) Standard negative control (No drug/formula); (b) Control exposed to inducer of ischaemia (Isoproterenol) and inducer of arrhythmia (Ouabain); (c) Controls pretreated with anti-ischaemic drug (Nifedipine) and antiarrhythmic drug (Quinidine) before inducing either condition.
5. After the period of pre-conditioning with either *T. arjuna* or *Collasyn*, ischaemia or arrhythmia was induced by exposure to Isoproterenol or Ouabain (incubation time -10 mins) to test the efficacy of the herbal formulation.
6. The cardiomyocytes were then observed microscopically for morphological changes and then trypsinised to analyse their viability using the trypan blue dye exclusion method.

Trypan blue dye exclusion method

1. An aliquot of cell suspension is suspended in 100 µl PBS and then diluted again by mixing with 0.04% trypan blue solution.
2. The suspension with dye is incubated for 2 mins and 10 µL of this suspension is immediately loaded onto a Neubauer chamber/ hemocytometer for cell counting.
3. The unstained (viable) and stained (non-viable) cells are counted separately in the hemocytometer.
4. The percentage of viable cells is calculated as follows: Percentage viability = No of viable cells/Total No. of cells x 100.

Statistical analysis

Each experiment was conducted thrice and the mean value obtained plotted along with the standard deviation.

Live embryo cardiac contractility assay performed as described in Study 1.

Anti-ischaemic property: See figure 3

Both *T. arjuna* bark as well as Collasyn seem to offer protection against *in-vitro* induction of ischaemia using 10 mM isoproterenol. The viability of cells was higher in cells pre-conditioned with either formulation and then stressed with isoproterenol as compared to those treated with isoproterenol alone.

There was an increase in viability on increase in concentration of the herbal formulation in both cases with the maximum viability seen when the cells are pre-conditioned with 100 μl of formulation (of a 10 mg/ml stock). The viability seen at the maximum concentration used was comparable to that obtained from cells pre-treated with Nifedipine (standard anti-ischaemic drug [10 μl of 10 mM stock was used]).

Anti ischaemic studies on live chicken embryonic heart: Figure 4

The percent change in contractility of intact embryonic chick heart is plotted. The increase in contractility observed when the heart is treated with an ischaemic inducer (Isoproterenol) is reduced in the case of pre-treatment with Nifedipine. However pre-treatment with *T. arjuna/Collasyn* seems to offer more protection against changes in contractility with a more pronounced effect seen in the case of *Collasyn*.

Anti-arrhythmic property: Figure 5

Both *T. arjuna* bark as well as *Collasyn* seem to offer protection against *in-vitro* induction of arrhythmia using 10 mM Ouabain. The viability of cells was higher in cells pre-conditioned with either formulation and then stressed with Ouabain as compared to those treated with Ouabain alone.

There was an increase in viability on increase in the concentration of the herbal formulation in both cases with the maximum viability seen when the cells are pre-conditioned with 100 μl of formulation (of a 10 mg/ml stock). The viability seen at the maximum concentration used was comparable to those obtained from cells pretreated with Quinidine (standard anti-arrhythmic drug [10 μl of 10 mM stock was used]).

It was also seen that the anti-arrhythmic effect of *Collasyn* and *T. arjuna* was comparable with no significant variation. It was also seen that there is a marginally increased anti-ischaemic effect in the case of *Collasyn* when compared to *T. arjuna*. This effect was more pronounced at lower concentrations tested: 10, 20 and 25 μl.

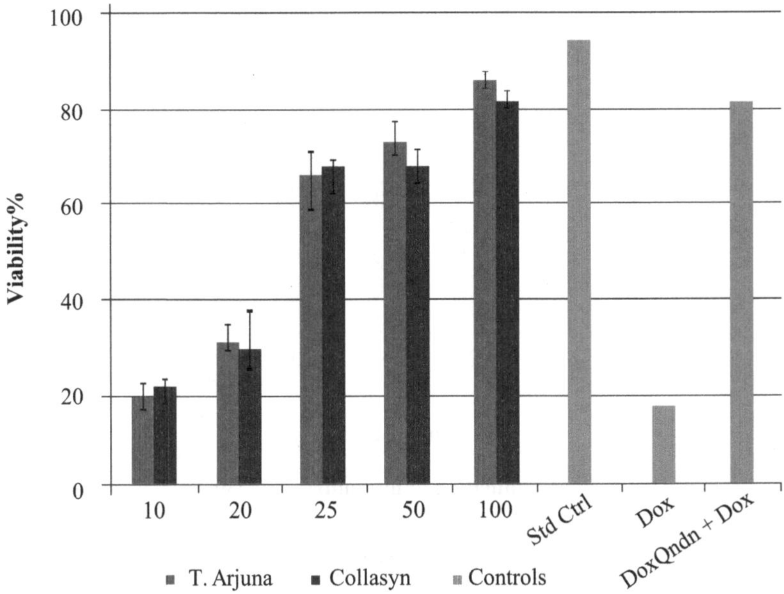

Figure 1

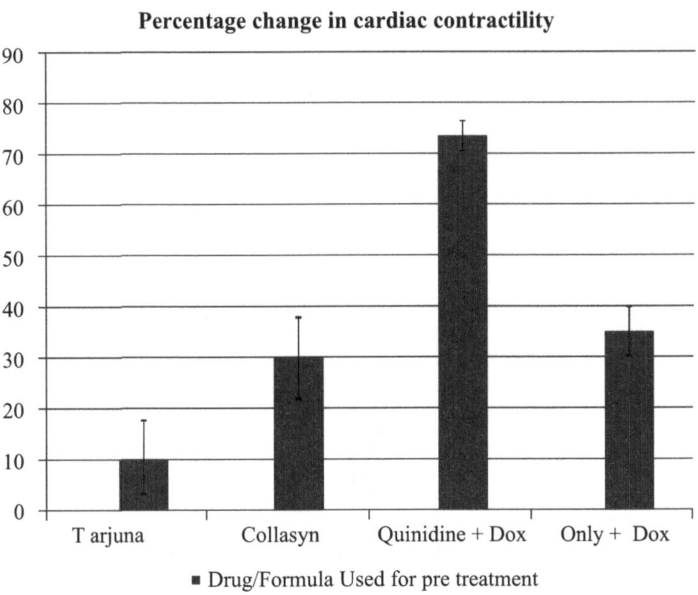

Figure 2

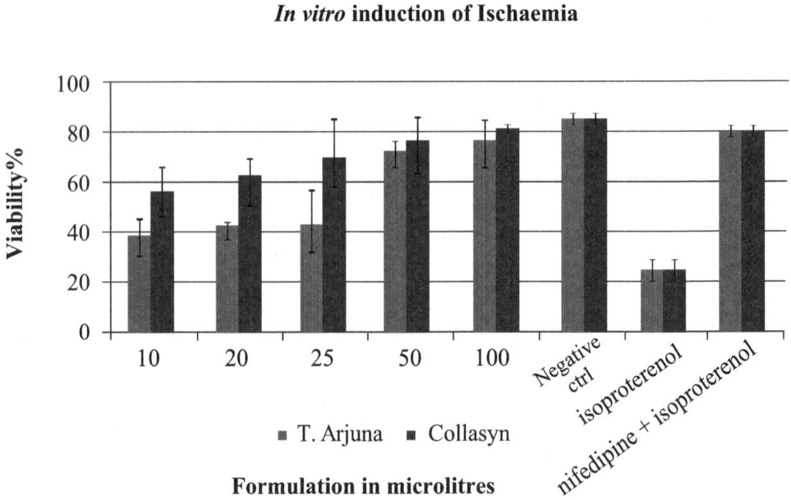

Figure 3

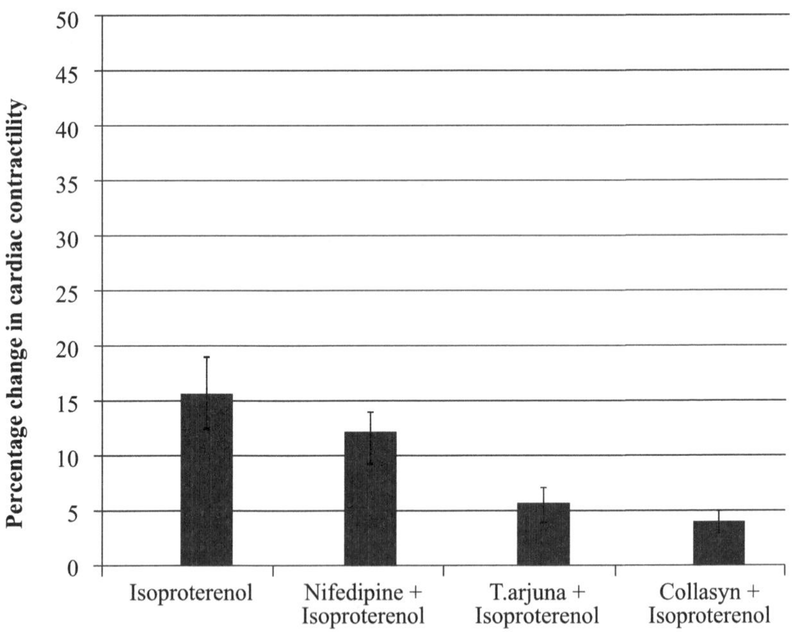

Figure 4

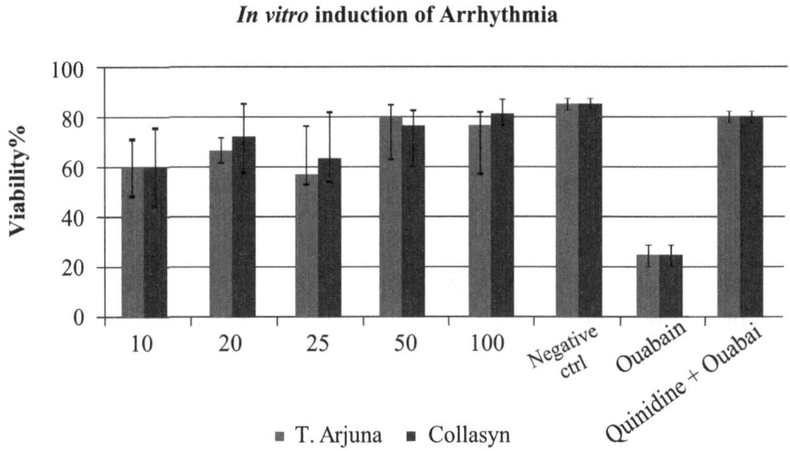

Figure 5

Additional study

Cardio-protective activity of formulations on Doxorubicin induced cardiotoxicity on a primary culture of chick embryonic cardiomyocytes

1. Chick embryonic cardiomyocytes were isolated from an 8-10 day old chick embryo and cultured in M199 medium with 5% FBS.
2. The culture was incubated at 370°C for 24 hours in a CO_2 incubator to obtain the primary culture.
3. The 24 hour primary culture was pre-conditioned with 10 mM Doxorubicin for 24 hours. Appropriate control experiments were performed. They included: (a) Standard negative control (No drug/ formula). (b) Control exposed to Doxorubicin.
4. After the period of pre-conditioning with Doxorubicin, the cells were treated with appropriate concentrations of *T.arjuna* or *Collasyn* for 2 hours.
5. The cardiomyocytes were then observed microscopically for any morphological changes and then trypsinised to analyse their viability using the trypan blue dye exclusion method.
6. The same experiment was carried out on chick embryonic fibroblasts as well to assess the cytoprotective effect of the formulations.

Results

1. The percentage viability of the cells was seen to increase upon treatment with either formulation, after exposure to Doxorubicin.
2. The effect of *T.arjuna* was more pronounced at 10, 20 and 25 μl concentrations as compared to *Collasyn* while at higher concentrations of 50 and 100 μl, Collasyn treated cells exhibited higher viabilities, (See Figure A).
3. In the case of fibroblasts, *Collasyn* showed marginally higher cyto-protection than *T.arjuna* against Doxorubicin induced cytotoxicity (Figure B).

In general, it is seen that *T.arjuna* and *Collasyn* confer a cyto-protective effect against cardiomyocytes and fibroblasts after Doxorubicin induced cytotoxicity in the study conducted.

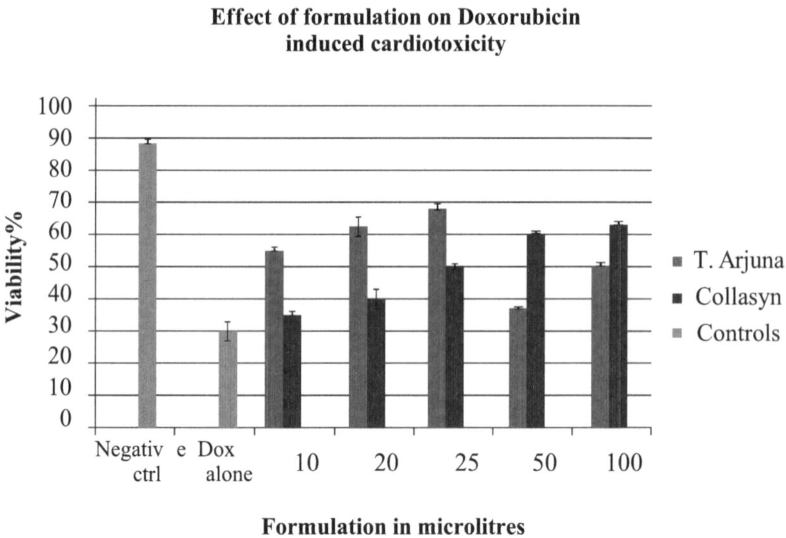

Figure 6 Pretreatment with Doxorubicin

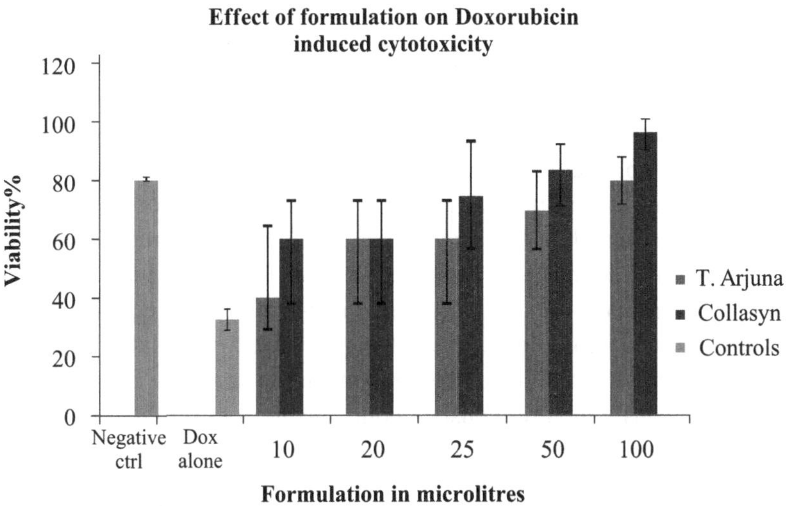

Figure 7 Study on fibroblasts

1. Alan L. Miller, N. D. 1998. Botanical Influences on Cardiovascular Disease, 1998. *Alternative Medicine Review*; 3(6): 422-431.
2. Han, S.Y., H. X. Li, Xu Ma, Ke Zhang, Zhi Zhong Ma, P.F.Tu. 2009. Protective Effects of Purified Safflower Extract on Myocardial Ischemia *In Vivo* and *In Vitro*, *Phytomedicine*, 694-702.
3. Gorelika, J. I. Vodyanoyb, C. Andrew, I. Shevchuka, A. Ivan, A. Diakonov, M. J. Lab, Y. E. Korchev, 2003. Esmolol is Antiarrhythmic in Doxorubicin Induced Arrhythmia in Cultured Cardiomyocytes Determination by Novel Rapid Cardiomyocyte Assay, *FEBS Letters*, 548: 74-78.
4. Long, S. R., R. A. Carey, K. M. Crofoot, P. J. Proteau, T. M. Filtz, 2006. Effect of Hawthorn Crude Extract and Chromatographic Fractions on Multiple Activities in a Cultured Cardiomyocyte Assay, *Phytomedicine* (9-10): 643-50.
5. Egon Koch, Fathi Abdul Malek, 2011. Standardized Extracts from Hawthorn Leaves and Flowers in the Treatment of Cardiovascular Disorders, Preclinical and Clinical Studies, *Planta. Med.*; 77: 1123–1128.

This study confirms the scientific basis for rejuvenation of different tissues through *rasayana* herb therapy. This formulation is used by hundreds of menopausal patients with great success. Experiments repeated and results are reproducible.

Twacha (Skin)

Twacha has been described as *upadhatu* of *rasa dhatu*. The status of *rasa dhatu* can be inferred from the health of the skin. Ayurveda described the nails and hair as its derivatives. The skin is important because of its function as a protective integument of the body. It helps in the prevention of injury and desiccation. The skin is the largest tissue of the body. It is composed mainly of two layers, *viz.*, the epidermis (outer epithelial layer) and the dermis (inner connective tissue layer). As with all living tissues in the body, the skin is always in a dynamic state of equilibrium. It constantly undergoes degradative changes with activity that is balanced by regenerative anabolic actions to maintain its structural integrity and function. Thus it requires constant nourishment from *rasa dhatu*.

Epidermis: It contains a series of layers. The inner most is the *stratum basalis*. This is the most active layer physiologically. The next layer is the *stratum lucidum*, which contains granules of the substance called keratohyaline. This keratohyaline produces a semi-fluid substance called eleidin. Eleidin is further transformed into keratin, which is the characteristic constituent of the outermost layer of the epidermis, which is called *stratum corneum*. The cells of this layer are clear, dead and scale like, and are constantly desquamated. In this layer, the nucleus and cytoplasm are replaced by keratin. Keratin is of two types, *viz.*, soft and hard. The epidermis of the skin is of the soft variety. Nails and hairs contain hard keratin. Keratin is an albuminoidal protein, which is insoluble in all reagents, therefore it makes an ideal protective covering. Soft keratin of the skin is poor in sulphur content; whereas the hard keratin of the hair is rich in sulphur. Hair fibres are mainly composed of dead cells, containing keratin micro fibrils. Sub-cutaneous tissues contain a large amount of lipids, of which one fifth are sterols. One such sterol is 7-D hydrocholesterol, which is converted into vitamin D by the ultraviolet radiation from sun light. Vitamin D is essential for the growth and calcification of bone, thus vitamin D is a lipoid substance.

This fact therefore validates the concept of Ayurveda, which states that *meda dhatu* (lipids) is the source for the formation of *asthi dhatu*.

Fatty acids, phospholipids and keratin are the constituents of the epidermis. Women have a higher percentage of triglycerides, whereas men have a higher percentage of cholesterol and phospholipids.

Sebum is an oily secretion of the sebaceous glands of the skin containing squalene, which is a hydrocarbon, cholesterol and other lipids. Cerumen or ear wax consists of 40% proteins, with the rest being lipids. Carbohydrates in the skin include glucose, pentose and glycogen. In conditions like psoriasis and other scaling diseases, there is excessive storage of glucose in the skin. Toxic heavy metals, *e.g.*, silver, lead and arsenic are deposited in the hair and skin.

Melanin: This is a brown black pigment of the skin, which is under neuro-hormonal control. Tyrosinase enzyme in the skin converts DOPA to Melanin. Melanin protects the skin from injury from ultraviolet radiations.

Dermis: This is the inner most layer of the skin. It is composed of dense, irregularly arranged connective tissue fibres. Connective tissue is formed due to embedding of insoluble protein fibres in the ground substance. The ground substance is a continuous fluid matrix. It is distributed in the dermis, tendons, ligaments, cartilage and the matrix of the bone. The strength and characteristic of a tissue depends upon the type of the fibrils of the connective tissue. The most connective tissue fibrils are made either of collagen or elastin. The greater the amount of collagen, the greater is the strength of the tissue. Cartilage is rich in the ground substance.

Collagen: Collagen represents 30% of the total protein of the body. There are five different types of collagen molecules serving the different functional requirements of different tissues. Abnormal biosynthesis of collagen leads to a variety of diseases. Its chief constituents are proline and glycine. Hydroxylation requires a proline or lysine hydroxylase, ascorbic acid, ferrous iron, alpha ketoglutarate and oxygen. The need for ascorbic acid in these reactions is evidence for its profound effects on scurvy, on connective tissue formation and wound healing. Scurvy can be prevented by vitamin C. On heating, collagen transforms into gelatine. If it is boiled in water for a long time, or in an acid solution for a short time, the collagen is converted into gelatine. Gelatine is a common component of food, which can be easily hydrolysed by pepsin and trypsin.

Elastin: This is a protein which has mechanical strength and high elastic property. Unlike collagen it does not contain hydroxylysine and contains only a small amount of hydroxyproline. It is not converted into gelatine, neither is it soluble in any solvent and does not undergo any chemical change.

Reticulin: This is the third fibrous protein, which is the component of the reticular fibres. The difference between collagen, elastin and reticulum is the content of lipids and carbohydrates in the latter.

Ground substance: (Fluid matrix): It is a proteoglycan, which is a modified dialysate of plasma. It contains some proteins derived from plasma through capillary action. It is unique for its high content of glycosaminoglycans or muco-polysacharides, which are 95% carbohydrate in origin. These poly-saccharides are synthesized by fibroblasts. The common muco-polysaccharides are hyaluronic acid and chondroitin sulphates A, B and C. A good example of ground substance is the synovial fluid which lubricates all the joints.

Skin is *twacha* of Ayurveda

It is *upadhatu* of *rasa dhatu*. The thickness of the skin layer is directly proportional to the nutrition level of an individual. Thus it is intimately associated with the functions of *rasa dhatu*. Just as we have noted that there are several layers of skin performing different functions, Ayurveda too has recognized seven layers of the skin, (*Sushruta Samhita*). These layers are described in relation to the diseases manifested in them.

1. ***Avabhasini*:** It is the location for *sidhma* (psoriasis) and *padma kantak* (papilloma),
2. ***Lohita*:** It is the location for *tilakalak* (small black moles), *nyacha* (black pigmented patches) and *vyanga* (freckles).
3. ***Shweta*:** It is the location for *charmadal* (ulcerative & exudative conditions), *ajagallika* (seborrhoea) and *mashak* (big black mole).
4. ***Tamra*:** It is the location of *kilas* (leucoderma with a pinkish tinge) and *kusta* (dermatoses).
5. ***Vedini*:** It is the location for *kushta* (dermatoses) and *visarp* (erysipelas).

6. ***Rohini***: It is the location for *granthi* (benign tumour), *apachi* (chronic lymphadenitis), *arbuda* (malignant tumour), *galaganda* (goitre), and *shleepada* (lymphedema of filariasis).
7. ***Mamsadhara***: This is the location for *bhagandar* (fistula *in ano*), *vidradhi* (abscess), *arsha* (fissure *in ano* and piles).

The individual thicknesses of all the layers is also described (*Sushrut Sh*. 4/4).

Every patient must be examined for the robustness of each of the seven *dhatus* and *oja*. *Twacha* (skin) should be examined for *rasa dhatu*.

Twaksara lakshanas (Signs of robustness of the skin)

Tatra snigdha shlakshna mrudu prasanna sukshma alpa gambheera sukumara lomaa saprabheva cha twak saranaam l Saa saarata sukha saubhagya aishwarya upabhoga buddhi vidya aarogya praharshana anyan aayushyatwam cha chashte ll (Cha. Vim. 8/103)

A *twaksara* person's skin is unctuous, smooth, soft, clear and thin, short, deep rooted, delicate hair, full of lustre. Robustness of the skin indicates that a person is happy, fortunate, powerful, pleasant, intelligent, knowledgeable, healthy, and cheerful and has a long life span.

Dosha dusti: Vitiation of *rasa dhatu* by *doshas*

Fever or *jwara* is the most important medical condition amongst all the conditions. It is rooted in disturbances of the *rasa dhatu* due to *vata*, *pitta* and *kapha doshas*.

Jwara: Pyrexia, fever

In many medical conditions, fever is the most common presenting symptom. Its incidence rises with vagaries in climate, exertion and indiscretions. It is caused by various etiological factors. Ayurveda on the other hand describes *jwara* as the king of all diseases.

The origins of *jwara* date back to the mythological *Daksha Yagna*, which was associated with the colossal dance of destruction and death all over the universe (macrocosm) due to uncontrolled anger of *Lord Rudra*. There was an associated large rise in temperature on earth, with disastrous climatic and environmental changes. Based on a similar theme at the microcosmic level of an individual, *jwara* manifests as *Rudra kopa* (anger of *Rudra*). Anger (*kopa*) is known to raise body temperature. In fever, the set point of the normal body temperature is raised to a higher level that makes an individual suffer great bodily pain, discomfort and agony. This is associated with obstruction to sweat secretion.

The concept of *Rudra* or *Shiva* is with associated heat. It is believed that when *Shiva* leaves the body, death ensues. A dead body is therefore called *shava*. Thus *Shiva* is considered central to body heat or the temperature control system in all living beings. The seat of temperature control of the entire body and that of *Shiva* are located in *shikha* (the lower level in the back of the brain). The centre for thermal control is located in the dorso-medial hypothalamus at the back of the lower brain.

Vishnur hridayam, Rudra Shikhah l

The location of Vishnu is in the heart and that of Shiva is the back of the head (*shikha*).

Mahamahopdhyay Gananath Sen interprets the mythological story of the *Daksha yagna* as follows: *Daksha* is the controller of all *indriyas*. *Vayu dosha* is the driver and controller of the organs of sense and action. Perturbed and vitiated *vayu* causes a disturbance to the thermal control centre (thermostat) leading to fever.

Another important cause for fever is the generation of *ama* in the gastro-intestinal tract. It is due to the vitiation of *samana vayu*. This obstructs the path of *pachakagni*. Semi-digested food, when absorbed into *rasa* leads to the release of toxins into the general circulation, raising the temperature, due to the hot (fire) quality of *pitta*, adsorbed by perturbed *vayu*. The circulatory system transports the heat to the tissues, including the skin and obstructs the sweat. Thus fever manifests with three symptoms, *viz*., a rise in temperature (*santap*), obstruction to sweating (*swedavarodh*) and body aches and pains (*sarvanga grahanam*).

With this background, let us now understand how modern science explains temperature control in the human body.

The thermostat that creates a set point temperature is located in the dorso-medial hypothalamus, which is the part of the lower brain. Any disturbance to this central thermostat causes a rise in temperature above the set point resulting in fever. The normal set point levels of temperature are: 37.5°C (99.5°F) - 38.3°C (100.9°F). Locations where temperature is normally recorded are otic, rectal, oral and axillary, with the otic (ear) being the most accurate.

Fever level: Maximum: 41°C (105.4°F) – 42°C (107.6°F).

Pyrogens are the agents that trigger pyrexial response. These are of two types: Exogenous (*Agantuka*) and endogenous (*abhyantara*).

Exogenous pyrogens: These are commonly the lipopolysaccharides that are derived from the cell walls of infection producing bacteria. These activate the arachidonic acid (AA) pathway and cause the release of prostaglandins (PGE2). This PGE2 disturbs the hypothalamic thermostat and causes a rise in temperature above the set point.

Endogenous pyrogens: Any invasion by a foreign substance leads to inflammation and the activation of the immune system associated with the release of cytokines, *viz.*, IL-1 and IL-6. These in turn activate the arachidonic acid (AA) pathway triggering the release PGE2. Thus release of PGs are at the root of pyrexial response in the body.

When the set point of body temperature is raised, shivering occurs due to muscular contractions as a result of activation of the autonomous nervous system with the release of acetyl choline and adrenaline causing peripheral vaso-constriction. This results in prevention of heat loss from the body. It also prevents sweat formation in the skin. As the fever subsides, the temperature returns to the set point resulting in the reversal of all the earlier processes. This reversal results in vasodilation with sweating, which cools the body. In rare cases seizures may occur in children during fever.

Beneficial effects of fever: Many consider fever to be a protective mechanism of the body. By raising the temperature of the body, it makes the environment hostile for the survival of many pathogenic organisms. Pyrexia may also help in causing leucocytosis, proliferation of T cells and enhancing phagocytosis, thus neutralizing endotoxins. Thus anti pyretic analgesics are not advisable in the early stages of fever.

Pathogenesis of *jwar*: *Jwara samprapti*

All the authors of *Vriddha Trayee* (Charak, Sushrut and Vagbhata) agree that *jwar* originates in *amashaya* (the proximal part of the GI tract, stomach and duodenum) with the accumulation of vitiated *doshas* (*vata*, *pitta* and *kapha*), which are provoked by their respective etiological factors. These *doshas* obstruct the channels in *pachyamanashay* (the middle part of the GI tract, small bowel) and transport *agni* to the periphery of the body (tissues and skin) through the circulating *rasa dhatu*. This leads to a rise in body heat. Blocking of sweat channels occurs simultaneously leading to stopping of sweating.

Vata, *pitta* and *kapha* are by products of digestion of food and its metabolism at different levels of *koshta*. These are *panchabhautic* in origin and are located in different parts of the GI tract. *Kapha* (*prithvi* and *jal*) is located in *amashaya*; *pitta* (*jal* and *tej*) in *pachyamanashay* and *vata* (*vayu* and *akash*) in *pakwashaya*. When there is homeostasis of *doshas*, it leads to health and their disharmony leads to disease. *Vata* is responsible for gene functions, including those of gene products and other regulatory and signalling mechanisms (neuro, hormone and immune). *Vata* is described as *yantra tantra dhara*. Cell division, morphological features of shape and size, cognition, and movement, *etc*., are governed and regulated by *vata*, *pitta* and *kapha*. *Pitta* is responsible for all translational or transcriptional activities, *viz*., metabolism, heat regulation and overall energy balance, vision, colouring of red blood cells and other pigments that are produced, intelligence and immunity. *Kapha* is related to all structural formation and mechanisms. It is responsible for growth, structural maintenance and stability, and allergies.

Improper digestion of food is associated with production of *ama* (toxic elements) that vitiate *doshas* and nutrient *rasa dhatu*. In *jwara* the *rasa dhatu* circulating throughout the whole body is primarily vitiated.

We know now that the intestine secretes a number of peptides that act like hormones to establish homeostasis of many physiological functions. One such example is of incretins, which are insulin like secretions of intestinal origin (GLP1 - glucagon like peptide, GIP- glucose dependent insulinotropic poly peptide).

Similarly *vata*, *pitta* and *kapha* (genes, gene products, cytokines, chemokines, hormones, neuro transmitters and varieties of enzymes *etc*.,) act in a similar way to some of the peptide like molecules. This hypothesis could be a subject of research. The intestines play a major role in immunology. Apart from the central and autonomic nervous systems, a third enteric neural system is now recognized, which is non adrenergic or non-cholinergic. Gut microbiome is currently a hot new research subject, which is developing into new subject. The gut is host to billions of microbes, whose volume of DNA far exceeds that of human specific DNA, providing another dimension to information transfer and signalling systems.

Pathogenesis of fever in modern medicine

Thermal regulation mechanisms: Heat, hypoxia, oxidative stress, exposure to toxins, nutrition deprivation and infections result in release of heat shock proteins (HSPs), which play a key role in regulation of multiple pathways of signalling systems. These include phosphorylation of NF-kB and binding it to TNF, MAPK, JAK-STAT, CDK1, *etc*.

Induction of fever is due to a coordinated interplay of the innate immune system and the neuronal circuitry of the central and peripheral nervous systems. Innate immune cells (macrophages, polymorphonuclear, and dendritic) through toll like receptors recognise the lipid polysaccharide cell wall of bacteria, viral RNA and fungal sugars, *etc*., and release PGE2, IL-1, IL-6, TNFα. These act on median preoptic neurons in the hypothalamus and raise the temperature. They also act on the parasympathetic acetyl choline and sympathetic nerves to cause shivering and vasoconstriction. RANKL (cytokine receptor activation of NF-kB ligand) is yet another pathway of inducing fever through release of COX2- EP3- PGE2.

Thermal stress causes activation of the immune system, first there is the innate then the adaptive immune response. The macrophages are induced with the entry of pathogen specific T-cells, with Th1 cell polarization leading to the release of IFNγ, IL-6 and increasing the cytotoxity of NKcells.

Return to homeostasis

The immune system responds to a rise in temperature by activating the inflammatory machinery (macrophages) through the release of cytokines. This leads to dampening of heat stress mechanism. Beta adrenergic receptors are present on the immune cells. Once the synthesis of cytokines stops, the process is reversed with the temperature coming back to the set point with the onset of sweating, (Ref. Fever and Thermal Regulation of Immunity - Immune System Feels Heat – Sharon S. Evans, Elizabeth A, Repaksy, & Daniel T. Fisher, *Nature Reviews Immunology*, 15,335-44, 2015).

Fever is a hallmark inflammation response of the body. It is orchestrated by integrated physiological, inflammatory molecules and mechanisms of neuronal circuitry. It provides an individual with survival benefits. A 1°C rise in temperature requires a 10-12.5% increase in the metabolic rate. Evidence is mounting in favour of raised temperatures up to 4 degrees giving better resolution of infection, with improved survival rates. Use of antipyretics early in fever is associated with a 5% rise in the mortality rate. Many viral fevers have a limited period of 3-4 days of pyrexia, after which the homeostasis returns. Hence antipyretics, *e.g.*, paracetamol, *etc.*, are contra indicated in the early stage of fever. In rare circumstances the temperature may rise very rapidly to a very high level, endangering life. In such cases aggressive treatment with cold compresses, antipyretics and even hypothermia is advised.

Rasa dusti is seen in all fevers. When *doshas* get vitiated harmful toxins are released into circulation. Fever is a sign of this toxaemia and is associated with a large amount of proteins breaking down. These products (amino acids), which are the result of the proteins breaking down, over crowd the liver, producing the premonitory symptoms of loss of appetite, nausea and vomiting. In order to correct the vitiated *rasa, langhana* or fasting is advised. It appears to be a very interesting concept. As it is, loss of appetite, nausea and vomiting continue, and the patient is unable to take oral feeds. If a patient suffering from fever is force fed, it will only further add to the load on an already overburdened liver. Hence, avoidance of food by a patient suffering from fever is beneficial, but hydration and electrolyte balance must be taken care of. During the period of *langhana*, Ayurveda advises hydration with an oral drink, *Shadanga paneeya*. It contains six, mild antiviral, antibacterial and antipyretic herbs. These herbs are *Musta* (Cyperus rotundus), *Parpatak* (Fumaria parvi flora), *Ushir* (Vetivera zizanoids), *Chandan* (Santalum album), *Shunthi* (Zinziber officianale), *Sugandhi Vala* (Pavonia oderata), (*Charak Chi.* 3/145). These herbs have an antipyretic and analgesic action comparable to salicylates along with mild antimicrobial activity. They also possess antiemetic action and help to restore the electrolyte balance, while improving the liver function. Fasting is a method of detoxification. It also helps autophagy. Autophagy is a natural regulating mechanism of the cell that disassembles unnecessary or dysfunctional components and eliminates them. In the light of this information, there is a need to revisit the concept of *langhana*, practiced by Ayurveda. *Langhana* and *shadang paneeya* therapy need a thorough clinical trial to establish their validity *versus* present methods of managements of fevers with harmful antipyretic analgesics and antipyretics.

The modern approach to all fevers in the initial stage is administration of paracetamol tablets after food. Paracetamol is known for its hepatotoxic property. Food is already shown to aggravate the load on an over loaded liver. Over and above this, administration of a known hepatotoxic drug is absolutely unscientific and hence not warranted. There is a need for an Ayurvedic antipyretic drug that can replace the universal use of paracetamol tablets.

Chapter : 32

Rakta Dhatu

Rakta dhatu is the second important *dhatu* or primal tissue.

Dehasya rudhiram moolam rudhirenaiva dharyate l

Tasmat yatnena samrakshyam raktam jeeva iti sthitih l
(Su. Su. 14. 44)

Verily *rakta* or blood is life. It upholds the body. Hence all efforts are needed to safe guard it.

The term *rakta* comes from its red colour. Iron pigment, haem of haemoglobin is responsible for this red colour. Blood circulates throughout the body, it carries oxygen to tissues and returns carbon dioxide to the lungs for excretion. It nourishes all tissues and removes all the waste products of tissue metabolism. It provides the body with an immune defence system. Blood is kept in a fluid state in the vascular system through balanced haemostatic mechanisms.

According to Ayurveda, it originates from the *rasa dhatu*. It is formed by the action of *ranjak pitta* and its *dhatwagni* on *rasa dhatu*. *Pachyamanashay* refers to an area between the stomach and the large bowel. This comprises the duodenum, small bowel, liver and spleen. Sushruta has enumerated the liver (*yakrut*), spleen (*pleeha*) and red bone marrow (*sarakta meda/rakta majja* of *asthi*) as the sites of erythropoiesis. Vagbhata also mentioned the role of a factor in the stomach in the formation of blood (erythropoiesis). Sushruta has advised the use of liver preparations as therapy in cases of anaemia, giving it a prime role in erythropoiesis. *Ranjaka pitta* gives blood its red colour. It appears from the description given above, that Ayurveda *acharyas* had some understanding of the process of erythropoiesis, and the blood bile relationship, roles of the liver and spleen. The physical qualities of *rakta dhatu* are as follows:

Indragopaka prateekaasham asamhitam
avivarnam cha prakrutistham janeeyat l
(Su. Su. 14/22)

Tapaneeyendragopaabham padmalaka sannibham l
Gunja phala savarnam cha vishuddham viddhi shonitam ll (Charak)

Its properties are as follows: It is 1. Liquid in consistency *(drava)*. 2. Flowing in nature (*sara)*. 3. Unctuous *(snigdha)*. 4. Slow *(manda)*. 5. Soft (*mrudu*). 6. Viscous *(pitchila)*. 7. Red in colour, like the insect, *indragopa* (red velvet mite). 8. Salty sweet in taste. 9. Has a fleshy smell *(visra gandha)*. Its panchabhautic consistency is *agneya*.

Functions: Its main function is to supply oxygen and remove carbon dioxide from the tissues. It is responsible for the growth of body tissues. It provides a substrate for muscle tissue (myo- haemoglobin and proteins from plasma). It enhances skin complexion and tactile sensation. In a person suffering from anaemia, one can observe the pallor and poor neural sensations.

Modern understanding of erythropoiesis

Blood is red because it contains red blood corpuscles. They are suspended in plasma along with other cellular elements, *viz.*, white cells and platelets. In the foetus, red cells are formed in the liver and spleen apart from the bone marrow. It is interesting to note that all the authors have quoted these two organs as the seat of formation of blood. Only Susruta talks of *sarakta meda* (red bone marrow) also as one of the sites. By the age of twenty most of the red marrow in the long bones is converted into fatty yellow marrow. Only the upper ends of the humerus, femur and flat bones contain red marrow, which actively participates in blood formation during adult life. The area of the bone marrow is as large as that of the liver. It contains pluri-potent, uncommitted stem cells and uni-potent committed stem cells. It is these committed cells that develop into RBCs and other blood cells.

Red blood cells are biconcave discs, 7.5 milli microns in diameter and 2 mill microns in thickness. Each RBC contains 29 pg. of haemoglobin. The average RBC count is 5.4 million/μL in men and 4.8 million/μL in women. There is, on an average, 900 grams of haemoglobin in an adult individual. It performs the function of an oxygen carrier.

Erythropoiesis

Erythropoietin is a glycoprotein hormone secreted by the kidneys and to a small extent by the liver. It promotes differentiation of stem cells in bone marrow to erythrocytes. It operates by various feedback mechanisms. Hypoxia, as seen at high altitudes and anaemia stimulate erythropoiesis.

High circulating RBCs inhibit the process of erythropoiesis. Stem cells responsive to erythropoietin are converted into pro-erythroblasts. The hormone (erythropoietin) stimulates mRNA synthesis. Four additional factors that regulate erythropoiesis are colony stimulating factors. Of the cytokines IL-3 is also an important factor. Proerythroblasts progress in stages to late normoblasts, reticulocytes and finally into mature red cells. Red cells lose their nuclei before entering into circulation. The average life span of these cells is 120 days. Any abnormal shape of RBCs, *e.g.*, spherocytosis, causes increased fragility. Deficiency of the enzyme G6PD can also cause haemolysis with the use of certain drugs *e.g.*, anti-malarial group of drugs. Sulpha and certain analgesics also cause the lysis of red cells.

Spleen

The spleen is the largest lymphoid organ in the human body. Its rich and diverse population of immune cells and its ingenious anatomy enables optimal surveillance and phagocytosis of circulating blood elements. Thus it plays an important role in the defence against pathogens. It is a blood filter. It removes all abnormal red cells including spherocytes. It contains many platelets. It also plays a significant role in immune processes. The sinusoids of the spleen contain phagocytes and lymphocytes. These cells induce immune responses. The different aspects of splenic functions are summarized below. There are three functional zones in the spleen; 1. Red pulp. 2. White pulp. 3. Marginal zone.

Functions of the spleen

Red pulp

Extra medullary haematopoiesis if necessary

Facilitating an environment wherein erythrocytes rid themselves of solid waste material

Blood filter for foreign material and damaged and senescent blood cells

Storage site for iron, erythrocytes, platelets, plasma blasts and plasma cells

Rapid release of antigen-specific antibodies into the circulation produced by red pulp plasma cells

Defence against bacteria using the iron metabolism of its macrophages

White pulp

T cell zone (periarterial lymphatic sheath) and B cell zone (follicles)

Storage site for B and T lymphocytes

Development of B and T lymphocytes upon antigenic challenge

Release of immunoglobulins upon antigenic challenge by B lymphocytes

Production of immune mediators involved in clearance of bacteria such as complement, opsonins, properdin and tuftsin

Marginal zone (MZ)

Phagocytosis of circulating microorganisms and immune complexes by MZ macrophages

Development of marginal zone B lymphocytes upon TI-2 antigenic challenge

Blood trafficking of B and T lymphocytes

Release of immunoglobulins upon antigenic challenge by splenic B lymphocytes

Liver

The liver is the second largest organ of the body after the skin. It is the chief organ of metabolism. All the nutrients are absorbed from the intestinal villi into the portal vein and are transported into the liver, where they are broken down into simple carbohydrates, amino acids, and fatty acids. It converts glucose to glycogen and stores it to provide energy as and when required by the body. The liver cells produce bile, which is concentrated and stored in the gall bladder. Bile is a dark green to yellow coloured fluid. Fatty acids in the duodenal canal stimulate endocrine cells to release the hormone cholecystokinin (CCK). Secretin stimulates the duct cells in the liver to release bicarbonate into bile. Bile aids the digestion and absorption of lipids in the food in the small intestine. It is responsible for the elimination of waste products of haemoglobin, bilirubin, biliverdin and excess cholesterol. It is a very important site for producing plasma proteins and clotting factors. It detoxifies all the noxious elements including drugs. The primary functions of the liver are as follows:

- Bile production and excretion.
- Excretion of bilirubin, cholesterol, hormones, and drugs.
- Metabolism of fats, proteins, and carbohydrates.
- Enzyme activation.
- Storage of glycogen, vitamins, and minerals.
- Synthesis of plasma proteins, such as albumin, and clotting factors.

Haemoglobin: It transports oxygen in the body. All the life processes depend upon it. It is interesting to note that Ayurveda equated blood with life (*Raktam jeeva iti smrutah*). It is a pigment that contains iron, and is made up of four sub units of the haem moiety conjugated to a polypeptide (globin). The polypeptides exist in two forms of chains *viz.*, α & β. The α chain has 141 amino acid residues and the β chain has 146 amino acid residues. Normal adult human haemoglobin (HbA) has two sets of α & β chains; hence it is designated $\alpha2\ \beta2$. Haemoglobin A1c has a glucose molecule attached to the terminal valine in each β chain. It is of special significance in diabetes mellitus. Foetal haemoglobin has a greater affinity for binding to oxygen than that of adult haemoglobin. This is due to the fact that the β chain of adult Hb is replaced by a γ chain in foetal haemoglobin.

Haemoglobinopathies: Globin genes determine the peptide chains. These can result into abnormal peptide chains leading to different haemoglobinopathies.

Thalassemia: Amino acid chains are normal in structure, but are produced in decreased numbers or are absent due to defective globin genes. A decrease or absence of certain polypeptides in the α chain, leads to α-thalassemia. Similarly, β-thalassemia occurs when there is abnormality in the β chain.

Sickle cell anaemia: This is very common in certain African countries. It is due the presence of haemoglobin S (HbS), in which the α chain is normal, but the β chain is abnormal.

Haemoglobin reactions

The iron in Hb is in the ferrous form and it binds to O_2 forming oxyhaemoglobin. Haem is also a part of myohaemoglobin and the cytochrome C enzyme. CO (carbon monoxide) has a greater affinity to bind to Hb than O_2.

Catabolism of haemoglobin

Globin is split from the haem first. Haem is converted to biliverdin which further undergoes a change to become bilirubin. It is then excreted into bile, which is yellowish in colour. This yellow coloured bile is equated to *pitta* in Ayurveda by some people. All these changes happen in the liver. Hence the *acharyas* had thought it prudent to associate all these four entities, *viz*., *rakta* (blood), *pitta* (bile), *yakrut* (liver) and *pleeha* (spleen) into one functional system. According to the texts in Ayurveda, it takes 24 hours to form *rasa dhatu* from digested food. *Rakta* requires five days to be made from *rasa dhatu* by interaction with *agni*. It gets its red colour from *ranjak pitta*, which is responsible for the haemoglobination of RBC. All these processes occur in the liver and spleen. It is pumped throughout the body through blood vessels along with the *rasa dhatu*. Its volume is eight *anjalies* (*Charak Sharer*. 7/15). It is sweet in taste, unctuous, red in colour, heavy and malodorous. It is one of the ten *pranaayatanas* (source of life). It gives the body strength, complexion, zest and life. It is the source of the strength of the muscles. Its *upadhatus* are tendons (*kandara*) and blood vessels (*siras*). *Mala* of the *rakta* is *pitta dosha*.

Haemostatic mechanisms

An important function of the blood is coagulation or thrombosis. Whenever any injury occurs to blood vessels, the thrombotic mechanism comes into play to stop the bleeding with the formation of a clot. There are certain factors which are coagulant or thrombotic, and others that are opposing factors, called antithrombins. Vascular injury causes immediate constriction of the vessels, which activates factor VII resulting in thrombin. Thrombin activates platelets, factor V and factor XI on the platelet surface, and a fibrin mesh is formed by converting fibrinogen to fibrin. The formation of a clot is due to platelet aggregation plugging into the fibrin mesh at the haemorrhage site. Thus with the formation of a clot, bleeding is controlled. Endogenous antithrombins are protein C, protein S, antithrombin and fibrinolytic system, cytokines, *viz.*, IL-4, IL-10. The balance of these two opposing systems maintains blood in a fluid state while in circulation. Any defect or disturbance to this system can cause different bleeding disorders or thrombophilias, which include haemorrhagic disease or deep vein thrombosis. *Rakta pitta* and *rakta dushti* are probably comparable to varieties of thrombophilias.

The blood in an individual can be in different states.

Rakta saara

Blood in its perfect or healthy state is described as *rakta saara*.

Karnakshi mukha jivha naasa oashta paani paadatala nakha lalaata mehanam snigdha rakta varnam shreemad bhrajishnu rakta sarata l Sa saarata sukha muddhatam medhyam manasvitwam saukumaryam anatibalam aklesha sahishnutwam ushna asahishnutwam chachashte ll (Cha. Vi. 8/104)

In an individual with *rakta saara*, the complexion is pink in colour and it glows. The face, eyes, ears, mouth, tongue, lips, nails, hands, feet and genitals *etc.*, are pinkish, red in colour. A person with *rakta saara* is physically strong, well composed and intelligent, gentle, but cannot tolerate severe hardships and heat.

Rakta kshaya

Rakta kshaye hrut peeda kampa shoonya trushna cha l

Shonita kshaye twak parushyam amla sheeta prarthana shira shaithilyam cha l (Su. Su. 15/13)

Acute blood loss causes pain in the chest and palpitations associated with loss of consciousness and excessive thirst. Continued chronic loss makes the skin rough and hard to the touch. The blood vessels are fragile and there is a desire for eating sour and cold substances. Use of the term *rakta* in the first line and *shonita* in the second line, is probably to differentiate between normal blood and menstrual blood loss. *Shonita* here refers to menstrual blood.

Anaemia can be due to either poor blood formation or due to blood loss. Blood loss can be acute in cases of trauma and haemorrhage. This can cause hypovolemic shock. Chronic blood loss can also occur as in cases of piles, menorrhagia and hook worm infestation leading to anaemia. Anaemia can occur in conditions such as thalassemia, abnormal hemoglobin opathies, abnormal types of red cells, *e.g.*, spherocytosis, sickle cell anaemia *etc.* Defects in blood formation due to nutritional deficiency (protein, iron, vitamin B12 and folic acid), aplasia of bone marrow or cancer of the blood (leukaemia) also cause anaemia. The patient becomes pale and complains of lassitude and body ache. The skin becomes rough and there is a tendency to crave cold and sour foods.

***Rakta vriddhi*: Polycythemia**

Rakto ativruddho: raktanga akshitam shira poornatwam cha l
(Su. Su. 15/19)

Excessive *rakta dhatu* is associated with flushed eyes, redness of all body parts and eyes and large blood vessels.

When the number of RBCs is excessive, it results in a condition called polycythemia. This happens due to over production of red blood cells in red bone marrow, which leads to hyper viscosity and intra vascular coagulation. It is associated with an abnormally enlarged spleen and liver. Physiologic polycythemia occurs at high altitudes. Such a person's face looks flushed and the body is seen to be full of blood vessels. Polycythemia Vera is pathological, and presents with the classic symptoms of itching and burning in the hands when exposed to heat. Gouty arthritis and peptic ulcer may also be associated with this condition. Primarily, the treatment is phlebotomy in cases of high viscosity, or intra vascular coagulation.

***Rakta doshaja roga*: Diseases of abnormal blood**

Kushta visarpa pidaka rakta pittam asrugdarah ll

Guda medhraasya paakascha pleeha gulma atha vidradhih l
Neelikaa kaamala vyangah piplavah tila kalakah ll

Dadruh charma dalam shwitram paamaa kothasramandalam l
Rakta pradoshajjayante ll (Cha. Su. 28/11-13)

Diseases due to vitiation of the blood or *rakta dushti*, are as follows:

Dermatosis, erysipelas, pimples, haemothermia, menorrhagia, inflammation of the anus, penis and mouth, enlarged spleen, mobile tumours, abscesses, bluish black moles (sub-cutaneous hemorrages), jaundice, freckles, port wine marks, moles, ringworm, skin abrasions, leukoderma, papules, wheals and red circular patches.

From the above list of diseases, one thing seems very clear, that inflammation is at the root of all the diseases (infections) of vitiation of the blood. A certain amount of toxemia exists in all the blood related inflammatory diseases.

New research studies have found a type of iron dependant programmed cell death, ferroptis, after depletion of glutathione peroxidase activity. Ferroptosis is characterised by the production of a reactive oxygen species (ROS) from accumulated iron load and lipid peroxidation in the cell. New pathways by which ferroptosis causes cancer are being discovered. It has now come to light that those who donate blood twice a year have less chances of developing cancer because of the low iron load, (Prof. Shinyo Toyokuni). Interestingly Ayurveda advocates *rakta mokshan* (blood letting by venesction), as one of the five procedures (*panchakarma*) for the promotion of positive health. This new research throws light on the usefulness of the procedure of *rakta mokshan.* Ayurvedic *rasayanas* are powerful antioxidants. They can prevent ferroptosis through their *jeevaneeya* property (antioxidant).

Chapter : 33

Mamsa Dhatu

***Mamsa dhatu*: Muscle tissue**

This is formed from *rakta* by the action of *mamsagni*. It takes about ten days to form. Its function is to provide cover and shape to the body, and strength to the next *dhatu*, the *meda*. *Mamsagni* converts *rakta* to *mamsa*. It is *parthiva* (earth *mahabhoota*) in consistency. *Sthula* (gross), *sthira* (steady), *guru* (heavy), *khara* (rough), *kathina* (hard) and *slakshna* (smooth) are its characteristics. It functions are *shareera pushti* (gives body strength), *meda pushti* (nurtures lipoid tissues), *shareera lepa* (it gives the body its contours) and *mala pushti* (nourishes its *upadhatus* and excreta). Its *upadhatus* are *vasa* (fat) and *twacha* (skin). Muscles or *mamsa* originate from *snayus* (tendons) and skin. Its *malas* (excretions) are ear wax and discharges from the eye.

Mamsa saar

Acchidra gatram goodha asthi sandhi
mamsopachitamcha mamsena l (Su. Su. 35/18)

When the *mamsa dhatu* is in a perfect state, it is called *mamsa saar*. Such persons have a sturdy, well-formed muscular body with strong and stable joints, and a handsome demeanour. They are endowed with qualities such as forgiveness, steadfastness, good health, wealth, knowledge, a long life, *etc*., and they have a charitable nature without greed.

Mamsa kshaya

Mamsa kshaye sphik manda oashta upastha uru vakshah kaksha
pindikodara greeva shushkata raukshya todau gatranam
sadanam dhamani shaithilyam l (Su. Su. 15/13)

Excessive depletion of *mamsa dhatu* results in cachexia. All parts of the body, *viz*., the buttocks, waist, lips, vulva, thighs, chest, and abdominal wall, all become emaciated. It is associated with dryness, roughness of all body parts and also aches and pains. Arteries pulsate very feebly.

Sarcopenia

This is a degenerative loss of skeletal muscle mass resulting in wasting, usually associated with aging. It also happens due to severe protein deficiency and malnutrition ending in cachexia. Wasting of the cheeks and buttocks, pains in the joints and complaints like giddiness are the signs and symptoms of loss of *mamsa dhatu*. Under nutrition, wasting, *kwashiorkor* and the final stages of TB, HIV- AIDS are a few examples.

Mamsa vriddhi

Sphikgganda oshta upastha uru bahu janghasu
vruddhm guru gatramcha l (Su. Su. 15/19)

When *mamsa dhatu* is excessive, it causes a strong muscular body, heavy weight, increase of the trunk region and swellings in the neck region. Cervical lymphadenitis, tumours (myoma, and fibro adenoma), cysts and swellings in the abdomen are but a few of the conditions associated with an abnormal increase in this *dhatu*.

Diseases that arise from the morbidity of *mamsa dhatu*

Adhimamsa arbudam keelam gala shalookashundike l
Pootimamsa alaji ganda gandamala upajivhika ll
(Cha. Su. 28/14)

Granuloma, malignant tumours of muscle tissue, piles, warts, rotting flesh, dry gangrene, enlarged nodes and multiple lymph nodes are the morbid clinical manifestations of *mamsa dhatu*.

Muscle tissue is made up of muscle fibres. Each muscle fibre is a single cell. It is multi- nucleated, with a long cylindrical shape and is surrounded by the membrane called sarcolemma. Each muscle fibre is further divided into filaments, which are made up of contractile proteins. These proteins are myosin, actin, tropomyosin and tropin. Myosin is a complex actin binding protein. The source of energy for contraction of the muscles is ATP. Muscle can be excited chemically, electrically and also mechanically to produce action potentials. A major part of the body musculature is made up of striated muscle or skeletal muscle. It is under voluntary control and can contract only by nerve stimulation, because of the fact that it lacks anatomical and functional connections between the individual fibres. Destruction of nerve supply leads to wasting of muscles, as typically seen in lower motor neuron lesions. Cardiac muscle has striations, but it functions as a syncytium due to the presence of pace maker cells in it. These cells discharge rhythmically and spontaneously causing the cardiac muscle to contract rhythmically. The smooth muscle of hollow viscera is different from cardiac muscle due to the fact that it does not possess the striations and its pace maker cells discharge impulses irregularly.

Chapter : 34

Meda Dhatu

Meda dhatu: Lipoid tissue

This is the fourth *dhatu* for which *mamsa dhatu* is the substrate. *Medagni* converts *mamsa* into *meda*. In *meda vaha srotas meda dhatu* is formed due to the action of *medagni* on *mamsa dhatu*. The kidneys, trunk and omentum are mentioned as the sites of its production. Its volume is about two *anjalies* (*Charka sharer* - 7/15). It is *aapa* and *parthiva* in its *panchabhautika* constitution. It is *drava* (liquid), *snigdha* (unctuous) and *slaksna* (smooth) in character. Its functions are to provide nourishment and unctuousness (*snehana*) in the body, strengthen (*dhrudatwam*) and give shape to the body. It is also responsible for the generation of sweat (*sweda kaaraka*) and is a substrate for the development of bone tissue and fills the bones (*asthi pushti*). Bone develops from the periosteum. The mineralization of bone and its conversion from cartilage to bone is under the control of vitamin D, which is a sterol (lipid). Now one can see the relation of the *meda* as a substrate for the formation of bone tissue. Lipid tissue is made up of adipocytes. Adipose tissue is undoubtedly the *meda dhatu*. Its *upadhtus*, or minor by-products of *meda* are ligaments, joint capsules, blood vessels, sweat glands and fat.

Meda saara: Robust state of *meda*

Snigdha mootra sweda swara bruhat shareeram
aayaasa asahishnum medasaa l (Su. Su. 35/18)

Persons who have *meda saara* have unctuous urine and sweat. Their voice is soft and they have a large body. They are very gentle and delicate with low endurance power and are usually wealthy. The *mala* (excretion by-product) of *meda* is sweat.

Meda kshaya

Meda kshaye pleehabhivriddhih sandhi shoonyata raukshyam
medura mamsa prarthanacha l (Su. Su. 15/13)

In *meda dhatukshaya* persons, there occurs splenic enlargement, dryness of the body and instability of the joints. Such a person desires fatty and fleshy meals.

Meda vriddhi

Medah snigdhaangata udara parshwa vriddhi kasa shwasadeen daurgandhyam cha l (Su. Su. 15/19)

Excessive *meda dhatu* increases unctuousness in the body along with obesity of the trunk. Dyspnoea on slight exertion and cough are common complaints. These people emit a foul body odour. *Meda vriddhi* can be seen either localized as lipomas or as general obesity.

Meda janya roga

Medah samshrayamstu prachakshmahe l
Ninditani pramehanaam poorva roopani yani cha ll
(Cha. Su. 28/15)

The excess storage of *meda* leads to prodromal signs of difficult to treat clinical conditions known as *pramehas* (obesity, diabetes and other urinary tract diseases).

Cellular lipids

These are mainly of two types. Structural fats mainly form cell membranes and also parts of the cells. The depot fats are made up of stores of neutral fat in the cells that are called adipocytes. These are dynamic tissues, where continuous resynthesis and breakdown of lipids occurs. Biologically important lipids are neutral fats (triglycerides), phospholipids and sterols. Phospholipids help form the cell membranes. Naturally occurring fatty acids have an even number of carbon atoms. Saturated fatty acids do not possess double bonds, whereas unsaturated fatty acids have a number of double bonds. Sterols are the substrate for all steroid hormones and cholesterol. There is also a special type of lipid known as brown fat, which is found only in very small quantities in an adult, but is more abundantly found in infants. It is located between two scapulae at the nape of the neck, the great vessels in the thorax and abdomen and many other scattered locations. These cells are extensively innervated with sympathetic nerve fibres. They also have large numbers of mitochondria and are capable of producing great amounts of energy with less ATP. In contrast to ordinary lipocytes, the brown variety has many fat droplets. These cells respond to sympathetic stimulation and also to food by generating more heat. This may be the reason for its role in the development of obesity. Adipocytes also produce a serine protease, which signals the appetite control system through the satiety centre. In fat depots, fatty acids are formed from glucose, and converted into neutral fats (triglycerides). Triglycerides are also broken down as and when energy is required and are released into circulation. Fatty acids are broken down in mitochondria to form acetyl CoA, which requires the participation of lysine. Outside of the mitochondria, the fatty acids are broken down in microsomes. This process requires the presence carnitine. Mitochondria of many tissues can synthesize fatty acids from acetyl CoA. Acetyl CoA is a coenzyme that participates in many biochemical reactions in the body. Adipocytes are also found to be a new source of mesenchyme stem cells. Currently these play a very important role in regenerative medicine.

Plasma lipids and lipid transport mechanisms

After a meal, the digested food is converted into chylomicrons in the intestinal mucosa. Chylomicrons are a variety of lipoproteins. Neither triglycerides (TG) nor cholesterols dissolve in blood, so they need to be carried in plasma by proteins, called lipoproteins, which transport the lipids through the lymphatic ducts into circulation. After a meal, the plasma has a milky appearance, and hence is called milky plasma. The lipoprotein, lipase in the presence of heparin acts on the chylomicrons to break them into free fatty acids (FFAs) and glycerol. These FFAs are re-esterified in the adipose cells to become depot fats, and are broken down again into FFAs as and when required. They are transported bound to albumin. Triglycerides, cholesterol and phospholipids are bound to apoprotein, which is a lipoprotein. LDL cholesterol is required by the tissue cells for the formation of cell membranes and the production of steroid hormones. Over load of plasma LDL can cause atherosclerosis. A number of environmental and physical factors trigger the release of oxygen free radicals into circulation. These react with the LDL cholesterol and cause its oxidation, injuring the endothelium of the vessels (arteries) in the process. These injured vessels signal the immune system to release WBCs to initiate an inflammatory reaction. Macrophages involved in the inflammatory process ingest the oxidized cholesterol and are transformed into foamy cells or foam cells. Cholesterol, inflammatory debris and foam cells adhere to the arterial vessel walls and form an atherosclerotic plaque. This leads to hardening and narrowing of the vessels. It is one of the main causes of hypertension. Damage to the inner endothelial layer of the blood vessels results in generation of insufficient quantities of nitric oxide (NO). Generation of NO is essential for maintaining the tone and elasticity of blood vessels. Nitric oxide synthase is required for the generation of nitric oxide gas from arginine, an amino acid.

Lipoproteins are classified on the basis of their densities. Very low density lipoproteins (VLDLs) transport the triglycerides that are synthesized in the liver to adipose tissues and muscle. Low density lipoproteins (LDLs) transport cholesterol from the liver to all the peripheral tissues. High density lipoproteins (HDL) transport cholesterol from the peripheral tissues to the liver.

Lipid peroxidation

During the metabolic processes, unpaired electrons of oxygen are liberated. They are called reactive oxygen species (ROS) or free radicals. ROS in turn oxidize the lipids. This can be compared to the mechanism that makes butter rancid. It causes harmful effects like atherosclerosis. Environmental pollutants, ultraviolet radiation, nuclear radiation, *etc.*, are some of the several sources of ROS. ApoE is a class of proteins involved in the metabolism of fats in the body. It is synthesized by astrocytes in the brain, the spleen cells and cells in the lungs, adrenal glands, ovaries, kidneys and liver. It helps in the regeneration and repair of nerves.

Metabolism of free fatty acids

Catechol amines, ACTH, TSH, LH, serotonin, glucagon, vasopressin, growth hormone and thyroid hormone sensitize the enzyme lipase through cyclic AMP and protein kinase and activate it. Lipases are of two types, the first is endothelium based lipase, which hydrolyses both the TGs in the chylomicrons and VLDL into FFAs and glycerol, releasing them into circulation. These are reassembled in the fat cells in the depots. Another lipase is the hormone sensitive, intracellular lipase of the adipose tissue, which catalyses and breaks down stored TGs into fatty acids and glycerol, and then releases them into circulation, which is how the cycle functions.

Cholesterol metabolism

This is an essential constituent of all the cell membranes and a precursor of steroid hormones and bile acids. It is only found in the animal kingdom. Its chief sources are egg yolk and animal fats. It is synthesised by the liver and other tissues. Biliary cholesterol is also absorbed from the intestines. Most of the cholesterol in the liver is in the form of VLDL.

Linoleic acid, linolenic acid and arachidonic acid (AA), and the poly unsaturated fatty acids (PUFA) are the essential fatty acids. Eicosanoids or the prostanoids are fatty acids derived from AA, having a chain of twenty carbon atoms. They are the precursors of prostaglandins, which are mediators of inflammation. Prostaglandins are very powerful local hormones with many biological actions. In rheumatoid arthritis they are produced in excess. The prostaglandins and thromboxane are formed due to the action of an enzyme called cyclooxygenase. The other pathway of arachidonic acid metabolism is by lipoxygenase, which results in the production of leukotrienes, which are the mediators of allergy and inflammation.

Cortisol inhibits both the PGs and leukotrienes because it acts at the level of inhibiting the release of AA. NSAIDs inhibit only cyclooxygenase (COX). Aspirin by acetylation, irreversibly inactivates the COX. *Sallaki guggulu* is an Ayurvedic herb that is commonly used in arthritis for pain relief. It acts through the inhibition of the lipoxigenase pathway.

Obesity: Sthaulyam

Rasa nimittam eva sthaulyam karshyam cha l

Tatra shleshmala aahara sevino adhyashanasheelasya avyayamino diwa swapnaratasya chaam evaannaraso madhuratarascha shareeram anukraamannati snehaan medo janayati l Tad atisthaulyam aapaadayati l

Tam ati sthoolam kshudra shwasa pipaasa kshut swapna praswedagaatra daurgandhyakrathan gatra saada gadgadatwani kshiprameva vishanti saukumaryan medasah sarva kriyastu asamarthah; kapha medo nirudhamargatwaacha alpavyavaayo bhavati, aavrutta margatwat eva shesha dhatavo naapi anyante atyatrathamato alpa pramaano bhavati, prameha pidaka jwar bhagandar vidradhi vata vikaraanam anyatamam prapya panchatwam payati l Sarva evan cha asya rogaa balavanto bhavati aavruttamargatwat srotasam, atah staulyotpatti hetum pariharet ll (Cha. Su. 15/37)

Both obesity and emaciation are due to abnormal *rasa dhatu*. Excessive consumption of substances that promote *kapha*, over eating before digestion of food consumed earlier, sleeping in the day time, lack of exercise cause the chyle to become excessively sweet in taste and this in turn increases unctuousness in *rasa dhatu*, leading to excessive production of lipoid *meda dhatu*. Due to obstruction to body channels by *kapha* and *meda* all the *dhatus* other than *meda* are formed in small quantities, leading to obesity. Such a person is excessively obese, becomes breathless on slight exertion, complains of excessive thirst and hunger, sweats copiously and emanates a foul body odour. These are the hallmark symptoms of an obese person, who usually complains of body aches and pains, has a stuttering, feeble voice, is easily tired and prefers to rest. Such a person is very gentle and soft, unfit to undertake any hard work, unable to exercise, is deficient in sexual prowess and is prone to the following diseases: Diabetes, boils, carbuncles, fever, fistula in *ano*, abscesses, neurological diseases (paralysis *etc.*). In order to avoid these difficult complications due to obesity it is advisable to take all preventive measures.

Shilajatu guggulu gomootra triphala loha rajas (loha bhasma) rasaanjana madhu yava mudga koradooshaka shyamaa uddalakaadeenam virukshana chedaneeyanam dravyaanam vividha upayogo vyayaama lekhana basti upayogascheti ll (Su. Su. 15/38)

Shilajatu, *guggulu*, *gomutra* (cow's urine), *triphala*, *loharajas* (*loha bhasma*), *rasanjana* (*daru haridra*), *madhu* (honey), *yava* (barley), *mudga* (chick peas), *koradushak* (cereal grains), *shyamak*, *uddalak*, *viruksha* (vegetables), *chedaneeya* (thinner substances), depleting enemas and importantly exercise are the modes of treatments advised by Sushruta.

Modern understanding of obesity: Patho-physiology of obesity

Obesity is an exaggeration of normal adiposity and is responsible for insulin resistance and diabetes, dyslipidaemia, atherosclerosis and hypertension, due to excessive secretions of adipokines. It affects a number of organs like the liver, heart and many endocrine and reproductive functions.

If the fat makes up more than 20% of the body weight in males and 25% in females, it is defined as obesity. It is a metabolic disorder. Such people have elevated triglyceride (TG) and LDL levels and low HDL levels, with insulin resistance. Men with abdominal obesity and waists measuring more than 91 cms (36 inches) and high levels of TGs are prone to atherosclerotic cardiovascular diseases.

Before the discovery of the leptin hormone gene in J.M. Freidman's laboratory, much of the pathophysiology of obesity was not understood. *Lepto* is derived from a Greek word meaning thin. It is chiefly produced in adipose tissue and the small intestine and helps to regulate the energy balance by inhibiting hunger. It was observed that in obese individuals leptin was over expressed, indicating that there was leptin resistance. It is important to understand the regulation mechanisms of appetite. Ghrelin, which modulates short term appetite control, is produced in the stomach. This initiates appetite when the stomach is empty. When the stomach is full or distended, satiety sets in and a person stops eating. Adipose tissues produce leptin, which controls the fat tissue reserves in the body through long term control of appetite. When fat tissue reserves are low, there is a greater urge to eat and when fat reserves are high appetite is decreased. There are many other mediators apart from ghrelin, *e.g.*, insulin, orexin, pyy3-36, cholecystokinin and adiponectin, *etc.* Adipokines are produced by adipose tissue and are mediators that modify obesity. Leptin deficiency, in experimental animals, is seen to be associated with obesity, but in humans it is seen to be associated with leptin resistance. Leptin and ghrelin control the appetite through the central nervous system, in particular the hypothalamus.

The immune system and obesity

Currently, obesity is considered to be a low grade, chronic inflammatory state. There are increased numbers of circulating pro-inflammatory factors. Excess fat accumulation leads to insulin resistance, an increase in macrophages, mast cells, neutrophils, and T & B lymphocytes and a decrease in eosinophils and T lymphocytes. Obesity induces hypoxia in adipose cells causing a switch to anaerobic metabolism stimulating inflammation, and increasing M1 macrophages. It is interesting to see that Ayurveda has given a lot of importance to prevention of obesity. Sushruta says that a lean patient is better than an obese patient. That obesity is a difficult condition to treat was well recognized by the eminent *acharyas* of the past.

Treatment advice for obesity

Nutrition and lipids

An average individual requires about 50-60 grams/day of dietary fat, which will provide 9.3 Kcals/gram of energy. In contrast, proteins and carbohydrates provide only 4 cals/gram of energy. New research has indicated that a diet should provide 30% of its calories from the fats. The contribution of each class of fats should be as follows: Mono unsaturated fats (MUFA) 15%, poly unsaturated (PUFA) 8% and saturated fats (SFA) 7% of calories.

Dietary fats

Dietary fats are classified into three types, as follows:

Saturated fats (SFA): Animal fats, of which butter, cream, dairy products and meat are the chief sources. They also occur in vegetables, *e.g.*, palm oil and coconut oil. Hydrogenated oils are also saturated fats. A high content of these fats in the diet is unhealthy and hence these are termed as bad fats.

Mono unsaturated fats (MUFA): Olive oil, sesame seeds, corn oil, groundnut oil and nuts are good sources of MUFA. Though they are high in calories, they lower the LDL cholesterol without affecting HDL cholesterol.

Poly unsaturated fatty acids (PUFA): Fish oil, sunflower oil, nuts and seeds containing oil in liquid form at room temperature are sources of these fats. They contain essential fatty acids (EFA), *viz.*, Omega-3 and Omega-6, which are not synthesized in the body. Therefore, these should form a compulsory part of an individual's diet. Alpha-linoleic acid (sources: Soya beans and olive oil) and decosa hexanoic acid (DHA) are Omega-3 fatty acids (source: Fish oil). Cereals, vegetable oils, whole grain bread, eggs and poultry products are good sources of Omega-6 fatty acids.

Oleating substances and *ghruta* or *ghee*

Sarpih tailam vasa majja sarva snehottama mataah l
Eshu chaiva uttamam sarpih sanskarasyanuvartanat ll

Ghrutam pitta anila haram rasa shukra ojasahitam l
Nirvapanam mrudukaram swara varna prasaadanam ll
(Cha. Su. 13/13-14)

Ghee, vegetable oil (sesame oil), animal fat and marrow are the best oleating agents. Of all these, *ghee* is the best due to its ease in making therapeutic formulations. It pacifies both *pitta* and *vayu*, and it promotes *rasa* and *shukra dhatus* as well *ojas*. *Ghee* enhances the voice and complexion of the body and appeases any burning sensation and softens the passage of stools.

Ghee/Ghruta is a form of clarified butter. It has a special significance in Ayurveda, as it an excellent pacifier of *pitta dosha*. The nutritional value of one tablespoon is 469 Kj or 112 Kcal. 100 grams of *ghee* contains 3.678 grams of MUFA, 0.473 grams of PUFA and 0.04 grams of protein, and 1 mg of potassium, 1.447 mg Omega 3 fatty acids (FA), 2.247 mg Omega 6 FA and 25.026 mg of Omega 9 FA. The vitamin A content is 3069 IU, vitamin E content is 2.8 mg, vitamin K content is 8.6 mg and cholesterol content is 256 – 375 mg (Wikipedia). Cow ghee is now believed to be anti-atherogenic and have a high nutritional value. Many Ayurvedic formulations are made in *ghee*. Cow's *ghee* is considered to be the best amongst all. It has a high smoking point.

Ghee contains conjugated linoleic acid (CLA), which is a micro nutrient that regulates the metabolism. This helps to reduce inflammation (*pitta shaman*), formation of tumours, cholesterol levels and hypertension. It contains short chain fatty acid (SCFA) butyrate that increases the immune functions, decreases inflammation, raises energy levels and decreases weight. Healthy people can consume up to 10 grams a day or two teaspoons daily.

Madhu meha

Madhu meha or diabetes has been known since ancient times and is described in ancient texts of Ayurveda as a chronic disease that is resistant to treatment and has a familial origin. Diabetes is seen in our country in epidemic proportions to the extent that one in three persons is a diabetic.

Diabetes is now recognised as a group of metabolic disorders that are characterised by high blood sugar levels for prolonged periods, associated with increased frequency of micturition, thirst and hunger. This can have very serious complications of acute keto acidosis and hyperosmolar hyperglycaemia (increased levels of blood sugar) leading even to death in some cases. There are many chronic complications associated with diabetes that affect a number of body systems and organs, such as cardiovascular disease, stroke, kidney disease, sexual dysfunction, diabetic foot ulcers and eye complications (diabetic retinopathy).

Until recent times diabetes was thought to be due to a deficiency of the insulin hormone secreted by beta cells of islets of Langerhans in the pancreas. Recent developments have shown that this is not the case. Diabetes is now believed to be due to an imbalance between two opposing hormones that maintain the balance in blood sugar levels, *viz.*, insulin and glucagon. In some cases of diabetes, there is an increased level of insulin (hyper insulinaemia) associated with obesity, which is due to resistance to insulin in the tissues.

Insulin is secreted by beta cells of islets. It helps the extra cellular glucose to enter into the cells and thus helps to provide fuel for the metabolic processes in the cell. It helps the liver to convert glucose into glycogen, which is the form in which glucose is stored. It helps lipid (fat or adipose tissue) formation and causes anabolic effects in the muscles.

When food enters the digestive system, the hormone, GLP-1 (glucagon like peptide) or incretin is secreted by intestinal entero endocrine L- cells and certain neurones within the nucleus of the solitary tract in the brain stem. It flows into the hepatic portal circulation and has the ability to enhance the secretion of insulin and decrease blood sugar. It is a glucose dependent mechanism.

Glucagon is a hormone secreted by alpha cells of islets. It causes an increase in blood glucose levels by discharging more glucose into blood circulation, either due to break down of glycogen or by producing glucose from non-carbohydrate substances, *viz.*, glycerol, lactate, propionate and certain amino acids. It causes the breakdown of fatty acids (lipolysis) into ketones. It increases protein metabolism in the liver and production of urea. Glucagon controls the metabolism by reducing food intake and increasing energy expenditure. There is yet another hormone that is secreted in delta cells of islets, called somatostatin. This suppresses the glucagon. Thus homeostasis of blood sugar is a very complex mechanism that depends on the balance of both opposing hormones. Hence diabetes is primarily a state of imbalance between insulin and glucagon, so treatment should address this imbalance and not just insulin deficiency.

The causes of diabetes

Ayurveda describes a group of twenty diseases under *prameha*, one of which is *madhu meha*. In *madhu meha* or diabetes mellitus, urine tastes sweet like honey. The main cause is the disturbed *kapha dosha* that affects *rasa dhatu* (plasma and other body fluids), *meda* (lipoid tissue), *mamsa dhatus* (muscle tissues) and organs, mainly *basti* (urinary tract), *sweat* and sebaceous gland secretions. Other very important causes according to Charaka are *agnimandya* and *vishamagni*. Currently dysbiosis (that leads to improper digestion of food) due to disturbed gut micro biota is observed to be associated with type 2 diabetes. The species, Butirivibrio, Bifidobacterium bifidum and Megasphaera in gut micro biota stimulate production of short chain fatty acids (SCFAs). SCFAs in turn stimulate secretion of the crucial peptide GLP-1 that stimulates insulin secretion and lowers blood sugar.

Sushruta described two types of *pramehas*. The first type is a lean diabetic called *sahaja*, which fits the description of type 1 diabetes. It is transmitted from parents through abnormalities in gametes (*beeja dushti*). The second type is an obese diabetic, which fits type 2 late onset diabetes. It is due to improper food habits, abnormal life styles, a sedentary life and obesity. Eating excess of sweet, salty and sour foods that are unctuous (oily) and heavy to digest predispose one to this type of diabetes. New food grains, meat of wet land dwelling animals, *gur*, milk, curd and wine, *etc*., that cause an increase in weight, predispose a person for diabetes. A lazy person who does not exercise sufficiently is a likely candidate for diabetes according to Ayurveda.

Types of diabetes

1. **Pre-diabetic:** Blood sugar is high but not high enough to label a person as a diabetic.
2. **Type 1 diabetic:** When the pancreas produces very little or no insulin. Usually seen early in life. It is genetic in origin.
3. **Type 2 diabetic:** It is usually a late onset, middle age disease. Very often there is a family history. In small birth weight babies, diabetes is commonly observed in middle age.
4. **Gestational diabetes:** In some cases, pregnancy may trigger diabetes.

Diagnosis

In ancient times urine, which attracted ants was diagnostic of the condition. Today it is done by estimating blood glucose levels and urine sugar levels. There are different tests for blood sugar levels, *viz*., fasting, two hours post lunch (post prandial) and random. A glucose tolerance test is carried out by giving 100 grams of glucose orally and testing the blood sugar levels every half an hour to detect pre diabetic condition and 75 grams of glucose to rule out gestational diabetes. Normal fasting blood sugar is 100-110 mg and a post lunch blood sugar level up to 120 mg is considered normal.

Glycosylated haemoglobin (HbA1C) test

This blood test indicates your average blood sugar level over the past two to three months. Normal levels are below 5.7%, so a result between 5.7 and 6.4% is considered pre diabetic. An A1C level of 6.5% or higher on two separate occasions means a person is diabetic. For a diabetic person the diabetes levels should be checked once in three months. Screening is also recommended for people who are under the age of 45 years and overweight, if there are any other problems, such as heart disease, a sedentary lifestyle, a family history of type 2 diabetes, a personal history of gestational diabetes or blood pressure above 140/90 mm Hg. In addition to the HbA1C test, blood pressure and blood and urine should be checked periodically for cholesterol levels, thyroid function, liver function and kidney function. Regular, periodic eye and foot examinations also are important.

Treatment

Monitoring blood sugar on a regular basis is very important for all diabetic patients.

Most prevalent methods to manage Type 2 diabetes

Weight loss: A sustained weight loss of 7% or more of the weight of a diabetic person, seems to be ideal. That means someone who weighs 82 kilograms would need to lose a little less than 5.9 kilograms to make an impact on blood sugar levels. This is the surest way to regulate blood sugar levels. Controlling the size of the portions one eats and eating healthy foods are simple ways to start losing weight.

Healthy eating habits: Restricting calories is very important. Vegetables are very important, refined carbohydrates, sweets and aerated drinks should be avoided. Saturated fats should be restricted. Up to 10 grams of cow's *ghee* daily, is healthy for a diabetic patient.

Fruits for a diabetic patient: Papaya, watermelon are low calorie value fruits, so they are suitable for a diabetic person, so also guava, orange, pomegranate, pine apple and apple are of medium calorie value in moderate portions. High calorie value fruits, *e.g.*, mango, banana, dates, *etc.*, should be avoided. Eating fruits provides energy and fibre. Fruit juices and sugary drinks are contra-indicated. Honey, though sweet in taste is advised for providing quick energy as it is chiefly fructose and it is safe in quantities of up to 10 grams a day. Cane sugar is contra-indicated. Ayurveda can differentiate between the character of sweetness of honey and cane sugar.

Physical activity: A sedentary life is harmful. One should aim for at least 30 to 60 minutes of moderate (or 15 to 30 minutes of vigorous) aerobic exercise most days of the week. A combination of exercises - aerobic exercises, such as walking or dancing on most days, combined with resistance training, such as weigh lifting or yoga twice a week - offers more benefits than either type of exercise alone. Ayurveda advises heavy manual labour for all diabetic persons who are overweight.

Diabetes medications and insulin therapy

Sulphonylureas, glipizide and glimepiride act by increasing insulin secretion and biguanides helps the body to effectively use insulin in cases that are resistant to it. These are the main drugs for diabetics. Possible side effects include, nausea, diarrhoea and gastro intestinal upsets, and hypoglycaemia. There are other agents, *e.g.*, thiazolidinediones, DPP-4 inhibitors, which are used when the primary drugs fail to regulate blood sugar levels. These drugs cause severe side effects ranging from heart failure, pancreatitis and cancers. The most recently developed drug is SLP-1 receptor agonist, which needs to be injected. It has severe side effects of pancreatitis and heart attacks.

Insulin

Discovery of insulin brought about a revolution in the treatment of diabetes. We have already described the mechanisms of action of insulin. When oral anti-diabetic drugs fail to control the disease, insulin is added to the regimen. There are many types of insulin, some of them are short acting and others long acting. Often, people with type 2 diabetes start using insulin with one long acting shot at night, such as insulin glargine (Lantus) or insulin detemir (Levemir). It is necessary to watch out for hypoglycaemias while on insulin therapy. Strict supervision by a diabetologist is absolutely necessary when a patient is on insulin.

Bariatric surgery

A person with type 2 diabetes and a body mass index (BMI) greater than 35, is a candidate for weight loss surgery (bariatric surgery). Dramatic improvements in blood sugar levels are often seen in people with type 2 diabetes after bariatric surgery, depending on the procedure performed. Surgeries that bypass a portion of the small intestine have a greater effect on blood sugar levels than do other weight-loss surgeries. Drawbacks of surgery include its high cost and risks, including a small risk of death. It also requires drastic lifestyle changes. Long-term complications may include nutritional deficiencies and osteoporosis.

Pregnancy

It is very important to look out for a history of oversized babies in previous deliveries to rule out gestational diabetes and also intra uterine growth retardation (IUGR) of the unborn foetus. There are many complications that can occur during pregnancy both to the mother and baby. Growth restricted, smaller birth weight babies are known to become diabetic in middle age. Proper antenatal care is thus a preventive measure of importance for diabetes. Women with type 2 diabetes may need to alter their treatment during pregnancy. Many women will require insulin therapy during pregnancy. Oral anti-diabetic medicines are contra indicated. Diabetic retinopathy may worsen during pregnancy. Visits to an ophthalmologist during the first trimester of pregnancy and at one year post-partum are recommended.

Ayurvedic treatment of diabetes

Numerous Ayurvedic medicines and treatments claim to help people with diabetes. Ayurvedic therapy is effective more as a preventive and as a supplementary measure in chronic cases.

Preventive diet advice: *Pathya* (strict diet regimen) is very important. *Mitam* (measured) and *hitam* (beneficial) food items should be consumed. Food articles with a low glycaemic index are indicated. Sushruta advised old *shali* rice, *ragi*, high protein pulses, *e.g.*, *chana*, *moong*, *arhar* and *kulthi*, oils such as *sarson* (mustard) and *atasi* (flax seed), astringent vegetables, *e.g.*, *vata shrung*, *patola*, *karela*, *etc*., and lean meat.

Medicines: A combination of *amla*, *haldi* and honey is the best for all diabetics. The sweetness of honey and that of cane sugar are different. That honey is recommended, whereas cane sugar is forbidden for a diabetic, is a glowing example of the wisdom of Ayurveda. There are many other herbs in Ayurveda that are hypoglycaemic and which are useful. *Jambool* (Syzygium cumini), *neem* (Azadirachta indica), *vijayasaar* (Pterocarpus marsupium), *methi* (Trigonella foenum graecum), *shilajatu* (mineral pitch), *mesha shrungi* (Gymnema sylvestre) are some of the herbs used in many anti diabetic formulations.

Chapter : 35

Asthi Dhatu

Asthi dhatu, originates from *meda dhatu*. Bone is an important site or location for *vayu dosha*. The most important symptom of vitiated *asthi dhatu* is pain in the bones and joints. Bone is the hardest of all tissues. It is *parthiva* (earth element) in origin. Its qualities are *guru* (heavy in weight), *khara* (rough in consistency), *kathina* (hard), *sthula* (gross), and *sthira* (stable). Its functions are *dharana* (weight bearing and supporting the body), *majja pushti* (it is a substrate of the marrow and strengthens it). It is always covered by the *mamsa dhatu* (*mamsavalambaka*). It provides shape to the body (*moortimata*). Its main functions are giving stability to the body structure and nourishing the marrow. Hardness is also an important characteristic of *vata*. The fact that ergosterol or vitamin D is required for calcification of the bone confirms its origin from *meda dhatu*. Bone is laid from the periosteum. The fat and periosteum are intimately connected. The most important protein of the bone is collagen. Bone gets its hardness due to mineralization of this collagen matrix. As said earlier, all the proteins are nitrogenous. *Vayu* mainly originates from nitrogen. On the above basis, one can argue that bone indeed is made of *vayu*. Porosity of the bone could be another reason to connect bone to *vayu*.

The body hair at different locations, and the nails are described as the *upadhatus* of *asthidhatu*.

Asthi sara: Robust bone tissue

Maha shirah skandam drudha danta hanu asthi nakham asthi l
(Su. Su. 35/18)

Persons with *asthi sara* are very strong physically, very zealous and possesses great physical tolerance. They have strong bones, joints, teeth, and nails, with a tall and broad body frame.

Asthi kshaya: Loss of bone tissue

Asthikshaye asthi shoolam danta nakha bhango raukshyam cha l
(Su. Su. 15/13)

Loss of bone tissue leads to bone pain, breaking or falling of the teeth and nails, and it is associated with dryness in the body.

Asthi vriddhi: Increase in bone mass

Adhyaasthi adhi dantascha l (Su.Su. 15/19)

Over grown bones and extra teeth are signs of an increase in *asthi dhatu*. Exercise causes an increase in bone mass. Abnormal bone growth occurs in acromegaly due to excessive production of the growth hormone. Benign tumours of the bone are known as osteomas and malignant tumours are known as osteosarcomas.

Asthi dosha janya roga

Adhyasthi dantau dantasthibheda shoolam vivarnata l
Kesha loma nakha smashru doshascha asthi pradoshajaah ll
(Cha. Su. 28/16)

Hypertrophy or atrophy of the bones and teeth, pains and aches in the bones and teeth, abnormalities of hair, nail and pallor are the conditions associated with morbid *asthi dhatu*.

Bone and its physiology

Bone is a special form of connective tissue. It is made up of type-1 collagen that is impregnated with minerals salts, such as Ca^{+2} and PO_4. It is a dynamic tissue, wherein more than 2 million bone reforming units (BRU) are working actively. The old bone is constantly being resorped and new bone formation takes place. Type-1 collagen in the bone is similar to that present in the skin and tendons. Osteoblasts are the cells that secrete collagen and form the matrix of the bone. Calcium salts are impregnated into this matrix and the resulting cells are called osteocytes, which form the new bone. Osteoclasts are multinucleated cells, which cause bone resorption. Interleukins 1β activates the osteoclasts. Nearly 75% of the bone is the dense outer part, the compact bone. The inner 25% of bone is spongy or trabecular bone. There are two types of bone, *viz.*, membranous and cartilaginous. The bones of the skull are formed by ossifying the membranes. The long bones are modelled and ossified from the cartilage. The shaft of the bone is called the diaphysis, whereas both the distal ends of the long bones are called epiphyses. There is an actively proliferating cartilage between the epiphysis and diaphysis called the epiphyseal plate. At different times, in an adolescent, the epiphysis gets ossified in different bones. This is how bone age is calculated. Growth hormones, which are insulin like growth factors help in the formation of bone collagen and cause proliferation of the epiphyseal plate. Vitamin D helps in calcification of the bones and is actively involved in absorption and transport of Ca and phosphate. It is interesting to note that the vitamin D is formed from 7-dehydro cholesterol in the skin by the action of sun light. It is not surprising that our seers have established the origin of bone to *meda dhatu* (lipoid tissue). Reduced mineralization of the bone can be due to vitamin D deficiency. It may result from inadequate exposure to sunlight or from failure of the liver and kidneys. If it happens in childhood it causes rickets.

Parathormone (PTH): This is the hormone secreted by the para thyroid glands. It is a poly peptide hormone. It causes bone resorption, demineralization of the bones and raises the serum levels of calcium. Deficiency of PTH can cause neuromuscular hyper excitability and tetany. It can happen with parathyroidectomy. Excess secretion of this hormone causes osteoporosis and hypercalcemic urinary calculi. It can also cause the formation of cysts in the bones.

Calcitonin: This is yet another hormone of importance in bone metabolism. Its action is opposite to that of PTH. It prevents formation of osteoclasts in the bone. It has receptors in the bones and kidneys. It increases calcium excretion in the urine. It reduces the activity of osteoclasts and thereby prevents osteoporosis. It reduces the circulatory levels of calcium and the phosphates.

Chapter : 36

Majja Dhatu

Majja dhatu refers to the bone marrow. It is also referred to as the seat of *vayu*. *Vayu* is the cause of all the neurohormonal functions of the body. The brain, spinal cord and all the neural tissues necessarily come under the description of *majja dhatu*. *Majja* is the tissue that is enclosed within bones and also fills the inside of the bones. Its volume is about one *anjali*. It takes about twenty-five days to form. It nourishes the *shukra dhatu,* fills the bones, and is the cause of strength (immunity), the sense of affection and love.

Majja sara: Robust bone marrow or nervous system

Akrusham uttama balam snigdha gambheera swaram saubhaagyopapannam maha netram cha majja l (Su. Su. 35/18)

Persons with *majja sara* are reasonably built and yet very strong. They possess a fair, bright complexion, wide attractive eyes and a pleasing soft yet commanding voice. They are tall, strong and have symmetrical joints and usually have a long span of life.

Majja kshaya

Majja kshaye alpa shukrata parvabhedo asthinistodo asthi shoonyata cha l (Su. Su. 15/13)

When there is excessive depletion of bone marrow, there is poor generation of semen, severe pain in the joints, severe bone pain and loss of sensation in the bones.

Majja vriddhi

Sarvanga netra gauravam cha l (Su. Su. 15/19)

This leads to heaviness (*anasarca*?) of the whole body and heaviness of the eyes.

Majja dushti

Ruk parvaanam bhramo moorcha darshanam tamasatata l
Arusham sthoola moolanam parvajaanaamcha darshanam ll
(Cha. Su. 28/17)

Pain in the joints, giddiness, syncope, blurred vision, and ulcerative, painful deep seated joints occur due to morbid *majja dhatu*.

We now study bone marrow in detail.

Physiology of bone marrow

It is the largest (comparable to the liver) and most active tissue in the body. It consists of uncommitted pluripotent and committed unipotent stem cells. It is from these stem cells that all the different types of blood cells are formed. Today, stem cell research and regenerative medicine are developing into a promising new field of medicine. The myeloid series, which are progenitors of white blood cells account for 75% of bone marrow cells and the erythroid series, which is responsible for erythropoiesis, forms almost 25%.

White cells

Granulocytes: The granules in these cells contain biologically active molecules. These molecules are involved in inflammatory and allergic reactions.

Basophils: Granules in these cells contain histamine and heparin. When activated by T-lymphocytes, they release histamine, which gives rise to a hypersensitive allergic reaction.

Eosinophils: These cells are increased in certain allergic disorders, *e.g.*, eosinophilia, worm infestation, *etc*.

Neutrophils: These cells form the most important and first line defence system of the body against the bacterial invasion. Daily production of these cells is to the tune of 100 million. The components of the complement system, *viz.,* leukotrienes, polypeptides from the lymphocytes, mast cells and basophils stimulate the production of neutrophils in the bone marrow. Opsonisation means making a particular thing tasty for ingestion. The plasma factors *e.g.*, immunoglobulins (IgG) and complementary proteins opsonise the bacteria so as to aid phagocytosis by the neutrophils. Degranulation is another mechanism by which these cells kill the bacteria. The granules are discharged into the extracellular medium by activating the enzyme NADPH oxidase, which is bound to the cell membrane, causing the release of toxic oxygen metabolites, *viz.*, singlet oxygen free radicals and H_2O_2. These toxic oxygen metabolites, along with the proteolytic enzymes released from the granules are responsible for the powerful bactericidal action of neutrophils. The other enzymes of importance are myeloperoxidase and elastase. Elastase attacks the collagen. Neutrophils are also involved in the generation of thromboxane and leukotrienes. Thromboxane increases vaso constriction and aids platelet aggregation. The leukotrienes increase vascular permeability.

Monocytes: These cells are produced in the bone marrow, enter into circulation and remain there for a period of three days. Thereafter they transform into tissue macrophages. The life span of a macrophage is about three months. Giant cells in tuberculosis, Kupffer cells, and pulmonary alveolar macrophages, osteoclasts in bone and microglial cells in the brain are a few examples of tissue macrophages. Earlier, these cells were called reticulo endothelial cells. Lymphokines produced by T-lymphocytes activate macrophages, which in turn produce hundreds of different substances, *e.g.*, prostaglandins of the E series and clot promoting factors.

Colony stimulating factors (CSFs): These regulate the production of various types of blood cells. These are granulocyte macrophage colony stimulating factor (GM-CSF), G-CSF, M-CSF, interleukin (IL-3) (multi CSF). IL-3 stimulates uncommitted stem cells to form committed stem cells to produce a particular type of cell. These CSFs also sustain the viability and activity of mature cells.

Lymphocytes: During foetal life, the precursors of these cells are formed in the bone marrow. They migrate into the thymus and bursa fabricius. The bursa fabricius is an organ found in birds, but not in mammals. In humans the B-lymphocytes are formed in the foetal liver and spleen. Later on they are formed in the lymph nodes and bone marrow. Therefore they are designated as T and B lymphocytes respectively. After birth, most lymphocytes are produced in the lymph nodes, thymus and spleen.

T-lymphocytes: There are four types of T cells. T-helper/inducer cells, T-suppressor cells, T- killer cells and T-memory cells. B-cells form plasma cells and B-memory cells. The first two types of the T cells are also called T4 cells. These produce the anti-bodies. T-killer cells are called T8 cells. The key component of the immune system are the lymphocytes.

Immune mechanisms

There are two types of immunities: Humoral and cellular.

Humoral: It forms a major defence against bacterial infections. The circulating antibodies, which are the basis for humoral immunity, are present in the γ globulin fraction of plasma proteins.

Cellular immunity: T and B cells form the cellular immunity. This is a major defence against viral, fungal, certain bacterial infections, *e.g.*, tuberculosis, and also tumours.

Major histocompatibility complex (MHC)

This is located on the short arm of chromosome 6 and is of two types. Class-1 MHC is present in all nucleated cells. It needs to be presented with a foreign protein (antigen) to activate the T8 cells. Class-2 MHC is present in macrophages, B-cells and activated T cells. When presented with an antigen it activates the T4 cells.

Mechanism of humoral immunity

Macrophages ingest bacteria and viruses and the foreign protein in them forms the antigen. When this antigen unites with MHC, it activates the T4 cells, which in turn stimulate the memory and plasma B cells to secrete immunoglobulins, which are mainly as follows:

IgG: It fixes the complement. Main potentiator of humoral immunity.

IgA: It is produced in the intestine and tears.

IgM: Its function is complement fixation. First line of defence. Aid to phagolytosis.

IgD: It helps B cells to recognize the antigen.

IgE: It has the action of a reagin. Reagin is an antibody involved in allergic reactions. It causes the release of histamine from the basophils and mast cells.

Mechanisms of cellular immunity

IL-2 activates the T8 cells and converts them into cytotoxic or the killer cells. This is how the T8 cells mediate cellular immunity. Suppressor T cells suppress or terminate the immune response by dampening the immune response of T and B cells.

Monoclonal antibodies: This is a method by which, the pure antibody against a specific antigen can be produced in the laboratory through the creation of hybridoma. Plasma cells can be fused with B lymphocyte tumour cells (myelomas) to form a clone. This clone is a hybridoma, which can be programmed to produce the desired antibody in large amounts.

Complement system: Certain plasma enzymes partly mediate the antigen antibody reactions. These enzymes are divided into nine types, as C1- C9. There is yet another pathway of the complement system, called the properdin system. Properdin is a circulating protein that stabilizes the activating enzyme system.

Lymphokines and cytokines

Lymphocytes, macrophages, endothelial cells, neurons and glial cells, *etc*., secrete hormone like substances which act as chemical messengers. These are the cell to cell communicators. When produced by lymphocytes they are called lymphokines. When other cells produce these chemicals they are called cytokines. They are known as interleukins and interferons.

IL-1 activates T4 cells and B cells.

IL-2 enhances the synthesis and maturation of T8 and B cells.

IL-4 is the B cell differentiation factor.

Interferon α & β are anti-viral in function.

IFN-interferon is a very potent activator of macrophages.

α-interferon enhances the action of NK cells and is of great significance in cancer therapy.

Chapter : 37

Shukra Dhatu

Spermatogenesis and rejuvenation in Ayurveda

Shukra dhatu is the last of the seven *dhatus*. It is formed from the *majja dhatu*. In an earlier chapter, we have seen how important the functions of *majja dhatu* are. All the blood cells, white cells and immune cells are formed from the bone marrow. Ayurveda hypothesized that *shukra dhatu* has its origin in *majja dhatu*. It is shown that totipotent cells from the bone marrow can be induced to become sperms. Spermatogonia in germinal epithelium of the testes and oocytes in ovaries could have their origin in totipotent cells in the bone marrow. The soft texture of the testes and ovaries, brain and other neural tissues could also be the reason to connect them to marrow. However, there is now a more compelling reason to connect *majja* to *shukra*. Sushruta states that when the development of *majja dhatu* (marrow) is complete, *shukra dhatu* begins to form. By the age of 16 in females and 20-25 years in males, *shukra dhatu* is fully developed. This state of adolescence is termed as *samarthagat veeryatwa*, meaning the state of reproductive competence, (Sushruta).

Pancha vimsho tato varshe pumaan naari tu shodashe l
Samatwagata veeryai tau janeeya kushalo bhishak ll
(Su. Su. 35/15)

In a child, the bone marrow in all the bones is red. In the teenage years, the red marrow is converted to yellow fatty marrow in the shafts of all the long bones. According to modern endocrinology, the yellow marrow is an important source for extra gonadal steroidogenesis. The estradiol produced in fatty marrow in a girl child during adolescence, activates the hypothalamus pituitary gonadal axis. This heralds the onset of puberty with the first menstruation, called menarche. The onset of menarche usually occurs between the ages of 12- 15 years. Thus the *majja shukra* connect can be explained scientifically. In boys this axis becomes active later in their teens.

All the Ayurvedic texts describe two types of *shukra*, *viz*., one that pervades the whole body (*sarva daihika*) and the other in the gametes (*beeja shukra*). Charak in *Viman Sthana* gives the origin (*mool*) of *beeja shukra* to be in the testes (*vrishan*) and penis. It is formed in *shukra dhara kala* (germinal epithelium) in the testes. It takes one month for the formation of *shukra dhatu*. However, the exact anatomy of ejaculation was probably not understood. According to the description available in all the texts, *shukra* is described to be emanating from the whole body and is ejaculated through the penile passage at the time of intercourse.

Sarva dehika shukra is responsible for the various biological and psychological functions described below and its volume is half an *anjali*.

1. *Deha balam* (Strength of the body) – *Ashtang Samgrah Su*. 19.
2. *Priti* (Love/Affection/Passion)
3. *Prasannata* (Equipoise/Contentment/A pleasant state of mind)
4. Handsome, good muscular body, glistening teeth and strong bones
5. Well nourished body
6. Fair in complexion
7. Soft skin texture
8. Very potent
9. Very fertile

All the above functions agree very well with actions of the steroid hormones, *viz*. testosterone and estrogen, which result in a positive nitrogen balance and increased libido. Hence the *Sarvadehika Shukra* concept can be equated to the actions of steroid hormones and also to the neuro muscular, psychological and hormonal basis for libido.

Shukram shuklam guru snigdham madhuram bahulam bahu l
Ghruta makshika tailabhyam sad garbhaya ll
(Ashtanga Hru. Shar. 1/17)

Perfect *beeja shukra* that is capable of fertilizing a normal ovum and forms a normal embryo has the following characteristics.

Crystalline and white in colour.

Liquid in form.

Sweet in taste.

Heavy, viscous and unctuous in character.

Has an odour of *ghee*, honey and oil.

Shukra saara purusha

Snigdha sahataraveta asthi danta nakham bahul kamam prajam shukrena l (Su. Su. 35/18)

A person with robust *shukra dhatu* possesses the following qualities. He is unctuous with well-formed bones, teeth, nails and a strong well-knit body. He is excessively sexy and has large progeny.

Shukra kshaya:* Depletion of *shukra

Shukra kshaye medhra vrushana vedana ashakti maithune chiraadwa prasekah praseke cha alpa rakta shukra darshanam l (Su. Su.15/13).

When there is depletion in *shukra dhatu* there is pain in the testes and penis. The person is unable to perform intercourse. Even when he does, he takes a long time to ejaculate, there is very little ejaculate and sometimes it is mixed with blood.

Shukra vruddhi

Shukram shukrashmareem atipradurbhavameva l (Su. Su. 15/19)

An excessive increase in *shukra dhatu* results in stone like formation of semen and spermatorrhoea.

Shukra dosha janya vyadhi

Shukrasyadoshat klaibyam aharshanam l
Rogi va kleebam alpaayu viroopam va prajayate ll

Na cha asya jayate garbhah patati prasravat api l
Shukram hi dushtam saapatyam sadaaram badhate naram ll
(Cha. Su. 28/18-19)

Semen that is afflicted with *doshas* causes impotence, failure of erection and other male sexual dysfunctions. Such a person is usually infertile and even if he does impregnate a woman, the pregnancy may abort. He may also be the source of sexually transmitted diseases.

The description of *beeja shukra* fits the modern description of seminal fluid. Its function is described as *garbhotpadan* (causing pregnancy through gametogenesis). Various etiological factors, beginning from *beeja dosha* (defective sperm/genetic abnormality) to environmental factors affect the balance of *tridoshas* to vitiate the *shukra*. The vitiated *shukra* is an important factor in male infertility. Over exertion, grief, fear, stress, a sense of guilt, suppression of natural urges, excessive and improper sexual indulgence, poor nutrition, a spicy and/or dry diet with an excess of sour, bitter and astringent foods are all factors that vitiate *beej shukra*. A recent history of an acute illness, chronic disease processes, and surgery can affect the fertility potential of *shukra*. Dosha affliction of semen causes changes in colour, odour, viscosity, volume, *etc*. It also affects the fertility potential of an individual.

Historical

Until about the 15th century A.D. in Europe, people believed that the fumes emanating from the semen caused pregnancy. There was also a belief amongst the medieval Italians that a miniature foetus existed in the ovary of a woman. In contrast, all the Ayurveda texts described the *beeja shukra* (seed for procreation in semen) as being responsible for impregnation of *aatav* (*stree beej*/ovum). Though the precise anatomy of the sperm was not known, the origin of *beeja shukra* in the testes was known. It was only after the discovery of the microscope by Antony Leuwenhok in 1670, that the morphology of the sperm was understood. Artificial insemination in camels was performed by Arabs as far back as the 14th century A.D., for improving camel breeds. The first artificial insemination in humans was done in 1780 A.D. by Sir John Hunter.

Spermatogenesis

After the red bone marrow is completely converted into yellow marrow, the dynamic portion of *majja dhatu* is acted upon by the *shukra dhatwagni*, and it undergoes biotransformation in the testes, to form *shukra dhatu*. It takes a total of about ninety days to form *beeja shukra* from *rasa dhatu*.

Modern understanding of spermatogenesis

Spermatogenesis is a complex process involving subtle interactions between the endocrine, paracrine and autocrine regulators, which act on different cell populations in and outside the testes. It is a testosterone dependant process. Sperms are formed in the seminiferous tubules. These tubules are lined by primitive germ cells. The other group of glycogen containing cells is called Sertoli cells. Leydigs cells produce the testosterone. Sertoli cells secrete androgen binding protein (ABP), inhibin and Mullerian Inhibiting Substance (MIS). MIS causes regression of Mullerian structures in intra uterine life. Both FSH and androgens are required for spermatogenesis. In the early stage of spermatogenesis a high concentration of testosterone is required, whereas in the later stage it requires the action of FSH on the spermatogonia. LH acts on the Leydig's cells to secrete androgen. Transformation of spermatogonium into a mature sperm requires 74 days on an average. Sperms completely mature during their sojourn through the epididymis. Dihydrotestosterone (DHT) is required for this purpose. In the female genital tract it is capacitated and enabled to achieve fertilization of the ovum.

Biosynthesis of testosterone

In the Leydig cells, cholesterol is converted into androgen by the action of the 17 α-hydroxylase enzyme, whereas in the adrenal cortex 11-21 hydroxylase enzymes cause this conversion.

Mechanism of action: Testosterone binds to the intracellular receptors to form a complex with DNA in the nucleus to facilitate the transcription of various genes. Body muscle mass, male sexual drive and libido depend upon the testosterone levels in the body. 5α reductase converts the testosterone into DHT (dihydrotestosterone), which amplifies the action in the target tissues. The target tissues are the external male genitalia, Wolffian duct structures, prostate, penis, and facial hair. DHT also causes the recession of the temporal hair line. Congenital deficiency of 5α reductase causes an anatomical abnormality, where the internal male genitalia are present along with the external female genitalia. Androgen hormones can be equated to *sarvadehika shukra*.

Control of testicular function: Puberty changes in the male child set in from the time the red marrow in the long bones is converted into yellow marrow. This fatty marrow is the source of extragonadal steroidogenesis. These steroids cause the activation of the hypothalamus pituitary gonadal axis by a positive feedback mechanism. Due to the stimulation of GnRH from the hypothalamus, the anterior pituitary produces FSH and LH. FSH is tropic to the Sertoli cells. Gametogenesis occurs under the influence of FSH and androgen. LH is tropic to Leydig cells. Testosterone reduces the levels of LH in the plasma through a negative feedback mechanism. Inhibin secreted by Sertoli cells inhibits FSH. The testes also produce oestrogen by aromatization of testosterone. Testosterone has positive nitrogen (protein) anabolic and growth promoting actions. It also causes the epiphyseal fusion in the long bones, finally leading to the arrest of their further growth.

Seminiferous tubular fluid: It is rich in androgens, oestrogen, K^+, inositol, glutamic acid and aspartic acid. The blood testicular barrier maintains its characteristic composition and it also protects the germ cells from the harmful agents and antigenic products of cell division. It also helps the sperms to attain maturity.

Seminal vesicular fluid: It comprises 60% of the volume of the seminal fluid. It contains fructose (1.5 - 6.5 grams/ml), ascorbic acid, flavones, prostaglandins, phosphoric choline, ergothiamine, *etc*. This provides nourishment to sperms.

Prostatic fluid: It forms 20% of the volume of the seminal fluid. It contains spermine, citric acid, acid phosphate, zinc, fibrinolysin, fibrinogen, cholesterol, phospholipids, and hyaluronidase, bicarbonate and phosphate buffers.

Micronutrients: These are very essential for spermatogenesis. Zinc appears to be the most important of all the trace elements. The concentration of zinc in the sperm is the highest as compared to that in any other tissue cell of the body. Nearly 200 enzymes depend on it for their actions. It is an essential component of DNA, RNA polymerases, all dehydrogenases, including carbonicanhydrase and superoxide dismutase (SOD). It is vital for the activity of many of the hormones, *e.g.*, thymic hormone, glucagon, insulin, growth hormone (GH) and sex hormones. The sperm membrane is richer in calcium, sulphur and zinc. Sperm mitochondrial spectrum of the trace elements consists of calcium, phosphorus, sulphur, iron, magnesium and manganese. Capacitation of sperms requires calcium and magnesium. It is very important for the motility of the sperms. The flagellar motor protein, Dynin requires Mg^{++} ATPase activated by calcium calmoduline. Deficiency of zinc impairs the synthesis of vitamin A, causes inhibition of prostaglandin synthesis, abnormal sperm morphology, motility and count. It is important for the formation of folic acid. Zinc deficiency in intrauterine life can lead to crypto-orchidism, malformed sperms and immune deficiency for the next three generations. Human milk is the best source of bio-available zinc. If a new born child is deprived of breast milk, it suffers from poor development of the germinal epithelium and immune deficiency. The sperm membrane is richer in Ca^{++}, S^{+++} and Zn^{++}. The head of the sperm is richer in Na^{+}, Cu^{++} and Zn^{++} and the sperm tail is richer in Ca^{++}. Trace elements in the mitochondria consist of Ca^{++}, P^{++}, S^{+++}, Fe^{++}, K^{+}, Mg^{++} and Mn^{++}.

Semen analysis: The best method to collect semen is by masturbation in the laboratory. Physiological frequency of accustomed intercourse amongst normal couples is twice a week. A minimum period of 48-72 hours of abstinence is advised before semen is collected for examination. The specimen should be examined within 20 minutes from the time of collection. It should be collected in a clean, wide mouthed glass bottle. Plastic containers should always be avoided due to the fact that they may be toxic. If the semen is collected at home it should be transported carefully. Cooling affects the sperms, hence during transportation the container should be kept close to the body. The normal parameters of WHO for semen are as follows:

Parameter	**Normal values expected**
Volume	≥2ml
pH	7.2- 8.0
Vitality	>75%
Morphology	>30% normal
Sperm density	≥20 million/ml
Total sperm count	≥40 million/ejaculate
Motility	> 60% forward progressive
WBC	< 1-3/hpf
Total fructose	>13 mmol/ejaculate
Immuno bead test	< 20% sperms with adherent particles
Antiglobulin reaction	< 10% sperms with adherent particles

Based on these parameters the semen sample is classified into the following categories:

Azoospermia: Absence of sperms in the semen sample, whether it is due to failure of production or due to obstructive pathology in the transport system, is called as azoospermia. Azoospermia should only be confirmed after two examinations are carried out at least three months apart.

Oligozoospermia: A count of less than 20 million sperms per ml. for any specimen qualifies for this category. A mild case is when it is between 10-20 million/ml., moderately severe is when it is more than 5 million/ml. If it is less than 5 million/ml. it is considered as severe.

Asthenozoospermia: When the sperm motility is low, it is called asthenozoospermia. According to Macleod criteria there should be at least 60% of sperms with forward progressive motility. There are four grades of the motility.

Grade 4. Excellent swift progressive motility.

Grade 3. Moderate progressive motility.

Grade 2. Struggling progressive motility.

Grade 1. Immotile.

If the linear velocity of sperm motion is less than 25 μm/sec., it can be a cause of infertility. If the number of motile sperms is less than 20%, it is a significant cause of infertility. 40 -50% of motile sperms is a borderline fertile sample. Motility in sperms is due to the presence of a flagellar protein called dynin. In absence of this flagellar protein the sperms lose their motility, *e.g.*, Kartagener's syndrome.

Teratozoospermia: When more than 70% sperms with abnormal morphological appearance are present in a semen sample, it is termed as teratozoospermia. There may be abnormal large heads, pin heads, double heads, heads with a very low amount of acrosome, amorphous heads, abnormal mid pieces, broken or coiled abnormal tails. Normal sperm head is smooth oval in shape with dimensions of 3.5x2.3 μm. 40-70% of the head should be filled by acrosome. It should not contain a very large cytoplasmic droplet. The neck and mid piece should be well formed and tail should be single and normal. At present there is no modern therapy available to improve the morphology of sperms.

Etiological factors in male factor in infertility

Disorders of testicular control

Defects in hypothalamus

Defects in pituitary

Hyper prolactinemia

Primary testicular disorders

1. Idiopathic
2. Varicocele
3. Crypto orchidism
4. Chromosomal anomalies
    a. 47xxy (Kline felter's syndrome)
    b. Androgen receptor gene on X chromosome
    c. Microdeletion on Y chromosome
    d. Gene for cystic fibrosis with congenital absence of vas deferens due to defective autosome 7
5. Physical and chemical agents, *e.g.,* heated atmosphere of work place, drugs *e.g.,* Nitro- furantoin
6. Chronic infections and illness
7. Immunological disorders
8. Absent dynin arms

Duct obstruction

1. Congenital absence of vas deferens
2. Surgery
3. Inflammation
4. Kartagener's syndrome: Sperms are immotile due to defect in dynin. Immotile sperms block the passage of sperm transport leading to azoospermia.

Coital defects

1. Low frequency
2. Use of lubricants
3. Impotency
4. Hypospadias
5. Retrograde ejaculation

Psychological factors and drug abuse

Many infertile males have a combination of these various abnormalities, including those of morphology, motility and sperm density *etc*. The age of the patient is important. Most infertile male patients fall in the age group of 25-40 years. A history of trauma to the testes is a major factor. A past history of mumps, smallpox and typhoid should be ruled out. Traumatic or inflammatory epididymo-orchitis can cause testicular atrophy. In all cases of male infertility cryptoorchidism should first be ruled out. The incidence of this condition varies between 0.86% and 3%. Presence of filarial disease, hydrocele and hernia should always be looked for. A history of surgery for congenital hernia is very important. Many times the vas deferens can be damaged during surgery. Sexually transmitted diseases, *e.g.*, Gonorrhoea can cause obstructive pathology in the sperm passage. Certain occupations can be responsible for hypo function of the testes, *e.g.*, boiler and steam engine operators (heated environment). Even the use of tight nylon under garments can cause hypo function of the testes by raising the temperature of the environment. Genetic ailments, *e.g.*, Klinefelter syndrome should also be considered. Diabetes mellitus and the resultant impotence are important factors in male infertility. A detailed marital and sexual history is a must in all cases of infertility.

Examination: Hypospadias, cryptorchidism, varicocele, hydrocele, hernia, *etc*., should be ruled out.

Testicular volume: This is the most important feature of any clinical examination. Normal adult testes should have a volume of at least 15 ml and can be up to 30 ml. It should be compared with a series of graded plastic ellipsoids called, orchidometers. If the testicular volume is less than 5 ml and the sperm density is less than 5 million or if the patient is azoospermic, the following etiological factors should be suspected.

1. Previous bilateral crypto orchidism.
2. Klinefelter's syndrome.
3. Other chromosomal disorders.
4. Pubertal gonadotropin deficiency.
5. Miscellaneous post traumatic or post orchitic atrophy of the testes.

If there is azoospermia or the sperm density is less than 5 million/ml., associated with good testicular volume, the following conditions should be looked for.

1. Recent transient illness
2. Obstruction to the sperm transport passage
3. Accessory gland dysfunction
4. Idiopathic

If the sperm density is between 5-20 million/ml, and the testicular volume is normal, the following factors need consideration.

1. Recent illness
2. Idiopathic
3. Varicocele
4. Infection
5. Crypto orchidism
6. Chronic illness
7. Hyper prolactinemia
8. Sperm motility defects
9. Accessory gland infection

Colour of the semen

It is greyish white in colour. Any green or yellowish discolouration, is suggestive of infection. If there is any reddish tinge or discoloration it is suggestive of haemorrhage. Ayurvedic texts have also mentioned that semen can be abnormal due to vitiation by *vat*, *pitta* and *kapha*. In *pitta dushti* (infection and inflammation) the colour of the semen can be yellowish or greenish.

Odour

Semen has a typical odour. Ayurveda described it as *madhu gandhi* (a honey like smell). Infection can cause a putrid odour of the semen. Putrid semen is described in *pitta dushit shukra*.

Volume

The normal volume of semen is between 2 – 5 ml per an ejaculate. A volume less than one ml is considered low volume. Low level of androgen can be responsible for the low semen volume. HCG therapy 2000 IU weekly for 8 weeks is used to improve the volume. Testosterone is not indicated as therapy. In patients with good sperm density with low volume, artificial insemination with the husband's semen is best. If the volume is more than 5 ml, it dilutes the sperm density and motility. Excessive volume may be due to over secretion by the seminal vesicle, possibly because of inflammation. In such an event it is recommended to use the first sperm rich split ejaculate for artificial insemination of husband (AIH). Drugs described as *shukral* can be useful in this condition, *e.g.*, Asparagus ascendance.

Viscosity

Normally seminal fluid is viscous. But in infertile males the viscosity may vary from watery to a gel. Thin watery semen is described in *vata dushti* and highly viscous gel like semen is described in *kapha dushti.* The excess viscosity traps the sperms and this results in poor post coital (PCT) tests. This is an important cause of infertility. In such cases seminal fluid is passed through 18-19 gauge needles and used for AIH. Alternatively the first portion of split ejaculate, which is sperm rich and less viscous, may be used for AIH. Treatment of seminal fluid with mucolytic agents can also reduce the viscosity of the seminal fluid.

Liquefaction

Liquefaction is different from viscosity. Semen, when discharged is in the coagulated state, due to the action of enzymes secreted in seminal vesicles. The prostatic enzymes cause its liquefaction. Failure of liquefaction is a very important cause of infertility. It was accidentally noted that saliva causes the liquefaction of semen. Therefore 4% amylase in Loke's solution as a post coital douche or in the form of a vaginal suppository is a useful method for treatment of delayed or absent liquefaction of the semen. Alternately, another method is to use sperm free normal seminal plasma in the artificial insemination husband (AIH) procedure.

Examination for the other cells

Immature germinal cells and the leucocytes appear as round cells. The only way to differentiate between them is by PAP staining. Other cells are the epithelial cells, RBCs, bacteria and protozoa. Bacteriology of semen should consist of ruling out N. gonorrhoea, U. urealyticum, Mycoplasma homnis and Chlamydia by taking a culture. More than, 3000 gram negative pathogens/ml or 10,000 gram positive non pathogens is suggestive of significant infection.

Fructose

This is an indicator of the health of seminal vesicles. Absence of fructose associated with azoospermia is an indication of ejaculatory duct obstruction. *Madhura rasa* or the sweet taste of semen, described in Ayurveda, is due to the presence of fructose.

Sperm agglutination

This is graded into four types. When all the sperms are freely motile it is labelled zero. If all the sperms are seen to be agglutinated and immotile it is labelled as four. In such cases immunological testing for IgA and IgG antibodies should be carried out. These antibodies on the surface of sperms impair the motility, cause poor zona penetration by the sperms and also poor PCTs. The immune bead test is positive in 50% of infertile patients. Sperm wash, and the use of proteases to digest the surface antibodies can be useful methods for treating this problem. Various herbal immunomodulators can play a major role in this situation.

Electron microscope study of seminal fluid

The electron microscope has helped us to understand many details of the micro-anatomy of the sperm and also the embryo. The centriole in the embryo is of paternal origin. With the advent of the electron microscope, the role of the paternal centriole in embryogenesis is becoming clearer. It is a self-reproducing entity. It organizes the cytoskeleton, micro tubules. It is the principal organizer of the mitotic apparatus. Defects in the centriole can cause chromosomal aberration, abnormal spindle formation, and micro or multiple nuclei formation in the embryo. It is responsible for de-condensation of nuclei and defects in it can cause failure of this process. Immobility of dynin arms may be the result of defects in the centriole. Mitochondria in the embryo are of maternal origin.

Sperm function tests

These tests are done to assess the fertilizing capability of the sperm. They are recent developments in the investigations for the male factor in infertility.

Hypo-osmotic swelling test: Membrane integrity of the sperm is important for acrosomal reaction, penetration and the successful fertilization of the female gamete by the sperm. Normally sperms treated with hypo-osmotic solution swell. 60% or more sperms swell in a normal sample. Less than 50% of swollen sperms in a sample, is considered as abnormal. This test correlates well with the zonafree hamster egg penetration assay.

Test for acrosin activity: Acrosin digests protein because of its content of various proteinases. Because of the acrosin reaction the sperm is able to fertilise the egg. When treated with the protein, gelatine, normal sperms develop halos when viewed under a phase contrast microscope.

In *vitro* sperm nuclear chromatin decondensation test: Soon after the penetration of the sperm into the oocyte, the nuclear chromatin of the sperm decondenses. This is the most important step for successful fertilization of the oocyte. When the sperm sample is treated with borate buffer, EDTA- SDS mixture and glutaraldehyde borate buffer, the chromatin in 70% of the normal sperms will be seen to be decondensing. This test is indicative of the capacity of the sperm to undergo nuclear decondensation during the process of fertilization.

Sperm mitochondrial activity index test: Mitochondrial enzymes are essential for providing energy for the sperm's motility. Lack of them can cause sub-fertility. Nitroblue tetrazolium precipitation helps to determine the mitochondrial activity index. More than 50% activity is indicative of a fertile sample.

Reactive oxygen species (ROS), free radicals and infertility

Spermatozoa mitochondria are only partially bestowed with natural antioxidant defence mechanisms. Though SOD and glutathione peroxidase are present, the sperm lacks the catalase enzyme. Accumulation of ROS causes damage to the components of sperm cell systems. It leads to immature abnormal sperms and impaired fertility. Genito-urinary tract infections also cause oxidative stress through the action of the leucocytes.

Oxidative damage to sperms leads to oligoasthenozoospermia resulting in infertility. The main concentrations of mitochondria are in the middle area of the sperm. The ability to generate ATP depends on the optimal functioning of mitochondria. Here the antioxidant supplementation plays a major role. There are studies which have shown the beneficial effects of vitamin E and Ubiquinone (Co Q10). Similarly *cap. Sujat*, a very powerful herbal antioxidant, an innovative formulation made by the author showed very encouraging results in achieving superior conception rates. A study presented by Dr G. Lavaztihgam, *et al.*, at the International Conference on Free Radicals, in 2001 showed that the cytoprotective and antioxidant action of *Amlaki* (Embelica officianalis) is superior to that of vitamin C and vitamin E. *Cap. Sujat* contains *Amlaki* as its chief ingredient, along with other herbs with known anti-oxidant properties. Another preparation, specifically aimed to improve spermatogenesis and potency, also formulated on the basis of Ayurvedic texts, is *Rejuspermin*. It is also replete with anti-oxidants.

Rasayan **(Rejuvenation) and virilification (*vaji karan*)**

Ayurvedic texts have described both virilification and rejuvenation in detail. An interesting observation made by Charak in the chapter on *Rasayana* is that those rishis, who left the forest to settle in urban dwellings suffered in health and their life spans were shortened. That urbanization as a cause of many environmental, life style induced diseases and short life spans was appreciated in the period of the *Samhitas* is very interesting. Two methods of rejuvenation or *rasayana* are designed to rejuvenate a person thus afflicted. An indoor therapy mode is called *kuti pravesh rasayan.* The therapy consists of *panch karma*, diet regulation and *rasyana* herb treatment. *Panch karma* consists of initial oleation and sudation followed by *vaman* (emesis), *virechan* (purgation), *basti* (enemata), *nasya* (nasal therapy) and *rakta mokshan* (blood letting). It is now established that ferroptosis, due to excess iron load is a cause for free radical damage and cancer. Regular blood donation twice a year helps in the prevention of cancer. These procedures are meant to cleanse the body of the accumulated toxins (detoxification). The diet consists of *shali* rice, wheat and barley amongst the cereals, *masha*/black gram (phaseolus mungo) amongst the legumes, cow's milk, clarified butter (*ghee*), meat and soups. *Kutipravesh rasayan* is believed to rejuvenate a person with improved spermatogenesis and virilization.

Herbs

***Aswagandha* (Withania somnifera):** It tastes sweet, astringent and bitter, its *vipak* is *madhur*, it is *ushna virya* and has specific *gunas* which are catabolic and unctuous. It is described as *jeevaniya* and *rasayana*. It increases bone marrow cellularity and causes proliferation of stem cells. It stimulates the haemopoetic growth factor IL-3. It is an immune stimulant and helps in protection against the infections. Steroidal lactones in it prevent lipid peroxidation, by protecting natural antioxidant enzymes, *e.g.*, SOD, catalase and glutathione peroxidase. It regulates thyroid function. It is also a GABA mimetic nuero pharmacological agent. It contains iron, zinc and iodine. It enhances radio sensitivity in cancers.

***Kraunch beej* (Mucuna pruriens):** It is *guru*, *snigdha*, *madhur* and *tikta rasa*, *madhur vipak*, *ushnavirya* and *tridosha shamak.*

Chemical composition: The seeds contain L-DOPA, proteins, oil and traces of manganese. Because of its L-DOPA content, it causes sustained penile erection. It is acclaimed as the best aphrodisiac.

***Shatavari* (Asparagus racemosus):** Its *rasa* is *madhur* and *tikta* (bitter), *virya* is *sheeta* and its *vipak* is *madhur* (neutral pH?). Its characteristics or *gunas* are *guru* (anabolic) and *snigdha* (unctuous). It is very nutritious. It contains beta carotene and vitamin A. It is an excellent antioxidant. It prevents depletion of natural antioxidants. It stimulates the reticuloendothelial system and immunity and also protects against infections as an immunomodulator. It has good anti-oxytocic properties and enhances the secretion of Prolactin. It has anti ADH activity.

***Vidari* (Ipomoea digitata):** Its *rasa* is *madhur*, its *vipaka* is *madhur* and its *virya* is *sheeta*. Its characteristic *gunas* are again *guru* (anabolic) and *snigdha* (unctuous). It contains beta carotene and vitamin A. It is highly nutritious. Magnesium is the most important micronutrient present in it.

***Amlaki* (Embelica officianale):** It is an anti-ageing agent par excellence and also cytoprotective. It is useful in building the collagen matrix. It has high bioavailable content of vitamin C. 8.7 mg of *amlaki* is equivalent to 100 mg of ascorbic acid. It is also a potent antioxidant due its property of enhancing SOD, catalase and glutathione peroxidase enzymes. The flavonoids and phenols in Embelica are responsible for its antioxidant action, thus preventing damage to the cell membrane. It is also an immunomodulatory agent. It tastes of all the five *rasas*, except *lavan* (salt), it is *madhur vipaki* (pH neutral post digestion) and the characteristic *gunas* are catabolic (*laghu*) and dry. Apart from vitamin C, K, Ca and Mg are also present.

***Bala* (Sida cordifolia):** Its *rasa* is *madhur*, the *vipaka* is also *madhur*, *virya* is *sheeta* and its characteristic *gunas* are anabolic, unctuous and sticky. It contains ephedrine. It has special anti- convulsion and antipyretic actions. An important micronutrient in it is potassium.

***Anantamool sariva* (Hemidesmus indicus):** It tastes sweet and bitter, its *vipak* is sweet, its *virya* is *sheeta* and it is anabolic and unctuous in character. It is also a good antioxidant. It neutralizes free radicals. In Ayurveda it is specially used as an antipyretic. The essential oil in it is antimicrobial especially towards G.I. tract infections. It is very valuable in pregnancy since the gut becomes sluggish and prone to infections under the effect of progesterone.

***Gokshuru* (Tribulis terrestris):** It is sweet in taste and *vipak*, its *virya* is *sheeta* and is characterized by anabolic and unctuous properties. It is an important *rasayana* in Ayurveda. It is a good diuretic, which acts by increasing the glomerular filtration rate (GFR), without resulting in any sort of electrolyte imbalance. It contains six essential amino acids, and harmine which is a MAO inhibitor. Normally monoamine oxidase prevents the conversion of L-DOPA to dopamine. Dopamine is important for the formation of the growth hormone and also testosterone. Tribulis terrestris aids the conversion of L-DOPA to dopamine, being a MAO inhibitor. Dopamine in the brain causes mood elevation and sustained penile erection. Testosterone is an essential factor in spermatogenesis. T. terrestris also contains two other important ingredients, *viz.*, Terrestrioside F3, which enhances the libido and Fructonol-biglucoside, which aids spermatogenesis. The combination of Mucuna with T. tribulis is an excellent example of the herbal wizardry of Ayurveda.

***Guduchi* (Tinospora cordifolia):** It is bitter and astringent in taste. It is *ushna virya* and sweet in *vipak*. It is catabolic and dry in character. Its special property is that it is antitoxic. It is an acclaimed *rasayana*. It stimulates the reticuloendothelial system, bone marrow cellularity and proliferation of stem cells. It also enhances the haemopoetic growth factor, IL-3. It is also a good antioxidant by virtue of its capacity to enhance GSH and vitamin C. It decreases plasma TBARs, and enhances ceruloplasmin and alpha-tocopherol. By raising the general immunity, it helps to fight infections.

***Pippali* (Piper longum):** It is a powerful *rasayana*. It is pungent in taste and sweet in *vipak*, its *virya* is described as *anushna sheeta* (it does not raise body heat), and its special *gunas* are catabolic, unctuous and acute. It is an acclaimed *rasayana* and anti-allergic. It effectively suppresses cutaneous anaphylaxis in animals. It relieves bronchospasms and protects mast cells. It is a hepato protective drug. It is also a very good bio-enhancer. It has no cidal action against the Entameba hystolytica, but it helps in enhancing the immune system, which restricts and controls the parasitic growth. It also has an essential oil which is antifungal.

***Shilajit*:** It is an exudate from Himalayan rocks. It is acclaimed as a very good anti-aging *rasayana* in Ayurvedic literature. It contains fulvic acid and it is a good anti-stress agent, as well a good NO captodative agent. It provides many vital micronutrient elements and essential amino acids. It is also a very good antioxidant, and it improves memory.

***Punarnava* root (Boerrhavia diffusa):** Its *guna* is *ruksha*, *tikta kashaya rasa*, *sheeta virya* and *katu vipak*. It is *vata kaphahara* and *shothaghna*. Acetone extracts of *punarnava* are anti-inflammatory. It increases ATP in the liver, and phosphohydrolase activity. It is a diuretic and causes coronary vasodilatation. It is useful in chronic renal failure and dropsy.

***Sunthi* (Zingiber officianale):** Its *gunas* are *laghu*, *snigdha*, *rasa katu*, *vipak katu* and *virya ushna*. Its anti-histaminic and anti-prostaglandin effects are well documented. It is anti-emetic and helps in vertigo. It also has antiviral activity. It is an excellent bioavailability enhancer. It is one of the three components of *trikatu*.

***Vasa* (Adhatoda vasica):** It is *laghu*, *ruksha*, *tikta kashaya rasa*, *katu vipak*, *sheeta virya*, *kapha shamak* and *vata vardhak*. It contains bromhexin and terbutaline, which are known for their expectorant property, and which are also known to improve sperm motility. It also causes thrombocytosis. It is considered to be the best *rakta pitta shamak*.

***Safed musli* (asparagus ascendance):** *Guru*, *snigdha*, *madhur tikta rasa*, *madhur vipak*, *ushna virya*, *tridosha hara*. It is the best spermatogenic agent.

Novel technology of Ayurveda to provide micronutrients

Herbal roots are the source of many vital micronutrients. The roots absorb the micronutrients from the soil. The content of micronutrients in different herbs depends on the variety of soil. Asparagus racemosus is rich in β-carotene, Withania somnifera is rich in iron, zinc and iodine, Glycerrhiza glabra is rich in calcium, *etc.* The animal kingdom gets these essential elements from plants. Ayurveda used this knowledge while creating various formulations In *Brahma rasayana* intended for rejuvenation, the main constituents are Terminalia chebula and Phylanthus emblica. Nearly fifty roots of different groups of herbs are used in the form of a decoction and are added to the main constituents. These roots are the source of all the important micronutrient elements required for the prevention of ageing. The main micronutrients are copper, manganese, chromium, cobalt and selenium. Copper is essential for all the oxidase enzymes. These include cytochrome oxidase, SOD, spermine oxidase, ferroxidase (ceruloplasmin), *etc.* SOD in cytosol is Cu^{++} and Zn^{++} based. Manganese is a cofactor for several enzymes. Mitochondrial SOD is Mn^{++} based. Chromium deficiency is known to cause age onset diabetes mellitus. Vitamin B12 (cynocobalamin) requires cobalt for its formation. Selenium is part of glutathione peroxidase, which is a powerful lipid peroxide inhibitor. Selenium and vitamin E are acclaimed anti-aging factors. The use of nitrogen based fertilizers in agriculture is believed to be responsible for the current world wide zinc deficiency. Food processing, *e.g.*, the milling process, removes 80% of zinc from wheat. Food preservatives, *e.g.*, acid pyrophosphate, tripolyphosphates and tartarazine, a food additive chelate Zn^{++} and cause the Zn^{++} deficiency. The modern techniques of supplementation of micronutrients in inorganic form have not shown good comparable clinical results and these elements are not in bio-available form. Herb roots, therefore are a very good source of bio-available, essential micronutrients. The use of herb roots as a source of essential micronutrients is indeed a novel technology developed by our ancient seers.

Clinical trial data of Rejuspermin

Cap. Rejuspermin, a commercially available herbal *rasayana* was tried in 80 cases of male infertility. Most of the patients were suffering from infertility for more than 5 years. In most of the patients, the sperm density varied from 0.1 million/ml to less than 20 million/ ml. Three patients suffered from azoospermia, but their testicular volume was normal and their FSH levels were within normal limits. Also, they did not have any obstructive pathology in the sperm passage. All the patients received three capsules in a day over a duration of three to nine months. Varicocele and infections were ruled out before taking them on to the trial. Their diet was supplemented with a cup of milk at least once daily. The results are as given below.

Results	No. of Patients 80	Therapy for		
		3 months	6 months	9 months
Count Improved	30 (37.5%)	18 (60%)	5 (16.6%)	7 (23%)
Motility	29 (36.25%)	13 (44.8%)	5 (17.24%)	11 (37.93%)
Conception	20 (25%)	14 (70%)	3 (15%)	3 (15%)

Conclusion

The results confirm the significant improvement in conception rates and also in the rate of improvement in motility and density of the sperms.

Chapter : 38

Ojus

Tatra rasaadeenam shukrantanam dhatunaam yat param tejastat khalu ojah

Tadeva balam iti uchyate l (Su. Su. 15/24)
Tatra balena sthiropachita mamsathaa sarva cheshtaaswapratighaatah swara varna prasaado bahyanaam aabhyantaranaam cha karananaam aatma kaarya pratipattir bhavati ll (15/26)

The robust essence of all the *dhatus* from *rasa* to *shukra*, which is the most effulgent and brilliant is called *oja*. It is also called *bala* (strength). It endows a person with strength, both in terms of a well-formed muscular body, fitness and the capacity to undertake hard work, a pleasing appearance and a glowing skin colour. The self (*atma*), all the external ten *indriyas* and internal equipment of the mind and intellect are in a perfect state of coordination and function.

Ojus is not described as a *dhatu* because it does not nourish or support any tissue of the body. At the same time it permeates the whole body and helps in preserving the vitality of the all the body systems. Hence it is classified as an *upadhatu* of *shukra*. It is described as *uttama* (the best), and *pranayatan* (the very seat of life). Its loss can cause death. Its deficiency leads to wasting and aging of the body. *Ojus* is especially deficient in patients suffering from *madhu meha* or diabetes mellitus.

Characteristics of *ojus*

***Ojus* has the following characteristics:**

Ojah somatmakam snigdham shuklam sheetam sthiram saram l
Viviktam mrudu mrutsnanam cha pranayatanmuttamam ll

Dehah saavayavastena vyapto bhavati dehinaam l
Tad abhaavaascha sheeryante shareerani sharirinaam ll
(Su. Su. 15/26-27)

1. *Somatmak* (Watery). 2. *Snigdha* (Viscous). 3. *Shukla* (White). 4. *Sheeta* (Cold). 5. *Sthira* (Stable). 6. *Sara* (Flowing). 7. *Vivikta* (Well selected). 8. *Mridu* (Soft). 9. *Mritsna* (Slimy). It is the most important *pranayatanam* (source of life). It encompasses all the organs of the body. Its deficiency causes wasting of the body.

It is of two types:

1. ***Para ojus***: It is also called *ashtabindu ojus* (8 drops). Its seat is the heart. Its loss results in instant death.
2. ***Apara ojus***: It is also known as *shleshmic ojus*. It is half an *anjali* in volume. It circulates all over the body. Its main location is in the ten main *dhamanis* attached to the heart.

Satwa sara purush

Smruti bhakti pragya shaurya shaucha upetam kalyanabhinivesham satwa saaram vidyat l
(Su. Su. 35/18)

When all the *dhatus* are in a robust condition, a person has a good memory, is devout, brilliant, and chivalrous. Such people are very conscious of their hygiene and are welfare minded.

Causes of *dhatu kshaya* leading to wasting

Vatala aahaara sevino ativyaayaayam ati vyavaaya cha adhyayanam bhaya shoka dhyaana raatri jaagarana pipasa kshuda alpa ashana prabrutir upashoshito rasa dhatuh shareeram anukraamaan alpatwannpreenati, tasmat iti karshyam bhavati,

So atikrushah kshut pipaasaa sheetoshnavata varsha bhara aadaneshu ashishnuh vata rogprayo alpa pramanascha kriyasu bhavati,

Shwasa kasa shosha pleeha udara agnisaada gulma raktapittanam anyatamamaasaadya maranam upayaati l
(Su. Su. 15/39)

Vata promoting diet, excessive hard work, excessive sexual indulgence, excessive involvement in studies, fear, grief, worry, staying awake late at night, thirst, hunger, and eating a meagre quantity of food, cause excessive depletion of *rasa dhatu*. Therefore it is unable to provide adequate nourishment to body tissues, leading to *karshyam* or *wasting*. Such a person cannot tolerate hunger, thirst, cold, heat, and rain, loses the ability to do any work and becomes prey to *vata* based diseases. Dyspnoea on mild exertion, cough, wasting, splenic disorders, ascites, digestive disorders, tumours, and blood dyscarias complicate this condition leading to death.

Payasya ashwagandha vidarigandha shatavari bala atibala nagabalanam madhuraanam anyasaam cha aushadheenaam cha, ksheera dadhi ghruta mamsa shalishashtika yava godhoomaanam cha brahmacharya vyayaama brumhana basti upayogashcheti ll
(Su. Sh. 15/40)

In wasting disease, herbs of *madhura rasa*, such as *ksheera kakoli*, *ashwagandha*, *vidari kanda*, *shatavari*, *bala*, *atibala*, and *nagabala* are advised, along with a diet of milk, curd, *ghee*, meat, *shali* rice, barley, wheat, *etc*. Exercise, celibacy and impletion enemas are also advised.

Oja visramsa

Abhighatat kshayat kopaat dhyanat shramat kshudha ojah samksheeyate l

Hyebhyo dhatu ghrahanaanih srutam l
Tejah sameeritam tasmat visrasyati dehinah ll
(Su. Su. 15/28)

Due to trauma, *dhatukshaya* (cachexia/wasting), anger, worry (stress), excessive exertion and hunger, the *ojas* is depleted from *dhatus*. By the provocation of *vayu* (*vata dosha*) the *teja* (*ojas*) exits from its place and causes a disability in a person of *oja visramsa*. Impairment of *ojus* results in the following clinical scenarios.

Sandhi vishlesho gatraanaam sadanam doshachyavanam kriyaa sannirodhashcha visramse l

Sandhi vishleshna (looseness of joints), *gatra sada* (body ache), *dosha chyavan* (displacement of *doshas* causing pathology) and *kriya nirodha* (difficulty in actions).

Ojovyapath

Stabdha guru gaatrata vaata shopho varnabheda glaani tandra nidrashcha vyaapanne l

If the *doshas* vitiate the *ojus*, the following clinical symptoms occur: *Stabda guru gatra* (heaviness and a numb sensation in the body and limbs), *vata shopha* (anasarca), *varna bheda* (pallor/discoloration), *glaani* (mental fatigue), *tandra* (drowsiness), and *nidra* (somnolence or desire for sleep).

Oja kshaya
Moorcha mamsa kshayo mohah
pralaapo maranam iti cha kshaye l
(Su. Su.15/29)

Loss of *ojus* results in loss of consciousness (*moorcha*), wasting (*mamsa kshaya*), stupor (*moha*), delirium (*pralap*) and finally death (*mrityu*).

The most important characteristic of ojus is *bala*. Bala is the strength of the body. It is of two different types

1. *Vyayama shakti* or tolerance of exercise.
2. *Vyadhi kshamatwa* or resistance to disease.

Charak has described this *bala* of the body as depending on three causes.

Sahajam kalajam yuktikrutam cha l

Sahajam yat shareera satwayo prakrutam, kalakrutam
rutu vibhaagajam vaya krutam cha, yukti krutam
punahstat yat aahara cheshta yogajam ll
(Cha. Su. 11/36)

***Sahaja* or genetic:** Genetically bestowed strength (immunity) to both the body and mind.

***Kalaja* (Temporal or seasonal):** This depends on the age of a person, or the season. Immunity in a child is greater than that in an old person. In *adankal* during *shishir* (autumn), *vasant* (spring) and *greeshma* (summer), the immunity is lower than the normal level. In the colder season, the *visarga kal* during *varsha* (monsoon), *sharad* (post monsoon) and *hemant* (winter), the immunity level is higher.

***Yuktija*:** Good habits, *e.g*., cleanliness and good hygiene, proper nutrition, exercise, a proper life style and intelligent use of special therapies, such as *rasayana* therapy, *etc*., can improve the immune power. Therapy with *rasayana* herbs has shown great promise in management of HIV/AIDs in some recent research studies.

Modern scientific medicine also believes that a healthy diet, good nutrition, proper lifestyle management, a supportive family, good counselling, and stress control measures help reverse the damage already done to the immune system.

It is worth while learning what constitutes *achara rasayana*, which includes both *sadvritta* (rightful moral behaviour) and *swastha vritta* (a life style conducive to promoting good health).

Healthy life style

Fortitude and just behaviour

Unselfishness

Charitable nature

Truthfulness

Forgiveness

Helpfulness

Good hygiene (Asepsis)

Good hygiene or good standards of cleanliness described in Ayurveda are no different from those described in modern medicine. The concept of asepsis, first introduced by Semmelweiss, has revolutionized the practice of modern surgery. It is quite surprising to learn that similar asepsis is practiced as 'touch me not' in elite Hindu Brahmin households and temples from time immemorial. The traditional greeting form of *namaste* by Indians with folded hands is probably a result of the principle of asepsis in day to day life. But the credit of establishing its relevance in modern medicine should no doubt go to Semmelweiss.

Ahaar rasayana **(Food as a drug):** Diet in *ojakashaya* - black gram, milk, *ghee*, meat soups of forest-dwelling animals are advised. It is well known that black grams are a good source of alpha-lipoiec acid. *Ghee* plays an important role in increasing the *ojas*. Medicated *ghees* are probably used to express the fat soluble molecules from the various herbs. *Ghee* gives a lipid coating to the drug molecules as well as an enteric coating drug delivery system (lipophylisation). The nutritional value of cow's ghee is very high and needs to be reassessed in relation to contemporary knowledge. It cannot be equated to oils.

***Dravya rasayana*:** Herbal drugs, especially the *rasayanas*, act through multi-dimensional mechanisms. An eminent physician, Dr R. D. Lele, hypothesized four ways of action of these drugs, *viz*., anti-inflammatory, anti-oxidant, immuno-modulator, and anti-glycation end products

The foregoing shows that the concept of *ojus* is a net total of celluar, humoral and all other immune mechanisms in the body. The description of all these mechanisms has already been discussed in the chapter on *majja dhatu*.

There is enough evidence to show that many of the *rasayana herbs* are capable of strengthening the human immune system. The table below shows the mechanism of action of some selected herbs.

No	**Immunomodulation** **(Differentially modulate cytokines)**	**Activation** **Polymorphonuclear (PMN) Monocytes (MN), MC, Macrophage system**	**Adaptogens** **(Increase in non-specific resistance)**
1	Withania somnifera	Withania somnifera	W. somnifera
2	Asparagus racemosus	Asparagus racemosus	A. racemosus
3	Tinospora cordifolia	Tinospora cordifolia	T. cordifolia
4	Piper longum	Achorus calamus	Piper longum
5	Allium sativum	Piccrorrhiza kurroa	Occimum sanctum
6	Azardarachita indica	Terminalia chebula	Term. chebula
7	Glycyrrhiza glabra	Embelica officianale	Emb.officianale
8	Gmelina arborea	Commiphora mukul	

Plants produce antioxidants to protect themselves from damage due to oxidation. Many herbs possess antioxidant properties, which are also known to be anti-HIV specific. Curcumin is one such example. It depresses the trans-activation of HIV1 LTR. It also increases the survival of CD4 cells and prevents their apoptosis, thus inhibiting HIV replication. Other important antioxidants are selenium, glutathione and certain aromatic herbs, spices and N-Acetyl-L-cysteine *etc*.

Part - V

Excretory Elements, Patho-physiology of Diseases & Clinical Diagnosis

Chapter : 39

Malas

Malas form the last of tripod consisting of *doshas* and *dhatus* and *malas*, that represent human physiology and biochemistry. *Malas*, also called *kitta*, represent the waste products of digestion and metabolism in the body. They are as follows:

1. *Purisha* (Faeces)
2. *Vit sneha* (Faecal fat)
3. *Mutra* (Urine)
4. *Sweda* (Sweat)
5. *Vata* (Gases)
6. *Pitta* (Bile)
7. *Khamalas* (Secretions from various passages)
8. *Prajanan malas* (Secretions from genitals)
9. *Lomakupa mala* (Secretions from hair follicles)
10. *Kesha* (Hair of the scalp)
11. *Smashru* (Body hair)
12. *Nakha* (Nails)

Interestingly Acharya Charka advises that the *mool malas*, be protected at all costs It is a well- known fact that any great loss of these excreta can result in serious medical conditions. Severe diarrhoea can be life threatening due to dehydration and electrolyte imbalance. Excessive loss of urine in diabetes insipidus can cause severe dehydration, and excessive sweating can cause electrolyte imbalance.

Mootra kshaya mootra kruchram mootra vaivarnyameva cha l
Pipasaa badhayate chaasya mukham cha parisushyati ll
(Cha. Su. 17/71)

In the condition where the urine formation is very poor (oliguria-anuria), symptoms of dysuria and discoloration of urine, increased thirst and dryness of the mouth are observed.

Ksheene shakruti cha aantraani peedayanniva marutah l
Rookshasu unnamayan kukshi tiryak uurdhwam cha gacchati ll
(Cha. Su. 17/70)

When the faeces are not well formed and deficient in a dehydrated person, *vayu*, which is dry in nature flows in the reverse direction (upwards) and causes abdominal distension and colic. Similarly all other *malas* when deficient, cause symptoms of emptiness, lightness, and dryness of the receptacles of each secretion.

A very important instruction to all those who want to remain healthy is "do not supress any natural urge." Restraining natural urges (*vegavarodh*) is believed to be the main cause of many pathologies. Undue holding of excreta in the body, not only causes severe discomfort, but it can also act as the triggering mechanism for various diseases. A lot of gastro-intestinal pathology may be initiated due to suppressing sleep, hunger, micturition, defecation, *etc*. Suppression of hunger can lead to acid-peptic disease. Dyspepsia and other disorders of the digestive system can result due to suppression of the urge for defecation. How does suppression of the natural urges cause various pathologies? Let us take an example of acid-peptic disease. For a long time antacids have been used to treat hyperacidity without realizing that antacids increase the secretions of hydrochloric acid by stimulating the mucosal cells of the stomach to secrete more acid. When an antacid is given, it may give temporary relief, but the stomach will respond to this increase in pH with a greater amount of acid secretion. It becomes an unending cycle. In a normal person hydrochloric acid secreted in the stomach is so strong that it can dissolve an iron nail. Yet it does not cause an ulcer in the stomach. The reason for this is that the stomach mucosa is protected against this acid as long as its pyloric sphincter is continent. The sphincters in the gastro intestinal tract are vital to maintain the integrity of this long GI tract. Gastric acid clears all the infections and therefore below the pylorus to the ileoceacal valve, the entire small gut is sterile. Below the level of the ileoceacal valve in the large gut there are billions of populations of microorganisms. This marvel is only possible due to the proper continence of valves at different levels of the GI tract.

We know for a fact that despite hydrochloric acid being present in the stomach, in cases of acid-peptic disease a microbe called H.pylori thrives and colonises. How is this possible? It is only possible, if the conditions in the stomach are disturbed and the pH of the stomach becomes favourable for the organism to form a nidus. Due to constant repression of urges like defecation, hunger, *etc*., pylorus becomes incompetent and thus allows alkaline bile to regurgitate into the stomach, making the gastric pH alkaline. This causes soddening of the gastric mucosa and thereby helps the acid to punch an ulcer. The modern method of treating hyperacidity with antacids is not correct, since it is not based on physiological facts. Instead of giving antacids a mild acid like buttermilk or vinegar will be more appropriate in hyperacidity. All the tissues of body contain many channels (*srotas*) through which all the tissue elements are transported. These channels are both microscopic and macroscopic. The state of abnormality of tissues and their channels is described in Ayurveda as *srotovaigunya* or *srotodushti* (abnormality or vitiation of channels). This abnormality is the result of obstruction, which is termed as *srotovarodh*. A common experience can clarify this concept. If the flow in a wash basin or sink is proper, there is no stink. The moment there is an obstruction in the passage of water in the sink, it begins to stink due to the accumulation of saprophytic bacteria. Unless there is an obstruction to a passage, it is not possible for the bacteria to colonise. Abnormal restraining of natural urges (*vegavarodh*), *e.g*., hunger, sleep, defecation, *etc*., can lead to blockage of the *srotasas* and affect the continence of sphincters. Suppression of the urge for urination can likewise cause urinary tract pathology relating to the continence of the internal sphincter of the bladder.

Prevention of *vegavarodh* can probably help in prevention of incontinence of the sphincters by preventing obstruction and abnormality in *srotasas* or body channels. Disease producing microbes are ubiquitous. They only get a foot hold in a particular site of the body, if it is afflicted by obstruction in its various micro or macro channels. They cannot invade unless the tissue is devitalized. Koch's postulates explain how a disease producing microbe produces the disease but fails to answer as to why a particular microbe gets a foot hold in the body tissues and thereby are able to establish a pathological process. Thus the concept of *srotorodh* and *dushti* establish the wisdom of Ayurveda, which in future could prove to be rewarding in prevention of a large number of pathologies. In conclusion, the cause of all bacterial disease could primarily be the obstruction or abnormality of the channels, including sphincter or valvular incompetence.

Chapter : 40

Nidaan Panchak

(Five Steps to Diagnosis)

Diagnosis or *rog vinschaya*

There are five tools described for the purpose of diagnosis of a disease.

1. ***Nidaan* (Aetiology):** It is the cause of the disease. Identifying the cause is the first and most important tool.
2. ***Purva rupa* (Premonitory symptoms):** These are generalized symptoms which precede the disease, but are not specially assigned to particular *doshas*.
3. ***Roopa* (Clinical picture of a disease):** The true clinical picture with all the signs and symptoms will be present.
4. ***Upashaya* (Relief of symptoms and signs):** Either due to natural resistance or due to therapy the disease resolves, resulting in relief of the symptoms. This can be achieved by therapy which may be directed against the cause (*hetu viparita*) or the disease (*vyadhi viparita*) or both. Therapy may be such that it is similar to the cause or disease yet it gives relief and comfort. It is called disorders *viparitharthakari* therapy. This principle of *viparitarthakari* seems to resemble the homeopathy principles.
5. ***Samprapti* (Pathogenesis):** How the disease process begins, progresses and finally resolves is defined as *samprapti*. Six *kriyakalas*, which form the *samprapti* will be explained later.

Pathology in Ayurveda

Nidaan is to diagnose or ascertain the cause of disease. Man is a combination of a triad, *viz.*, *satwa* (mind), *atma* (soul) and *sharir* (body). Disease has many synonyms in Ayurveda. It is called as *vyadhi*, *papma*, *gada* or *roga*. *Vyadhi* is described as the state when the body and/or the mind is in pain and misery. Diseases are caused by the imbalance of the three *doshas*, *viz.*, *vata*, *pitta* and *kapha*. Imbalance of *doshas* occurs due to three main reasons.

***Asatmendriyartha samyoga*:** Excessive indulgence (*atiyoga*), disuse (*hinayoga*) and perverse use (*mithya yoga*) of organs of cognition and conation and the objects of the five senses.

***Pragnaparadh*:** Judgmental errors leading to wrongful actions and volitional transgression, *e.g.*, committing abnormal, unnatural or sinful acts. It is the most important of all the causes.

***Parinama*:** It is a result of changes in the environment, climate, ageing, *etc.*, which affect the *doshas*.

Susruta Samhita enumerates various causes for the spread of communicable infectious diseases. Examples of these diseases are *kushta*, fever, wasting disorders, conjunctivitis, *etc.* Various methods of communication of infection are described such as conversation (droplet infection), touching of the body (*gatra samsparyat*), sharing beds (*saha shayyat*), sharing clothes, *etc.*, which cause the propagation of contagious diseases.

Classification of diseases

There are seven types of diseases.

***Adibala pravritta*:** These are caused due to defects in the sperm or egg. They can be termed as being of genetic origin or a hereditary nature.

***Janmabala pravritta*:** These are due to improper environment, nutrition and care of the mother during the antenatal period. Congenital diseases are an example.

***Dosha bala pravritta*:** Errors in diet (*ahara*), life styles (*vihara*) and behaviour (*achara*) disturb the homeostasis of *doshas*, *dhatus* and *malas* causing diseases. These are further divided into organic (*sharirika*) and psychic (*manasika*).

(The three types given above are grouped under *adhyatmika*.)

***Sanghata bala pravritta*:** Traumatic diseases fall into this category. Poisoning also comes under this category.

***Kaalabala pravritta*:** Time of the day and seasons dictate the strengths and weakness of *doshas* causing diseases. *Kaalabala* refers to time or season and age related diseases.

***Daivabala pravritta*:** Where the cause is not obvious it is called *daiva* or providential. Epidemics and pandemics (*janapadodhwamsak*) are examples.

***Swabhava bala pravritta*:** Naturally occurring diseases as seen in old age or childhood.

The commonest cause of disease according to Ayurveda is improper digestion of food. Indigestion results in *aama dosha* (toxicity). For *agni* to function normally, the normality of *samaana vayu*, *kledak kapha* and *pachak pitta* are essential. Following the proper digestion of food the *saara* (useful essence) is retained and absorbed as the chyle and waste matter is excreted as *mala* by *apaana vayu*. *Aama* formation occurs when *agni* is abnormal and improperly digested elements are absorbed into the entero portal circulation, breaching the *pittadhara kala* (mucosal barrier) in the *grahani,* causing the *saama* state of *doshas*, *dhatus* and *malas* leading to disturbance to the homeostasis in the body, which results in innumerable *saama* (toxic) diseases. The entire diagnosis of a disease in Ayurveda depends on identifying the *saamata* of different *doshas*, *dhatus* and *malas*. This description fits into dysbiosis following the disturbed or altered gut microbiome.

***Samprapti*: Pathogenesis of the disease**

Disease progresses and also resolves in stages. The different time frames, when therapeutic interventions are made are known as *kriyakalas*.

Kriyakala* I:** It is the stage of accumulation of *doshas* or *chaya.** In this stage the *doshas* accumulate at their own site and stagnate at one site or place. This *kriyakal* in infections is suggestive of the site or portal of entry and colonization by pathogens.

Kriyakala* II:** It is the stage of excitement or *prakopa.** In this stage the stagnant *doshas* get aggravated. Probably this is the stage of incubation, when the symptoms are vague and ill defined.

***Kriyakala* III:** This is the stage of spread or *prasar* (stage of toxaemia). In this stage the toxins circulate through the blood stream, giving generalized symptoms, *e.g.*, fever, body ache, pains, *etc*.

***Kriyakala* IV:** It is a stage, where localization (*sthana samshray*) of pathology occurs due to *sroto vaigunya* (defect in the channel leading to its abnormal state).

***Kriyakala* V:** It is a stage of expression (*vyakti*) or manifestation of the disease. Signs and symptoms of the full blown disease are now visible.

***Kriyakala* VI:** It is a stage of resolution (*bheda*) or termination, where in the disease is either completely resolved, becomes chronic or incurable, and even cancerous. In some cases it may end in the death of a patient.

As can be seen from what has been stated above, these *kriyakalas* have a parallel in modern understanding of the pathological process of an infectious disease.

Shat *kriyakalas* & *pragnyaparadha*

Sanchay	:	Accumulation of inflammatory molecular machinery
Prakop:		Setting up of inflammation process
Prasar	:	Toxemia with blood stream invasion
Sthana Samsraya	:	Localisation of pathology
Vyakti	:	Full blown clinical picture
Bheda	:	Termination – homeostasis, chronicity, cancer, death

Pragnyaparadh* and *shat kriyakala

Ayurveda describes sensing or informational and intelligent systems elaborately. The three types of coding and processing mechanisms of information are described as *trigunas*, *viz.*, *satwa*, *rajas*, and *tamas*. These are the operative elements that regulate the faculty of the mind at the gross body level and also at the cellular intelligence at a microscopic level. Information processing pathways of the mind consist of receiving, storing and analysing information with the help of the faculty of recall of previously stored information (*smruti*) after which a judgement is made. Thus knowledge is generated. All actions are knowledge based. This applies to all actions even at the cellular level. We have at length discussed these intelligence systems of *satwa*, *rajas* and *tamas* in relation to the modern understanding of mechanisms of intelligence based actions even at the cellular level in earlier chapters. Informational intelligent systems initiate actions of molecular elements, *viz.*, *vata*, *pitta* and *kapha*. Various biological processes in the body become observable. *Vata* represents regulatory, *pitta* transcriptional and *kapha* the structural (stromal, cellular and vascular) mechanisms operating all the biological processes in the body.

Currently all the disease processes (pathology) in the body are considered to originate from inflammation. Inflammation also progresses and terminates in phases, similar to *kriyakalas*. Below I present an article on the subject of inflammation sent to me by a very dear friend, the late Prof. George St. Laurent III., University of Washington, for the benefit of the readers.

Inflammation is a complex biological process and an immune response to stress that affects the body adversely to create a disease. The objective of this protective response is to bring back the stressed or traumatised tissue to the state of homeostasis once again.

The figure below explains how tissue responds to inflammation. This is called the tissue cycle.

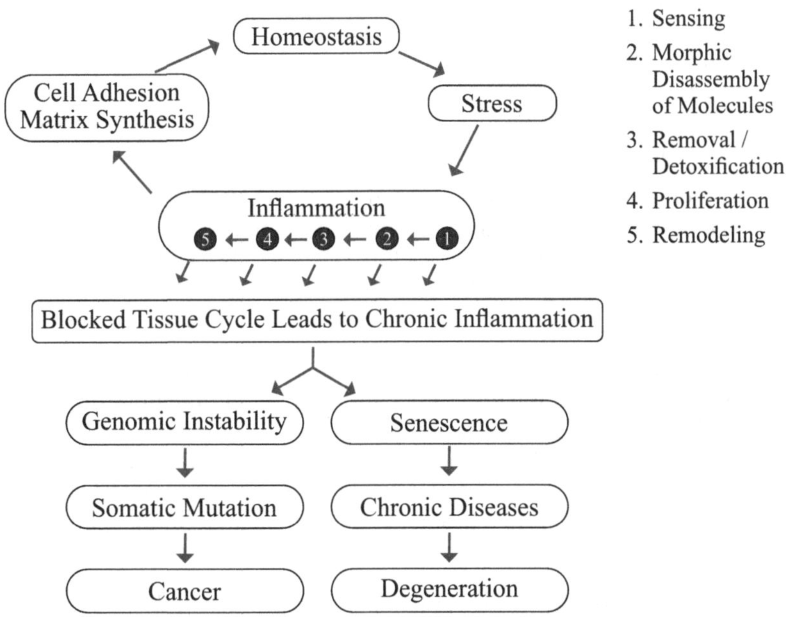

Normal tissue cycle

The first step in the inflammation is the sensing of damage to tissue by any stress or trauma. According to Bartel D.P. (2004) cellular intelligent systems (mi RNAs/nc RNAs) sense the damage and mediate the inflammation response. This results in gene expression and release of a number of gene products and their receptors. Proper gene expression depends on perfect pairing of miRNA with that of mRNA, whereas incomplete pairing can lead to suppression of translation. Thus noncoding RNAs (ncRNA) and miRNA play a major role in inflammation.

1. Morphic disassembly of molecules in tissues caused due to stress or trauma is sensed by miRNA. The alteration in morphological patterns in several miRNAs and mRNA trigger expression of genes and gene products. This in turn causes tissue response associated with leukocyte infiltration and the activation of the immune system followed by release of cytokines, B-cells, T-cells, monocytes and polymorphs etc. The resident macrophages that migrate in to tissues are of two types. Th-1 proinflammatory are M-1 type of monocytes that stimulate LPS (lipopoly saccharides), interferon γ and GM-CSF (Granulocyte macrophage colony stimulating factor). M1 types will inhibit cell proliferation and restrict angiogenesis.

   M2 macrophages, when activated stimulate production of IL-4, IL-3, IL-13 and M-CSF (macrophage colony stimulating factor), which promote angiogenesis and anti-inflammatory Th-2 response through signalling of FGF (fibroblast growth factor) and PGF (placental growth factor). Balance of Th-1 and Th-2 response is necessary for bringing back homeostasis.

   Tumor angiogenesis is associated with TAMs (Tumour associated macrophage), which is a phenotype of M-2 macrophage. It is capable of releasing proangiogenic factors, *viz.,* VEGF, TNF α, FGF, and IGF (insulin like growth factor). Thus inflammation can terminate in a cancer.

2. **Detoxification:** With all the elements of inflammation in full swing, the inflammatory process leads to elimination of debris of damaged tissue and harmful elements. This is the beginning of the process of healing. It is called *bheda* or termination of disease process. Termination of disease may also lead to complete healing or homeostasis or to chronicity or even death of the patient in some cases.

3. Neo vascularisation, cellular proliferation along with remodelling of the adhesive matrix complete the healing process.

Thus coherent coupling between informational systems and the elements of inflammatory molecular machinery is vital for complete healing and return to homeostasis. This is called the tissue cycle. Loss of coupling of the both the systems leads to a blocked tissue cycle. It can lead to either genomic instability or to senescence. Genomic instability leads to somatic mutation causing cancer.

Senescence can lead to degenerative and chronic pathology.

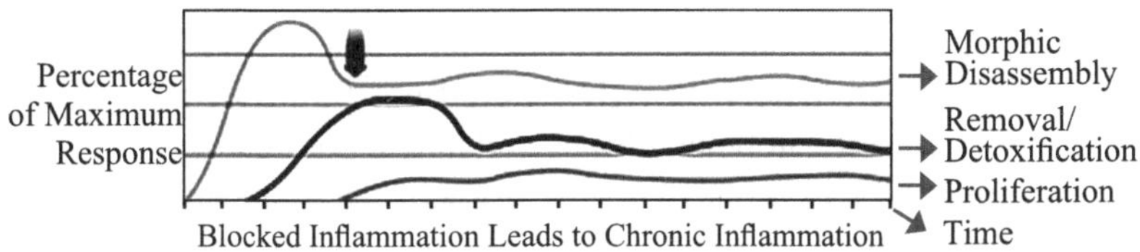

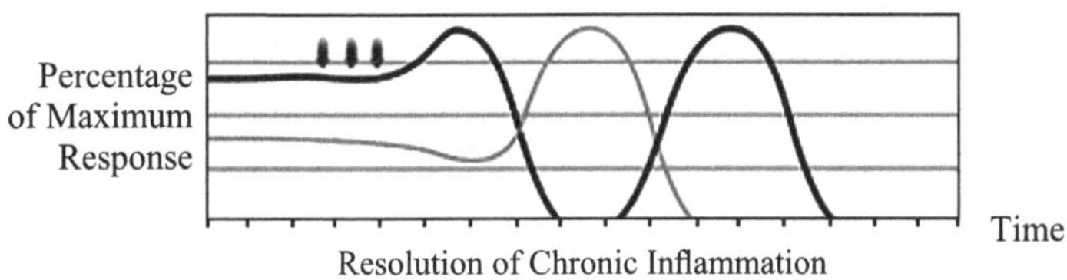

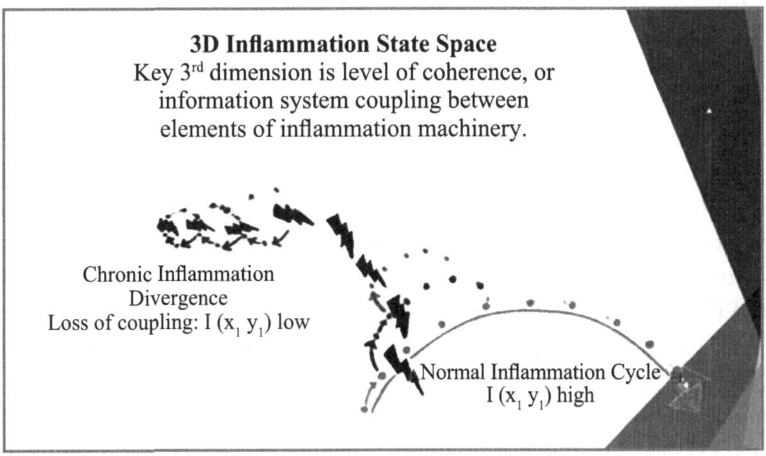

We often create a situation of divergence of coupling by the premature use of anti-inflammatory (NSAID) drugs and antibiotics causing loss of coherence to either create chronic inflammatory disease or cancer. The current increase in the incidence of both these conditions is now attributed by many studies to rampant misuse of anti-inflammatory drugs and antibiotics.

(Late Prof. George St. Laurent III, (Washington University, USA)). We pay our tribute to him.

The commonest causes of inflammation are trauma and microbial infections. If the inflammation is the protective mechanism, then we should support this natural protective mechanism. Thus the current use of anti-inflammatory NSAIDs should not form the basis of the treatment. Unfortunately analgesics and anti-inflammatory drugs are used rampantly. This is one of the reasons why the tissue inflammatory cycle is obstructed due to the loss of coherence between information systems and elements of inflammation machinery. The divergence leading to loss of coupling causes a chronic inflammation state, which leads to either cancer or senescence and finally death. The incidence of cancer is growing at a galloping rate. One of the reasons could be the rampant use of anti-inflammatory drugs.

Molecular elements of inflammation

Vitiated *tridoshas* (*vata*, *pitta* and *kapha*) disrupt the homeostasis and release various molecular elements of inflammatory machinery at the site of stress. *Vata dosha* is described as *tantra yantra dhara*, meaning it is both the process and the effector. Genes and their products, neural transmission, endocrine, autocrine and immune mechanisms fall in the orbit of regulatory mechanisms of *vata*. *Pitta* is all about transcription and transformation mechanisms. The number of transcription factors, *viz*., hypoxia inducible factors (HIFs), NFkB and NO are required for angiogenesis. Angiogenesis is the key factor in inflammation. The genes involved in angiogenesis are the vascular endothelial growth factor (VEGF), stromal cell derived factor (SDF-1), platelet derived factor (PDGF), IL-1B and COX-2. TNF-α, macrophage inflammatory protein (MIP-2), inter cellular adhesion molecules (ICAM), vascular adhesion molecules (VCAM), chemokines and inducible nitric oxide synthase (iNOS) are the other pro-angiotic factors necessary for healing of inflammation. These are all induced by NFkB. All mechanisms and their processes in inflammation exhibit reciprocal regulations.

Accumulation or *sanchaya* is the presence of any one or more of the *doshas* in excess, which cause disequilibrium. This is the first stage of *shat kriyakaal*. This leads to imbalance of *doshas* (*prakop* or aggravation), heralding the premonitory symptoms (*poorva roop*). Generalised symptoms, *viz*., fever, body ache, *etc*., along with localised symptoms of redness (*rubor*), heat (*calor*), pain (*dolor*) and tumours (swelling) develop. This part of the process of inflammation is described as *prasaar* (extension into general circulation of the blood or toxaemia) and *sthana samshraya* (localisation of the disease process associated with the development of specific signs and symptoms of the disease (*vyakti*). *Bheda* is the termination of the pathology. In conclusion, *pragnyaparadh* is the loss of coherence between the information and intelligent systems and molecular systems at the cellular and tissue level, apart from the mind level. Thus it is the most important player in the genesis of all diseases. Homeostasis is the return of coherence. Homeostasis is complete healing.

Arbuda or cancer

Cancer is equated to *arbuda* in Ayurveda.

Description of *arbuda*

Circumscribed in shape (*vrittam*), long standing (*sthiram*), mildly painful (*manda rujam*), large (*mahantama*), deep rooted (*unalpa-moolam*), continuously increasing in size (*chiravruddhi*), non-inflammatory (*apakam*) are the signs and symptoms mentioned by Sushruta. Largely this description fits benign and malignant tumours. Benign tumours grow slowly, do not extend into adjacent tissues by invasion and do not metastasize into distant locations as malignant tumours do. Sushruta described *adhyarbuda*, and *dwirarbuda*. These can probably be correlated to malignant tumours or cancer. Malignant tumours spread rapidly and they are variegated in appearance on histopathology. Etiopathogenesis of *arbuda* is based on a highly vitiated state of *tridoshas*, *viz.*, *vata*, *pitta*, and *kapha*. *Kapha* is the predominant *dosha* in the tridiscordance of *doshas* opines Sushruta. Therefore *arbudas* do not suppurate. With the affliction of *kapha* the structural mechanisms are affected.

Mithya ahara and *vihara*, including abnormal lifestyles associated with lowered immune levels, promote the vitiated states with up-regulation of *doshas* resulting in tridiscordance of *doshas* leading to cancer. When *vata*, the regulatory force behind cell division is deregulated, normal cell division is altered into abnormal division and mutations. In an earlier chapter we have explained how the blocked inflammation cycle causes genomic instability leading to cancer. Let us now understand the mechanisms proposed in modern medicine with regards to genesis of cancer.

For a normal cell to become a cancer cell, it has to undergo six alterations.

1. Acquiring growth signal that makes it proliferate with an autonomous drive. Mutated ras, myc genes are examples.
2. It becomes insensitive to growth inhibitor signals, *e.g.*, inactivation of Rb gene.
3. Evasion of apoptosis or programmed cell death.
4. Acquiring limitless replication potential or immortality.
5. Sustained tumour angiogenesis.
6. Tissue invasion and distant metastasis by obtaining mobility.

Before a cell becomes cancerous, it undergoes a number of changes from the precancerous stage to the cancerous state. Papaniculou recognised the value of examination of cervical and vaginal smears to study the exfoliated epithelial cells in them to identify this precancerous stage, which is termed as cervical intra epithelial neoplasia (CIN). Detection of the CIN stage can help us to prevent cervical cancer. USG in peri- and post-menopausal patients can help to identify the early stage of excessive endometrial proliferation, which precedes carcinoma of the uterus. Even ovarian cancers can be detected early in this way, and can be treated satisfactorily. With the advent of the Human Papilloma Virus (HIV) vaccine, a new preventive strategy is available.

In the case of breast cancers a mammography can detect early suspicious lesions. Identifying a mass through self-examination of the breast is an important education for women towards early diagnosis.

Chronic inflammation is known to predispose to cancer. Inflammation is a protective mechanism designed to achieve cellular homeostasis, when the equilibrium is disturbed by any injury, either external or internal. If the process is blocked by any means, *e.g.*, anti- inflammatory drugs, antibiotics *etc*., the normal cycle of inflammation is not completed and it ends up as an unresolved chronic inflammation. The cell either goes into a degenerative state or senescence, or the cell genome gets destabilized and it will end in cancer.

In cell division there is duplication of chromosomes.

Oncogenic positive genes: myc, neu, her-2, fos, ret, akt, ras. Hyper-activity of these mutated genes cause cancer.

Tumour suppressor genes: P53, Rb, VHL, APC. Inactivation or suppression of these genes can also cause cancer.

DNA molecules from cancer cells bind to calcium phosphate, enter into a normal cell and transform it into a cancer cell. This is called transfection. Introduction of exogenous genes into a mouse embryo, in the very early embryonic stage, was shown to be associated with modified genes. This resulted in transgenic animals.

There are number of exogenous carcinogens, tobacco use, X-rays, asbestos, chimney soot, chemicals and viruses *etc.*

Hereditary cancers

Certain cancers run in families, *e.g.*, retinoblastoma. Retinoblastoma (Rb) is of two types. 1. Inherited 2. Sporadic. Two copies of the Rb genes are present in each pair of chromosomes. In the familial variety a child is born with a defective Rb gene thus predisposing them to the disease early in childhood. In the sporadic type, it requires inactivation of both genes. Thus it appears later in life.

The BRCA-1 gene is found in almost 1% of women. It is linked to breast cancer.

Acute promyelocytic leukaemia (APL): In APL there is translocation of a fragment of a gene on chromosome 15, which is fused with a gene fragment on chromosome 17. Thus it is called chimeric oncogene. It encodes a protein that binds strongly to transretinoic acid. Transretinoic acid is a maturation factor for promyelocyte to mature granulocyte. Therefore transretinoic acid is used to cure APL.

Her-2, and neu are two names for the same gene, the human epidermal growth factor receptor.

Identification of protein kinases as potential onco-proteins led to the discovery of target directed therapeutic strategies. Humanized monoclonal antibodies are now successfully targeted against a number of protein kinases.

Herceptin is now used against Her-2 positive genes in breast cancer. It also up regulates cell cycle inhibitor genes, *e.g.* P21, P27. It is marketed as Trastuzumab.

Gleevec is the market name for Imatinib. It is the choice of treatment for chronic myeloid leukaemia (CML), acute lymphocytic leukaemia (ALL), which is positive for the Philadelphia gene bcr-abl.

Recombinant DNA: Through this technology genes can be shuttled from one organism to another, manipulated and engineered. Human genes can be transferred into bacteria (E. coli) and many complex proteins can be synthesized, *e.g.*, Insulin, growth hormone, clotting factors *etc.*

Resistant infections

Infections were a great challenge before the advent of antibiotic therapy. Slowly a new problem is appearing, *viz.*, resistance to antibiotics. Can Ayurveda provide an alternative?

Ayurveda also used herbs to fight infections when infections got established. Many herbs with antimicrobial activity are used to fight infections. One good example is *panchavalkal*, which is described as the best to fight infections, especially in the female genital tract. A group of five Ficus plants (*panchavalkal*) is known to effectively treat inflammatory conditions in the female genital tract. Taking this into account, a drug development plan was formulated. The plan of action was to verify whether these drugs actually act *in vitro* on various infecting agents cultured from the female genital tract. Swabs were collected from patients attending the gynaecological clinic of a large teaching hospital and studied for the minimum inhibition concentration of the extract of *panchvalkal* required to effect antimicrobial action. Our study revealed that *panchavalkal* has a wide spectrum antimicrobial action.

Spectrum of *panchavalkal* (Ficus plants)

Staph. Aureus	Cl. Welchii
Streptococcus	Cl. Perfringens
Esch. Coli	Cl. Difficile
Pseudo. Aeruginosa	Bacteroides Spp.
Kleb.Aerogenes	Mycoplasma Pneumoniae
Salm. Typhi	Candida Albicans
Trichomonas Vaginalis	-

This study was then reconfirmed by four different laboratories of repute. The next stage was to test its potential of toxicity. Acute and chronic toxicity studies in mice showed that it is absolutely nontoxic.

An *in vivo* study to test its ability to protect infected animals from death was conducted in rats. Animals were give *panchavalkal* extract orally for one week and subjected to intra peritoneal infection from para typhoid and typhoid cultures. In the control animals there was 100% mortality, whereas 60% of the animals in the *panchavalkal* group survived, establishing its protective effect against powerful infections.

A test was conducted in which the extract was mixed with a sperm suspension in Ham-F 10 solution, centrifuged and incubated. This suspension of sperms was studied for changes, if any, in sperm motility and morphology for a period of 72 hours. The study revealed that the extract did not affect any of the parameters studied.

Clinical studies were carried out with regards to its local and systemic effects as a chemoprophylaxis and therapeutic agent in different inflammatory conditions afflicting different systems of the body. It was found that this drug is effective in treating vaginitis, chronic pelvic inflammatory disease and as a chemoprophylaxis in minor and major gynaecological surgeries. It was also found to be very effective in treating chronic resistant osteomyelitis.

Pharmacological studies have shown that it contains an anthroquinoneglycocide, which causes the breakdown of the cell wall of bacteria, proving its bactericidal action. *Albizzia lebbec*, an ingredient of *panchavalkal* protects the mast cells from degranulation, prevents histamine release and allergy and brings down IgE levels.

From the Ayurvedic point of view it possesses three important properties, *viz.*, *shodhan* (removing inflammatory debris), *ropan* (healing with granulation) and *varnya* (improving the lustre of the overlying skin). How is the lustre of the skin enhanced? It involves the mechanism of capillary growth by its angiogenic factor. Therefore one can safely infer that *panchvalkal* should also help the capillary network to grow rapidly due its action of *varnya*. Thus Ayurvedic terminology needs to be interpreted on the basis of modern physiology.

There are certain herbs which have been tested against various viruses. Curcumin of Curcuma longa, Glycerrhizin of Glycerrhiza glabbra and Punicalin of Punica granatum are but a few examples.

Plants develop many phytochemicals for their own defence against the various types of infections. Fungi and moulds are known to possess an antimicrobial action. The first fungus, to show antibiotic activity was the Penicillin notatum. Alexander Fleming was the first person to recognize this bactericidal action of a mould, which inhibited a bacterial growth almost magically. It was in fact a metabolite secreted by the fungus which was subsequently named Penicillin. This discovery in 1941 revolutionized modern medicine with the development of many powerful antibiotics. Antibiotics act by two mechanisms.

1. **Bactericidal:** When an antibiotic causes disruption of the cell wall of bacteria and kills it, it is called bactericidal. Examples are penicillin and cepholosporins
2. **Bacteriostatic:** Some antibiotics alter the chemical environment inside the bacteria and thereby prevent bacterial growth, reproduction and multiplication. Examples are tetracyclines and streptomycin.

Now a third mechanism for antimicrobial activity has been discovered, Quorum sense inhibition.

Quorum sense inhibition (QSI): This is another mechanism to fight infections. It is a novel approach to target bacterial resistance too. Quorum sensing (QS) is a cell density dependent expression of species of bacteria mediated by hormone like compounds called auto inducers (AI). Bacterial infections are mediated by QS. This process involves QS regulated gene expression mediated by the recognition of a signalling molecule, acyl homoserine lactones (AHL). Swarming, biofilm formation, secretion of virulence factors and acquiring resistance by the bacteria are all QS based. Just like animals and humans, plants are also constantly exposed to bacterial infections, and they possess a variety of anti-QS metabolites or phytochemicals, *viz*., phenolics like gallic acid, caffeic acid and glucosinate hydrolysis products (GHP), *e.g*., isothiocyanates (ITC) and flavonoids are reported to possess antibacterial, antiviral, antioxidant and anti-inflammatory properties. QSI potential is believed to be antibacterial without killing bacteria and enables circumventing the problem of bacterial resistance. Pentaphyte (*panchavalkal*) has been tested for its anti QS inhibition capacity and found to be a powerful inhibitor of QS.

Increasing and indiscriminate use of antibiotics is leading to the development of resistant organisms. In the veritable race between microbes and antibiotics, the microbes seem to be gaining the upper hand. A species of Staph. aureus, resistant to vancomycin, which is considered to be the most powerful broad spectrum antibiotic, has been identified. Most infections are poly-microbial. When an antibiotic is administered the organisms that are sensitive to it are inhibited, but those which are resistant begin to proliferate. Thus a quest for an ideal and effective antimicrobial is a distant dream. Here the role of Ayurveda comes in. It is this reason that prompted the author to pursue the research with *panchvalkal* and create an effective antimicrobial in the form of Pentaphyte P-5. It acts in multiple pathways from being QSI to bactericidal. Thus it is an ideal agent in all the resistant chronic infections and even in allergies.

Many communicable infections today are preventable by prophylactic vaccination. Has Ayurveda ever conceived the idea of anything similar to vaccination?

Novel technology of vaccination in Ayurveda

Panchagavya prashan, a traditional religious practice, has been in vogue amongst devout Hindus for millennia. It involves oral administration of a preparation called *panchagvya*, consisting of five cow products, *viz*., dung, urine, milk, curd and *ghee* mixed together and prepared in a copper vessel. A small quantity in a dose of 0.5 ml. is administered to all people orally on an empty stomach, once in a year during the monsoon. Why this not so very pleasant practice of oral administration of *panchgavya*, was promoted and continued for so long by the most enlightened Brahmin community, is a matter of great interest. It definitely needs an answer. This practice was expected to deliver a person from all their sins. Sin in Sanskrit is *papa* or *papma*. *Papma* is a synonym for disease. Was it conceived to prevent diseases during the monsoon? Can we try and decode the purpose and the basis of this practice in modern scientific language? Dr Edward Jenner had hypothesised that the cowpox infection conferred immunity against smallpox. This ritual interestingly is practiced once every year during July and August at which time the

Vaccinia viraemia is at its peak in cows. Was this practice used as an alternative technology of active immunization?

***Panchagavya* – Alternate technology of vaccination**

Probable mechanisms of action of *panchagavya*.

Fresh cow dung	Enteric organisms including typhoid, tetanus, tuberculosis. *etc*., plus Vaccinia virus, polio virus, *etc*.
Urine	Acidic, antitoxic mechanisms attenuating microbes.
Milk	Nutritive medium alkaline in reaction to protect attenuated organisms.
Curd	Nutritive medium protects attenuated organisms. Being acidic in reaction the medium is neutralised.
Ghee	Provides enteric coating protecting bacteria from gastric acid.
Copper vessel	Ionisation of copper aids attenuation of microbes.

Cow dung is expected to harbour all the enteric organisms. Since it is a season when the vaccinia is rampant in cows, it is expected that the Vaccinia virus is secreted into all the secretions and bodily excretions of the cow. When the dung is treated with acidic urine, especially in a copper container, which ionizes the dung, organisms undergo definite attenuation. Attenuated intestinal organisms in cow dung will include typhoid, tetanus, tuberculosis, vaccinia virus and poliomyelitis virus, *etc*. The polio virus is an intestinal virus. The milk and curd act as a neutral nutritive media for sustaining the attenuated cultures of organisms. The addition of *ghee* gives it an enteric coating effect, so it can safely reach the intestine. When these attenuated organisms reach the intestinal villi and Payer's patches, they stimulate active general immunity, as well as specific immunity. In modern scientific terms, this ritual resembles an alternative technology for active immunization. In other words it is a method of oral vaccination. Repeating the process once year is like giving a booster dose of a vaccine.

Our group studies on 16S rDNA at NCCS, Pune, on fresh *panchagavya* have shown that this technique eliminated pathologic bacteria and increased the density of beneficial lactobacilli. It is eminently suited to transplanting the beneficial cow bacteria into human gut microbiome. Further research is expected to unveil more important information. It is quite possible that results may prove this hypothesis correct. If so, then, the practice of "*panchagavya prashan*" could be a safe alternative mode of vaccination with a booster dose given every year to prevent a number of monsoon related infectious diseases. Indeed the word vaccine is derived from the word *vaca*. In Latin *vaca* means the cow.

Vaccination has its origin in variolation. It was in vogue all over the orient, much before the advent of vaccination by Edward Jenner. Variolation consisted of exposing a person to the scabs and pustular fluid of a patient suffering from small-pox. The process was expected to confer immunity. Though variolation was used, its scientific basis was not well understood till Jenner introduced the cowpox vaccination. Moreover the crude way in which it was practiced sometimes led to the development of disease itself. Therefore it did not become very popular.

References

1 Chinmayi Joshi, Pooja Patel, H S Palep, Vijay Kothari (2019). Validation of the anti-infective potential of a polyherbal 'Panchvalkal' preparation, and elucidation of the molecular basis underlining its efficacy against Pseudomonas aeruginosa. BMC Complementary and Alternative Medicine, 19(1):19.doi.org://10.1186/s12906-019-2428-5.

2. Pooja Patel, Chinmayi Joshi, Hanmanthrao Palep, Vijay Kothari (2018). Anti-infective potential of a quorum modulatory polyherbal extract (Panchvalkal) against certain pathogenic bacteria. Journal of Ayurveda and https://doi.org/10.1016/j.jaim.2017.10.012.

3. Hanmanthrao Palep, Vijay Kothari, Swati Patil (2016). Quorum sensing inhibition: A new antimicrobial mechanism of Panchavalkal, an Ayurvedic formulation. Bombay Hospital Journal, 58(2): 198-204.

4. Pooja Patel, Chinmayi Joshi, Snehal Funde, Hanumanthrao Palep, Vijay Kothari, Prophylactic potential of a Panchgavya formulation against certain pathogenic bacteria, F1000Research 2018, 7:1612 Last updated: 31 DEC 2018 (https://doi.org/10.12688/f1000research.16485.)

5. Dr.H.S.Palep, "Scientific Foundation of Ayurveda". The Chaukhamba Ayurvijnana Studies (64). Chaukhamba Sanskrit Pratishthan, Delhi, 48-49,170-171, 2004.

6. Panchagavya preparation Nitya Karma Pooja pranalika, Published in 2014. By Geeta press, Gorakhpur.

7. Gajbhiye SP, Padmanabhan U, Kothari S, Patil A, Palep H, Chowdhary A, Immunostimulant activity of a medical preparation panchagavya, Int J Res Pharm Sci 2014, 5(3) ; 1 – 5.

8. Swati Patil, Hanmanthrao Palep, Snehal Funde, Panchagavya: An Unexplored Pathy in Healthcare (International Journal of Pharmacy and Pharmaceutical Science) [Manuscript accepted, yet to publish]

9. Shrikant P. Gajbhiye, Vivek S Vishwe, Jayashree A, Chetan R Zope, Sunil Mansighnka, Abhay S. Chowdhary and Usha Padmanabhan, Isolation of Micro-Organisms from Components of Panchagavya, International Journal of Current Advanced Research Vol 5, Issue 12, pp 1565-1569, December 2016.

Chapter : 41

Dasha Vidha Aatura Pariksha: Ten Modes of Examining a Patient

Dooshyam desham balam kaalam analam prakrutim vayah l
Satwam saatmyam tatha aaharam awastha pruthagvidhaa ll

Sukshma sookshmaah sameekshya eshaam
dosha aushadha niroopane l
Yo vartate chikistyaanam sa skhalati jaatuchit ll
(Asht. Hr. Su. 12/67-68)

Tasmaat aaturam parikshet prakrutishcha, vikrutishcha, saaratashcha, samhanatashcha, pramaanatashcha, saatmyashcha, satwatashcha, aahaara shaktitashcha, vyaayaama shaktitashcha, vayasthashcheti, bala pramaana visheshasha grahana heto ll
(Cha. Vim. 8/94)

A thorough examination of a patient involves ten aspects for consideration.

1. The very first is *prakruti* or constitutional make up. How to examine and identify one's *prakruti* has already been described. Based on *prakruti*, which *vikruti* is treatable can be determined and then a customized treatment can be prescribed.

2. *Vikruti* is *dosha vikruti* that can be identified through the manifestation of disease. Treatment in Ayurveda is based on bringing the deranged *doshas* back to normalcy.

3. *Saara* is the status of different *dhatus* or tissues affected by the disease process. Whether a particular tissue is affected moderately or severely determines the type of treatment needed to correct the damage and render the tissues healthy again.

4. *Samhana* is related to the nutrition level of a patient. Nutritional advice is of utmost importance, along with proper medications.

5. *Pramaanata* is about the various parameters of the body, *e.g.*, height, weight and girth. These parameters are very important in prescribing the various dosages of drugs in therapies. BMI is calculated based on height and weight. It is person's weight in kilograms divided by height in meters square.

   BMI = kg/m^2. A BMI more than 25 is considered obese.

6. *Saatmya* is a congeniality or homologate substance to a person. Some persons are allergic to certain substances. Knowledge of *saatmyata* is very important to a treating physician.
7. *Satwa* is all about the mind, level of consciousness, mental and intellectual state of the patient. It is very important to know this before any treatment measures are undertaken.
8. *Aahara shakti* is all about the status of digestion of food. This is dependent on the strength of *agni* or the digestive fire. *Mandagni* or *vishamagni* needs to be identified and a treatment regimen is prepared after due consideration.
9. *Vyayama shakti* is the amount of exercise a patient can tolerate. Is the patient bed ridden and needs help for his normal activities? Does the patient tire easily on slight exertion and even get dyspnoea?
10. *Vaya* or the age of the patient is very important. Diseases that are common in childhood are different from those of an aged person. Old age needs special consideration. Thus age is an important consideration for any diagnosis.

Vagbhata has added two more criteria for examination. They are *desha* or location of the patient's residence and *kaala*, the time of the day or the season.

Thus a physician must examine a patient minutely on all above mentioned heads, and only after that will a wise physician arrive at any diagnosis. What a holistic approach for the examination of a patient!

Examination: The method of examination of a patient to arrive at a correct diagnosis in Ayurveda is much more elaborate than the contemporary methods of examination and involves the following: Taking the history of the patient by *prashna* (asking relevant questions). Inspecting and examining all the *srotasas* and their function (*darshanam)*. Examination by palpation (*sparshanam*) of all the body parts of the patient is also an important mode of examination. Examination of a patient making full use of all the organs of cognition is advised. Use of auditory, olfactory, tactile, visual and taste sensations in diagnosing a disease is well explained with regards to many diseases. The auscultation method, using a stethoscope is a new addition. This method of examining a patient is now an essential part of a physical examination. Indirect evidence is used in some cases, *e.g.*, in *madhu meha* the sweetness of urine is inferred on the basis of ants invading the sample of urine. Certain bedside clinical tests like *tailabindu pariksha* of urine by putting a drop of oil in the urine to roughly estimate the specific gravity are also described.

A New Integrative Approach for medical education and health care in India is the need of the hour.

Many years ago a renowned *vaidya* observed that Ayurveda and modern medicine are two different, incomparable sciences. For every science, there is a different method of approach and evaluation measures. He said that Ayurveda and modern medicine are like cloth and oil. To measure the first, one needs a tape and for the other, one needs a flask. Hence the two can never meet. They are two opposite shores of a river; two opposite poles. The conclusion is that there should be no integration of the two sciences.

As opposed to this view I feel modern medicine is the result of continued enquiry started by our ancient seers, right from the Vedic period. In this book I have tried to present an evolution of the different streams of science so as to bolster each other. Today's modern medicine is the culmination of an evolutionary progress of basic sciences. That Ayurvedic *sutras* provide the seed for this evolved knowledge can be seen all throughout the book. In my opinion the apparently bizarre ideas need to be researched for the possibility of some meaningful messages. This is science.

At the heart of science is an essential balance between two seemingly contradictory attitudes -an openness to new ideas, no matter how bizarre or counterintuitive they may be, and the most ruthless sceptical scrutiny of all ideas, old and new. This is how deep truths are winnowed from deep nonsense. -- Carl Sagan

I hope that this work helps in clearing a lot of confusion about Ayurveda and its basic principles of human physiology. I conclude this book with the Sanskrit verse by non other than Mahatma Vidura.

Natu aham kaamaye rajyam, na swargam na punarbhavam l
Kaamaye dukkha taptaanam praaninaam arti naashanam ll

I do not want a kingdom, nor heaven, not even rebirth, but I want all the suffering sick humanity to be free from the pain and misery of disease.

AUM SHANTI

Glossary

Sanskrit	Meaning	मराठी
Aachaara rasayana	Enriching life style	आचार रसायन
Aadibala pravrutta	Genetic diseases	आदिबल प्रवृत्त
Aahaara rasayana	Food that rejuvenates	आहार रसायन
Aahara shakti	Ability to digest food	आहार शक्ती
Aama/Saama	Undigested, semi-digested toxic food	आम /साम
Aamashaya	Upper part of gasatro intestinal tract	आमाशय
Aananda	Bliss	आनंद
Aap	Water element	आप
Aapta praman	Authoritative opinion or textual evidence, intermediate information	आप्त प्रमाण
Aasana	Physical posture of different yogic exercises	आसन
Aatma	Soul/Self	आत्मा
Aayu	Life	आयु
Aditya	Sun	आदित्य
Agni	Metabolic fire	अग्नि
Agneya	Hot	आग्नेय
Agni sankalpana	Concept of digestive power	अग्नि संकल्पना
Ahankara	Ego, recognition of self from nonself	अहंकार
Ahitam	Unwholesome	अहितम्
Akash	Sky, quality of which is sound and its resonance	आकाश
Alochaka pitta	Pitta that causes thought process in the mind	आलोचक पित्त
Amla	Tangy, sour	आम्ल

Sanskrit	Meaning	मराठी
Anantam	Infinite	अनंतम्
Anna	Food	अन्न
Anna visha	Toxic food	अन्न विष
Anubandha	Association of past deeds	अनुबंध
Anumaan	Evidence derived from inference	अनुमान
Apaan vayu	The one that causes all the excreatory function	अपान वायु
Apana	Types of Vayu and Force that has a downward flow or pull like gravity	अपान
Apara ojus	Cellular immunity of the body	अपरा ओजस्
Apatyam	Child	अपत्यम्
Artha	Achieiving material success	अर्थ
Asatmendriyartha samyoga	In appropriate combination of sense organs with their objects leading to abnormal actions.	असत्मेंद्रियार्थ संजोग
Ashtanga	Eight disciplines	अष्टांग
Asthi dhatu	Bone tissue	आस्थिधातु
Asthika	Believers in Vedas	आस्तिक
Aum	Resonance of sound, pranava mantra	ओम्
Avalambak kapha	Type of kapha that provides stability to body	अवलंबक कफ
Baala	Child - Paediatrics	बाल
Balam	Strength	बलम्
Basti	Enemata	बस्ति
Bheda	Termination of disease in cure, chronicity, cancer or death	भेद
Bhrajaka pitta	Pitta that improves colour and lustre of skin	भ्राजक पित्त

Sanskrit	Meaning	मराठी
Bodhaka kapha	Taste buds of tongue (chemical receptors that recognise tastes)	बोधक कफ
Brahmanda	Galaxy	ब्रह्मांड
Brahme muhurt	Early morning period before dawn	ब्राम्ह मुहूर्त
Brahmn	Cause of creation	ब्रह्मन्
Buddhi	Intellect, power of judgment	बुद्धि
Chala	Motile or mobile	चल
Chaya	Accumulation	चय
Chintan	Thought process or processing of information	चितंन
Daiva bala pravrutta	Providential or act of God	दैवबल प्रवृत्त
Damshtra	Bite - Toxicology	दंष्ट्र
Darshana	Philosophy	दर्शन
Dasha vidha aatura pariksha	Ten types of clinical parameters for examination of a patient	दशविधा आतुरप-रिक्षा
Dhaarana	Fixation of mind on a singular objective	धारणा
Dhaari	Synonym of life	धारी
Dharma	Code of conduct prescribed by a religious or cultural group	धर्म
Dhatu kshaya	Depletion of dhatus	धातुक्षय
Dhee	Mind's faculty of receiving information/ emotional reaction or control	धी
Dhruti	Mind's faculty of storing information /volitional control on actions	धृति
Dhyaana	Meditating	ध्यान

Sanskrit	Meaning	मराठी
Dosha	Disease causing elements vata, pitta & kapha /molecular mechanisms	दोष
Dosha prakruti	Unique physical and mental make up due to predominant dosha	दोष प्रकृति
Doshabala pravrutta	Due to imbalance of vata, pitta and kapha doshas	दोषबल प्रवृत्त
Dhatu	Tissue	धातु
Drava	Liquid	द्रव
Dravya	Substances	द्रव्य
Dravya rasayana	Drug that rejuvenates	द्रव्य रसायन
Dushit agni	Deranged metabolic fire	दूषित अग्नि
Garbha	Embryo, foetus	गर्भ
Graha	Planet	ग्रह
Grahani	Small intestine	ग्रहणी
Greeshma rutu	Summer season	ग्रीष्म ऋतु
Guna	Attribute	गुण
Guru	Heavy	गुरु
Gnyanam	Knowledge	ज्ञानम्
Gnyeyam	The objective to be known	ज्ञेयम्
Gnyanendriya	Sense organ	ज्ञानेंन्द्रिय
Gnyata	Knower	ज्ञाता
Hemanta rutu	Winter season	हेमंत ऋतु
Hetu	Cause of disease	हेतू
Hita	Wholesome	हित
Hitam	Wholesome	हितम्
Indriya	Organ of senses and action	इंद्रिय
Indriyaartha	Object of organs of sense / Objects of enjoyment	इंद्रियार्थ

Sanskrit	Meaning	मराठी
Jagat	World	जगत्
Janmabala pravrut-ta	Familial or congenital dis-eases	जन्मबल प्रवृत्त
Jara	Old age - Geriatrics	जरा
Jeerna	Digestion	जीर्ण
Jeevitam	Life	जीवितम्
Jwara	Fever	ज्वर
Kaaya	Body, agni or fire, internal medicine	काया
Kalaa	Unctous membrane structure in tissues and organs like intestine and other organs	कला
Kalaja	Temporal (Relation to time)	कालज
Kale	Timely	काले
Kama	Personal desire and ambition	काम
Kapha	Structural mechanisms of body constituted by aapa and earth Mahabhootas that is unctuous in nature like mu-cus/kapha dosha	कफ
Kapha kara	That which causes, stimulates or provokes kapha	कफकर
Karma	Action	कर्म
Karmendriyas	Organs that perform actions	कर्मेंद्रिय
Kashaya	Astringent	कषाय
Katu	Pungent	कटु
Kayaagni/Dehaagni	Body temperature	कायाग्नि / देहाग्नि
Kedari kulya nyaya	Law of sequential watering in square plots of rice field	केदारीतुल्य न्याय
Kesha	Scalp hair	केश
Kshaya	Depletion/Deficiency	क्षय

Sanskrit	Meaning	मराठी
Khale kapota nyay	Law of choice of pigeon to pick the grains of its choice	खलेकपोत न्याय
Kha mala	Secretion from various hollow organs	ख:मल
Khara	Rough or granular	खर
Kledaka kapha	Moistening agent of kapha/ salivary or mucus secretions	क्लेदक कफ
Koshta	Stomach & gastro intestinal tract, abdominal cavity/ abdominal cavity	कोष्ट
Kriya kala	Stage of pathogenesis	क्रियाकाल
Kshaya	Loss	क्षय
Ksheera dadhi nyay	Law of conversion of milk into curd	क्षीर दधि न्याय
Kundalini	Serpant power, represents central nervous system, (brain and spinal cord)	कुंडलिनी
Laghu	Light	लघु
Lavana	Salty	लवण
Loka	World	लोक
Loma Koopa mala	Sebaceous secretion	लोम कूप मल
Maatra	Measure	मात्रा
Madhumeha	Diabetes melitus	मधुमेह
Madhura	Sweet	मधुर
Majja dhatu	Bone marrow	मज्जा धातू
Mala	Excretion	मल
Mala	Bodily excretion	
Mamsa vaha srotus	Muscle tissue channel	मांसवह स्त्रोतस्
Manah / Manas	Mind	म न: / मनस्
Manda	Slow	मंद
Mandagni	Weak digestive fire	मंदाग्नि

Sanskrit	Meaning	मराठी
Manovaha srotas	Channels of the mind	मनोवह स्त्रोतस्
Mamsa dhatu	Muscle tissue	मांस धातु
Mamsadhara kala	That tissue which supports myocytes and muscle tissue	मांस धराकला
Marma	Vital points on body, injury to which can cause death	मर्म
Meda dhatu	Lipoid tissue or fat	मेद धातु
Mrudu	Soft	मृदु
Mimamsa	Philosophy of karma kanda	मीमांसा
Moksha	Detachment from all personal attachments	मोक्ष
Mootra	Urine	मूत्र
Mrutyu	Death	मृत्यु
Nakha	Nails	नख
Nashtartava	Menopause	नष्टार्तव
Nastika	Non believers in Vedas	नास्तिक
Nasya	Method of cleaning of nose by eerhines/snuffing	नस्य
Nidan	Etiology, cause of disease	निदान
Nidan panchak	Five steps to diagnosis	निदान पंचक
Nidra	Sleep	निद्रा
Nityaga	Eternal	नित्यग
Niyama	Disciplined practice of rules	नियम
Nyaya	Logic/Law	न्याय
Oja visrama	Loss of immunity due to sudden loss of tissue strength	ओज विश्रम
Oja vyapatha	Immune deficiency	ओज व्यपथ
Ojah/Ojas	Inherent immune strength of the body	ओजः / ओजस्
Ojus/Oja	Most robust essence of all dhatus	ओजस / ओज

Sanskrit	Meaning	मराठी
Paapma	Sin, disease	पाप्मा
Pachak pitta	Type of pitta	पाचक पित्त
Pachakaagni/ Jatharagni	Digestive fire	पाचकाग्नि / जठराग्नि
Padartha	Object of perception	पदार्थ
Pancha gavya prashan	Oral administration of five cow products (dung + urine + milk + curd + ghee)	पंचगव्य प्राशन
Pancha karma	Five methods of detoxification (vaman, virchan, basti, nasya & rakta mokshan)	पंचकर्म
Pancha valkal	Barks of five ficus plants, vata, ashwatha, udumbara, plaksha, pareesha	पंचवल्कल
Pancha mahabhoota	Five proto elements	पंचमहाभूत
Para ojus/Ashta bindu ojus	The very source of life	परा ओजस / अष्टबिंदू ओजस्
Parinaama	Results of environmental changes	परिणाम
Pinda	Micro level of matter/embryo	पिंड
Pitchila	Sticky or greasy	पिच्छिल
Pitta	Transforming molecular mechanism constituting Tej + Aap forming pitta dosha	पित्त
Pitta	Bile	पित्त
Pitta dhara kala	The kala that produces digestive secretions in the stomach and intestine	पित्त धरा कला
Pittakara	That which causes, provokes pitta	पित्तकर
Pleeha	Spleen	प्लीहा
Poorva roopa	Premonitory symptom	पूर्वरूप

Sanskrit	Meaning	मराठी
Praana	Life force	प्राण
Praana vaha	Life sustaining channels that carry the life principle	प्राणवह
Praana vayu	The vayu that is located in the upper part of the body and head	प्राणवायु
Pragnyanam	Infallible superior knowledge / intellect	प्रज्ञानम्
Pragnyaparadh	Volitional transgression/ Failure of judgement/ judgmental error	प्रज्ञापराध
Prajanan mala	Secretion from genitals	प्रजनन मल
Prakopa	Provocation	प्रकोप
Prakruti	Dynamic material source element of an organism/nature	प्रकृति
Prakruti	Dosha dominant based cluster that dtermines ones constitution.	प्रकृति
Pramanata	Related to body measurements. *e.g.,* weight, *etc.* for calculation of dose of drug	प्रमाणता
Prana	Types of vayu and life force	प्राण
Prasaar	Stage of spread of pathology throughhout the body, via circulation	प्रसार
Prashamana	Resolution/Relief	प्रशमन
Pratyahara	Withdrawal from worldy enjoyment	प्रत्याहार
Pratyaksha pramaan	Evidence through direct observation	प्रत्यक्ष प्रमाण
Prithvi	Earth element	पृथ्वी
Pureesha	Feaces	पुरीष
Pureesha dhara kala	That tissue which holds the feaces	पुरीष धरा कला

Sanskrit	Meaning	मराठी
Purush	Self or the sentient element	पुरुष
Purusha	Sentient element (concious-ness)	पुरुष
Purushartha	Primary objective of human life	पुरुषार्थ
Rajas	Duality of mind's processing power /poor judgment power	रजस्
Raja	Menstruation	रज
Rakta vaha	Blood circulation system	रक्तवह
Rakta dhatu	Blood tissue (Red blood corpuscles)	रक्तधातु
Rakta mokshan	Blood letting/venesection/ application of leeches	रक्तमोक्षण
Ranjaka pitta	Pitta that gives colour to rasa dhatu and converts it to red colour of blood. haemoglo-binization of erythrocytes	रंजक पित्त
Rasa	Taste	रस
Rasa dhatu	The first dhatu of the body that nourishes all body tissues	रसधातु
Rasana	Tongue	रसना
Roopa	Clinical manifestion	रूप
Rutam	Relative truth	ऋतम्
Ruksha	Dry	रुक्ष
Saara	Inherent strenght of tissues	सार
Saatmya	Congeniality/Acceptability	सात्म्य
Sad vritta	Moral code of conduct	सदवृत्त्
Sadhaka pitta	The pitta that provides mental power to an achiever	साधक पित्त
Sahaja	Natural/Genetic	सहज
Satkarya vaad	The argument that there was always existence. From ex-istance only existance is born.	सत्कार्यवाद

Sanskrit	Meaning	मराठी
Sama	Balance/Homeostasis	सम
Sama agni	Balanced digestive fire	समअग्नि
Samaana	Type of vayu and force	समान
Samaana vayu	Vayu that aids metabolic fire (pachakagni) to digest food	समान वायु
Samadhi	Stage of final surrender to the almighty	समाधि
Samasthagata veeryatwa	Adolescence, stage of sexual maturation	समस्थागत वीर्यत्व
Samavaya	Inherent, inseparable combination	समवाय
Samhana	Good nutrition status	सहन
Samprapti	Pathogenesis of a disease	संप्राप्ती
Sandra	Compact	सांद्र
Sanchaya	Stage of accumulation of vitiated doshas	संचय
Sanghata bala pravrutta	Traumatic or infectitious diseases	संघातबल प्रवृत्त
Sankhya	Philosophy of numbers	सांख्य
Sapta dhatu	Seven body tissues of importance	सप्त धातु
Satwa	Best quality of mind's information processing power	सत्त्व
Satwa	State of mind	सत्त्व
Satwam	Mind	सत्त्वम्
Satyam	Truth	सत्यम्
Shaakha	Extremities	शाखा
Shabda	Resonance of sound, word	शब्द
Sharad rutu	Post monsoon season	शरद ऋतु
Shareer	Body	शरीर
Sheeta	Cold	शीत

Sanskrit	Meaning	मराठी
Shishir rutu	Autumn season	शिशिर ऋतु
Shivlinga	Physical symbolic representation of Lord Shiva	शिवलिंग
Shleshma dhara kala	Mucous membrane, surface which produces the lubricating fluid	श्लेष्म धरा कला
Shleshmaka kapha	That which binds tissues	श्लेष्मक कफ
Shoonya vaad	Argument supporting a view that from non-existence came all existence	शून्यवाद
Shreshta	Superior	श्रेष्ठ
Shukra dhatu	Semen and male sex hormones	शुक्र धातु
Shukradhara kala	Germinal epithelium of the testes that produces spermatozoa	शुक्र धरा कला
Slakshna	Fine, amorphous	स्लक्षण
Smashru	Body hair of different parts	स्मश्रु
Smruti	Recall of information, memory	स्मृति
Snigdha	Oily	स्निग्ध
Stanya	Breast milk	स्तन्य
Sthana samshray	Localization of pathology	स्थान संश्रय
Sthira	Stable	स्थिर
Sthoola	Gross	स्थूल
Stree shukra	Oocytes and female sex hormones	स्त्री शुक्र
Strotas	Secreting glands or transporting channels, cystic cavities can be microscopic or macroscopic	स्त्रोतस्
Shukra	Semen	शुक्र
Sukshma	Subtle	सुक्ष्म

Sanskrit	Meaning	मराठी
Supraja	Well-born population	सुप्रजा
Surya	Sun, Aaditya	सूर्य
Sutra	Aphorism (that which provides condensed knowledge)	सूत्र
Swabhavabala pravrutta	Naturally occuring disease	स्वभावबल प्रवृत्त
Swapna	Dream	स्वप्न
Swastha vritta	Code of conduct for a healthy life	स्वस्थ वृत्त
Swastha	Health	स्वस्थ
Sweda	Sweat	स्वेद
Tadvidya sambhasha	Medical seminar	तद् विद्य संभाषा
Tama / Tamas	Poorest quality of mind's information processing power	तम् / तमस्
Tantra	Process	तंत्र
Tarpaka kapha	Lubricating/Nourishing type of kapha	तर्पक कफ
Teekshna	Acute	तीक्ष्ण
Teekshnaagni	Excessively acute digestive fire	तीक्ष्णअग्नि
Tej	Fire and light element	तेज
Tikta	Bitter	तिक्त
Tridosha	Three molecular meachanisms that cause disease in a person	त्रिदोष
Twacha saara/ Twak saara	Quality of rasa dhatu	त्वचा सार / त्वक् सार
Twak or Twacha	Skin	त्वक् / त्वचा
Udaana vayu	Vayu located in neck and chest/Respiratory function	उदान वायु
Udana	Type of vayu and force that has a upward flow	उदान

Sanskrit	Meaning	मराठी
Upachayam	Nourishment	उपचयम्
Upanishad	Vedanta text dealing with enquiry of self and its relation to the Universe	उपनिषद्
Upashaya	Relief of symptoms and signs	उपशय
Updhatu	Derivative from dhatu that also nourishes certain entities	उपधातु
Ushna	Hot	ऊष्ण
Uttara Mimamsa	Vedanta - Philosophy of understanding origins of life	उत्तर मिमांसा
Vahini	Duct or tract which allows secrection or flow of fluids	वाहिनि
Vaisheshika	Philosophy related to material world	वैशेषिक
Vaishwanar	Digestive fire	वैश्वानर
Vamana	Emesis	वमन
Vardhak guna	Quality that causes increase or over expression or up regulation	वर्धक गुण
Vardhaka karma	The one that increases action of a particular quality	वर्धक कर्म
Varsha rutu	Rainy season	वर्षा ऋतु
Varna	Colour or social class	वर्ण
Vasant rutu	Spring season	वसंत ऋतु
Vata	A regulatory molecular mechanism in the body. One of the doshas	वात
Vata	Farting of gases	वात
Vata kara	That which stimulates or causes or provokes vata	वात कर
Vaya	Age	वय
Vayu	Air element	वायु

Sanskrit	Meaning	मराठी
Veda	Ancient universal knowledge treasure	वेद
Veerya	Pharmacodynamic action of drugs/Selective potency of a drug	वीर्य
Vidya	Knowledge	विद्या
Vikruti	Abnormal dosha identification	विकृति
Vipaaka	Post digestive status of taste	विपाक
Virechana	Laxation	विरेचन
Visha	Poison	विष
Vishada	Transparent	विशद
Vishamaagni	Erratic digestive fire	विषमाग्नि
Vishnu	The God, who oversees, & maintains the universe	विष्णू
Vit sneh	Faecal fat	विट स्नेह
Vivek	Experiential true wisdom	विवेक
Vriddhi	Increase	वृद्धि
Vruddhi	Hypertrophy or increase size	वृद्धि
Vrushya	Aphrodisiacs - Rejuvenation	वृष्य
Vyakti	Clinical manifestion of diseases	व्यक्ति
Vyana vayu	Located all over the body controls blood circulation	व्यान वायु
Vyana	Types of vayu and force that circulates all over the body and extremities	व्यान
Vyayam	Exercise	व्यायाम
Vyayama shakti	Exercise tolerance	व्यायाम शक्ति
Yakrut	Liver	यकृत

Sanskrit	Meaning	मराठी
Yama	Rules for self conduct	यम
Yantra	Equipment	यंत्र
Yoga	Philosophy of mind control	योग
Yukti	Intelligent reasoning	युक्ति
Yukta	Balanced	युक्त
Yuktija	Intelligent ways to create therapy	युक्तिज

Bibliography

1. Charak Samhita
2. Sushrut Samhita
3. Kashyap Samhita
4. Ashtang Hriday
5. Madhav Nidan
6. English Translation of Charak Samhita - Dr P.M. Mehta
7. Introduction to Kayachikitsa - Dr C. Dwarkanath
8. Ayurveda and Modern Medicine - Dr RD. Lele
9. Ayurvedic Healing - Dr Dawid Frawley
10. Ayurvedic Healing for Women - Atreya
11. Kaumarabhrirya Tantra - Nirmala Rajwade
12. Dravyaguna Vijnan - Vaidya VM.Gogte
13. Bhavapraksha Nighantu - Bhava Mishra
14. Progress in Obstetrics and Gynaecology
15. Upanishads (Chhandogya, Aitareya, Taittiriya, Katha, Kena, Mundak, Mandukya, Amritabindu, Prashna and Kaivalya Upanishads) English Translation by H.H. Swami Chinmayanand
16. Effectiveness of P-5 (Ayurvedic) Vaginal Pessaries in Vaginitis - H.S. Palep, M.H. Palep *et al.* Bombay Hospital Jour., Vol.34, No.2, 1992
17. HIV/AIDS and Ayurveda, Promising Leads; Dr H. S. Palep. Seminar on "Journey to Dialogue on HIV/AIDS and Traditional System of Medicine" 10th Nov. 2000.
18. Post-menopausal Problems in Ayurveda. Dr H. S. Palep All India Ayurvedic Conference, Hyderabad 2001
19. John Ecceles: Evolution of Consciousness Proc. National Academy of Science, USA Vol. 89, pp 7320-24, Aug. 1992.
20. Man and Medicine-A History- Farokh Udwadia 2000.

21. Prof. David Barkar- The Developmental Origins of Adult Disease. J. Am Coll Nutr 2004; 23: 588-95

22. Max Planck Physicist Nobel Laurate, Quotes

23. Rene Descartes- French Philosopher- "Principles of Philosophy" 1644.

24. Karl Marx: German Philosopher- Consciousness and Life , JSTOR 1995

25. Fred Hoyle's Universe- Jayant Narlikar 2010

26. Ignaz Semmlweiss, Hungarian Physician, "Herald of Hygienic Medicine"- E.A.Carson- 2018

27. Alexander Oparin, Russian Biochemist, "Origins of Life"

28. Pancha Gavya Prashan- Dharma Sindhu

29. Cannon – Bard "Thalamic Theory of Emotions: A Brief Genealogy and Reappraisal by Otniel C Dror, Dec.17 2013

30. James Jeans- British Physicist - "Mysterious Universe" 1930, Cambridge University Press

31. Carl Jung, Swiss Psychotherapist, "Psychologyand Alchemy" Vol. 12 1944, Wikipedia.

32. Bhagawad Geeta.

33. Thyroid Hormone Regulation of MetabolismNCBI-NIH, 2014, Am. Ass. Physiology.

34. Siddhartha Mukherjee, "The Gene, An Intimate History"

35. Dr Hall, Dr Roshbach, Dr Young. "Molecular Mechanisms Controlling Circadian Rhythms" Nobel Laurates 2017

36. Osheil M Turner- Progress in Gynecology Vol. 12

37. Frish & Revelle, "The Right Weight, Body Fat, Menarch and Fertility" 1971. Cambridge University Press.

38. Dr H. S. Palep, "Scientific Foundation of Ayurveda". The Chaukhamba Ayurvijnana Studies (64). Chaukhamba Sanskrit Pratishthan, Delhi, 2004

Recommended Reading

(Prepared by Dr Ashok D.B. Vaidya)

Traditional Medicine in Asia: Eds. Ranjit Roy Chaudhury and Uton Muchtar Rafer, WHO, Regional Office for South Asia, New Delhi 2002.

Lele RD: Ayurveda and Modem Medicine, Bharatiya Vidya Bhavan, Mumbai, 2nd Edn., 2001.

Dahanukar SA and UM Thatte: Ayurveda Revisited, Mumbai Popular Prakashan; 3rd Edn. 2000.

Singh RH: Holistic Principles Ayurvedic Medicine, Chaukhamba, Varanasi, 1998.

Ayurvedic Pharmacopoeia of India (Part 1 & 2): Ministry of Health, Government of India, New Dellii, 1986 & 2000.

Essential Ayurvedic Drugs for Dispensaries & Hospitals, AYUSH: Ministry of Health & Family Welfare, Government of India, New Delhi, 2000.

Handa SS: Indian Herbal Pharmacopoeia, Vol I & 2, Mumbai, IDMA. 1998 & 1999.

Svoboda RE: Ayurveda - Life, Health and Longevity, Penguin Book, New Delhi 1993.

Gogte VM: Ayurvedic Pharmacology and Therapeutic Uses of Medicinal planes (Dravyagunavijnan), Bhavan's SPARC Mumbai 2000.

Charak Samhica, (Ed.) Vaidya V.D. Shukla, 2000, Chaukhamba, Varanasi, 2000.

Bhaishajya Ratnavali, (Ed) RD Shastri, Chaukhamba, Varanasi, 1985.

Bhavan's SPAARC, Selected Medicinal Planrs of India, CHEMEX CJL, Mumbai 1992.

Chopra RN: Indigenous Drugs of India. Academic Publications, Kolkara, J 982.

Dash B: Basic Principles of Ayurvedic Concept, New Delhi, 1 980.

Desai VG: Aushadhi-Sangraha, IT Acharya Mumbai, 1927.

Kulkarni RD: Principle of Pharmacology in Ayurved,, Kulkarni, Mumbai 1977.

Sharma PV: Dravyagunavijnan, Chaukhamba, Varanasi, 1978.

Svoboda RE: Prakriti - Your Ayurvedic Constitution, Motilal Bana rasidas, New Delhi, 1993.

Index

About the Author

Dr Hanmanthrao S. Palep, founder chairman of Dr Palep's Medical Research Foundation Pvt. Ltd was born in Polasa, Telangana, (India) in the year 1938. He graduated in Ayurvedic Medicine and Surgery from the renowned R. A. Podar Medical College (Ayurvedic), Mumbai in 1962. Thereafter he completed his MBBS and MD in modern obstetrics and gynaecology from the prestigious Grant Medical College, Mumbai in 1973. He held the post of Hon. Professor at Grant Medical College and was also a part time professor at R. A. Podar Medical College for more than two and a half decades. He has been a teacher and examiner for undergraduate and postgraduate courses in the specialty of obstetrics and gynaecology in both allopathic medicine and Ayurveda at Mumbai University for over three decades. He is the only recognized teacher at the Mumbai University in both the faculties of modern medicine and Ayurveda. He is a renowned gynaecological surgeon, an eminent obstetrician and infertility specialist. Currently he is the National Professor and visiting scientist at the Haffkine Institute for Training, Research & Testing, at Parel, Mumbai.

Dr Palep has spent a major part of his prolific years in imparting knowledge both in India and abroad. It is therefore no wonder that the Ayush department of the Government of India deputed him to conduct short training courses in Ayurveda for the medical students at prestigious US medical schools like Boston, Harvard and Johns Hopkins in the summer of 2007. This training program was jointly sponsored by AAPI (Association of American Physicians of Indian Origin). Subsequently, in 2008, he was also invited to deliver lectures at a number of medical schools in the USA. His relentless research efforts have led to finding novel Ayurvedic solutions, based on modern scientific parameters, for various ailments of a stubborn nature. This has resulted into a number of highly popular standardized Ayurvedic formulations, *viz.*, *Sujat*, *Torchnil*, *Pentaphyte* and others, manufactured by Dr Palep's Medical Research Foundation, a research based organization, which he has successfully headed since 1997. Many more research projects and clinical trials are presently under way. Dr Palep has presented and published many research papers in conferences, seminars and journals, both national and international. The medical research foundation has held more than a hundred CMEs to educate practitioners and specialists of modern medicine to spread the message of the scientific basis of Ayurveda. In 2005, he authored and published a book titled "*Scientific Foundation of Ayurveda*," which received great acclaim from academicians. Now he proudly presents another book titled, ***Dosha Dhatu Mala Vignyan: Integrative Human Physiology***.

Praise for the book

The book, *Dosha Dhatu Mala Vignyan: Integrative Human Physiology* by the eminent doctor, Dr H. Palep, is an outstanding piece of work on the subjects of Ayurveda and holistic medicine. The book goes into depth regarding the multiple aspects of Ayurveda, and is divided into five parts. Each part provides a preamble to intricate concepts that are discussed and well-explained, and a scientific basis for the inculcation of Ayurvedic remedies and methods is provided. As such, this is one of those rare books that merges the diverse concepts of Ayurveda and western medicine in a way that appeals rationally to a reader. The book is well written, concise and much to the point. Towards the end of the book, empirical results are also presented, which make the book indispensable to every practitioner. The book stresses on holistic living, lifestyle regimen, *doshas*, tissue elements, *dhatus*, and *malas*. All in all, this is a great effort that can potentially become a must-have, not only for students of Ayurveda, but also for the layman.

– ***Prof. Ashwin Gumaste, FNAE,***
Institute Chair Professor
Department of Computer Science and Engineering
Indian Institute of Technology, Bombay, Mumbai, Powai

Dr Hanmanthrao S Palep's text book on Ayurveda takes the reader from the beginning and moves step wise through the historic origins of the universe to the evolution and sustenance of life. Interspersed between these complexities is life itself that is made up of various physiological sentient matter and its relationship with the environment, seasons, climate, time of day and daily practices. The book introduces concepts of Ayurveda in a manner that can be readily grasped by both Indian and western readers. I am particularly enthused by Dr Palep's ability to simplify complex concepts, some of which are supported by relevant figures and diagrams. Due to the pandemic, everyone wishes to lead a healthy life and adopt an alternate lifestyle that offers optimal living. Ayurveda provides a very good alternative and Dr Palep's book is timely as it seeks to underscore the harmony between the body, mind and spirit.

Back in the early 2000's when I chose to study Ayurveda (despite having a busy life as a neuroscience researcher), we were facing an acute shortage of good Ayurveda text books in English that included verses from Charaka, Sushruta, Vagbhat and others. That problem will not arise with Dr Palep's book as the concepts are thoroughly supported by Sanskrit verses from these texts in the relevant areas. Furthermore, in Ayurveda conferences, fellow members ridiculed me for quoting verses from non-Ayurvedic texts like the Bhagavad Gita or the Upanishads. So, I was very happy to see Dr Palep adding relevant *shlokas* from non-ayurvedic texts as well.

In essence, this is a first-rate text book of Ayurvedic medical theories and practices presented as an organized system of healing principles and clinical interventions. While it appears to be a large book that looks somewhat intimidating, once you begin reading it, you will be captivated on knowing how human life is intricately connected to the universe and all its living and non-living inhabitants. The book will make essential reading not only for physicians and students of Ayurveda, but also for anyone who is interested in leading a healthy life style.

– ***Dr Rammohan Rao, PhD (Neuroscience)***
C-AP (Certified Ayurveda Practitioner)
RYT (Registered Yoga Teacher)

Best-selling author of Good Living Practices:
The Best from Ayurveda, Yoga, and Modern Science
for Achieving Optimal Health, Happiness and Longevity

This book titled "*Dosha Dhatu Mala Vignyan: Integrative Human Physiology,*" is a bold attempt to view the ancient Ayurvedic physiological concepts from the point of view of the modern medical system. Dr H.S. Palep is a "*savyasachi*" like Arjuna, he is thoroughly educated in both Ayurveda as well as modern medicine and only he could dare to undertake this task! He has boundless energy and an inquisitive, restless mind, always ready to experiment and analyse; a true scientist! Ayurveda is an amalgam of philosophy, art and science of human life with a rich tradition of over six millennia and has a very holistic way of studying and managing human life in health and disease. Dr Palep has covered the vast expanse of ancient knowledge in various chapters covering the basic concepts of life, its creation and manifestation and the art and science of Ayurveda. Extensive quotes of *shlokas* and *ruchas* from the Vedas and Upanishads, with interpretation and correlation with modern concepts in physics, biology, genetics *etc.*, makes interesting reading. Ayurvedic concepts of homeostasis at the atomic, molecular, cellular, body and cosmic level resulting in total health, and how imbalance of these results in diseases and disorders, is very nicely explained and correlated with modern concepts. Principles of examination of a patient in the Ayurvedic system are also well presented.

When a student of modern medicine tries to study Ayurveda, the Sanskrit language is the first hurdle. Secondly, over almost the whole of the last millennium, Vedic philosophy, the tremendous pioneering achievements in all fields of science in our country and Ayurveda have been systematically denigrated and suppressed, resulting in total apathy, guilt and suspicion about our ancient heritage. It is books like this and patronage in the form of AYUSH initiative, which will help in restoring the glory our ancient heritage!

– ***Dr Sharad Gogate***

Former Professor of Obstetrics & Gynaecology
Geneticist & Prenatal Diagnosis Specialist
LT Medical College, Mumbai

Ayurveda is ancient science (as old as the human race), practised in India. Much of it has been lost over time (it is still is being practiced in Hindu houses as, "*Ajicha Batwa*") due to various reasons. I feel that the invasion of the country by the *Moghuls* and later, the British Raj are crucial factors for this loss of knowledge, as creativity was destroyed. The knowledge of the ancient saints and *rishis* was not popularised in their writings in simple language which could be understood by the common man, and hence they did not have many followers. Since the advent of the Covid-19 pandemic, more people are focussing on Ayurveda as it stresses the importance of healthy living, good habits, yoga, and a healthy diet, which increase immunity and lead to a lower rate of infection and a better recovery rate.

An understanding of human physiology is the basis of medicine to treat diseases. My friend Dr H.S. Palep has done a remarkable job of writing this book, *"Dosha Dhatu Mala Vigyan: Integrative Human*

Physiology." I am proud of him and thankful that he gave me a chance to read the script.

I am of the frank opinion (after a more than 40 years of experience of teaching medical and paramedical students) that all medical students, health care workers, and practitioners must read this book. I am confident that everyone who reads it will appreciate that understanding human physiology, in the context of Ayurveda, is more practical and open to a new avenue of understanding, treating diseases and preventing their recurrence.

– ***Dr Y S Nandanwar*** *M.D. (Ob/Gy.)*
Consultant Obstetrician & Gynaecologist
Ameya Polyclinic Prof. HOU D.Y.Patil Medical College, Nerul
Navi Mumbai Ph.D Guide D.Y.Patil University, Navi Mumbai

Medical Suptd. D.Y.Patil Hospital, Nerul Member
Academic Council D.Y.Patil University, Nerul

Chairperson Ethics Committee PT Hospital Mumbai Member Ethics Committee NIRRH (ICMR) Mumbai Ex- Prof. HOD L.T. Med. College, Sion Mumbai Ex-Prof. Seth G.S.Med. College, KEM Hospital Parel. Mumbai

I am very thankful to Prof H S Palep for inviting me to write a review of his latest book titled "*Dosha Dhatu Mala Vignyan: Integrative Human Physiology*." I have always believed that in order to understand and interpret Ayurveda in its right perspective, one has to have expertise in multiple disciplines of science. Prof Palep is exactly endowed with this quality and, therefore, I immediately agreed to review his present book.

Whenever I read a book I always prefer to start from the introduction since it provides the thought process of the author behind penning the book. In this case also the first line of the introduction reads:

"Ayurveda, the Hindu system of medicine, is the proud heritage of India". This sentence itself clarified that the book has been written with spiritual and nationalistic fervour. I could also expect the validation of ancient Ayurvedic principles and its holistic approach by their scientific interpretation in the book.

Being very passionate about Ayurveda myself, I have always felt that interpretation of the basic concepts of Ayurveda in the language of science is a huge gap that needs to be filled.

In my view an aspiring country needs seven attributes:

1. Healthy people
2. Younger population
3. Natural resources
4. Able leadership
5. An educated society
6. Disciplined social atmosphere
7. Ethical and moral values

In order to achieve these attributes, the following enablers are required:

- Good teaching practices
- Good learning practices
- Good behavioural aspects
- A healthy life style
- Communication skills
- Social integration
- Inter personal skills
- Spiritual values and practices

All the above attributes and traits constitute the ethos of Ayurveda, which is why Ayurveda is a complete knowledge/science of life, and not a mere system of medicine or science of health.

The present book by Dr Palep, which has 41 chapters spread over five distinct parts, beautifully expands and explains the evolution of Ayurvedic philosophy and its development.

The titles of the chapters are self-explanatory. Part I "The Scientific Foundation of Ayurveda," has 10 chapters. Part II "Ayush *Kaameeyata*" has 8 chapters and deals with the guidelines and ways to achieve a long and healthy life. Part III "*Tridosha Vignyan*" has 8 chapters and deals primarily with *tridoshas* and the concept of *Prakruti.* Part IV "*Saptadhatus* or Seven Prime Tissue Elements of the Body" deals with *saptadhatus* which are the seven prime tissue elements of the body and has 12 chapters, which include subjects like *Rasayana, Ojas* besides the seven *dhatus*. Part V "*Malas*" has 3 chapters and deals with the very important subject of *malas* (waste or excreta) and 10 modes of examining a patient.

Since, my student days I have always wanted to understand the scientific interpretation of the transformation of the seven *dhatus* in sequential order from the food we eat. I am very happy to share that for the first time Prof Palep in his lucid manner has been able to explain this subject, and the most interesting part is the explanation of the development of solid tissue like bone from tissue in the liquid state like *majja*. The scientific explanations provided by Prof Palep at each and every transformation step reflect his thorough and in depth knowledge of multiple scientific disciplines and are worth reading.

To me any definition of health is incomplete without understanding the concept of waste/excreta, which in Ayurveda is referred to as *malas*. This important aspect of health has been ignored by scientists and physiologists of modern medicine but has been the hallmark of the definition of health in Ayurveda. Dr Palep has dedicated a complete chapter to *malas* in this book and has explained their importance.

In his zeal to validate almost all the ancient practices and principles, Dr Palep has used the latest scientific developments, *e.g.*, explaining the harmony between nature and human beings he describes how carbon has been replaced by silicon. People may debate on it, but Dr Palep has at least tried to explain *Lok Purush Samyata* in a scientific manner.

The book will be very useful for all those who are well versed in the basic principles of Ayurveda but did not have an opportunity to understand its scientific interpretation, to boost their confidence.

The book is an essential read for all stakeholders of Ayurveda, from graduate students to post-graduate scholars. It also holds a treasure of knowledge for teachers of Ayurveda, because after reading this book the teacher will be able to explain the basic principles of Ayurveda with more conviction. It will, therefore, help in creating better Ayurveda students, more confident Ayurveda practitioners and teachers and it will also enlighten Ayurveda researchers.

Initially the book reads almost like a spiritual text but as we go deeper and deeper, we enter into a higher level of science, with interpretations with which an analytical person may or may not agree, but certainly cannot ignore.

Personally, I do not agree that Ayurveda is a Hindu system of medicine, considering its universal scope and expanse but it also depends on the interpretation of the word "Hindu". As I mentioned earlier as to what the reader can expect in the book, Dr Palep has pursued his thought process throughout the book in a highly convincing manner.

I wish to congratulate Dr Palep for presenting a scholastic narration of Ayurvedic principles and their scientific interpretation/validation in his present book and for an excellent piece of work, and wish him the best of luck for the success of the book.

– ***Chandra Kant Katiyar***
CEO Health Care (Technical), Emami Ltd, Kolkata

Former Director, Herbal Drug Research
Ranbaxy Research Labs, Gurgaon and
Former Vice President and Head
Dabur R&D Centre, Dabur India Ltd, Sahibabad

I have gone through the draft of the book *Dosha Dhatu Mala Vignyan: Integrative Human Physiology* authored by Dr Hanmanthrao S Palep.

It is generally seen that most students pursuing Ayurveda studies come with a background of modern science after passing a course in biological sciences. Ayurveda was originally written in Sanskrit, and though translated into different languages, the technical words remain the same. Hence, it requires a good knowledge of both Sanskrit and science to understand and interpret the subject, and to explain it to both students and patients. Even then it is often difficult to explain the technical subjects. If the subject matter of Ayurveda is explained in the language of modern science that the students know, it may be easier for them to assimilate it and become good practitioners. This kind of explanation and interpretation is possible only if experts have thorough knowledge of Ayurveda as well as modern medicine.

Dr Palep has a command over Ayurveda as well as modern medicine by virtue of his qualifications and self-study. He has therefore been able to give logical explanations of human physiological matters described in Ayurveda with correlations to modern medicine and science in a lucid manner. The elucidation of the basic concepts of Ayurveda like *prakriti*, *purush*, primal qualities, *panchamahabhut*, *etc*., with references from the Upanishads and Darshanas, and their simplification is noteworthy. Ayurvedic philosophy has been dealt with using the concepts of western philosophy and biochemistry. All the components connected with digestion and metabolism, *dosha*, *dhatu*, *mala*, *prakriti* etc., are scientifically clarified in the light of genetics.

Some research studies on cardio-protection, male infertility and antimicrobial & anti-inflammatory effects carried out by the author and his team at Dr Palep's Medical Research Foundation, have been included, supporting the doctrines of Ayurveda. Unlike modern medicine, Ayurveda is customized to each person on the basis of several factors including individual *prakritis*. Besides the actual subject of human physiology, Dr Palep has also included topics like *swasthavritta*, *dravyaguna*, *nidanapanchak*, and the examination of a patient. He has also described the principles of general treatment on the basis of abnormal states of *dosha*, *dhatu* and *mala*.

This book authored by Dr H.S.Palep is a book on human physiology with a novel approach and modern understanding. I congratulate Dr Palep for bringing out an excellent book and am sure that this book will be useful to undergraduate and post graduate students, as well as to teachers of Ayurveda. It will certainly give an insight into Ayurveda to non-ayurvedic medical professionals interested in learning about Indian medicine.

I hope that Dr Hanmanthrao S Palep will bring out more such books with a modern ken.

– ***Prof. Dr V V Prasad*** *M.D.(Ay.), Ph.D. (BHU)*
Ayurveda Specialist, Swami Vivekanand
Health Mission's Hospital, Uttarakhand

Formerly
Professor, S.V. Ayurveda College, Tirupati
Professor, J.S. Ayurveda College, Nadiad
Director, Rashtriya Ayurveda Vidyapeeth
Ministry of AYUSH, Govt. of India, Delhi
Advisor (ISM), ESIC, Ministry of Labour
& Employment, Govt. of India, Delhi